CONFINED SPACE

Deryn Collier

A TOUCHSTONE BOOK

PUBLISHED BY SIMON & SCHUSTER

NEW YORK   LONDON   TORONTO   SYDNEY   NEW DELHI

Touchstone
A Division of Simon & Schuster
1230 Avenue of the Americas
New York, NY 10020

This Touchstone export edition June 2012

TOUCHSTONE and colophon are registered trademarks of
Simon & Schuster, Inc.

For information about special discounts for bulk purchases,
please contact Simon & Schuster Special Sales at 1-800-268-3216 or
CustomerService@simonandschuster.ca.

Designed by Akasha Archer

Manufactured in the United States of America

10   9   8   7   6   5   4   3   2   1

ISBN 978-1-4516-6947-3
ISBN 978-1-4516-6949-7 (ebook)

For Guy

1

"Her name is Belinda Carlisle," he said.

"No way! Like the singer?" Sparky laughed.

He stared down at the girl, bound and asleep on the couch. So pretty. Chubbier than Sparky usually went for, but pretty.

"What should we do with her now?" he asked.

He watched Sparky's eyes. They shone. Too brightly. He knew that look.

"Don't you have some work to do?" Sparky asked.

He shrugged. "I guess."

"Just leave her with me for a while. I'll look after everything," Sparky said.

He started to shake his head but found himself nodding instead. It had always been that way. He backed away from Sparky, and from the girl on the couch. It was never good when Sparky looked after things, but he did have work to do. There was always work to be done.

•

From the roof of the bottle washer, Gavin Grayson could see the whole bottle shop. It was quiet today, Labor Day Monday, but even after only a month on the job, he already had a sense of the familiar rhythm of each machine when it was running—its role, its purpose in the larger system of making beer. A good millwright listens to the machines, Gavin's mentor had told him during his apprenticeship, and Gavin believed him.

The bottle washer was two stories high and as wide as two lanes of traffic. He felt like he owned the place, standing there. He loved the Bugaboo Brew crest on the chest of his navy-blue coveralls. He loved the fact that though he was new to the job, they had asked him to work a weekend overtime shift already. Patch the bottle washer on the outside, Conrad had said. But Gavin wanted to do better than that. He wanted to do more for his new team, his new family. He was used to way harder repairs on the oil rigs. It would be nothing to go inside and fix the leak up right.

He'd performed a simple lockout before climbing the metal ladder that clung to the side of the machine. Now he slid open the trapdoor on the roof of compartment number four. The powdery smell of the caustic soda solution crept into his nasal passages. He looked carefully at the long trays, like elongated dishwasher trays, at the top of the compartment. Each one held forty plastic cups, and each cup nestled a recycled beer bottle. Easy enough. If he took out a dozen trays, there would be enough room for him to crawl inside.

Once this was done, he pulled out his cell phone and checked it one more time. Still no message from Belinda. He started to dial but then disconnected the call. He clipped the phone to the back pocket of his coveralls, slid on his neoprene gloves, and pulled down his face shield.

The compartment was a narrow, vertical tunnel. Gavin barely fit inside, and once down there, he did not have much room to maneuver. He was surrounded on all sides by the remaining trays and their beer bottles, and he stepped carefully around these to find solid footing on the floor of the machine. Once this was done, he crouched down to have a closer look at the leaking seam. Belinda's face came to mind, but he pushed the picture away. She was on her way. She was. Sometimes she did things in her own time, that was all. If they were going to be married, he'd have to get used to that.

He pulled a mini flashlight from his pocket to check the seam. If he welded a little patch there, that should do it. Really, he thought, it should hold for years. No need to wait until a shutdown to repair it. A little action with the blowtorch and it would be good as new. He'd tell Belinda when she finally got there—how the new job was going so well. That it really was a fresh start.

He tried again to push the thought of her away, but it was more insistent this time. When he brought his gloved hand to his forehead, as though to rub the memory out, he came up against his face shield.

Such a simple thing, really. A button. The button open on her blouse. One button too many, and the bra that he saw peeking out underneath was the dusty rose one he'd ordered for her from the Victoria's Secret catalog. It was the fact that she must have gone home after work to change before going to the bar, because she'd never wear a skirt that short to work. But why would she dress like that when she wasn't expecting him back for another couple of days? Her eyes burned brightly with a glow he'd seen in the manic eyes of the guys on the rigs after they'd been out for too long. A look he'd had himself once or twice, but one he'd never expected to see on a girl. On *his* girl.

Gavin breathed deeply behind his shield, trying to calm himself. He looked around at the cups cradling the recycled beer bottles. It felt like they were closing in around him. He needed to get out for a minute.

But he couldn't stand up straight. Something pinched him from behind, and he realized, twisting back, that his cell phone was stuck on the lip of one of the cups. He tried to shuffle his hips forward, but the phone did not release. He quieted himself and focused, picturing the phone clip. It couldn't be more than half an inch that had him stuck, but if he wanted to get loose without tearing the phone apart, he had to move slowly.

Just then, he heard a loud, shuddering thud, and the hollow beat of a recent pop hit echoed from above. The compartment seemed to brighten. Someone had turned on another bank of lights. Someone else was out there.

He was sweating. The face shield slipped down until the strap covered his eyes. He stopped his gentle rocking and pulled the shield off, lifting his head toward the opening to feel the cool air on his face. Finally, with one last rock and a slight shift to the left, the clip of the cell phone unhooked itself from the cup. It happened fast, and Gavin stuck his hand out to keep from falling forward.

He pulled himself up and, reaching out of the machine, hooked his hand on the handle of the compartment door. One swift movement and he'd be out in the air and space of the bottle shop.

Then he heard a hiss. A gurgle, like the pause between a tap opening and the water starting to flow. Something shifted above him and a stream of caustic sprayed him full in the face. Blinded, he propelled his body upward in the motion it had already begun. He managed to keep his purchase on the door handle. The caustic poured onto his torso and fell into the chamber below, taking with it his last breath, his last heartbeat, his last thought. As the compartment filled he hung motionless, one arm dangling from the handle, and his face, already ragged and burned, turned toward the light above.

As the tank filled, his body began to float, as if in a bath bubbly with corrosives.

2

Porridge. That's what the smell was. The smell of a Sunday morning pot of porridge that was reheated throughout the week. The smell of the slow fermentation of unrefrigerated porridge.

Don't be ridiculous, Belinda. Gavin's voice, scolding her. *Porridge doesn't smell. Oatmeal has no smell.*

I can smell oatmeal. At least a week old. And something else too. Can't you smell that? Something wet and heavy. She straightened her head and sniffed.

Her skin stung when she moved. Like a spider bite. She went to press her hand to her abdomen, to lessen the pain of the sting, but she could not move her arms.

Awareness rushed in all at once. She was lying on her back. On something cushioned. Rough fabric pressed against her bare legs. A couch. Her hands were bound tightly in front of her, tied together by something soft that did not cut into her skin. She could move her arms up and down but could not separate her hands. She tried this now, moving her arms up, and was hit with a sharp pain in her shoulders and upper back. She lowered her arms back down and lay perfectly still.

Fine. I'll try opening my eyes. It took her a moment to gather

her courage. When she did open them, the sensation was like ripping off a Band-Aid. Her lids were crusted together and she blinked several times to moisten them. She looked around, then closed her eyes again in a panic. *Where the hell am I?* She listened for a moment. She could hear noises, but they weren't close by. There was a steady scraping sound, and occasionally the low rumble of a machine, like a truck driving past. She was close to the outdoors, to a road with regular truck traffic.

She forced herself to open her eyes again and look around. She was alone in a room surrounded by boxes. On her right was an open door. She studied the shapes she could see through its opening. Shelves. They were roughly built, like the ones in her dad's shed when she was growing up. He'd been a handyman on occasion, when he was sober enough to work, and he'd kept every spare scrap of material and partially empty can of paint he could get his hands on. *Can't let this good stuff go to waste,* he'd say. But then it would just sit there in his shed, doing exactly that.

Belinda shook herself to keep her thoughts on track. Her head felt larger than normal and her brain seemed to bounce around inside her skull with each movement. *Can't doze off. I've got to figure this out. What was I thinking of?* Paint cans, that's right. She stared into the opening again. Shelves of paint cans, several rows of them. A library of paint. And then a chain-link fence. This took a moment to think about. She looked up and could see the gray line of a concrete roof. An indoor fence. But a fence nonetheless.

She was suddenly alert. Her eyes followed the line of the fence upward, as far as she could see. There was a gap between the top of the fence and where the roof must be. A way out.

Then the door swung closed. She heard footsteps walking

away. She could no longer see the paint cans or the chain-link fence. But she knew they were there. She would find her way out. Slowly and painfully, she twisted her fingers and began to work at the knots in the fabric that secured her hands.

The package was sitting in the middle of her desk when Evie got back to her office after her morning safety inspection. The words "Evie Chapelle, Safety Manager, Bugaboo Brewery, Kootenay Landing" were printed neatly on the square white label affixed to the brown paper. Even before looking at the return stamp— "BevCo Corporate Office"—Evie knew what it was.

Deciding to savor the moment, she placed her coffee cup on her desk and began to collect the scattered safety inspections she had been working on into a tidy pile. She managed to find a spot for them amid the stacks of loose papers, binders, and files that covered the top of a long, low filing cabinet—the only other flat surface in her closet-sized office.

She slid off her safety glasses and slipped her earplugs out of her ears. As safety manager, she needed to set the standard of safety whenever she was out on the floor. But here in the confines of her tiny office, she could relax a little. She smoothed the part-cotton, part-Lycra Bugaboo Brew shirt over her slim hips and tugged the hem down over the top of her jeans. Karl, the brewery manager, had recently reminded them that their target customers were the young, hip beer drinkers of the West Coast. Bugaboo managers needed to look the part.

Evie wasn't sure how these two sets of appearances—safety and youth—were supposed to mesh. She did know that she had turned forty just a few months before, and Lycra was not something that should still be part of her wardrobe.

Finally she sat down and leaned back in her chair. It was a big chair, not quite ergonomic, and she kept meaning to get it replaced. Her feet barely reached the floor and she had to swing her legs to swivel from side to side. It made her feel like a child visiting her father's office, not a manager with almost twenty years' experience working for what was now the world's biggest brewing company. Twenty years and still moving up, she thought. And this, no doubt, will help. She pulled the package toward her, slid one finger under the edge, and lifted the side flap. Just as it popped up, her office door swung open. Conrad Scofield ducked his head around the door and grinned at her.

"Good weekend, Dragon Lady?" he asked.

As he plopped himself down on the chair in front of her desk, Evie noted that he wasn't wearing his safety gear. His safety glasses and earplugs swung from cords clipped to the collar of his golf shirt.

"Dragon Lady? That's a new one. Is that what they're calling me these days?" she asked.

He rubbed the bridge of his hook nose and smiled at her from under a fringe of sandy hair. That grin, she thought, lets him get away with just about anything. "You bet. Dragon Lady, Crazy Lady. A few other choice names that I won't share with you. Dragon Lady because you breathe red tape rather than fire."

Evie laughed. "Actually, that's pretty clever. Did one of your union guys think that up?"

Conrad looked away. His fair skin blushed easily, and two red circles popped up on his cheeks now. "Uh, no." He picked up his safety glasses on their string and spun them around between his thumb and forefinger. "So how was your long weekend?" he asked.

"Oh, fine—don't tell me." Evie sighed and looked at her package. She fingered the other edge and slipped the second flap open. "My weekend was the same as always. I worked, from home. For three days instead of two," she replied.

Conrad nodded. "Dirk still out of town? I'm starting to miss him. I had to watch the game without him on Sunday. When's he coming back?"

Evie shrugged and tucked a lock of her dark-brown hair behind her ear. "And that's something I don't want to talk about. How about you? How was your weekend?"

"I left this place on Friday afternoon and didn't give it one moment's thought until I got here this morning." He held up his cell phone and rolled his eyes. "Of course, I'm paying for it now. BevCo has never heard of the Labor Day holiday, apparently."

Conrad leaned the chair back so it balanced on two legs, then propped a foot on the side of her desk. "Last weekend of the season at the trailer. Bunch of the guys came up the lake. Barbecue Sunday night. It was great."

"Quality control? Product sampling?" Evie asked.

"Plenty of product sampling. Plus some of my ultra-select home brew, which Dirk will be sorry he missed," he said. "So what's in the package? You going to open that thing, or what?"

Evie tipped her head and smiled. "Want to see?"

Conrad tapped the screen of his phone and held it up to her. The display showed a timer counting down with seven minutes left. "Only if you can get it open before the guys come back from their coffee break. We've got a jam on the bottle washer, so I sent them a little early while Steve fixes it." He paused, shaking his head. "I can't imagine what Christmas morning must be like at your house. Take all day."

Evie swung her legs to spin her chair so she was facing the filing cabinet. She rummaged on its surface until she found the paper she was looking for. "I wanted to talk to you about this fax, anyway. Have a look while I open this," she said.

The paper she held out to him read "Kootenay Landing Answering Service" in bold letters across the top. Conrad sat up, leaned over the paper, and started reading out a list of names.

"None of my guys are on here, Evie. Brewing guys, steam engineers, a few managers. Why give this to me?" he asked.

"Because none of your personnel are on that list. And so I just wanted to double-check that you didn't have anyone working over the long weekend." Evie lifted the last flap of paper and smoothed it flat on her desk. The hem of her shirt crept over the band of her jeans with the movement and she pulled at it impatiently with her free hand.

Conrad shrugged and handed her back the paper. "What's it a list of?"

"People who called in to the answering service to register that they were working alone in the brewery over the weekend," Evie replied. She leaned forward to take the paper. "Did you have anyone working alone this weekend, Conrad?"

"Aw, Christ, Evie. This is just what people mean. You've got to make everything so damn complicated."

"What's complicated about calling in to let someone know that you're working alone? It's the procedure we all agreed on, not to mention a requirement of the Workers' Safety Board," she said.

Conrad ducked his head down and started tapping his thumb on the screen of his phone.

"Look, Conrad, I know it's Karl's job, not yours, to make sure these guys follow procedure. Just tell me—did any of your guys come in and work on the weekend?"

Conrad would not look at her.

"Conrad?" she asked.

He sighed. "The new guy, Gavin. He came in to fix the leak on the bottle washer."

"Did you tell him to follow the procedure? Does he even know about it? He's only worked here for what, a month?" she asked. She knew she sounded strident as the questions tumbled out.

"We gave him the usual spiel," Conrad replied.

"Does the usual spiel involve training on the proper procedure for working alone on a weekend?" Evie did not try to hide the anger in her voice.

"Okay, okay. I'll tell him. You must have the training document in your pile of papers there. You do, don't you?" Conrad gestured to the stack of papers on Evie's filing cabinet.

She dug through them until she found the one she was looking for, then she scrawled Gavin Grayson's name across the top in her loopy, left-handed script. "Here it is. Have Gavin review it and sign off. And make sure he understands, would you, Conrad?"

Conrad stood up and saluted. "Aye, aye, Dragon Lady," he said wryly, but he smiled at her as he waved her off. Then he held up his screen again. "Still two minutes left. Are you going to let me see what that thing is, or what?"

Evie took a deep breath and closed her eyes. Then, without looking and ever so slowly, she clasped the sides of the framed object and flipped it over. Conrad whistled softly. Evie opened her eyes. The gold-colored frame surrounded a mat of deep blue, which held in place a thick cream-colored certificate stamped with both the BevCo and the Bugaboo logos.

BEVCO SAFETY AWARD
IN RECOGNITION OF 500 ACCIDENT-FREE DAYS
AT THE BUGABOO BREWERY

"Nice job, Dragon Lady," Conrad said. When he swung the door open, the sounds of the bottle shop made their way in. "My time's up. Gotta run. Hey, why don't you come with me? Do a spot inspection of something? Let's go for another five hundred days," he said with a smile.

She knew he was humoring her, but his smile almost made her believe it mattered to him too. She stood up and grabbed her safety glasses and earplugs, then pointed at Conrad's, still dangling from his shirt. "Only if you put those on."

He winked at her but did what she asked.

They paused at the entrance to the bottle shop. The normal rattling rhythm of the production floor was quiet. The machines idled; rows of bottles on the stalled conveyors clinked expectantly against each other, waiting to be filled.

"Help!" a voice called from deep within the acres of machinery. "Help!"

Evie and Conrad looked at each other. For a moment, it seemed as though they were frozen in place. Then Evie's limbs caught up with her mind and she began to move toward the voice, fast.

"Help!" the voice cried again.

She began to run.

3

Bern Fortin crouched down and tapped another yogurt lid into the soil at the end of the row of late-harvest spinach. It was supposed to be ready in time for the Thanksgiving feast at the food bank, but if the slugs kept up their work, there would be nothing left but the little nibs of the stems. He tipped the beer bottle over the lid and slowly poured until a small pool of liquid filled the base of the container. Then he stood to survey his work.

A dozen white plastic lids, each filled with a dose of Bugaboo Brew, dotted the rich soil along the base of the three rows of greens. Bern brushed at the dirt stains on the knees of his jeans and stretched his arms up to the sky. He held the beer bottle up at an angle. The image of the mountains on the label caught his eye, and he compared it to the real mountains that surrounded him. He spun in a slow circle, comparing the two, until—there—he matched them up. Bugaboo Glacier.

He'd had every intention of climbing it that summer, but somehow the days had marched by, always one step ahead of him. He had not expected the tiny seedlings to grow into the tumultuous, and demanding, jungle that lay before him. And his supposed part-time job—the reason for his move to this mountain town at the other end of the country—was weaving him, thread by thread, into the fabric of the community. He had not expected that either.

He tipped the beer bottle again and watched the morning sun glint against its side. Still a little left. He thought of his former regiment and wondered what the brave soldiers of the Royal 22nd would think of Lieutenant-Colonel Bern Fortin, now retired, wasting good beer to kill slugs. Especially Bugaboo Brew. Even back on his early tours—Rwanda, Bosnia—when soldiers were still allowed two beers a day, it was rare that they'd get their hands on a popular brand like Bugaboo. Now with the new no-alcohol policy on tours, his guys still in Afghanistan would be lucky if they saw a beer a month.

Bern raised the bottle to the morning sun, to the mountains, to his men and drank back the last of the beer, stale and warm as it was. *Santé.*

As was usual when he was alone in his garden in the early morning, his thoughts flowed in his native French. The return to English would no doubt come as a shock, as it did every day. He'd been living in Kootenay Landing for six months already, but it obviously took longer than that to counteract close to forty-five years of having both languages alive all around him. He was not sure he'd ever get used to the loss.

He surveyed the mountains again. Those he had gotten used to—and grown to love. From where he stood they surrounded him, solid and reassuring. Below him stretched a wide valley bottom. The morning mist had risen, revealing fields of alfalfa ready for harvest. Around him were the rolling hills of the Kootenay Landing town site, its leafy-treed streets dotted with quaint older homes built by the original settlers over a century before.

The tallest buildings in town were the two grain elevators—one white, one red—which stood watch next to the train tracks that skirted the hillside.

Bern's own house was a tiny bungalow that, with a few modest renovations, he'd adjusted to suit his needs. It was just on the edge of town. From his front door he could see the brewery, which was one of the main employers. Beyond it, orchards and vineyards stretched all the way to the base of the eastern mountain range in one direction, and to the American border in the other.

He'd fallen in love with the backyard at first sight. Much larger than the house itself, it started at the steps of his back porch and made its way down to the edge of the creek that was his property line. Almost a full acre, very rare in town, the real estate agent had told him. Almost a full acre of rich, dark soil. Perfect for gardening.

Bern took to gardening as though it could save his life, and sometimes he thought perhaps it would. He'd made the promise to himself on his last mission, in an outpost bunkered from the hard-fought desert by sandbags. With shades of brown in every direction, he'd made a promise he could barely articulate. Each day, as he planned operations—as he sent some teams out to train Afghan soldiers, others to rebuild roads and schools and bridges, and then waited to see if all of them would return, and in one piece—the promise grew. A certainty within him, something solid. The answer lay in growth, and in beauty. In color. In life, though he dared not hope for that much.

Beer bottle in hand, he began his daily inspection, a wayward drill sergeant making his rounds. The rows of vegetables fell into formation, clipped and weeded, the soil under them tilled and loose. The squash spread on mounds of almost-black earth, dozens of them fattening for harvest day. Bern did not like squash—or potatoes, for that matter. All of these would go to the food bank. He'd harvested the garlic the week before; it was drying in large bunches from the rafters under the porch. That so much growth came from so little, he could not fathom. That each harvest contained within it the seeds of its own survival, the promise of more life—it was more than he'd ever thought possible.

He crouched near a row of lavish tomatoes. Here he had failed. A small brown spot dotted the end of each of the otherwise perfect fruit. Bern picked a few overripe specimens and tossed them in a high and lazy arc to the open compost bin. Turning the compost: another job that waited for him. Even from where he stood he could smell the sweet, funky odor, a combination of rotting fruit and moldy leaves. It was a stench that could take him down roads he did not want to travel.

He looked over the tumbledown fence that separated his garden from Mrs. Kalesnikoff's next door. He'd offered to replace it when he first moved in. A soldier knew how to build good and solid fence, after all. But Mrs. K. had refused. "You'll see," she'd said cryptically.

He did see now. Sweet peas—masses of them. They populated the whole length of the invisible line that separated his garden from Mrs. K.'s. Tiny jewels of color clinging to the grayed fence boards, pulling them inevitably downward.

Mrs. K.'s garden started just past the riot of flowers. She spent much less time weeding and tying and pruning than he did, and yet her garden looked tidier, more restrained, as if the plants had somehow sensed the force of her will and responded. The slugs too seemed to pick up on some invisible signal. Their damage ended at the line between the two properties.

He carefully chose a blemished tomato. No doubt Mrs. K. would have something to say about it. He took long strides toward the gate that always hung open between the two gardens, leaving the empty beer bottle on the gatepost. Mrs. K. was not out yet. He knew she would be inside, waiting for him with thick Russian coffee in a veined mug and some sample of baking that she needed him to test. But first, he had to look after her woodpile. He placed the tomato on an out-of-the way log and got to work.

She was perfectly capable of chopping her own wood, of course. She'd done it since she was a child, she'd told him gruffly, and she wasn't that old. But Bern couldn't sit by and watch a seventy-year-old woman split firewood.

The ax was waiting for him. It felt good to stretch to his full six feet and three inches. Arms extended and with an effortless swing, he allowed the ax blade to find the spaces between the fibers of wood and slice them clean apart. He chopped enough for one week of winter fires and stacked the logs carefully, close to the back door. Then he retrieved the tomato and went inside without knocking.

"You were up all night," she said to him without looking up. She was standing at the counter in her housedress, a flowered apron tied carefully at her stocky waist. Her dark-gray hair was pulled into a tight bun at the nape of her neck. It was a kitchen day, not a garden day. The same restrained chaos of the garden prevailed in the kitchen. The massive counter was spread with baking—chiffon cakes, nut loaves, yeast breads, and, Bern was happy to see, homemade cinnamon buns cooling on racks. Next to them a pile of Styrofoam trays and a roll of plastic bags stood at the ready, for freezing tidy packages once the baking cooled. On the counter next to the sink, dozens of glass jars, gleaming from their recent washing, waited to be sterilized and filled with garden harvest. On the opposite side of the oversized sink, an old wooden crate held a bushel of tomatoes, each one perfectly red, round, firm, and blemish-free.

He kept his boots on—she insisted, though he suspected she mopped the floor each morning after he left—and walked through the kitchen, as large as a mess hall, to the small dining table. He pulled out a padded, well-worn chair and sat down. He placed the tomato in front of him.

"Good morning, Mrs. K.," he said. He ran his fingers through his dark curls, which were longer than they'd been since he was a child.

She tutted in response and pushed a coffee cup in front of him. He smiled, wrapped his long fingers around the thick mug, and waited.

"You were up all night," she said again, reaching for the tomato. "You water too much," she said gruffly. "And you water the leaves. The leaves don't drink. Roots drink."

She bustled off to the oven and pulled out a cake large enough to feed a platoon. She pressed a finger to the surface and, dissatisfied, slid it back into the oven. "Larry Berg?" she asked.

Bern shook his head. News traveled fast in Kootenay Landing.

"He had a heart attack. I sat with Connie until the kids could get here from Calgary," he said.

"He wasn't very old," said Mrs. K.

Bern shrugged. He wasn't supposed to talk about his work,

but he was finding that he usually didn't need to say anything at all. He took a sip of the strong, sweet coffee. Left to his own devices, he took his coffee black, with no sugar. To Mrs. K., good coffee was sweet and white, no discussion.

"But he didn't look after himself," said Mrs. K. "Connie never had a garden, you know. All store-bought food. Prepared. Eating out." She made a guttural sound in her throat as she said this. "Not good for the digestion."

"Can I still use the tomatoes?" Bern asked. "For soup or salsa or something?"

"What is this salsa? No one needs salsa," she replied. "Winter, you need stewed tomatoes." She gestured toward the sink. "Twenty jars today."

Bern smiled. "Stewed tomatoes, then. Can I still use them for that?"

She approached the table again. This time she placed a plate before him; on it lay a cinnamon bun the size of a person's head. She picked up the tomato again and eyed it critically. "Cut off the blossom end. That's all you can do." She looked at him through narrowed eyes. Drawn to her full height, she was at his eye level when he was seated. "Seeds won't be any good, though. I'll have to save some of mine for you." Subject closed.

She took the cake out now, and Bern sat back and watched her work. She slid a knife cleanly around the edge of the pan and the cake popped out, almost of its own volition, when she'd barely tipped the pan over the cooling rack. He thought back to his fledgling gardening career to date. It seemed that everything he had learned—and it was a lot, though not nearly enough—had come through these tiny bits of wisdom shared almost grudgingly by Mrs. K.

"You work too hard, you know," she said now. She slid a foam tray along the counter and carefully arranged two cinnamon buns on it.

He shrugged and took another bite of his bun. "I'm the coroner now. I need to go when they call."

"They call a lot," Mrs. K. said. "And you don't let them go, the dead." She always said the exact number of words needed to get her point across, and never more.

Bern closed his eyes and allowed the fatigue of the night before to roll over him. His cell phone, always present since he'd taken the job as Kootenay Landing's coroner six months before, chirped. He reached for it and had it to his ear in one swift motion.

"Bernard Fortin," he answered. The French pronunciation of his name slipped out before he could stop himself.

"Bern, that you?" The line was full of static and background noise, but there was no mistaking the rasping shout of Alvin Resnick, head of the local police detachment.

"Staff Sergeant Resnick, what can I do for you?" Bern asked.

"How fast can you get here?" Resnick barked.

"Well, that depends where you are."

"Don't joke with me, Fortin." When Resnick said Bern's surname, he made it sound like the name of a chain of American grocery stores. "We've got a situation here. A deceased person, male, early thirties, or so we think. Not a natural death, so you can cross that off your form."

Bern cupped his hand over the phone to keep Mrs. K. from hearing. She was deftly slipping a plastic bag over a loaf of nut bread with one hand and swirling a twist tie in place with the other. It looked like she was paying absolutely no attention to him, but he knew otherwise.

"So a dead body, but not going anywhere, *oui*?" Bern said quietly. He chewed on his tongue slightly as the French phrasing slipped out again.

"No, not going anywhere," Resnick snapped. "But it's disintegrating faster than the polar ice cap."

Bern held the phone between his ear and shoulder. "Did you say disintegrating? Resnick, where are you?"

"Bugaboo Brewery. Go to the main entrance," Resnick said. "Hurry up."

Bern flipped the phone closed. He leaned his nose down to his coffee cup and inhaled deeply. He took one sip, then another. He looked down at his gardening jeans, the thick flannel work shirt that had been fresh yesterday but was none too clean now, and his leather hiking boots, which were coated in dust. No time to change.

"I have to go," he said.

Mrs. K. tilted her head at him. "Last day for fall fair entries today," she said.

He tilted his head back at her and shrugged. "And?"

"And you need to enter," she said firmly.

He smiled at her. "But not tomatoes."

She shook her head once. "Squash, potatoes, garlic." She counted each off on a finger. "Onions, too soft. Spinach, too many slugs. Some of your flowers are good: bachelor's buttons, zinnias. Dahlias not big enough. Maybe tomato soup," she said. "Yours is not bad. Salsa, if you want."

He smiled at her concession. "So what do I need to do?" he asked.

"Come back before five o'clock. I'll get your form ready." She shrugged. "You have to sign it and pay."

He had no idea what he would be walking into in a few minutes, or how long it would take, but one thing he could be certain about in his day: he would be back in this kitchen before five o'clock.

Bern nodded. "Thank you. Believe me," he said with a wink, "I've got to run." He took a last sip of coffee and stood, leaving his mug and plate on the table, because that was what she expected. As he walked out the door to the garden, she called after him.

"You will eat when you come back. I'm making borscht."

In five long strides, he was through the open gate and the patio doors and into the kitchen of his tiny house. He grabbed his car keys off the counter and his metal briefcase from the second bedroom, which he'd opened and converted into an office. Two more steps and he was through the living room and out the front door. He left it unlocked.

He hopped into his truck and backed out of the driveway. It was only two blocks to the front entrance of the Bugaboo Brewery.

4

At some point, she became aware of a deep rumbling sound. Morning? Afternoon? She had no way of knowing. A train's plaintive whistle pierced the thick cement bunker that contained her. After a while the rumble became a background sound that lulled her. She drifted off, staring into space.

Her head snapped to the side and her eyes opened wide when, with a shuddering thump, the rumbling came to a complete stop. All was quiet. No sounds of passing trucks. No trains. But the smell was still there. The stink of oatmeal, and something new. The smell of something burnt.

The thoughts were coming more clearly and she could hang on to them longer. Body, sore. Lips and throat, parched. Whatever it is they gave her was in the water. She would barely sip when they brought it, though she was desperate for something to drink. The last time the one with the gruff voice slapped her on the head.

She thought of Gavin's eyes. More than brown, they were flecked with the same color as the strawberry blond of his hair. And for a big lug of a guy he was always kind of helpless around her. Or at least had been, until things got out of hand.

Belinda groaned when she thought of how quickly her life had fallen apart. What a way to get clean. If she got out of here—*when* she got out—she would never touch coke again in her life. She might not even take a painkiller for a headache. In the concrete bunker, as she had come to think of her cage, her skin felt chilled by the cold air. She could not imagine ever being warm again.

She could remember driving Brad to Edmonton. Was that Saturday? What day was it now? Was Brad doing this to her? Something had happened in Edmonton. Brad was mad at her, she knew that much. But would he be doing this? *This?*

The bandages were not tied so tightly this time. They were soft, some kind of fabric. She started to move her wrists in small circles. Tiny, slow movements. She fell asleep at one point but woke up again and remembered. Eventually, she was able to slip one wrist and hand out of the restraint. She left the other one in, the extra length of fabric looping loosely. She could slip her hand back in if he came back. He must not know she could get her hands free. It was her only advantage. She allowed her fingers to travel her cold skin, exploring the painful edges of the blistered holes that dotted the soft flesh of her stomach.

What were they doing to her? Her fingers traveled the small circle again. The size of the tip of her finger. She pressed her finger firmly into one hole and a warm, thick liquid wetted her fingertip. She inhaled sharply.

The door clanged and a dim light crept into the room. Belinda worked her free hand back into the bandage. Her eyes adjusted and she saw once again the outline of the couch, the flat-screened TV, the wall of boxes. The row of paint cans and the chain-link fence were visible through the door, and then blocked as the man moved in front of the light and walked silently toward her, carrying a bottle of water.

"Drink up," the shadow said. The light was behind his head and she could not see his face. She pretended to drink. Then she lay, with her eyes closed, and waited.

"Bern Fortin," he said with a smile to the woman behind the reception desk. He handed her a card. She took it between manicured nails without looking at either it or him.

"I'm not sure if we'll need that," she said into the phone, which seemed to hang in midair between her shoulder and her ear without creasing her pale blazer or mussing her equally pale blond hair. She held a pencil in her hand and tapped it three times on the desk in front of her.

She still did not look up. Bern watched her closely. Maybe it was all the time he'd spent in the army, away from them, but Bern loved to look at women. He loved to look for that one striking feature that made each woman beautiful and unique.

The nameplate in front of her said Gemma Burch. She was a few years older than him, getting close to fifty, he thought. The skin around her eyes was delicate and thin, the lines of her cheeks were drawn downward this morning, but the round apples of her cheekbones suggested a tendency toward optimism. He admired how carefully she looked after the details of her appearance, from the pink-tipped nails that held the pencil to the seamlessly combed and dyed, almost-white hair. A woman confident in her looks as she aged, but still not taking anything for granted.

Bern watched as she finally scanned the card in her fingers. She mouthed the words "BC Coroners Service," and her pale painted lips formed a perfect O. "Hold, please," she said into the receiver, tapping a button on the phone with the end of the pencil.

"You're the coroner?" she asked. Her eyes were lined in a soft chocolate brown, which was carefully highlighted with a paler eye shadow, minimizing the wrinkles in her eyelids. The eyes beneath were hazel and looked intelligent. They traveled from Bern's wild black hair to the thick wool work shirt and then down the full length of his faded jeans, pausing at the grass stains on his knees. "I thought you were coming to fix something," she said, jutting her chin at his metal briefcase.

He smiled at her and shrugged. "I was in the garden. Staff Sergeant Resnick told me to get here as fast as I could."

She held the receiver of the phone over her shoulder and smiled quickly. The phone started to ring. "They're expecting you. Are you wearing closed-toed shoes?" She lifted herself several inches out of her seat to inspect his shoes. He lifted the cuff of his jeans to expose a snug-fitting leather hiking boot. "Good," she said. "Head through those doors behind me." She waved the pencil toward a steel door. A sign above it read Bottle Shop. "Turn right, then right again. You'll hear them."

Bern bowed slightly, a gesture that was lost on the woman, who was already answering the next call. He picked up the briefcase and headed in the direction of the door. As directed, he turned right down a long hallway made of cinder blocks that had been thickly painted bright white and were covered with framed awards and certificates. Bern slowed down to inspect them and found, ironically, that they were safety awards.

The hallway quickly went from display gallery to factory at the place where the cinder blocks stopped gleaming with coats of glossy paint. Within two shorts steps, Bern found himself in an industrial zone. The floor at his feet was painted with yellow traffic lines. Following them, he turned a corner to the right. Before him opened up an enormous space, filled at intervals with machines such as he had never seen before, all connected by conveyor belts.

The ceiling was two stories high. The banks of fluorescent lights seemed as distant as a passing aircraft. It felt to Bern like the very air in the place was gray, trapped by cinder blocks, machinery, and vast pockets of space where humans traveled a narrow, predetermined path. Bern knew nothing about breweries, but these machines seemed old to him and vaguely clunky, as if they'd been built from scrap parts in someone's garage. He imagined some small man in a hidden room filled with spare parts, working night and day keeping those machines going.

The place looked as if it could raise a din when it was running, but everything was quiet as Bern walked along the cement floor. He could hear voices in the distance; words echoed and bounced around the cavernous space. He followed the yellow arrows painted between the yellow dividing lines on the floor. The path skirted a machine. Bern could not guess its name, but its purpose was clear. The conveyor belt leading to the machine was lined with cases of empty beer bottles. Once the bottles left the machine, they were free of their cases, which lay in toppling piles in a wheeled bin next to him. Above the bin was a small metal platform, the heart of the machine, or so it seemed to him. At the place where the bottles were freed by some unknown process from their cases, he saw a ghetto blaster and a small stool. The process involved human assistance, though there was no one on hand at the moment.

"There you are!" Staff Sergeant Alvin Resnick was in front of him all of a sudden. There was something about the man that annoyed Bern. Resnick stood next to him now, and Bern straightened instinctively to his military bearing, lifting himself to his full height until he towered over the shorter man. The RCMP officer's close-set eyes bristled with frustration; his gray hair was carefully shaved into a buzz cut more suitable to a new recruit. Resnick's uniform was crisply pressed, but it stretched at the waist where his shirt buttons strained to cover some extra flesh. He had strategically placed his duty belt to cover the gap where his shirt opened. Time to order the next size up, Bern thought but didn't say out loud. It was just the kind of comment that he felt like making around Resnick but would never dream of saying to anyone else.

"What have we got?" Bern asked instead.

"We've got a guy floating in a tank of chemicals. An employee, or so we think. We won't know for sure until we get him out of there." Resnick waved in the direction Bern had been headed, past the newly freed bottles and toward the back of the factory. They started to walk toward more enormous machines that lay scattered like dinosaurs felled by an ice age.

"Sounds like he came in on the weekend to fix the machine and it got filled up while he was in there." Resnick crouched down into a deep squat and shifted under a conveyor belt. Bern followed, or tried to. He was too tall to make the move easily and almost banged his head as he stood up.

Resnick watched this with a smirk on his face. Bern brushed his pants off as he stood and asked, "Does the machine fill up automatically, or is it done by a person?"

"That's one of the things we are trying to sort out," Resnick said. They were passing through a narrow corridor between two rows of conveyor belts. Resnick was walking quickly, and Bern took long strides to keep up.

"Who found him?" he asked. Resnick stopped suddenly, and Bern almost bumped into him. They had reached a monstrous machine that stretched off as far in the distance as Bern could see. There were people clustered in small groups at its base, a few of them wearing blue coveralls and safety glasses. Several RCMP officers mingled about as well, and some people dressed in studiously casual clothes, as if they were on their way to a barbecue at a country club and had gotten sidetracked.

Resnick surveyed the scene and jutted his chin at a man in blue coveralls. The man stepped toward a police officer and said a few words. He was young, in his twenties, with blond hair that hung down into a face whose features Bern could not make out at such a distance.

"Steve Ostikoff found him." Resnick practically spat out the man's name.

"Ostikoff," Bern repeated. "You know the guy?"

Resnick shrugged. "Enough to know I don't like him."

"Did anyone touch the body?" Bern asked.

"C'mon, Fortin. We know our jobs better than that," Resnick snapped before he stalked off in the direction of the machine.

When Bern caught up with Resnick, he was stepping onto a ladder that was welded to the side of the machine and reached all the way to the roof of the monster, ten feet above floor level. Bern surveyed the ladder. There was no way to get his case up there. He found a dry spot between two soapy puddles on the concrete floor and laid his case down. He took out a pair of thin latex gloves and shoved them into the back pocket of his jeans.

Then he shut the case tightly and followed Resnick up the ladder.

There was no railing at the top. The roof of the machine was just a flat steel expanse, as long and wide as a ballroom. It was divided into sections, each with a slightly raised trapdoor with a metal handle on it. The fourth door was open, and Resnick was standing next to it. At his feet were several long, thin objects that looked like dishwasher trays full of beer bottles. A light had been set up on a tripod and was shining down on the opening in the machine. Two other police officers were talking to a woman in civilian clothing a few steps away.

"What is this machine?" Bern asked as he approached Resnick. Stepping past the officer, Bern saw the arm. He looked away quickly, then looked back slowly, taking in the sight in incremental bits.

"It's a bottle washer. For returned beer bottles," Resnick was saying. He pointed to the long trays that lay by his feet. "He needed to take those out to get in. There's not much space in there, and it sounds like he was a pretty big guy."

Bern could barely hear him. He started with the hand. The fingers, icy and white, were thick, with strawberry-blond hairs sprouting from each knuckle. They gripped the metal handle tightly. Resnick crouched down next to the opening, and Bern stepped around the tripod and joined him. From this angle he could see where the blood had pooled at the base of the palm, a sign that this arm had been there for some time. The forearm was encased in a blue canvas sleeve, and it dangled from the midpoint between elbow and shoulder into the tank below. Bern leaned forward to see the rest, but the arm ended with a jagged stump, the blue canvas in threads.

"Dear God," he said quietly.

He looked inside the tank. Something was floating beneath the thin skein of soap scum that covered the surface of the gray water. The fumes that wafted up made his nostril hairs tingle and his eyes tear up. Bern blinked three times and held his breath. There were some sticks floating on top. He leaned back, took a deep breath, and closed his eyes.

"Bones?" he asked quietly.

"From fingers," Resnick replied.

"We've got to get him out of there." Bern held his breath and leaned forward again to take in a bit more. He tilted his head to keep from looking at the arm. Under the surface was a large object, its exterior peeling and raw. His mind closed around the image, but the interpretation came slowly. He was looking at a hump of shredded flesh, which he gradually understood to be hunched shoulders. There would be a head somewhere below the surface, and the rest of the torso and legs were completely submerged in the tank.

The smell was overpowering and Bern fought the urge to escape. The building was huge; he was surrounded by space and yet he felt trapped. A cold sweat spread over his body. Dread formed a stone in the pit of his stomach and the memories hit him in a wave. He closed his eyes and found a different body floating behind his eyelids. Whole families of mutilated corpses bobbing on the shores of a murky river. Arms and legs separated from their torsos, forever anonymous.

"How deep is it?" Bern asked. Each word was a pebble.

"Close to ten feet. He would have been standing on the bottom," a quiet voice replied. A woman's voice. Bern kept his eyes closed and let the sound wash over him like the call of a bird in his garden in the morning. "Are you okay?" she asked. "You look dizzy or something."

"What's the chemical?" he asked, ignoring her question. It felt like he was moving in slow motion, each word a chore to form.

"Sodium hydroxide. A three percent solution," the musical voice replied in a deeper tone. Serious stuff.

Bern opened his eyes and, carefully avoiding the arm, focused on the place where the sound was coming from. Crouched across from him, the opening to the caustic bath between them, was the woman who had been talking to the police officers. His first impression was one of smallness: she was as tiny as a child. She wore jeans and a blue V-necked shirt with an embroidered B just under her left shoulder. Her hair was almost black and curled around her face. Gray hairs intermingled with the black, and Bern realized she was older than he first thought. Her eyes were such a clear blue as to be almost purple. The color of the bachelor's buttons that bloomed around the perimeter of his garden. He'd known a woman with eyes like that once. He kept his gaze locked on hers for a moment only, then looked away.

His eyes fell next on the peeling stump of the arm, the fingers gripping the handle as though they could still pull the man free from his fate.

"And you are?" he asked.

"Evie Chapelle, safety manager for the Bugaboo Brewery," she replied.

"So it was your job to make sure this didn't happen?" He barked the words. The voice of a commander.

Her eyes widened, but she did not reply. Then she nodded slowly and only once, as though conceding his point.

Another wave of memories, another pile of bodies came to

him now. Bern closed his eyes again and put a hand down to steady himself. His senses, now on overdrive, could pick up the sickly sharp smell of battery acid, with an undercurrent of death. Piled outside force command headquarters, the bodies were being set upon by the packs of feral dogs that roamed the streets. "Get rid of them," his commanding officer had ordered, "before they make us all sick."

He opened his eyes again and focused on the woman. He could see her before him, tiny and tidy and watching him intently with eyes the color of flowers. Her lavender eyes held him, steadied him. The double vision receded as quickly as adjusting a set of binoculars. He felt the heat leave his body, and though he was covered in sweat, he was suddenly cold.

Resnick stood behind him, waiting. They were all waiting for him. Waiting for the coroner to tell them what to do next. The body in the tank floated before him, slowly disintegrating. The arm, still whole, waiting for him to restore to it what dignity he could.

Bern stood up, taking his bearings. He spun slowly around. The factory was edged with a metal catwalk. It was lined with people—staff members, he presumed, who had stopped their work to watch what was going on. They would get more than they bargained for if they hung around much longer.

The investigative process snapped into place in his mind. Irrefutable. Something to hang on to. The coroner's first task is to find out who died.

"Who is it?" he asked the lavender-eyed woman. Damn, he couldn't remember what she said her name was.

"Gavin Grayson. A millwright," she said.

"When did it happen?"

She looked down for a moment. When she answered, her voice was very quiet. "Sometime over the weekend. I'm not sure when."

"Huh," Bern replied. "Do you have a chemistry department? Any stats on how quickly this stuff eats through flesh?" She did not squirm under his stare.

"The supplier might have something. I can contact them. I don't think our corporate office will have that kind of information." She paused, as if about to say something else.

Resnick, who had been watching, barked at her. "This man is in charge," he said, pointing at Bern. "You tell him everything. Got it?"

She nodded. "It's just that . . . sometimes a mouse will get caught in there. We do our best to keep them out—there are traps everywhere—but with all the grain around, there are bound to be a few."

Resnick rolled his eyes.

She looked at him steadily and said, "You said to tell him everything."

Bern felt something inside him soften toward her. "About the mice," he prompted.

"When a mouse goes through, it's just bones at the end of the twenty-minute cycle," she said.

Resnick snorted, but Bern nodded. It gave him something to work with. All at once, he made his decision. "I want this place shut down," he said. "Everything." He turned to Resnick. "You've got photos?"

Resnick nodded.

"Okay. Let's drain the tank. I want someone taking shots as the water level goes down. Let's get that poor guy out of there."

•   •   •

Steve Ostikoff stripped off his gloves and dropped them into the plastic evidence bag that the police constable held out to him. She was short and kind of stocky. She looked a little older than him, maybe the same age as his older sister. He wanted to tell her that the caustic on the gloves would burn through the plastic in minutes, but just then he caught sight of a small clump of residue on one fingertip of the right-hand glove. The feeling of Gavin's skin, like the thin skin that forms on cooling soup barely holding back the liquid beneath, was a memory that would be with him forever now. As would the hand gripping the door handle, and the arm eaten by caustic until it separated from the rest of the body. His stomach rolled and the bile was at his throat in seconds. He cupped his hand over his mouth and pointed at the side door.

"Just don't go far," the constable said. "And don't talk to anyone. We'll want to interview you again soon."

Once he was outside, the contrast with the air of the bottle shop was so sudden that Steve forgot all about being sick. It was sunny and warm, a full summer day. He leaned back against the outside wall of the brewery. The front of the building was U-shaped, with a small, grassy courtyard at the center. Across from him, at the opposite end of the U from where he was standing, was the employee locker room, the lunch room, and the long hallway he had walked down just an hour ago to reach the bottle shop. It seemed like it was three minutes ago and yet two years ago all at the same time.

He stood up straighter and took a few deep breaths. He felt much better, which was great, because just then Shandie Greene opened the door from the pub and led a group of tourists out to the parking lot. Steve blushed at the unexpected sight of her, and at the thought of how close he'd been a moment ago to kneeling in the grass and puking.

The Bugaboo Brewery tour was popular with tourists. Shandie gave a tour at least every hour during the summer months. They would slow down, but not end completely, now that school holidays were over.

Steve watched her talking to an old couple at the front of the group, and she pointed off to the mountains, toward the Bugaboo Glacier. They listened intently to her every word. People did that with Shandie—in awe, Steve thought, of how damn gorgeous she was. He knew this part of her spiel well. She had mimicked it just the other night when they were out for a drink, and he'd laughed at how funny she could be. "That's why the beer tastes so crisp and fresh, because of the water that comes from the glacier." She'd echoed the words lightly, tossing her long, dark hair back and forth. "They fall for it every time," she'd said, laughing.

Steve knew the water didn't come from the glacier. It was Kootenay Landing town water, which rolled off the mountains to the east and into the municipal reservoir. It was fresh, quality mountain water, sure. But it didn't come from the Bugaboo Glacier.

He checked his watch. Forty-five minutes had passed since he'd found Gavin. He shivered as a picture of the soaked mess of the body spun before his eyes again. He looked down at his hands. He wanted to scrub them clean. He watched Shandie lead her flock to the parking lot, then he crossed the grass to the employee entrance.

The locker room was deserted. Banks of ancient beige metal

lockers lined the walls. Above them hung a collection of posters advertising Bugaboo Brew for the last fifty years. The effect was of a retro high school crossed with a bar bathroom. None of the lockers had locks on them, Steve's included. It was something Steve's father and uncle had taught him as a young boy. Union brothers do not steal from each other. And if one of his brothers needed something of Steve's, let him have it. Steve followed the advice, but in his own way. He didn't lock his locker, but he did lock his truck. And he kept his valuables in there.

He'd had gloves on when he'd reached out to Gavin, but his hands still felt filthy. He scrubbed them with too-hot water and a tangy-smelling disinfectant soap that left his skin raw. He ripped off enough paper towels to dry his whole body and wadded them as he patted his hands dry. He turned to his locker and stopped suddenly.

A small metal padlock had been slipped through the loop of his locker door and snapped shut. It lay there like an accusation. Steve looked over his shoulder, then back at the lock. He walked closer to it. He leaned forward to read the label but did not touch it. L. Ostikoff, it read.

Steve tapped his foot on the sparkling clean linoleum. The others were all in the lounge upstairs, drinking coffee and waiting to be questioned, speculating about what had happened. Anyone on the rescue team would be helping the police to somehow get Gavin's body out of the bottle washer. As a first aid attendant, he would be expected to help them.

Someone was trying to send him a message with that lock. And in the wrong hands, in the wrong context, the finger of accusation would point at him.

Steve reached into his pocket and pulled out his keys. He found the smallest key on the ring and inserted it into the lock, twisting it until it snapped open. He slid the lock out and let it fall into his pocket, then checked his watch again. No way he was going to take the blame for this. No fucking way.

From: Karl Ostikoff [plantmgr@bugbrew.ca]
To: Dave Porteous [vpwestern@bevco.ca]
Cc: Evie Chapelle [safety@bugbrew.ca]
Sent: Tuesday, September 8, 10:52 a.m.

Dave,
Following up on our phone call this morning, a fatality
has occurred at Bugaboo. A worker was found inside
compartment #4 of the bottle washer. The tank was
filled with a 3 percent caustic solution. Rescue efforts are
under way, and our team is cooperating fully with the
RCMP and Coroners Service, both of which are on site.
We are expecting an officer from the WSB this afternoon.
    I will keep you posted of possible need for a corporate
legal team.

Karl
Karl Ostikoff
Manager
Bugaboo Brewery—A BevCo Company

5

While Evie Chapelle organized the recovery, Bern stayed with the body. He recited the coroner's duties silently to himself: find out who died, how they died, when they died, and by what manner. It circled like a children's rhyme through his head. He repeated it over and over, trying to keep all other thoughts out.

From where he stood he could see small teams of people undertaking the tasks he'd laid out for them. After some debate over how to handle it, a paramedic had removed the arm, wrapping it in its own body bag for the time being, to protect it from the caustic the rest of the body had been exposed to. The tank was empty now, and it was time to get Gavin Grayson out. The coroner in his glory, caring for the dead. Even the RCMP officers, even Resnick, had to defer to Bern in the aftermath of a death. In Afghanistan, Bern had commanded an entire battle group. It wasn't as if the leadership role was unfamiliar to him. And yet, now that he was a civilian, it was different. Everything was different.

He watched Evie Chapelle lead a squad of workers in blue coveralls. She looked back to see if they were following. A fatal mistake. She ducked under a conveyor belt and approached a huge control panel along one wall. They followed, but Bern could see the tense set of the shoulders, the heads bent together, muttering.

That was the biggest difference, right there. In the army, you knew your men would follow. Refusing to obey your orders was tantamount to breaking the law. He'd had to lay charges against one of his soldiers only once in over twenty years. His chest tightened when he thought about it: the young man in jail, awaiting trial. In the military, duty came first. No matter what any individual might say is right.

But in the civilian world, the lines were not so clearly drawn. A leader needed to be more persuasive. There was always an element of personal choice. Your team could choose to follow you or not. Bern had spent his whole lifetime within an organizational hierarchy—first in Catholic schools, then in the military. Choice was a new concept for him, one he tried to explore a little more every day. Even the little things—longer hair, scuffs on his boots, dirt on the knees of his jeans—went against the grain of years of training. Each one a victory of sorts.

The rescue team approached the bottle washer now and hovered in a circle. Evie Chapelle stood at their center, orchestrating their movements. She looked like a kid bossing the grown-ups around, and they didn't seem to like it one bit. She made them sign forms, affix permits, check and double-check lockouts. Bern could see Resnick pacing behind them, growing impatient with the bureaucracy. Just when he thought the RCMP officer was going to go in and pull the corpse out on his own, she let them get to work.

She picked a small guy to go in. Full breathing tank. He climbed into the compartment from a side door at floor level.

His two helpers stood holding a hard-cased rescue stretcher and a body bag, which they would slide in when the small guy was ready. Two other workers climbed up the side of the bottle washer to join Bern on the roof. The blond guy Resnick had pointed out earlier and another young man, both in full harness and lugging equipment. Bern stepped aside to make way for them. They moved the light away from the opening and set up a larger tripod equipped with a winch. They attached themselves to it and dropped a rope down.

Then they waited.

It was a carefully choreographed dance. There was a long pause when nothing seemed to be happening. Bern knew that the small guy in the machine would be seeing, for the first time, what he would see in his dreams for the rest of his life.

A radio echoed: "On belay." Another pause. "Up, slow."

Bern nodded at them and the two young men began pulling up the rope. He held his breath along with them.

"Stop."

And there it was. The full and awful truth. The hard casing of the rescue stretcher, and in it a black body bag, hastily zipped to catch as much of the remains as possible.

They guided the stretcher to a horizontal position, and Bern asked them to open the body bag. He knelt down, steeling himself, and inspected the contents. Careful not to touch anything, he allowed his eyes to roam over the assortment of ragged flesh and bone, and felt nothing. Nothing but the present moment and the task at hand: to find out who died, how he died, when he died, and by what manner.

He nodded to the young men again and they zipped up the body bag. "Down, slow," came the radio order as they began to lower the stretcher down the outside of the bottle washer. The paramedics waited in a line at ground level like mourners in a funeral procession.

The front office was an oasis after the buzz of activity in the bottle shop. Evie ducked into the mail room and leaned against the photocopier. She took a deep breath and closed her eyes for a second. They flew open again as the image of Gavin's burned body filled her mind. She stared at the rows of mail slots on the wall and read each name. The slots were arranged alphabetically, for the most part—though anyone who had been there less than five years had a slot on the end, each one arranged in a vaguely chronological order from the employee's start date. That was the kind of sloppiness that drove Evie crazy.

Gemma strode into the mail room, a sheaf of papers in her hand. Her hand flew to her chest when she saw Evie.

"Oh, Evie! You scared me half to death!" she said. "Oh, I mean. No. I shouldn't say that. I'm sorry. Are you okay?"

Evie nodded. "Just taking a second," she said.

Gemma nodded and moved to the mail slots. She started slipping papers into them, her motions swift. She looked unaffected by the day's events, her smooth bob as sleek as ever. Evie pushed at her own straggly hair and watched Gemma at work. There was something reassuring about knowing that despite the horror they had seen that morning, some things still went on the same as always.

"Every day I think about putting these names in order. It would only take an hour or so to do it. But then, they've been

like this for so long, it's like my body has them memorized."
Gemma laughed. "So I tell myself I'm doing my part for productivity by keeping them where they are." She turned and smiled at Evie. "I probably shouldn't say something at a time like this, but did you meet the coroner?"

Evie nodded slowly.

Gemma rolled her eyes. "Did you even notice? That is one good-looking man. Those dark eyes? That lean body? That accent?"

A smile flitted across Evie's face, and she shrugged. "I wasn't really paying attention," she lied.

Gemma sighed. "Well, hard not to, I say. So have you had your moment now?" she asked.

Evie nodded.

"Good, because Karl wants to see you," she said, just as a voice hollered from the main office.

"Gemma!"

"There he is. C'mon."

"What are you doing?" Karl Ostikoff's voice boomed at them. He stood in front of Gemma's desk, a pile of documents in his hands. He was not overly tall. Blond, trim, and with startling green eyes, he was the image of a handsome man. But Evie had worked with him for years and knew that the image was just a thin veneer. While at first glance he looked as young as his son, Steve, who had just discovered the body, she knew Karl was pushing fifty. Her first impression of him, when she'd been transferred to Bugaboo, was of a snake in the grass. Five years later, she still hadn't lost that feeling. A year earlier, Karl had been promoted to brewery manager. He was now Evie's immediate boss.

"Just the mail and some filing," Gemma said. If Gemma shared Evie's impression of Karl, she certainly didn't let it show.

"I don't know how you can be filing at a time like this," he said. Gemma moved around him to get behind her desk and his eyes landed on Evie. "I need to talk to you."

She moved closer and stood before him. He seemed to age as she got closer, the lines on his face becoming more visible. He was impeccably dressed, as always, in casual trousers that were carefully pressed. The seam at the front was still crisp, unaffected by a morning spent climbing the bottle washer ladder. He wore his own type of uniform, a polo-necked BevCo-branded shirt. Today his shirt advertised a low-carb beer brewed in Mexico.

"Evie," he said. His voice sounded serious, but his face gave nothing away. "The Workers' Safety Board just happens to have an officer driving through Kootenay Landing this afternoon. He will be here by three o'clock."

Evie crinkled her nose. "It usually takes them a few days to get to the scene," she said.

Karl nodded, once, and a flash of annoyance crossed his face. "Tell me what he'll be looking at."

"Okay," she said slowly. "The main two regulations will be confined space and working alone. Whoever they send will go over those with a fine-toothed comb. Procedures and training documents will be the main ones. But they'll look at implementation documents too: sign-in sheets, lockout forms. That kind of thing."

"And what will he find?" he asked.

Evie sighed and ran her hand through her hair. "Well, we still don't know what we are dealing with here. I mean, how this could have happened. Overall, we are pretty compliant, but until we know how this happened—"

She stopped talking as Karl held up a hand. "I just want to remind you what the priorities are here."

She nodded and tried to focus on his words. "Find out what happened," she said.

He stared at her for what seemed like a full minute, not saying anything.

"No," he said. It came out like a slap—loud and forceful. He looked down and took a deep breath. "Your job is to protect the company," he said quietly, his anger reined in again. "No matter what. Your job is to prove that we as a team did everything we needed to do. Your job is to prove due diligence. That is all. What happened? Doesn't matter. What matters is your team. You are part of the team, right?" he asked. His voice had gone from barely restrained anger to friendly sports coach, with no visible change in the expression on his face.

"Part of the team," she repeated. Evie almost expected him to chuck her on the shoulder, but when he spoke again, his voice was ominous.

"That's right. So when the WSB comes, you say all the right things." The menace in his voice was barely disguised now. "And in the meantime, you stick to that coroner like glue."

She looked up at him, searching his face for clues. She could find none.

"And don't fuck it up," he whispered.

His eyes slipped away from her face. Evie watched the perfect creases at the back of his pant legs and his full head of blond hair walk away from her. From the back he looked like a young man again.

6

Bern pulled out an upholstered chair and sat down next to Resnick. The room was called the employee lounge, and judging by the decor, the company was doing well. It was as nice as the bar at a ski resort—thick wooden beams and deep club chairs scattered in the corners. The color scheme was predominantly blue, like a can of Bugaboo Brew. Someone had brought in doughnuts, which were piled high on a tray at the bar that blocked off one end of the room. Behind it, several glass-fronted beer fridges topped with Bugaboo signs blinked brightly.

"The beer fridge is locked. I already checked," Resnick said between bites of a jelly-filled doughnut. "But there's coffee."

Bern shook his head as he sat down and surveyed the room. Resnick's officers had set up quickly, and three of them sat at tables, interviewing witnesses. "Anything so far?" Bern asked.

"We talked to everyone who was on shift today. So far they're all sticking to the same story: the guy should not have gone in there by himself, and if he did, he should have locked out. Did you see this lockout everyone is talking about?"

"Yeah, I did," Bern said. "It's complicated. Anyone entering a machine is supposed to fill out a form and use a set of locks—like the lock you had on your high school locker. Seven lockout points and three forms to fill out before you go into the bottle washer. Not easy to remember the details, but easy to remember that you need to do something."

"So either he did know and decided to go in of his own accord, or he just didn't know," said Resnick. A blob of jam had got stuck to the edge of his lip, but he didn't seem to notice.

Bern looked away. "Or he did know and didn't care. Maybe that's the way they do it around here," he said.

"Yeah, there is that," said Resnick. He took a sip of coffee from a Styrofoam cup.

"Anything unusual stand out?" Bern asked.

"Yeah, that bugger Ostikoff. There's something up with him for sure."

"How so?"

"I just get a funny feeling about that guy. Not answering questions straight," Resnick replied. His face was twisted in a sneer.

Bern wiped at the corner of his own lip, hoping Resnick would follow suit. He didn't. "Maybe that's because you've got a bee up your nose about him anyway. I could tell when you first pointed him out to me. What's that about?"

Resnick shrugged. "Nothing. He just strikes me as an asshole through and through."

"Huh."

"Huh? What do you mean, huh?"

"Well, just . . . you know. When you start out like that . . ." Bern's voice trailed off.

"Start out like what?" Resnick demanded.

"Well, I'm just not surprised that you didn't get anywhere."

Resnick held the last bite of doughnut in his fingers and pointed at Bern. "You think you could do better?"

Bern shrugged. "I love a challenge," he said.

Resnick leaned back in his chair and stared silently at Bern. He popped the last bite of doughnut in his mouth and licked sticky icing from his fingers. In the process, he managed to clean the bit of jam stuck to his lip.

"Constable Schilling," he snapped, sitting up straight again. A uniformed officer, a young woman, appeared before them. She ignored Bern and stared fixedly at Resnick. "I'm going to send Ostikoff back in here. I want you to sit in while Fortin here interviews him."

Schilling nodded sharply. Bern thought there was something rebellious about her stance and slightly mocking in the way she said, "Yes, sir," as if she were holding herself back from rolling her eyes at her superior officer.

Resnick turned to Bern. "Find out what he's not telling us, Fortin," he said before stalking off.

Bern smiled at Constable Schilling, who nodded back. "You'll take notes, to remind me what he said?" Bern asked.

Schilling nodded and tapped her notebook. "Yes, sir," she said again, but this time with a smile. She sat down across from Bern, her notebook open, her pen armed and ready.

After a moment, Steve Ostikoff came in. Bern watched him as he stood in the doorway. Thick blond hair, square features, a trim figure—standard-issue good-looking guy. Bern waved to Steve and he walked to the table and pulled out a chair. He sat down and immediately slouched his shoulders. Bern smiled and opened his hands. "Make yourself comfortable. You've had quite a day. Do you happen to have a key to that lock?"

Steve sat up with a start. He glanced about nervously. "What lock? What are you talking about?" He looked at Bern and Constable Schilling out of the corner of his eye.

"The lock on the beer fridge. What other lock would I be talking about?" Bern asked.

Steve slouched back down and turned his sullen look at Bern. "Nothing, no other lock."

Bern looked over at Constable Schilling and cocked his head. Steve watched him.

"I just . . . I didn't think police officers drank on the job. That's all."

Bern studied him for a minute. Close up, he could see slight pouches below Steve's eyes, which were a bright green. Seasonal allergies. Or maybe a hangover. Definitely on edge.

"Well, good thinking, except I'm not a police officer. You know that, right? I'm the coroner." Bern's voice was easy, inviting.

"Like on *CSI*? You do the autopsy?" Steve asked.

"Well, no. Not like that, though it's a common misperception," Bern explained. "That's how they do it in the United States. But in Canada it's different, and in British Columbia it's different again. Here we have lay coroners, who are people who have some background in investigations and can help figure things out. An independent office, separate from the police."

"So if I tell you something, you won't have to tell the police?" Steve asked.

Constable Schilling looked up at this, alarmed. One of her hands reached instinctively for her duty belt, though Bern was sure none of the weapons and tools strapped there would help her in this situation. A little diplomacy, a little camaraderie. That's what was called for. No wonder Resnick was having trouble getting anything from this guy.

Bern looked quickly at Schilling and patted the air with his fingers. Take it easy. "Well, not necessarily. I would have to use my judgment. If what you told me didn't relate to breaking a law or committing a crime, I wouldn't have to tell the police."

"So what's yours?" Steve asked.

"Sorry, you lost me. My what?"

"Your background. You said coroners have an investigative background," Steve said. "What's yours?"

"I was a soldier. An officer."

Steve grunted. "So what do you want to know? I already told those guys everything."

"Did you now?" Bern asked pointedly. He reached for the interview notes that Resnick had left him and flipped through them.

"Yes, everything," Steve repeated.

"Well, help me understand a few things, then. Because this is my first time in a brewery. Before today my only experience with beer was as a consumer, and to tell you the truth, I liked it that way." Bern smiled helplessly. "Take me through your morning."

Steve recounted almost word for word what was in the notes that Resnick had given Bern. Schilling wrote it all down again in her notebook.

When he finished, Bern asked, "If you were going to go into that machine, would you lock it out?"

"I would never go into that machine. It's not my job," he said.

"So whose job is it?"

"A millwright. Maybe an electrician. Maintenance guys."

"So you don't know anything about what would need to be done to enter that machine?"

Steve shrugged. "I never said that."

Bern waited the silence out. Constable Schilling tapped her pen on her notebook and waited too. Steve looked around. There were two other employees being interviewed at the other end of the room. He leaned forward and spoke quietly.

"Okay. It's like what you saw today. Major deal. Lockout points, over behind the infeed; everything gets shut off. Permits, harnesses, supervisors, SCBA, radios. The whole shebang."

Bern leaned forward and kept his voice as low as Steve's. "So that would be pretty common knowledge? Not to climb in the machine without locking out?"

"Well, for someone who had worked here for a while it would."

"And for Gavin?"

Steve's eyes flashed and he fought to keep his voice low. "I don't know. I hardly knew the guy."

"Venture a guess?" Bern asked.

Steve was quiet for a minute. "No, no guess. I can't see a reason why he would go in on his own. Unless . . ."

"Unless what?"

"Well, he was a bit of a show-off. The machine was leaking pretty bad. We were waiting until the next shutdown week to put in a permanent fix. Gavin was supposed to put a little patch on the outside. But maybe he thought he could just fix it all on his own?" Steve sat back again, spread his hands on the tabletop, and started drumming his fingers.

Bern waited. Steve continued drumming. When he said nothing more, Bern asked, "Does that sound to you like something Gavin would do?"

"Like I said, I hardly knew the guy," Steve said. He crossed his arms and let them fall on his chest. The look he gave Bern was saying, *I'm all done here.* But Bern looked back: *Not till I say you are.*

"But from the little you did know," Bern said, "I'm asking you to speculate."

Steve sighed. "He was a bit of a show-off, like I said. Liked to brag, you know?" His voice trailed off, then came back stronger. "But then, I can't really see him doing anything way out of line like that, safetywise."

"Unless someone told him to?" Bern prompted.

Steve shook his head slowly. "Even then, I think he would have followed procedure."

"So maybe he didn't know the procedure?"

"Yeah, maybe he didn't know it," he said, nodding as he spoke. Then his brow furrowed in confusion. "Except you never heard me say that, okay?"

Bern smiled easily. He could see he was not going to get any more cooperation from the fellow. He held up his hands in mock surrender. "All right, all right. You never said that. One last question: Who fills up the machine?"

"There are three of us who run the bottle washer. One for each shift. One of us usually does it," Steve said slowly.

"Usually?"

"Well, sometimes. It depends. Sometimes we fill it up over the weekend. But this week, because we were running new bottles to start, there was time to fill it up in the morning—this morning—at the start of the shift. It could fill while we ran out the other line and be full by the time we made the change over to old bottles and started up the bottle washer. That way, no one needed to come in on the long weekend."

"Is that how it happened?" Bern asked.

"No."

"Why not?"

"Well, because when I got here, it was already full," Steve said slowly.

"But you hadn't filled it?"

"No." His voice was getting louder.

"Do you know who did?"

"No," he snorted. "That's like asking me if I know who killed him."

"Is that what you think happened? Gavin was in there and someone came and filled up the machine?"

Steve glared at Bern over his crossed arms.

"Well? Are you going to answer me?" Bern asked.

"I don't think he would have climbed in when it was full." Steve spat the words out.

Bern took a deep breath. Let it go, Fortin. Try another tack. You can interview him again later, when Resnick's crew isn't around.

"Anything else you want to tell me before we finish up here?" Bern asked.

Steve sighed. "I might as well tell you before someone else does. My dad is the manager here. Brewery manager, of the whole place."

"Okay. So your dad is the boss," Bern said slowly. "Something more I should know about that?"

Steve shrugged angrily. "I'm the one who started up the machine this morning. People are going to think that I did it and my dad is getting me off the hook. But I didn't do it. Okay?" His voice had taken on a plaintive tone. He twitched in his seat and looked around the room. "Can I go now? I want to get out of here."

"Why so upset?" Bern asked him.

"Look, I came into work and found a dead guy. That ever happen to you before?" Steve snarled.

Bern tipped his head. He leaned back like he was telling a story and spoke lightly. "Yes, that has happened to me before. In fact, there were a few months at my work where there were dozens of dead guys, and women and children, lined up at my front door every morning. So yes, you could say it's happened to me before, and yes, I know how you feel. You want to go home and be close to the people you love. You want to have a shower and a cold beer. And sleep, if you can. If the pictures in your head don't torment you and keep you up."

Steve didn't say anything. His arms remained crossed, face scowling.

"Just remember one thing: I have been there, and so I do know. And I know that if I had information that would help others understand what had happened, and prevent it from happening to anyone else, I would share it," Bern said.

"With the police?" Steve asked.

"Or with the coroner. Here's my card," he said. He looked over at Constable Schilling, who nodded once without looking up from her notes. "You may go. We will want to talk to you again, but you can go home for now."

From: [capitaineallouette@hotmail.com]
To: [bernfortin@bccoronerservice.bc.ca]
Re: re: re: re: re: re: Bonjour
Sent: Tuesday, September 8, 6:45 a.m.

I hope you are well. How is the garden coming? I still have trouble picturing it, but I guess we are all different outside of the jobs we have. Outside of the army. I have been spending some time thinking about what you said, and I asked about taking online courses, to keep me occupied until the trial. They said yes right away, like they were waiting for me to ask, which made me think maybe you'd put in a word for me? If you did, thank you.

I've been thinking a lot. I have time to do that here, more time than ever. I'm trying to understand why it is so wrong—what I did. I still don't think it was wrong, and if I dare say it, I don't think you really believed it was either. I hope I'm not offending you. It's just the truth how I see it.

A reporter came to see me. He said there was a lot of talk—about a deal around your retirement, and that maybe you wouldn't be called. Wouldn't come and speak up for me.

I don't know what to think about that. It goes around and around in my head, everything that happened that day, and after. I have to tell them the truth: if it happened again, I would do the same thing.

Wouldn't you?

My class starts next week. It will give me something to do, other than work out. I'm going to take philosophy. Do you think I will find an answer to my question?

Happy gardening, Lieutenant-Colonel.

Marcel Alais

7

He escaped from the brewery and gulped the fresh air. Relief washed over him as he slid his truck into gear and turned onto the road, away from the plant. He felt hurried, like he needed to get back there quickly, though his immediate duty to the dead was done. Resnick had things well under control, and Bern could take the time to change out of his gardening clothes and let Mrs. K. fuss over him for a few minutes.

Once he got home, the need to hurry seemed to leave him. He walked through the tiny house, enjoying the sight of each room. The cream-colored walls, the pale yellow cabinets, the 1950s-style Formica table in a deep pomegranate that made him smile every time he looked at it. There was something funny about him, Bern Fortin, setting up his own home for the first time in his forties and having a kitchen table worthy of June Cleaver.

He loved that he could stand in the center of his home and see every corner of it. In that way, it was not unlike the various officers' barracks where he'd spent many years living. And it was as tidy as barracks as well: that was a habit he'd likely never break.

The biggest change Bern had made to the bungalow was to

open up a wall between the living room and second bedroom. His desk was a broad board that stretched from one end of the former bedroom to the other. Above it was a wide window that looked out over the front of the house. On each side of the window he'd built bookshelves and stacked them with a carefully selected library culled from garage sales, secondhand stores, and library book sales. Books on gardening and food preservation. Books on medicinal herbs and bread making. Books on composting and keeping chickens in the backyard. These were all things Bern wanted to learn in his retirement. Each book was a talisman of his new life—a reminder of his promise. He had much to learn about growth and beauty, but he could not spend all his time there. Not yet. He still had a debt to tend to. A debt to the dead.

The office was his favorite part of the house. All that was on the expansive desk was a laptop, the smallest one he could find. He used it mostly to order seeds online, and to look up information on gardening from the clues dropped by Mrs. K. There were the inevitable emails as well: from his men, from fellow officers. Checking in, staying in touch, letting him know how they were doing. He knew there would be an email waiting for him now. Captain Alais got email access on Tuesdays. Bern didn't feel up to that just yet.

He opened the door to his bedroom. It was one area of his life that still needed to be decommissioned. You could bounce a nickel off his bedspread. Bern stripped down and put his dirty clothes in the closet hamper. He chose a clean pair of cords and a soft flannel shirt from those he'd hung as carefully as a quartermaster. He laid them on the bed and walked the three steps to the adjacent bathroom.

He looked at himself straight on in the mirror. It was a

challenge to himself, one he took on daily. Eyes, dark and intense; lids slightly hooded. Looks like you're keeping a secret, his mother used to tell him. Looks like you don't have a clue, his commanding officer would have said. Black hair, curling around his head, much longer than regulation would allow. His skin was kissed olive by the sun and shadowed by the hint of a beard. Straight, even features—like an aristocrat or a goddamn girl, depending on who you listened to. He turned away. The clippers were in the drawer, next to the straight razor, but he would not use either. Not today.

He'd carefully restored the original cerulean-blue bathtub and tiles with new caulking and a lot of elbow grease, but he'd upgraded the showerhead to one with multiple spray patterns and an intense massage feature. Some parts of military life were easier to let go of than others: the lukewarm, low-pressure, or nonexistent showers of in-theater operations were a thing of the past.

With fresh clothes on, the dirt of the garden and the pall of the brewery washed away, Bern was ready to face his email. He scrolled through the various new messages, only a few personal ones in among the special offers from garden centers. The one he was waiting for, from Captain Alais, was there. Bern sat back after reading it and let the words sink in. *Très bien,* he thought. Very, very good. Maybe something good will come of this after all.

He checked his watch and stood quickly, grabbing his cell phone from the charger. In the garden he stopped to pick a bouquet for Mrs. K. He started with bachelor's buttons, added sweet peas and a few marigolds, and rounded it out with cosmos. Then he followed the path to Mrs. K.'s downstairs kitchen door.

When he'd first heard her mention her downstairs kitchen,

Bern had no idea what she was talking about. But he soon learned that she had two full kitchens. The one in the basement, where he'd had coffee that morning, was as large as a church hall, with multiple counters, rows of cabinets and a dining room table. The lower floor also had a downstairs sitting room and Mrs. K.'s bedroom. Upstairs was the good kitchen and the good living room. Bern had never seen either of these rooms used, though they were of course immaculate and ready to be pressed into service at a moment's notice.

He let himself in without knocking. Mrs. K. was in her usual place at the counter, her head covered in a thickly woven hairnet. On the counter next to her was a crate full of peaches. The sink in front of her was filled with hot water and peaches too, and she pulled one out now and peeled its skin off.

Bern had never dared ask her age, but he guessed she was at least seventy. She was deeply tanned and solidly muscled from a lifetime of hard work. She rinsed her hands in the sink, dried them on her apron, and took the flowers from him without smiling.

"What do I do with these?" she tutted.

"Every beautiful woman needs flowers now and then," Bern said.

She pushed him toward the table. "Go sit," she said.

Bern laughed and shook his head but did as he was told. The fall fair form was waiting for him, filled out carefully in her block printing. She had him entering a whole variety of categories.

"Jam?" he asked. "I've never made jam."

"I'll show you," she said. She placed a tray in front of him. "Nothing to worry about right now. Eat in peace."

Bern took in the tray before him. A steaming bowl of borscht with a dollop of heavy cream. Fresh sourdough bread spread thickly with butter. A glass of homemade ginger beer. A delicate plate of butter cookies topped with maraschino cherries. He raised his shoulders in a resigned shrug and said simply, "I will."

It was only two blocks down an unpaved road to the back gate of the brewery. Bern walked slowly, enjoying the last of the warm summer day, the feeling of fullness in his belly from Mrs. K.'s dinner, and the knowledge that he'd somehow made his neighbor's day by signing his name dutifully to the fall fair form she'd filled out for him and handing over $7.50 in change to pay the entry fee. These were the threads that held him together for one more day.

The mountains were almost hazy in the heat. Not for the first time Bern imagined the mountains being wheeled in by unseen roadies, like enormous set pieces for a complex period movie. The perfect setting for a life of pottering in the loose, rich soil, fretting about aphids, and competing for the best tomatoes in the fall fair. A little coroner work on the side. At least, that's what he'd thought.

He reached the back gate and looked in at the rear of the plant. Only a few cars and trucks were left in the lot. Wide swaths of pavement lay bare between outcroppings of equipment and spare machinery. Several transport trucks were lined up by the warehouse, where they would stay until the WSB gave the staff the go-ahead to start production again.

The gate was locked by a simple combination keypad lock. He looked around to see if anyone might let him in. He couldn't see anyone in the brewery grounds. Behind him were street after street of employee houses. He could knock on any door, and someone inside would likely know the combination. The house on the corner caught his eye. A little white bungalow on a corner lot, its front windows with an uninterrupted view of the brewery yard. He thought he saw the edge of a curtain move slowly back in place. He could ask at that house, but of course those inside would have no reason to tell him.

Bern continued at his leisurely pace, following the chain-link fence around the perimeter of the grounds for close to ten minutes before he got to the front gate. He walked slowly through the front parking lot and in the main door. Gemma Burch was still at her post.

Bern smiled at her. "I'm sure you've had a tough day, but you look just as lovely as you did first thing this morning," he said.

"Ah, Mr. Coroner. Well, flattery will get you everywhere, I'm afraid," she replied with a smile. "The WSB officer is here. She's in the conference room with Evie and said for you to join them when you got back."

Bern held up a finger. "I'll go in just a minute, if you don't mind. But first, is there someone I can talk to about this lockout system that keeps coming up? Up until today, I thought padlocks were for sheds, but apparently there is a whole other aspect to them that I am missing."

Gemma laughed as she picked up the phone and punched in a few numbers. "Conrad, can you come to the front desk for a few minutes? Thank you," she said. "Conrad is just the person to explain it to you. He won't be long."

A minute later a friendly-looking man in his late thirties

walked quickly in through the door to the bottle shop. He shook Bern's hand as Gemma explained his request.

"Sure thing. Just come with me," he said. He went back out the door with equal speed, and Bern took a few long strides to catch up with him. He was dressed in the same outfit that most staff members seemed to wear—dress slacks and a T-shirt sporting a Bugaboo logo. Conrad seemed more at ease than most of the people Bern had talked to. He led the way from the bottle shop and down a hallway of offices. When the hallway opened up into a wide room, he came to a stop.

"This is the maintenance supply room. We keep our parts inventory here, and the millwrights and electricians each have their own sets of tools that they store here," he explained. "And here," he said, approaching a tall metal cabinet and pulling open its doors, "is where we store the lockout system."

Bern came closer and peered into the cabinet. Inside it were rows of metal shelves on sliders. On each one, carefully lined up and labeled, were sets of small padlocks, about four inches high. Across the base of each one stretched a white adhesive label printed with the name of an employee.

"Okay, you'll have to explain to me how this works," Bern said.

"I know it looks like the high school janitor's office on locker day. But these are more than your average lock. They are lifesavers really." Conrad picked up a lock at random and showed it to Bern. "Each employee who works in maintenance, or whoever needs to go into a confined space, is assigned his own set. The most lockout points are on the bottle washer—it has seven points—so each employee gets eight locks." Conrad handed him a lock. "They have an extra one, just in case." He laughed. "In case of what, I don't know. But just in case."

Bern held the lock in his palm, feeling its weight. "Hard to believe such a small thing could make such a big difference," he said quietly. "So tell me exactly? I want to be sure I get it."

"So if one of our maintenance guys is working on a machine—say he's fixing the bottom saw, which is the machine that cuts the bottoms off the return beer case—he needs to make sure that no one else will come along and start the machine up while he's working on it. On the saw, there are three places to lock out. Each one has a hasp that, when locked in place with this lock, will make it impossible to turn the machine on. So he locks out, then puts a tag on the lock saying who he is, what he's doing, and how long it will take."

"And the keys?" Bern asked.

"There is one set here," Conrad replied, "and a second set locked in the main office."

"So I'm just thinking out loud here. Is there any possibility that someone could have taken a lock off? I mean, with the extra set, or—"

Conrad interrupted him, talking more quickly and sounding less laid-back. "No. No chance of that. Seriously. It's just not done. Everyone knows that."

"Taboo?" asked Bern.

"Yes, that's it. Seriously taboo. Taking a brother's life in your hands if you do that." Conrad ran his hands through his hair.

"Thank you for explaining," Bern said. "It's a lot to understand for an outsider." He shrugged and smiled. "Is there anything else you think I should know?"

"I think that covers the basics. You really have to see it in action to understand. When it's a confined-space entry, it's very complicated," Conrad said.

Bern nodded. "I got a sense of that today, when the rescue team did the recovery. But I didn't understand fully. Now I believe I do. Thank you again," Bern said, nodding and backing away from the cabinet.

Conrad swung one door closed and was reaching for the other when Bern said, "By the way, can you just show me Gavin's locks?"

Conrad paused midmotion. "Uh, sure. Well, Gavin didn't have his own locks labeled yet. I was still working on that. But in the meantime, I told him to use Leroy's locks."

"Leroy?" Bern asked.

"Oh sure, of course. I think everyone knows Leroy, but of course you wouldn't. Leroy Ostikoff. He was the millwright Gavin replaced. He's off on long-term disability, but he won't be back before he retires." Conrad sighed. "He's not easy to replace. He worked here for his whole life, from when he was sixteen or something. Knows the place in and out. A poet with machines."

"What happened to him?" Bern asked.

Conrad shrugged. "Well, I probably shouldn't say, since it has nothing to do with what happened with Gavin. But I guess it won't hurt. His back is wrecked. He's all bent over. Too much time crawling under conveyor belts fixing machines, I guess."

"So can you show me his locks?"

"Sure thing." Conrad pulled open the door again and slid out a middle shelf. "That's strange."

Bern tilted forward to see what he was looking at.

"These are Leroy's locks. But one of them is missing," Conrad said.

"Have you ever noticed that before?"

"Can't say I have, no. But like I said, seven is the most we use. So it wouldn't have been a problem for Gavin. I mean, if Gavin had been following procedure," Conrad said. He looked quickly at his watch. "I've really got to get going. Can I walk you back to the office?" He closed the cabinet doors firmly.

"That would be good, so I don't get lost in this maze," Bern said. As they walked he asked, "So Leroy Ostikoff? He must be related to Steve Ostikoff, the young man who found Gavin."

Conrad nodded. "And Karl Ostikoff, the brewery manager. Karl and Leroy are brothers. And Steve is Karl's son."

They passed through a warehouse with pallets stacked to the ceiling. Three forklifts were parked between carefully painted parking lines on the concrete.

"It's funny, isn't it?" Bern remarked. "One brother in the union and the other running the place? Funny how things end up in families."

Conrad laughed. "Not funny if you know Karl. The guy was born to run things, no doubt about that. He was an even better millwright than Leroy, back in the day. But he made the leap from union to management." They reached the door to the main office and Conrad held it open for him. "Well, not a leap in Karl's case. It was more an effortless stride. And here I leave you, in Gemma's very capable hands."

With a quick nod, Conrad was out the door, swallowed back into the brewery.

• • •

Humorless. The word stuck in Bern's mind like gum on a shoe when he took his first look at WSB Officer Susan Byron.

"Does she bite?" he whispered to Gemma, who had shown him into the conference room.

"Be good," she whispered back. She was standing close to him and he could smell breath mints and her perfume, which made him think of spring. To Evie she said, "Here's Coroner Fortin for you. I'm going to wrap up for today. I think everyone else has gone home."

Evie looked up, her face even paler than it had been that morning. "Thanks for staying so late. See you in the morning," she said to Gemma.

Evie introduced Bern to Susan Byron. The safety board officer was stocky and overdressed for the weather in a burgundy wool pantsuit with a cream-colored polyester blouse. She made direct eye contact and shook his hand firmly. She did not smile.

Bern looked her over discreetly, trying to find something beautiful about her square frame, ill-fitting pants, and unflattering jacket. He finally settled on her feet, which looked small and delicate although tied rather tightly into clunky, steel-toed shoes. He smiled lavishly and held her hand for a moment too long.

"We're just wrapping up for the day," Evie said. She gestured out the window of the conference room. Night had come quickly; it was completely dark outside.

"So you've grilled her enough for one day?" he asked Byron with a wink at Evie.

"She's not the victim here," Byron replied. Bern watched as she tucked a few piles of papers and files into a giant lawyer's briefcase.

"We will resume at eight a.m., sharp. And I would like you here as well." Byron looked briefly at Bern as she slid another pile of documents into her case. How she fit so many in, Bern could not guess.

He bowed slightly. "Nothing would keep me away . . . well, with the exception of another untimely death in Kootenay Landing or surrounding area," he said.

Byron slammed her briefcase shut and twisted the numbers of the combination pad to lock it. "This isn't a joke, you know," she said as she headed to the door. Evie and Bern followed her out. "A worker is dead."

Bern nodded seriously as they walked together to the front door of the brewery. "When you've seen as much death as I have," he said quietly, "you begin to realize that it is no reason to lose your sense of humor."

Byron stopped walking and turned to face him. She opened her mouth to say something but seemed to think better of it and closed it again. She nodded once to Evie, who held the door for her, and left without another word.

"Well, you certainly seem to have made a good first impression," Evie said. "Are you leaving now too, or do you need to talk to me?"

Bern looked at her. Her face was pinched with fatigue. A tight crease of worry had drawn itself between her eyebrows, between those eyes that so reminded him of another pair of eyes from a happier time. He felt like reaching out and brushing it away with soft strokes of his fingers. He wanted to protect her from the ugliness of what had happened, from the relentless onslaught of the investigation, and from his own questioning, which had yet to begin.

"You look tired," he said. She nodded but did not reply. "But yes, I do have a few questions for you." He coughed once. "Did the humorless Officer Byron allow you time to eat supper?"

Evie laughed and shook her head.

"No, I thought not. Well, here is what I would suggest. I live not two blocks from here. How about we go sit on my patio, have something to eat, and go over my questions there?" he asked.

Evie shrugged. "Well, I am hungry. And my boss did say to stick to you like glue," she said.

"He did?"

Just then, a piercing alarm screamed through the loudspeakers. Bern watched as Evie placed her pale, ringless fingers into her ears to block out the sound.

"I'll have to check all the doors," she called over the sound.

Bern covered his own ears and shrugged. "Okay," he said. "Let's check all the doors."

They started by the employee entrance and checked all the doors that led to the front of the building. The shrieking alarm filled every space and precluded conversation. He followed Evie through the maze of machinery inside the plant until they reached an exit door at the back of the brewery. It stood wide open.

Bern pulled it shut while Evie punched the alarm code. The silence in the wake of the alarm shutting off was as soothing as a blanket. He stood next to her in an entryway that held three interior doors. One was open, and Bern could hear the roar of machinery within it. He looked inside and could see a series of three enormous boilers. Looking back at Evie, he saw that she was angry.

"What do you think happened?" he asked.

She bit her lip and shook her head. "This is a problem," she said. She pointed to the three doors. "This door goes to the boiler room, this one to the aging cellars, and this one to the bottle shop. And this"—she pointed to the exit door that had been left open—"is the quickest way for a lot of employees to get home. There is a back gate out there, and it's a shortcut for a lot of people."

"A shortcut for some, but a problem for you," he said.

She looked at him and he could see her relief at being understood. At not having to fight, to convince, to cajole her team. At having her words taken at face value.

She sighed. "Yes," she said. "Sometimes I've come and found that door simply unlocked. The plant is closed for the weekend, shut up tight, and that door is unlocked for anyone to come in. It's just hard to imagine what people must be thinking, to leave it like that."

Bern smiled faintly at her. "You know, I find that it's best not to speculate too much about what other people might think, one way or another. It inevitably leads to disappointment."

Again she looked up at him in surprise. Her features already seemed less pinched than they had just a few minutes ago.

"I hate to even suggest that we do this, but if we go out this door and through that back gate, we will get to sit down in comfort and eat some delicious food that much faster."

She smiled then, a real smile. A lovely smile. "Okay, how about we go out this way?"

Outside, the air was cold, so cold on her bare skin. A buzzing alarm pierced her mind.

She had managed to loosen the fabric that tied her wrists

together. No one had come all day. Once she'd freed herself, she had opened the door to the paint room, climbed over the chain-link fence, and crabbed down the other side to a concrete floor. She had crawled up some stairs and down a hallway. Her movements were slow, and each one made her want to curl up and hug her frozen, aching limbs to her tortured belly. She crawled to a door. Red letters swam above the metal frame. Exit. The alarm had started shrieking as she made her way outside.

It was nighttime. Full darkness was interrupted by piercing lights that made no sense. And forms, huge lumps and piles to navigate. She lurched down some steps and hugged the side of a railcar. She followed the length of it and, reaching the end, held the bottom rung of a ladder and swung around the back. She crouched down low for a moment. Her breath whistled in and out through dry lips. Her stomach heaved. She held it down.

The stairs she had come down were lit by a rectangle of light, coming through the door she'd left open. The alarm continued its shrieking, but there was no one following her. For now. *Move, move, move!* Past the railcar was darkness. She could not stay hiding there. Because wherever he was, he could hear the alarm too. And he would come looking for her.

Her legs cramped as she tried to stand. She forced through the pain and pushed herself forward. She limped, crouched low, a primate walk, her hands touching down on the tarmac. Pain tore through her. Her stomach rolled and lurched with each movement. She reached a stack of pallets and retched into the grass at their base. The pallets leaned up against another chain-link fence. This one was higher, but she'd scaled one already, so she could do it again. But no, this one had a gate. She weaved her fingers through the fence and pulled herself along. The mesh of the fence jingled as her arms and body shivered from the cold. Her teeth rattled. Her insides roiled again, but she forced herself to swallow the bile that rose up in her throat. Finally, she reached the gate.

Please, she whispered. Her throat burned from the acid that would not stay down in her stomach. She crabbed her hands up the fence and pulled her body up to the gate handle. She studied it carefully. A punch number combination lock. She leaned her head against the fence and groaned. She did not have the strength to climb. How could she climb it? A little rest. But something inside her screamed. *No! No rest.* And then whispered: *Try the handle.*

She studied the lock again. Round metal handle. The combination pad was for those on the outside. A gate to keep people from coming in, not going out. She reached for the handle. Her fingers slipped. She tried again. The cold metal burned her fingers as she grasped it. She turned the handle and the gate flapped open under the weight of her body and dragged her forward. She scrambled to keep up with the gate, then untangled herself and swung it shut slowly. She turned the handle again and the clasp shut noiselessly. At the same moment, the alarm stopped.

They're coming. *Move, move!*

Next to the fence was a field. Wide open, with scraggly grass that grabbed at her bare legs and feet. Some distance ahead, lights wavered outside a low structure. She lay down on her stomach, using the grass for cover, and slowly began to pull herself toward the lights.

8

Once outside, Evie still kept an eye out for the person, or people, who had caused the alarm to go off. She saw no one. There was no sound. Just the railcar of syrup standing watch. The darkness, punctuated by spotlights, swallowed the familiar view of the brewery yard: stacks of empty pallets; a few deserted stainless steel tanks, waiting to be reclaimed; a tidy stack of empty chemical totes, ready for shipment back to the supplier. The yard was surrounded by a chain-link fence, into which was punched a single gate—a back exit that gave way to the small nest of streets behind the brewery where many workers lived.

As they went out through the gate, she wondered when anyone had last changed the code on it. Or on the security system, for that matter. A man stood on the front steps of the house across the street. She could see only his silhouette in the darkness, but she'd recognize his half-bent stance anywhere: Leroy Ostikoff, brother of the brewery manager, Karl Ostikoff.

"Hi, Leroy," she said.

Leroy walked toward them, favoring one leg. He'd injured it years ago, working on one of the boilers with his dad when he was barely in his teens. Leroy was another one who'd worked at the brewery forever. His hips fairly creaked with arthritis, forcing him onto medical leave a few months back. His face was young-looking still too, like his brother's, thought Evie. She tried to remember from his file how old he was. His hair was still pretty blond, his body as wiry as a teenager's. The thought that brewery work might keep a man younger than his years flitted through her mind, but then she remembered Gavin. He would never get a chance to grow old—to find out whether his hair would go gray, whether his face would become lined, whether he'd be beset by injury or arthritis, like Leroy.

"Just heard the alarm. Wondered if I could help," Leroy said. He gestured behind him and across the street to a small white bungalow. It sat on a corner lot, directly across from the brewery's back gate. It was set within a wide square of precisely trimmed lawn.

"Did you see anyone?" Bern asked him.

He shook his head. "Nah, no one came out that I saw," he said. "But then, it's pretty dark."

"I don't suppose this combination lock actually keeps anyone out," Evie muttered.

"Suppose not." Leroy turned and loped off a few steps, then turned back. "You're the coroner, right?" he said to Bern.

"Bern Fortin." He took a few steps toward Leroy and held out his hand to shake. "I'm your neighbor, live just over there—"

"I know where you live," said Leroy. He ignored Bern's outstretched hand. "Only one in the whole neighborhood don't work at the brewery. Everyone knows where you live."

Evie watched Bern's curls spring as he tossed his head back and laughed. Leroy made a sound that was a cross between a cough and a grunt and walked away.

Bern called after him. "I might want to talk to you tomorrow."

"'Bout what?" Leroy paused.

"About Gavin Grayson and the bottle washer," Bern said.

"I don't know anything about that."

"Of course you don't," Bern said. "I know you don't work there anymore. But I'm told no one knows that machine better than you. I want to understand what happened."

"Guy was an idiot, that's what happened," Leroy said.

Evie saw a small smile of triumph flicker across Bern's face and then disappear. "But I want you to tell me exactly what kind of idiocy would get a man into that situation. Can I come by and see you tomorrow?" he asked.

Leroy shrugged, then started moving off again on his uneven gait. "Can't stop you."

Seated on one of Bern's cushioned deck chairs, a mug of tea in her hand and the smells of an abundant garden at night surrounding her, Evie began to slowly unwind. She sat cross-legged on the seat and noticed some dirt on the hem of her jeans. She could only imagine what a mess the rest of her must be. Her hair, usually frizzy by this time of day, must be making a dark halo around her head. While most people would have sun-kissed skin at the end of the summer, Evie was paler than ever. Summer was the busiest time of year in the beer industry, and she'd spent most of it indoors, working.

There would be no forgetting this day, ever. She did not want to forget the images and the knowledge that while she'd been sitting at home, working away on her laptop, one of her workers had died. The very worst—the one thing it was her responsibility to prevent—had happened.

She sipped at the tea, fragrant and sweet and perfectly served in a thick pottery mug. Evie—whose own mug collection consisted of the remaining seven of a set of eight that Dirk had bought at Canadian Tire when he'd first moved out on his own in his teens—loved the dual heft and fragility of the pottery. She'd been living on her own for years when she and Dirk had married. She must have had mugs, and she wondered now what had happened to them. She sighed and shook her head. Domestic details like that tended to escape her notice, much to Dirk's annoyance.

"What are you shaking your head about?" Bern asked from inside.

"Just how peaceful this is. What a contrast to the rest of my day," she said.

Bern came through the open screen door carrying a tray, which he gingerly laid on the table in front of her. On it were two steaming bowls of soup, a plate of sliced crusty bread, cheese, and pickles, and two cloth napkins, carefully rolled and secured with silver napkin rings.

"Wow, this is beautiful," she whispered. "Do you always eat like this?"

Bern shrugged. He carefully set a bowl, spoon, and napkin before Evie, then set a place for himself across the table. He put the plate of bread and pickles between them in the middle of the table.

"It's something I'm learning—to slow down and appreciate the little things. It's something I promised myself after my last posting. Simple, beautiful things are important," he said. "Especially when you've been touched by death. Please eat."

She thought about his words as she took a slurp of soup. Its flavor was familiar but enhanced somehow, filling each taste bud on her tongue and seeming to explode.

"What kind of soup is this?" she asked. "I've never tasted anything like it."

"Tomato soup. Fresh from the garden . . . well, sort of. I'm making it in big batches and canning them. I hope to make it last all winter," he said. "That's something else I'm learning from my neighbor—how to can food. Well, learning by watching. She won't actually let a man work in her kitchen." He laughed. "But I watch her and then try it on my own. We donate most of it to the food bank and just keep what we need to eat."

"The food bank? I didn't even know Kootenay Landing had one," Evie said. "It seems so strange, when you can grow everything here."

Bern nodded. "Up until recently, I thought tomato soup only came from the grocery store."

"It's really, really good." She took another spoonful of soup. And another. "Can I ask you something?"

He shrugged. "Go ahead."

"How do you do it? I mean, you must be touched by death all the time in your line of work."

He shrugged again, an unconscious movement that seemed to say something different each time. This one said, *That's just the way it is, like it or not.* "I eat like this often," he said. "It's important to appreciate beauty."

He looked right at her when he said it. It was disconcerting, really, the way his dark eyes searched for something in her features, moving from her eyes to her cheekbones and her chin, pausing at her lips, and moving back to her eyes, as though trying to build a composition. His accent was so slight, he could almost conceal it. But not from Evie.

"You're French Canadian, right?" she asked.

He tipped his head in a cross between a bow and a nod. "Most people think British, or possibly South African. I went to English school my whole life," he said. "But I'm from Montreal, and my family is French through and through."

"Do you see much of them?"

Bern lowered his eyes and shook his head. "That's a long story," he said. "One for another day."

"Okay. Can I ask you something else, then?" She hesitated but forced herself to carry on. "What happened to you this morning? When you first saw Gavin? It's like you were far away. You seemed confused. Almost lost."

He didn't answer right away. He just held his mug close to his cheek, gazing out into the garden. A shadow seemed to come over his features, which she saw now were quite delicate, a fact that was hidden by the wild dark hair that curled around his head. When his words came, they were even quieter than hers, a hoarse whisper.

"I was in the army for most of my career. Until not long ago—it's little more than six months since I retired. My first tour was many years ago now, in Africa. In Rwanda. I will never forget the things I saw there, and then later, in Bosnia, in Afghanistan." He shook his head. Evie leaned forward, straining to hear. "Some-times . . . well." He sat back and shrugged helplessly. "Sometimes the memories come back to visit, and there is nothing I can do but wait for them to leave again."

"But surely there is something you can do? To make that stop happening?"

He smiled sadly. "Maybe," he said. "But maybe it is best to let the memories live? And to be accountable for what happened, and to those who died?"

"Is that why you're the coroner now?" she asked.

"Yes," he said quietly. "Yes, it is. It is my duty. To tend to the dead."

He stood and cleared the table. He was gone for a few minutes, and when he came back, the moment had passed. He brought out a fresh pot of tea and a cordless phone. He refilled their mugs and sat down again, setting the phone next to him on the table.

"I'd like to ask you a few questions, if that's all right?" he asked. His voice was back to normal now, back to business.

She nodded curtly and sat up straighter.

"I'm just trying to understand what happened. What I can't figure out is if he fell in when the tank was already full or was in the tank when it got filled up," he said.

Evie thought for a minute, running through the preventive maintenance procedure on the machine in her mind.

"He was in there, and it got filled up," she said firmly.

"Tell me how you know this," Bern said as he took a sip of tea. He held the mug in his palms, and his fingers played loosely on the outside as though on the keys of a piano. Long, thin fingers, she noticed.

"The trays on the roof of the machine. That's one of the first steps in routine maintenance. Take the trays out to get inside. I think that's what he was doing," she said. "The tank would have to have been empty for him to get those out."

She sighed and tipped her head at Bern. The desire to just

start talking, to open up and let everything out, was so strong she could feel a pressure in her throat, the words piling up and hoping to escape. But she had to be careful. She had to remember her job.

"I think he'd planned to go in. He got the trays out, and once he was in there, he got stuck," she said. "Besides—" She held back the words.

"Besides?" he asked.

"Well, I didn't notice any splashing, did you? If he'd fallen in, there would have been splashes everywhere. And anyway, you saw the size of the door. A guy that big could not fall in through a trapdoor that small without getting stuck," she said.

"Good point." He tented his fingers and waited, staring at her face again. It made her nervous and she could not stop the words from pouring out.

"I mean, he could slip or trip, and maybe he'd get a leg or arm in the machine. And if it was full, he'd have been injured by caustic very badly. But eventually he would have made his way down the ladder and called for help," she said.

"Unless someone pushed him in," said Bern. He shrugged after he said it—some people do strange things in this world— and then took another sip of tea.

Evie shuddered. "That is just too horrible to think about. How could anyone push a big guy like Gavin into a bottle washer full of caustic? No, he would have fought back. It would be excruciating from the very first second his feet touched the caustic, but it would take a while to push a big guy like that in. No, I can't believe it."

"Unless he was pushed headfirst," Bern said. "He would have died almost instantly, with his first breath."

"But why?" Evie asked. "Why would anyone do something like that?"

Neither of them had an answer to that question. Her words reverberated through the night silence for a while. The night was cool and the hot tea warmed her. Evie felt exhaustion wash over her again. But no matter how tired she was, she doubted she would sleep that night.

"How are you holding up?" Bern asked.

"Me? I'm fine," she replied automatically.

"Really? You don't look fine," he said.

His eyes were probing, questioning, inviting her to talk. Evie wanted to tell him everything. About how scared she was—and how mad. About how just that morning she'd been harping to Conrad about the working-alone procedure. About how none of them ever listened to her. About how something like this was bound to happen eventually. She pulled her eyes away from him.

"What else do you need to know about the accident?" she asked.

She saw him change gears then, seamlessly. "Why would Steve Ostikoff be worried about a lock?"

Evie felt the weight of the teacup in her hands. "One lock?"

"Yes, just one," he replied.

She ran through possible scenarios in her head and could see no harm in telling him. "How much do you know about lockout procedure?" she asked him.

He shrugged. "A little, not enough."

"Normally, going into a confined space like the bottle washer would be a major undertaking. Three or four people, each with his own set of locks. And they would use them to shut off any systems that feed into the confined space—steam, caustic, hot water, electricity—so that even if someone pressed the start button, nothing would happen. There are seven lockout points on the bottle washer, so technically you'd need seven locks, per person, before someone went in. It's a safety measure, but it's also become a form of industrial etiquette. You see a lock, you know someone's inside. You don't touch the lock or the machine."

She fell silent and sipped her tea again.

"But one lock?" he asked.

"Well, the only place we do a lockout with one lock is what we call a lazyman's lockout," she said. "Some of our machines are outfitted with a hasp, like you'd find on a kid's locker at school. Operators can slide a lock through to close off the start button. It's for very routine maintenance—running maintenance, we call it. It's faster than fully locking out the machine. And it's supposed to be done only when the operator is in full view of the start button the whole time."

He digested this information with a small sip of tea. "Is there a lazyman's lockout on the bottle washer?" he asked.

Evie paused before answering. It would be hard to keep information from someone who understood things and their implications so quickly. "It's not to regulation anymore, but it's still there. It used to be okay, but with updates to the regulation . . . well, it needs to be removed," she said.

"But it hasn't been removed yet?"

"No, not yet."

Evie could hear a distant rumbling sound and the far-off cry of a train.

"What is Evie short for?" he asked. His voice was tender, his head cocked to one side. She felt as though he had reached out and touched her, although he had not moved. It was a long time since anyone had asked her that. Since anyone had cared to know something personal about her.

The train was closer now. Evie heard a long wail escape as it passed the uncontrolled crossing on the west side of town.

"Marie-Eve," she answered, her voice barely audible above the sound of the train. "It's short for Marie-Eve. My mother was French Canadian too."

But the train swallowed up her words. It passed right by them, through the field adjacent to Bern's house, its light cutting a tunnel through the no-man's-land of tough grass grooved with footpaths. Close enough to touch, thought Evie. Its piercing whistle felt like it cut right through her. The sound seemed to hang around long after the train had passed. Trapped by the valley, it bounced around between the two walls of mountains before floating away.

Just as the sound of the train died down, the phone rang.

Bern picked it up. *"Oui,"* he said quietly in French. *"Oui, ça va encore. Toi aussi?"* He stared right at Evie as he spoke, then switched to English. "Another day, my friend. We've made it for another day. Speak to you tomorrow."

She must have fallen asleep. She tried to move her arms, her legs—but she could not budge. The panic hit her full force and she struggled against the restraints, then realized they were gone. Her heart beat wildly. She flung her arms, kicked her legs, cried out. No sound escaped. Her mouth was as dry as the sharp blades of grass that poked into her bare arms and legs.

She flopped onto her back, her breath gasping and ragged.

Above her in the night sky endless stars were trapped between rows of mountains. They haven't caught me again, she thought. But she felt so cold—everything so cold and stiff, she could hardly move.

"Help," she whispered. "Gavin."

Gavin, Gavin, Gavin. Where was he?

She heard a sound. Far away, but there was something there. She rolled over again, and waves of nausea grasped her. I have to keep moving. She moved toward the sound, which was growing louder. She swallowed the bile that rose in her throat, choked, and spit. The spittle landed on her chin, foaming and sour. The dew had begun to settle on her exposed skin. She was so cold that each movement ached. She dragged herself forward. One pace. Two paces.

So weak and tired, she could not get up. Where was Gavin? She retched again and then lay still. Small noises, like the sound of a cat working out a fur ball, escaped her throat. She could not move and the noise was upon her now. The rumbling went right through her and got even louder until she thought it would swallow her up. That would be okay. That would be all right. I will just go to sleep for a little while. The rumbling was joined by a shriek, long and steady, that pierced the night air. That's okay. It's okay. It's okay now.

9

Evie didn't wake up on Wednesday morning. She just sat up. You can't call it waking if you never slept, she thought as she padded out of bed to the adjoining bathroom. Rory, her German shepherd, shifted in his sleep and made a little whinny sound in his throat.

"Go back to sleep," she whispered to him.

For all the interesting architectural detail on its exterior, Evie's house was quite simple on the inside. It was a standard suburban split-level home. The second level overlooked the valley, which, at this time of year, was slowly becoming a monochromatic landscape of fields in various stages of fall fallow. She had the same view from the bathroom as from the master bedroom. A long vanity with two sinks and, instead of mirrors, two windows that looked out at the valley bottom below. Evie did not miss having a mirror, and she rarely looked at the view anymore—the house was just too high up for her comfort. It hung on the edge of a cliff. The forty-foot drop-off was not quite vertical, but it seemed that way from the vantage point of the second floor.

She turned on the shower and hung her pajamas carefully on the hook next to the stall before stepping into the warm steam. She let the hot water work its magic. A ten-minute shower is better than eight hours of sleep, she told herself. Or one hour of sleep.

Her thoughts flowed with the water. She steered them away from Gavin and the horror of the day before. She'd be dealing with that soon enough. She thought of Bern, of the peace on his deck last night, of the lovely teacups. I want some teacups like that. The thought came from nowhere, and she quickly shoved it away. Someone died on your watch. You don't get to go shopping for pottery.

Her thoughts settled on Dirk. Should she do something? It had been almost seven weeks since he'd left to drive his nephews home after their visit, or so he'd said.

She'd first heard of Nate and John's visit the night before they arrived. Apparently their parents needed a break and Dirk had offered, knew she wouldn't mind, though of course she did.

"What will you do with them?" she'd asked.

"Oh, they can work with me in the shop. Don't worry about it," he'd said. She knew this was a dream of Dirk's—two teen-aged boys of his own to work in the shop with him and learn the ropes.

"I can't take time off work. I've got too much to do," she'd replied. This was an exaggeration. There was always a lot to do, but she had over a year's vacation coming to her. She'd never taken more than a few days at a time in the twenty years she'd been with the company. And even then, she took time only when she really needed to, like when Dirk's mother died, or when she was transferred and needed a few days to get settled. But she hadn't been transferred anywhere in five years.

The boys had come—no longer boys but men really, fifteen and seventeen. Evie was surprised by their polite way with her, and how enjoyable their company had been on the few nights she'd made it home from work before midnight. It seemed to help that when she did make it home for dinner, she brought boxes of pizza or stuffed, steaming bags from the A&W. They ate it all, no matter how much she bought.

Dirk even smiled at her a few times during their stay, laughed once when she tried their portable video game, touched her arm as she brushed past him one time with a mound of greasy wrappers and ketchup-stained napkins.

That was the night Nate and John scrambled up the cliff. She sat on the couch after dinner, savoring the silence that usually reigned supreme. Dirk had his back to her, facing the computer screen, shoulders hunched, updating his books. His business had been quiet, and Evie knew he worried about money. He didn't need to—she made more than enough for both of them. "But that's not the point," Dirk would say.

The couch backed onto a large picture window, which was flanked by a sill wide enough for a window seat. It was covered with potted plants around the edges; the center held a padded fleece oval pillow where Rory slept. Evie did not pay much attention to herself really—she didn't wear makeup or nice clothes or look after herself in any way that anyone would notice. But she looked after her dog and her plants. The plants palmed a rich canopy around the dog's bed. The leaves were fat and healthy, thick and dark or moss green, all shapes, painstakingly wiped down with a mixture of mayonnaise and warm water. Rory's coat was thick and gleamed from being brushed, and the pads of his paws were wiped daily with the same mixture that the plants received.

Sitting on the couch, Evie could hear Dirk's nephews yelling at each other outside and Rory barking at the top of the steep dirt path that crisscrossed the edge of the cliff. She had a briefcase next to her, a laptop unopened on the floor, a pile of documents waiting for her attention, and she sat quietly, not touching them.

"It's nice, having them here," she said to Dirk.

He stopped typing when she said this, then came to sit next to her on the couch, moving the briefcase to the floor. His hair was black, or rather had been black and was now flecked with gray in a way that suited him. Evie wondered at the injustice of it: Dirk seemed to be getting better-looking as he approached fifty. He kept his hair long, brushed back from his forehead; it fell below his ears. Last year he had grown a beard, which suited his square jaw and olive skin. She couldn't remember the last time she'd really looked at him.

"It's not too late, you know," he said. Evie froze in her seat. He leaned closer to her, put his hand on her knee. "You're only forty, Evie," he said. "Lots of women have babies when they're forty."

At that moment, the boys reached the top of the cliff. Their lithe adolescent limbs appeared behind Evie and Dirk in the frame of the picture window. They pumped their fists, waved their arms, then called to Rory to climb back up the trail. Evie could hear him barking below.

She'd gone out and marveled at them, grateful for the distraction. How had they done it? Weren't they afraid? And they'd told her in great detail about the trek they had made, the handholds, the slip of crushed rocks raining down, the thin sapling with strong roots that had saved Nate's life.

She'd insisted on taking a picture of them with scraped arms and hands, standing victorious at the top with Rory panting at their feet. She took it with her digital camera from work. It sat there still, saved with other, less lively pictures—pallets of beer piled high in front of an emergency exit, and a puddle of slick lubricant dripping down from a conveyor belt and pooling in a pedestrian walkway.

They had been so alive that evening, she and Dirk as well. The next morning Dirk had left to drive the boys back to Alberta. A twelve-hour drive. He said he would be away a few days. Over a week later, he'd finally called to say he'd found a job that paid really well and was going to stay awhile. That was almost two months ago, and as time went on, it became increasingly difficult for Evie to pretend that things were ever going to go back to how they'd been.

Evie turned off the water and stepped out of the shower. She dried herself off and pulled Wednesday's clothes off the shelf. She looked at the place she had carefully stacked her outfits just a few days ago. Four sets—for a short week—of jeans, Bugaboo golf shirts, and Bugaboo fleece vests. It seemed like a year ago that she had picked out her clothes for the week and placed them on the shelf. It was just one of her habits that drove Dirk crazy. *Don't you ever wake up and feel like wearing something different?*

Once dressed, she stood before the sink. She stared out the window to the black valley. Not even a wisp of dawn illuminated the fields below. It was four in the morning—not really morning at all—but if she thought this, if she let the fatigue in, there was no way she would be able to face the day. Backlit by the track lights behind her, Evie saw herself reflected in the windows, a ghost of a woman with wavering white skin, a halo of frizzy, thick hair, eyes ringed in dark circles. At the point where her pupils should have been, the glass revealed only blackness, and Evie imagined all that was contained beyond the window—the tumble of cliff, rock, and grass; the miles of farmers' fields broken by a meandering river; the cottonwood trees; the bridge; and then the ascent of mountains beyond—imagined all of it inside her, black and endless.

She sighed. Rory must have come into the bathroom while she was in the shower. He shifted on the floor and sighed too. He looked up at her with his sad moon eyes and lumbered to his feet. He padded over to her and laid his head on her thigh.

"Ready for breakfast?" she asked him. She ran her hands down his soft fur. "And maybe a little brush? Just a little one."

He looked up at her. Evie knew it would be another day when she left him outside. She had an arrangement with the neighbor, who would walk Rory with his own dog during the day. The rest of the time, Rory usually hung out in Dirk's shop and in the yard.

"You'll be okay," she said. "You'll have food and a walk, and it's going to be a nice day. You can hang out with Chester next door." She paused and looked into his eyes. They always looked sad to her. Dirk kept telling her they weren't sad; they were just big and watery. When Dirk was home, Rory would follow him around the shop all day. She thought of him as her dog, but he must miss Dirk too, she thought. "Okay, let's go downstairs and get this day started," she said.

The woman's body lay tangled in knee-high grass. She was splayed out on her stomach, with one arm stretched out before her, one knee tucked under her abdomen, as though she had been reaching, crawling, and had stopped midmotion.

"Don't you live around here?" Resnick asked Bern.

Bern gestured silently to his side gate, just a few hundred feet away. Sunflowers towered over the gateposts, their cheerful heads hanging down. Bern did not trust himself to speak. Two bodies in twenty-four hours was a lot, even for a coroner.

"She's so young," he finally said. It felt like his voice came from far away. He dared not close his eyes.

She *was* young—early twenties, maybe. Her hair was blond, cut into a bob and wet with dew. It hung in clumps in front of her face, which was planted in the dirt. Had she been alive, she would not have been able to breathe like that, and this thought made Bern feel as if he couldn't get enough air.

"You all right?" Resnick asked, looking at Bern. "You're not going to puke or anything?"

Bern shook his head and looked around. Resnick's officers were spread throughout the field, blocking the footpaths that were a shortcut to the town's main street, keeping people from passing through. Bern focused in on a police officer who was redirecting a few teenagers to take the road. They went on their way after a few glances toward Bern, Resnick, and the girl in the grass. Bern crouched down to get a closer look.

She wasn't wearing much: an architecturally complicated bra—all gusset and wire—made of a brocaded fabric in dark purple shot with gold threads, and a jean skirt stained with dirt and hiked up around the tops of her thighs. She had the perfectly dimpled skin of a fat girl—firm and plump.

"Her shoes are over there," Resnick said with a jut of his chin to the field. "Fell off, I guess."

Fatigue seemed to fill Bern with each breath. So many dead to care for in the here and now. And with each one, the nameless dead of the past seemed to revisit, threatening to spill out of the confines he had carefully drawn for them. *Can't you do anything about it?* Evie's words echoed in his mind. But if I forget, he thought, who will be held to account?

"Who found her?"

Resnick gestured to the other side of the tracks, where an old woman sat on a tree stump. She was wearing a cardigan sweater, which Bern knew to be hand knit, and a thick wool skirt. She carried a string bag—empty still. She'd been on her way to town.

"Mrs. Kalesnikoff," he said.

"You know her?"

"She's my neighbor," he said, walking away from Resnick and the young woman in the grass. Mrs. K. was with Constable Schilling. Bern nodded at her and sat next to the older woman on the stump. He put his arm around her shoulder.

She leaned her head against his chest. Her voice came out in a whisper. "She was just lying there like that. I thought, I thought—" She gulped down a wail. "I thought it was my granddaughter."

Bern looked up at the officer, who shook her head of mousy brown hair. She bent forward to talk to the old woman.

"Is it your granddaughter, Mrs. Kalesnikoff?" Schilling asked.

A shake of gray hair. "No, no. I looked. It's not her," she replied. "But she's so young!" She buried her head further into Bern's chest. "So young," she whispered.

"Did you touch her?" Bern asked.

Bern felt her forehead nod up and down along his sternum. He looked at Schilling.

"Where?" they both asked together.

"Her hair—it looked so much like my Katie's. I lifted it up to see her face," she said.

Bern let out the breath he did not realize he'd been holding. "But you didn't try to move her? Turn her over or anything like that?"

"No, no, nothing like that," she said. She lifted her head out of Bern's rib cage and sat up. "I'd like to go home now."

Bern looked at Schilling again and cocked his head. She nodded. "Let me walk you home," he said. Bern took her forearm and started toward her house. He saw Resnick from the corner of his eye, raising both hands in a hopeless gesture, but Bern ignored him. Mrs. K.'s house was within sight of the body, so he wasn't leaving the scene. Not technically, anyway. Sometimes the living had to come first.

They went in through the back door and he settled her at the table in the downstairs kitchen.

"Let me show you how a man can make tea," he said. He spoke to her quietly as he made his way around the kitchen. He talked about the food bank, a topic that was sure to distract her.

"Last night, a friend asked me why Kootenay Landing needed a food bank, when there is so much food grown here. It's not like there is not enough food," he said. He followed the well-worn path he'd seen her take so many times as she made him tea. As he placed the everyday good mugs on the table, she replied, as he knew she would.

"It is not food that people need. It is time. People rush everywhere. No time to prepare food. To put food by for later," she said.

He warmed the old, veined teapot first, then put in two tea bags and filled it with boiled water. Next came the sugar bowl with the missing lid and the souvenir spoon from the Queen's jubilee. It was a testament to the state of shock she was in that she let him complete all the steps.

He sat next to her and served them both tea. They drank in silence. He knew Resnick would be cursing him all the while, but he needed this moment. A moment with the living. A moment with no memories.

"Not bad," Mrs. Kalesnikoff said finally. "Not the same as mine. But not bad." She cleared the cups and clucked at him when he stood to help.

"Can I call someone for you? Your daughter?"

She shook her head.

"I hate to leave you all alone."

"I will be fine," she said stubbornly.

"Do you remember seeing anything unusual last night? Or hearing anything?" he asked.

She shook her head.

"Me neither," he said. "But it was so close." He watched her wipe the mugs dry and put them back in the cupboard for next time.

"You know, I'm going to be busy all day with this. I have tomatoes that need to be picked. I'm afraid they will go to waste," he said.

She folded her strong arms across her chest. "I'm not going to make salsa," she said.

Bern smiled at the serious figure she made in her going-to-town housedress, her freshly rolled hair, and the slightest dab of lipstick. Her eyes narrowed and she waited for his opinion on the subject.

"Salsa? Who said anything about that? Stewed tomatoes. That's what the food bank needs," he said.

She nodded firmly. "Shame to waste all those tomatoes. Even with the spots." She put her hands on her hips and waited for him to leave.

"So that's settled, then," he said.

She didn't reply, just got to work. When he left, she was piling jars on the counter, readying them for washing and sterilizing.

He returned to the scene, where Constable Schilling was taking photographs of the body while Resnick took notes.

"This is a little out of your league, hey?" he asked as Bern approached. He hiked at his belt and snapped out his cell phone. "Want me to call in the Cranbrook coroner? He's seen a little more than heart attacks in old ladies."

Bern raised his shoulders and dropped them back, instantly in marching stance. He stepped closer to Resnick, looking down on the shorter man. "Tell me what you've got," he said.

Resnick stepped back. He pointed to a trail of trampled grass that led to the body, then stopped. "Schilling followed this all the way back. It starts at the edge of the field over there. Close to the brewery. But that's just where the grass starts. Could have come from anywhere."

Following Resnick's finger, he could see the back gate that he and Evie had used the night before. They had not cut across the field but had walked along the road. He turned in the other direction. The path ended where the dead woman's fingers clawed at the grass. Across the tracks, less than a block away, was the police station. He shook his head.

"We have no idea what we are dealing with here," Resnick said. "We may need to hand it over to major crimes."

Bern crouched down close to what he could see of the woman's face. Her mouth was slightly open, the ground under it wet. He leaned as far forward as he could and sniffed. The sour smell of death brought the barely dormant memories within him to life. He looked up, at the field, the mountains, the terrain so similar in many ways to Rwanda. Fields and streams filled with the bodies of innocents. A panorama of death flitted in front of his vision, but he slammed that door closed. There was nothing he could do for those anonymous dead.

"Fortin? You still with us?"

Resnick, here and now. Bern allowed the wave to crest before he answered. "Could be relatively simple," Bern said. He pointed to the wet spot of vomit beneath her mouth.

"Asphyxiation?" Resnick looked toward the police station, as though measuring the distance. "Shit," he muttered.

Bern cocked his head toward his own backyard. "Death by asphyxiation within steps of the coroner's house and the police station?"

"Let's hope not," Resnick said.

"Did she crawl? Or was she dragged?" Bern asked.

Resnick nodded toward Schilling.

"I couldn't see any footprints. They wouldn't leave impressions on this ground, but you'd see the flattened grass. Sir," Schilling added.

"Anything else you can think of, Constable Schilling?" Bern suspected she had more good ideas in her head than Resnick would ever give her credit for.

The young officer pointed down the street from Bern's house. "We've had our eye on a house over there. Think it might be a drug house. Pretty recent—we're just watching it at this point."

Resnick stood. "Drug enforcement will want us to handle that carefully. We'll canvass the whole neighborhood, see if anyone saw where she came from," he said. His legs were spread out in a wide stance, and the shirt button that had been strained yesterday looked ready to pop right off today. "Or if they know who she is."

"We might be able to tell when we turn her over. Have you got all the photos you need?" Bern asked.

Schilling nodded. "Over to you, Mr. Coroner," Resnick said.

Bern slipped on some latex gloves and crouched low again. Keeping his fingers an inch away from her skin, he followed the pooling of blood in her body. He pressed one finger into the front of her thigh and pulled it away.

"Lividity is fixed. Dark purple. Could be from the temperature. We'll have to find out how cold it was last night," he said.

He lifted one of her arms. *Stiff and cold.* Then he moved one of her legs. *Still some motion.* He deftly checked the back pockets of her jean skirt. *Empty.*

"Let's turn her over," he said.

Bern kept his eyes on her face. Gradually, it revealed itself to him: one side bruised a deep purple, and under that a pert, upturned nose and pouty lips, only slightly blue from the cold. Bern imagined her eyes would have been blue as well. But they were closed. He had never seen her before.

Resnick whistled under his breath.

Bern turned his head to take in the rest of the body. Her arms had stayed in position, her legs relaxed only slightly. Turned on her back now, she looked like she was climbing a ladder. Schilling was at the girl's feet. He looked where she was looking.

The girl's bustier had stayed in place, with the exception of one shoulder strap, which had slipped down her arm. It left a snake of white on her shoulder where the elastic had stretched, preventing the blood from pooling. The rest of her exposed skin was mottled with lividity. The tight-fitting top ended just below her ribs. The jean skirt had twisted up even further as they turned her body; a stretch of abdomen and the full length of her thighs were exposed. She was not wearing underwear. Bern wanted to cover her.

He stood and went over to where Resnick was crouched. Interspersed among the dark purple blotches of pooled blood were bright red circles, tattooed into her skin. Each one was close to an inch across and edged with a white rim of heaped skin.

"What are they?" he asked.

"Cigarette burns," Resnick said. "Schilling, get a ruler or a lighter or something."

Schilling pulled a ballpoint pen from her pocket. Resnick lay this carefully on the girl's stomach, while Schilling started to take more pictures. Bern sat back on his heels.

"Could be self-inflicted," Resnick said. "The major crimes guys won't be happy if I call them out here for nothing."

Bern started to count the spots, which spread from the pillow of her belly across the tops of her thighs like chicken pox. Thirty-six cigarette burns. "But then you'd see stages of healing, or old scars. These are all recent. Self-harm like that is a habit, not something you pick up all at once." He moved back up to check her neck. The skin was unmarred and cold under his touch. "Seems to be otherwise unharmed," he continued. "No visible injuries or markings. No lacerations. No strangulation marks that I can see."

"Can you guess at the time? You think we'll need to call major crimes? They'll want to know," Resnick asked.

Bern sighed. He knew he needed to give them something to work with. "The cold makes a difference. And whether she crawled on her own or was dragged."

"Give me something. Estimate at least," Resnick said.

"Minimum eight hours. Twelve at the outside." Bern looked at his watch. "Between eight last night and midnight."

"So let's start our investigation right here, huh, Mr. Coroner?" said Resnick. "You live right there. Weren't you home last night? Didn't you hear anything or see anything?"

Bern cast his mind back to the night before. Eight o'clock? He thought of the alarm he and Evie had heard going off.

"Hello? Fortin?"

"Sorry," Bern said. "I was just thinking about last night. When I was finishing up at the brewery with Evie and the WSB officer, an exterior door alarm went off."

"And?" Resnick asked.

"And Evie and I checked all the doors but didn't find anything," he said.

Resnick reached into his breast pocket and pulled out a crushed pack of cigarettes. He pulled one out and put it between his lips.

"You can't smoke here," Bern said.

Resnick rolled his eyes. "God, I know. Don't remind me. It just helps me think." He sucked on the end of the unlit cigarette in silence for a moment, then looked up at Bern with his beady eyes. "What time was the alarm?"

"It was somewhere around seven o'clock. I can ask Evie; she might have a record of it," he said.

Resnick snorted and pulled the cigarette out of his mouth. "Evie, Evie, Evie. It's like there's an echo out here."

Bern ignored him. He scanned the body before him again, slowly this time. Familiarity bred resistance and he could look at her with some objectivity. The garish lingerie, carefully highlighted hair, pretty features, bruised-looking skin, and even the angry burns—he had gotten used to them. He was looking for something more. *There. Got it.*

"Yes," he said. There was no doubt about it. He pointed at her wrists. He had almost missed it. The tiny purple bruises where the blood had pooled were to be expected, as were the white lines between them where the bones had pressed up against the ground. But along those white lines, he could make out a minuscule crosshatch of angry red lines on the outsides of both wrists.

"Yes, you'll want to call in major crimes. I want her sent for a full autopsy," Bern said. He pointed to her wrists. "And we are looking for a primary scene. It looks like she was held captive."

He turned his head and followed the trail of crushed grass to its origin. It began by the back gate of the brewery.

"And we need to search that brewery. Every inch of it."

10

When Susan Byron arrived in the conference room at the appointed time, Evie had already been at the brewery for several hours. A night at the Kootenay Landing Hotel had done nothing to improve the WSB officer's mood. She glanced at Evie without a smile or a nod and began spreading the contents of her briefcase out before her on the conference room table.

Gemma stood in the doorway; she bit her lip and wrinkled her nose at Evie while Byron wasn't looking. "Need anything?" she whispered.

Evie shook her head. She needed to get this over with. It was her whole job distilled into one meeting. If she could show that the company had done everything it could to prevent an accident like this—that they had done their due diligence—she'd be a hero. If she messed up, there was a strong likelihood that she, and other managers, would be charged with criminal neglect.

"Can I get you anything, Susan?" Gemma asked. "Coffee?"

Byron nodded. "Yes, please," she said.

Gemma cocked an eyebrow at Evie. Evie shrugged. "Sure, why not?"

Once Byron had all her papers and files piled up to her satisfaction, she looked up at Evie. "First, you're going to show me all the training records and procedures," she said.

Evie nodded. "No problem."

Gemma came back in and put a mug of coffee before Byron. "Take anything in it?" she asked.

Byron shook her head quickly. She was wearing the same ill-fitting pantsuit from the day before, but this time with a black cotton mock turtleneck in place of yesterday's blouse. Her face was round and, it seemed to Evie, incapable of expressing any emotion other than annoyance.

Evie looked down at the ends of her own frizzy black hair, lying on the shoulder of her fleece vest. She looked at Susan Byron again. Is that how I look to people? That all I do is work and all I care about is compliance with regulation?

Gemma was in front of her all of a sudden, putting a cup of coffee before her. "Milk and sugar, just how you like it," she whispered. She winked when Evie looked up at her. Evie smiled gratefully. No, she thought. I'm part of a team. People know me and like me. They know how I take my coffee.

Gemma mouthed, "Good luck!"

Byron coughed. "When the coroner gets here"—she looked pointedly at her watch as she said this—"I'm going to want to interview all the operators again."

Evie swallowed a gulp of coffee. Gemma slowed to a stop by the door and turned around. "All of them?" they asked together.

Byron nodded once. "Anyone who has anything to do with the bottle washer—operations, maintenance, or management," she said. She took a sip of her coffee and put her cup down with a grimace.

"But you interviewed those people yesterday, with the police," Evie said.

"Yes, and I'm going to keep interviewing them until I understand exactly what happened here," Byron said.

Evie nodded slowly and looked up at Gemma. "Okay, so that's all the millwrights and bottle washer operators, including relief. Better get the filler operators too—they know how to run the machine if they need to. That should be it—"

"Management?" Byron interrupted. "Who knows how to fill that machine?"

Evie took a deep breath. "It's contrary to the collective agreement for a manager to do the work of a union employee," she said.

"And it's contrary to the safety regulation for someone to fill a machine with three percent caustic solution when there is someone inside it," Byron retorted.

The woman has a point, Evie thought to herself.

"So that's me, Conrad, Karl. I think that's it," Evie said. Inwardly, she groaned. That was at least twenty interviews; it would take hours.

Gemma nodded. "I'll look after it," she said as she left the room.

"Can't wait any longer for the coroner," Byron said. "Let's get started."

The morning dragged on. Bern did not arrive, and Byron's mood did not improve. Partway through the morning, Karl came in and took a seat at the table. He was wearing his own uniform—pressed slacks and polo-necked golf shirt, this one silk-screened with the imprint of a new BevCo brewery in China. Evie became aware of him watching her and remembered his warning from the day before.

They went through the procedure for each regulation the incident contravened, and then the training documentation. Susan Byron listened without comment and only occasionally asked a question. Now and then she made a note on a pad of paper in front of her. The way she turned her head from side to side without moving her eyes made Evie think of a reptile.

"Show me your working-alone procedure," Byron said, interrupting Evie midsentence.

Karl, who had been making a quiet exit, sat back down, adjusting the crease on his pants as he laid one ankle across the other knee. He crossed his arms and looked at Evie out of the corner of his eye.

Evie felt her chest tighten, and a roar like the engine of an airplane started in her head. When she breathed, it felt like there was not enough oxygen in the air. She looked over at Karl. He looked back at her, his face as expressionless as ever, but she could practically hear his thoughts: *Don't fuck it up.*

"Right now? Don't you want—"

"I want to see your working-alone procedure, right now," Byron said flatly.

Evie called the procedure document up on the computer at the end of the table and turned on the projector. The procedure appeared on the screen on the wall, each step in the process carefully numbered and detailed. Evie had written all these procedures: she'd spent two full years revamping the operational and safety procedures for the entire brewery. No one had ever shown this much interest in them before.

"We've retained an answering service. When an employee is working alone, he calls in to this service—"

"How?" Byron barked.

Evie took a short breath and tried to focus. The noise in her head had been replaced by an echoing silence, as if she were standing alone in one of the fermentation hallways. She picked up the laser pointer on the conference table and aimed the tiny red light at the second item on the screen. "Well, there's a direct-dial phone set up by the main employee entrance. He picks up the phone and tells the person on the other end that he is working alone."

Karl caught Evie's eye with his cold stare. Evie's chest tightened again.

"And who needs to call in?" Byron prompted.

Once again, Evie aimed the pointer at the projected screen. "Like it says here, all brewing operators and steam engineers on weekends. Maintenance when there is overtime scheduled, and bottle washer operators on cleanup shifts."

Susan moved her head again, not looking at the screen, and made another note on the growing list on her pad. "The victim is a . . ."

She waited in silence for Evie to fill in the blank.

"He's a millwright," Evie replied. "Rather, he . . . uh, he was a millwright."

"And he works for . . ."

Byron paused again and waited in the excruciating silence for Evie to finish her sentence. Evie felt the panic rising in her again.

She looked quickly at Karl, who was frowning at the procedure on the screen. He did not look over at her.

"Maintenance department. It appears that he came in to fix a leak on the bottle washer," she replied.

"I find your choice of words interesting. You say, 'It appears,' as if he decided to do this of his own accord. Would he not have been instructed to fix the machine by his supervisor? By his department manager? Or did he just decide, all on his own, to come in and fix the machine?"

Through the tightness in her chest and the eerie echoing in her head, Evie suddenly saw her way clear. She wanted to jump up and hug Susan Byron. Evie nodded. "Yes, it appears so," she said. Out of the corner of her eye, she saw Karl's head snap up and look at her.

"I find that hard to fathom," Byron said.

"Me too," said Evie. "But that is my understanding of what happened." *And you'll never be able to prove otherwise.*

"And the cleanup shift?" Byron said.

"Yes?" Evie asked.

"You said that when bottle washer operators come in on a weekend, they do a cleanup shift. Tell me about that," Byron said.

Karl started tapping his pen on the side of his hand.

"They change the caustic solution in the bottle washer," Evie said.

"So they empty it?"

Evie nodded. "Sometimes. Sometimes it gets emptied at the end of the last shift on Friday. So then the operator on the weekend just fills it up."

"And this time?"

"We know that it was emptied on Friday—" Evie said.

"And filled up on the weekend overtime shift." It was Byron's turn to finish Evie's sentences.

"None of the operators will admit to coming in over the weekend," Evie said.

"What do you mean they won't admit to it?" Byron snapped.

"They all say they did not do an overtime shift," Evie replied. "We have no record of anyone coming in."

Byron scribbled something on her page. She ran her fingers through her hair, which flapped up momentarily and then flopped back in place.

"I just don't see how that is possible. Did a ghost fill up the machine?" Byron spat out the words. She stood and walked over to Evie, leaning over the table. "Do you have so little administrative control over your system that you don't even know who was here on the weekend and who wasn't?"

Her words echoed in the room. Evie could feel a breath inching its way into her chest, this one going a little further than the last. Almost there, she thought.

"It could be that our administrative controls were not up to par over the weekend," she said quietly. "But it seems clear that an operator came in of his own volition to make a repair. And he did not follow procedure—for either working alone or lockout."

Byron took a step back. She paced the room, back and forth several times. Evie watched the unflattering cut of her pantsuit and the seams riding over the rounded bulge of her hips. Finally, Byron turned back to Evie.

"Let's go see your training documents, then. Right now," she said.

This is it, thought Evie. Pass or fail on this one.

"Okay, let's go, then," she said.

Karl followed them, and the three of them crowded into the small storage room off the main office. Byron stepped forward and removed the giant lock that she had put on the file cabinet the day before. Then she stepped back to let Evie open it.

"I always file the most recent training documents at the back," Evie said.

Byron nodded but did not say anything.

"That way, it's all chronological. And I can see, month to month, who needs to refresh their training, right?" Evie was speaking quickly. "So I'll just flip to the back here. August. That's when Gavin started working here."

Evie shuffled uselessly through the papers. She'd handed a training form for Gavin to Conrad the morning before. And by that point, Gavin had already been dead for some time. She grabbed a sheet at random and pulled it out.

"We test for understanding, you see. They have to fill out a quiz," she said. "I check every single one, and if there are mistakes, the supervisor reviews the training with the employee, and he signs off that he understands. See?" She handed the document to Susan.

Byron took it and quickly glanced at the name on the top. "Ed Farrell got all the answers right," Byron said. There was no hint of irony in her voice. "How about Gavin Grayson? Did he get all the answers right?"

Evie flipped to the back of the file and pulled out the last document.

"Uh," she said quietly. "Yes, he did."

There in her hand was a working-alone training document. Gavin's name was scrawled on the top in her own loopy handwriting, the answer to the multiple-choice questions circled crookedly in black ballpoint pen. Gavin's signature spread across the bottom of the page, not confining itself to the line that had been left for it. He had dated the document the eighth of August.

"He did, as a matter of fact," Evie said slowly, handing the paper to Susan. "He did get all the answers right."

This is wrong, she thought. She knew it was wrong. But Evie handed the document over anyway. And all she felt was relief.

From: Evie Chapelle [safety@bugbrew.ca]
To: Karl Ostikoff [plantmgr@bugbrew.ca]
Re: Environmental File
Sent: Tuesday, September 8, 8:23 a.m.

Karl,
The environmental audit is in two weeks. I still have not received the files from you. I would like to review them, and go over any questions I have, well before the auditors arrive. You know what these things are like—no stone unturned. I need to be fully prepared in order to get the best results for the whole Bugaboo team.

Let's get this handoff done.

Evie

11

The sound chirped just outside the room, scaring Leigh half out of her wits. She jumped off the recliner. So much for a little rest before going to work, she thought. She pawed through the laundry basket on the floor.

"What is that? What is it? A cricket? Hon! Jason? I think there's a cricket in the house!" she called.

It chirped again. Leigh had the laundry completely spread out on the floor now. The afternoon sun came in through the vertical blinds and washed the room in a red glow. Creepy, she'd always thought. But at least this rental came with blinds, not like the last one, where they had strung up sheets to cover the windows. That's a sure sign of poverty. They were moving up in the world again.

Another chirp. It seemed to be coming from the couch. Jason's backpack was there, just where he'd dropped it when he came home from school an hour before. Home from school and straight to his room.

"*Jay?* Hon, there's something in your backpack making a racket!"

"Don't touch my backpack!" he yelled.

Leigh's hands froze. She turned to her son. He was standing in the doorway of his room wearing only boxer shorts. He looked like a skinny little man-child. Fourteen years old. Too young to do the things he wanted, but too old to be mothered.

"It's making a racket, honey," she replied.

He shrugged, his skinny shoulders on impossibly long arms moving up once, then down.

"What is it?" she asked.

"A cell phone." His voice was sullen.

"A cell phone? I thought we decided you weren't ready for a cell phone."

"Found it," he said.

"You found it? Dear God, did you steal it? Are you . . . ? Did you—" Leigh stopped herself and looked up at him. *Are you turning into your father?* she thought. But what she said was "Tell me what happened."

He shrugged again, a wall of a shrug. A wall so high she wanted to pound her way in.

"I found it. In the alley behind the hotel," he said, shrugging once more.

Aren't your shoulders getting sore? she wanted to ask, but instead she said, "What did you plan to do with it?"

"Turn it in, I guess." He would not look at her.

"Okay." She stretched the word out, trying to stay calm. "That's a good idea. How about right now? You want me to drive you there?"

"Where?" he asked, looking truly confused.

"To the police station."

"Now?" he asked.

"Yes now!"

"But, Mom, it's not like I stole it," he exclaimed. "Couldn't it wait?"

"No, it can't wait," she said.

"It's just a cell phone!"

Leigh lost her mask of patience. "It is *not* just a cell phone. It's a slippery slope! You find something, you keep it, and you think it's yours. Then next thing you know, you're looking for things to find so you can keep them, and after that, you're finding things in places you have no right to be in, like people's houses and people's pockets. And then the next thing you know—"

"Yeah, yeah, I'm in the cell next to Dad. Okay, okay, I got it," he grumbled.

"So go get dressed. I'll drop you there on my way to work."

Somehow he managed to roll his eyes, shrug, and flop his hair all at the same time, before closing the door of his room.

"And hurry up!" she yelled through the closed door.

Who are you? The woman was covered now; a body bag shielded her exposed skin from the sun that had baked the rest of them all afternoon long. The scene-of-crime officers would work until nightfall, but it was pretty clear to everyone that they were searching for a primary scene—a place where the mystery woman had been held captive, and possibly murdered.

The sun stretched their shadows long, in one last fanfare of afternoon light. An ambulance waited for its cargo at the edge of the field, right by Bern's house.

"One of my officers was first on the scene. He'll go to

'Kelowna for the autopsy." Resnick stood behind Bern, watching. "We'll know by tomorrow or the next day what it is we're dealing with."

Bern nodded. "Hard to say how she died," he said quietly. "Or when." He knelt down and unzipped the top of the body bag. He tried to memorize her features. A healthy girl, pretty, with straight white teeth. Someone had looked after her as a child, had cared for her into an abbreviated adulthood. He held a curled lock of her hair between his thumb and forefinger. *I will find out who you are.* He made the promise to himself, and to her. The coroner's first task: find out who died. He zipped the bag closed and nodded to the waiting officer.

"Someone from out of town," Resnick said. "Passing through, probably—a city crime that happened to land here. Glad it's going on major crimes' budget and not mine."

He did have a point, thought Bern. Through the course of the day, officers had stopped several dozen people passing through the scrabble of field that served as a shortcut between Selkirk Street and the residential streets across the tracks. Officers had shown them a photo of the dead woman's face. No one had recognized her. If she had been in town for any length of time, someone was sure to have seen her before.

"We'll start canvassing the neighborhood tonight. It's right around dinnertime. We'll see what we can find out," Resnick said. Bern stood up and stepped out of the way as an officer and paramedic lifted the body bag onto a stretcher. He and Resnick watched as they rolled it unsteadily through the field.

"And the brewery?" he asked.

The long afternoon sun cast a shadow across Resnick's face,

making his expression unreadable. "I'll get a couple of officers to go through it with a fine-toothed comb. Do you want to go along?" he asked.

Bern thought about this for a minute. Then he shook his head. "I'll wait to hear the autopsy results. And to read the six-teen—twenty-fours," he said. It was the coroner's prerogative to request a full copy of all police notes during an open case.

"Whose?" Resnick asked.

Bern shrugged. "Everyone's. Have them type them up at the end of their shift. I'll come get them around midnight."

Resnick grunted. "What are you going to do until then?"

"Well, if you'll give me the key, I'll go check out Gavin Grayson's apartment. And stop by the brewery to talk to the WSB officer again."

Resnick shielded his hand over his eyes and looked up at Bern. "I don't see why you don't just let that one go. An accident. Brutal, and a disgusting way to go, but it *was* an accident. Let the WSB sort it out," he said. Then he slapped his forehead. "Oh, I get it. Of course. You want to see the safety girl again."

Bern did not reply. He watched an officer climb into a patrol car and follow the ambulance down the road. They were soon out of sight. Like pulling a shade, the sun suddenly dropped behind the mountains and Bern could see Resnick again, in all his bristly impatience.

"So can I have that key?" he asked.

Resnick raised his hands in surrender. "Fine, suit yourself. Check in at the front desk," he said, nodding in the direction of the police station. "Tell them I said to give it to you."

Bern watched as an officer walked toward them through the

field, collecting the small flags that they had placed at intervals throughout the crime scene. Soon there would be no indication of what had happened. It would go back to being a stretch of dry, trampled grass. Not a place in itself but a place between departure and arrival—a passing-through place.

12

Gavin's apartment was in a small box of units on a corner lot two blocks from the brewery. Three main-floor units opened to the street like the rooms in a tiny motel. There were three upper units as well, circled by a rickety balcony that spanned the upper floor. Six little boxes of life, thought Bern as he used the key to open the door, then gestured for Evie to follow him inside.

"Are you sure it's all right that I come in?" she asked.

Bern flicked on a light. The tiny apartment was stuffy from being closed up in the heat. There was a large window in the front. He took two steps toward it and pushed open the orange curtains, allowing what was left of the day's dwindling light into the room. Mountains looked back at him. Even the most dreary little apartment in Kootenay Landing had a stunning view.

"Probably not," he said. "At least not in Resnick's opinion. But I need you here. You might notice something that I wouldn't, since you at least knew Gavin." He gestured into the room. "Not that there is much to see, though."

The suite was depressing. The main room had a sofa under the window, its woven plaid fabric accentuating the rather startling orange of the curtains. In front of this, a low, faux-wood table was strewn with a garble of personal effects. Bern looked these over carefully: a pocketknife with the bottle opener attachment flicked open, a coffee cup, a cell phone charger, a half-eaten package of barbecue-flavored sunflower seeds, and a Kootenay Landing phone book. Under the table, three empty bottles of Bugaboo Brew were lined up in a row. A small television on a rolling cart completed the living room portion of the suite. A half wall separated the living room from the kitchen, which, judging by the dark-paneled cupboards and riotous wallpaper, had been slapped together in the mid-1970s.

Bern went into the bedroom—a lumpy-looking mattress on the floor, a faded comforter thrown on it. A door at the back of the room led to a tiny bathroom. He stepped over the coverlet and picked up a framed picture on the bedside table. It showed a girl sitting on the passenger seat of a truck. Her bare feet were up on the dashboard; a pair of cut-off jean shorts covered only a small portion of her tanned legs. The photo had been taken from the driver's side, and the door to the truck was open to a sunny day and a golden wheat field next to a highway. The young woman rested a beer bottle against her leg. Her other hand, the one closer to the camera, held a cowboy hat in place on the top of her head. Her head was tipped backward, and her tanned arm covered most of her features, except for a row of straight white teeth. She was laughing.

Bern grunted. It could be any happy, carefree young woman.

"Do you know anything about Gavin's girlfriend?" he asked.

"Just that we can't reach her. She's listed as his next of kin," she called back from the kitchen. Bern put the picture down and joined Evie in the kitchen. She was looking through a pile of papers next to the apartment-sized fridge. "I heard she was supposed to be coming here to join him, but I don't know the details." She was quiet for a moment, then said, "This is interesting."

"What's that?" Bern asked. Her hair had fallen in front of her face and she chewed distractedly on one lock. She held a calendar up to him.

"He's got his schedule marked here. He was on afternoons all last week. And he's got an overtime shift written in—four hours starting at two p.m. on Monday," she said slowly.

Bern walked around the wall and stood next to her. He bent down to see the calendar over her shoulder. "That looks pretty planned," he said.

"Yeah," Evie said quietly, "it does."

Bern's cell phone chirped. "Dear God," he muttered, "not another one." He pulled the phone off his belt and answered: "Bern Fortin."

He was greeted by the honey voice of the chief coroner's secretary. "Bern, just calling to remind you about your semiannual review on Friday. The CC is expecting you in the Kelowna office at eleven a.m."

"Claire," he said, "how nice to hear your voice. But you know I'm in the middle of two cases right now. I can't possibly make it for Friday. I'll have to reschedule."

Claire tutted on the other end of the line. "His understanding is that you are waiting for autopsy results, and that the RCMP have the rest under control. Meantime, you can pop over here for a meeting."

Bern smiled into the receiver. He knew that Chief Coroner Ogden Kumar was probably standing right by her desk, hands clasped behind him, balancing on the balls of his feet in his leather-soled dress shoes, listening.

"I'd hardly call a four-hour drive each way 'popping over,'" Bern said. "Can't it wait a few days? I've got this other case too."

"We understand that the other case involves a workplace accident. The chief is recommending that you give the WSB the space to investigate, and then work from their report. Let their budget absorb it," Claire said. He could almost see her looking up at Kumar and smiling as she said the words. "So take a day. We'll see you Friday morning. He says he'll even buy you lunch before you drive back."

She hung up before he could reply.

When they left Gavin's apartment, they walked the three blocks to Bern's house. They didn't plan it or talk about what they were doing. They just walked there together. Bern turned the handle and walked right in.

"You don't lock your door?" Evie asked him.

"Never," he replied.

The bungalow was tiny; Evie had not really had a chance to look at it the night before. The front door opened to a small living room with barely enough space for a couch and chair. There was no television but rather a tall, wide bookcase that spanned the wall shared by the living area and the tiny dining area. Behind the low, modern couch, which was upholstered in deep chocolate brown, was a 1950s-style kitchen table—complete with a wide stainless steel rim and a deep red top. Next to this was a kitchen outfitted with wooden cupboards painted in yellow. The doors to the porch were off the kitchen. A home office was open to the living room. Two doors led away from the dining area—both were closed. Bedroom and bathroom, thought Evie. The whole house was orderly and very clean. A stark contrast to the apartment they had just visited.

"Have a seat," Bern said. He motioned to the couch. "I'll make some tea."

Evie sank into the soft comfort of the couch. She was happy to be there. Very happy, for the first time that day.

Bern came in a few minutes later and placed the tea tray on a low, polished wooden cube table. His face had changed since the day before, Evie thought. His cheekbones were drawn down and looked longer. The skin under his eyes was dark, making his irises look black. He sat down on a chair across from her and ran his fingers through his wild curls, some of which stayed standing straight up when he pulled his hands away.

"It's been quite a day," he said.

"Can you tell me what happened?" Evie asked, pointing in the direction of the field where the girl was found.

"You know that we found the body of a young woman, yes?" he said.

Evie nodded. "And the police searched the brewery."

"I haven't heard the results of the search yet. If they found anything, I think they would have phoned me."

There was a plate of cookies on the tray—homemade, by the looks of it. He offered the plate to Evie and she took one.

"I can't imagine when you had time to make these," she said.

A brief smiled softened his face. "Just one reason to keep the door unlocked," he said. "My neighbor comes in and leaves me cookies."

"Can you tell me anything?" she asked. "About what happened?"

He shrugged. *A little,* the shrug said, *but not too much.* "I can tell you *when* it happened. Last night, likely while we were sitting on the deck. Do you remember hearing anything? Or seeing anything when you left?"

Evie thought for a moment about the peaceful moments they'd shared over a cup of tea the night before. All while a young woman lay dying nearby. "Just the alarm. And the train."

Bern nodded. "The alarm. I thought of that too. That's why they searched the brewery. Other than that, there's not much to tell. The RCMP have taken her to Kelowna for an autopsy. Right now, the biggest priority is to find out who she is."

"No clues?" Evie asked.

"Not the usual—no ID, no witnesses, no one who has recognized her," Bern said. "Resnick figures it's an out-of-town crime that just happened to touch on Kootenay Landing. But she doesn't match the description of any missing person—not that we've found so far, in any case."

"Do you agree with him?" she asked.

He shrugged expressively. *Not really, but I'm willing to play along,* this one seemed to say.

"Eh, bien," he said, standing up. "Do you really want tea?" He gestured to the tray. "I think I might like something a little stronger. Beer, maybe? I've got some, but it's not Bugaboo."

Evie laughed. "Don't tell anyone, but I really don't like beer," she said.

"Wine, then?" he asked.

"Sure."

He took away the tea but left the cookies. He came back

moments later with a bottle of wine and two delicate glasses. He pulled the cork expertly and poured them each a glass of a rich, dark red.

"Cheers," he said. "Now tell me—how is it going at the brewery?"

It was Evie's turn to shrug. "The WSB officer seems to be done. Byron says she won't be back—not tomorrow, anyway. She was called to another accident, one in Cranbrook. Before she left, she gave the go-ahead for production to start again."

"Did you do any interviews today?" he asked.

Evie took a sip of her wine and leaned back. She thought back to the two dozen or so interviews that she had done with Byron. "Lots. Nothing new. It's like—" She cut herself short.

She saw Bern's eyes skim her features with curiosity. He picked a cookie off the plate and took a bite, then held it up in the air. "An excellent pairing with the wine," he said with a chuckle. "So you were saying it's like . . . ?" he asked.

Evie sighed. "It's like the guys think if they keep quiet for long enough, it will all go away. And they might be right. The WSB is swamped—Byron spent a day and a half here, which is almost unheard-of these days. The Mounties have already got another death on their hands. Once the accident report is filed, I doubt we will ever hear mention of Gavin Grayson again."

Evie sat back and took another sip of wine. She'd said more than she'd meant to. His head was cocked and he was listening carefully. He listened, it seemed to her, not just to the words but to the meaning and emotion behind them. It made her want to talk forever.

"You don't agree that it was an accident?" he asked.

"I never said that," she answered.

He shrugged. "Not in so many words," he said. "You have doubts, then?"

"I just think it would be important to know exactly what happened, so that it doesn't happen again," she said.

Bern put his wine glass down and opened his hands wide. "But that's why the investigations—WSB, coroner's office, RCMP, even. To try to keep such things from happening again."

"It just feels like everyone is satisfied with knowing it was an accident. No charges to be laid. No one coming forward with caustic on his hands saying he did it. The company can prove due diligence. Case closed." Evie could not stop herself from talking. She could hear the anger in her words and wanted to take them back. I'm just as bad as them, she thought. She pictured Gavin's signed training document, with her own handwriting across the top. It was the very same document she had given to Conrad the morning before. She was sure of it.

"Ah, I understand," Bern said. "A conflict, perhaps, between what your heart tells you to do and what your job tells you to do." His words were quiet and hit the mark. "I've had that conflict before."

Evie felt all the frustration and anger and tension of the day flow out of her in that fraction of a moment of being understood. She was suddenly exhausted. She put her wine glass down and yawned.

"Have a nap if you like," Bern said. "You are too tired to drive home now."

How odd, Evie thought, as she lay down on the couch and pulled a couch pillow under her head. But it feels like the right thing. "I never really sleep," she said.

He began talking quietly as she lay there, his words comforting her as she slowly drifted off to sleep. "Yes, I've had that conflict before. In fact, it's why I left the army when I did. Twenty years of service—that's the earliest you can retire. I did twenty-two years and nine months. Do you know that in the army, if you are given an order, you must follow it? The whole military is based on this principle. Without it, nothing would work; the whole system would fall apart."

His French accent seemed to get heavier as he continued to tell her a story. About a young officer who faced an impossible situation. She listened to the lilting comfort of the words, too tired to focus on their meaning, until the thought floated to her mind that he was speaking in French.

A while later the phone rang. She heard him murmur, *"Moi aussi."* Then she drifted off into a deep sleep.

From: Dave Porteous [vpwestern@bevco.ca]
To: Evie Chapelle [safety@bugbrew.ca]
Cc: Karl Ostikoff [plantmgr@bugbrew.ca]
Re: Preliminary Accident Report
Sent: Thursday, September 10, 6:09 a.m.
1 Attachment: BevCoMajorIncidentReportTemplate.doc

Evie—
A reminder that the Preliminary Accident/Due Diligence
Report on the fatality at Bugaboo Brewery this week is
now overdue. Legal expects to receive a copy of this
within forty-eight hours of the incident. Please have
something to them by the end of the day. Understood
that there will be gaps, but need to get them something
to work with.

Let me know if you need support from my team on
this. I have attached the template for the report.

Cheers,

Dave
Dave Porteous
Vice President, Western Region
BevCo Canada

13

Chantel Postniuk dropped her purse in the middle of the desk and waited for Kelly to pack up her stuff. It was the same thing every time her shift started after Kelly's, which thankfully didn't happen that often. Usually Chantel worked the day, and Kelly the afternoon and evening. Overnight was covered by the dispatcher in Cranbrook. But with two dead bodies so far in the week, and the major crimes unit in town, both civilian receptionists had been asked to do twelve-hour shifts.

"Anything I need to know?" Chantel asked. She adjusted one of the metal studs on the wide black leather belt at her waistband. She had dressed with care: pencil-thin black trousers, a cropped jacket of quilted satin and a crisp white blouse. Serious, professional—but the belt and high-heeled black boots added flair. She looked Kelly over. It had been a while since the other woman's waist had seen a belt, but it looked like she'd taken some care over her appearance as well. She wore a dropped-waist dress in a thin corduroy—the kind Chantel remembered her elementary school teacher wearing. Under the jumper-style top she wore a long-sleeved T-shirt with a frilled collar. A pair of burgundy-colored penny loafers completed the look. Thank God, no kneesocks today, thought Chantel. She sat on top of the desk and rifled through her purse for some gum.

"Want some?" she asked Kelly.

Kelly shook her head, and her long hair, fraught with split ends, shuffled around on her shoulders. "No, thanks," she said. She moved around the desk collecting her things: photos of her kids—a girl with a gap in her teeth and a boy with braces; breath mints; a small plastic card printed with a watercolor sunset and the words "God loves us all, big and small"; a china teacup; and a small spiral notebook with "Kelly John" written in block letters across the top. All of these went into the second drawer; Chantel swung her legs out of the way so she could open it. Then Kelly locked the drawer and pocketed the key.

"These are copies of all the notes from yesterday's investigation," she said. "Coroner asked for them." Her voice became muffled as she reached below the desk for her purse. "He was supposed to come get them. But he didn't yet."

Chantel smiled. Kelly's crush on the coroner was well known in the office. The woman had been married to a plumber for twenty-odd years—happily, as far as anyone could tell—but she got flustered and started blushing whenever Coroner Bern Fortin came into the detachment. Chantel flicked some imaginary dust from her white shirt. Coroner Fortin was a treat to look at—and what an accent he had—but there was no sense getting all hot and bothered around him. That kind of thing never worked on a man like that.

"So he didn't come in?" She smiled when Kelly shook her head. "Something for me to look forward to, then," Chantel said.

At long last, Kelly looked like she was ready to go. Chantel adjusted the height of the office chair before sitting down. Then she brushed off the desk and looked around.

"Don't forget your cell phone," she said to Kelly. It was sitting in the middle of the desk.

"My cell phone?" Kelly asked. "Oh, sorry. I forgot to tell you. Someone turned that in. You know Leigh, who works at the Kootenay Landing Hotel? Her son found it, and they turned it in last night." She shrugged. "Maybe someone will claim it."

She walked toward Chantel as she said this, looking like she might settle in for a long chat. Chantel waved her away. "I'll look after it. You've had a long night. Time to go home now," she said. Once her colleague was gone, Chantel swung the seat around to face the desk again and reached into the pocket of her jacket for her own key—the one to the top drawer. She unlocked it and pulled out her stainless steel travel mug; a photo of herself, outfitted in a harness and making a face at the top of the bungee-jump platform at the Calgary Stampede; and a small container of sanitary wipes. She wiped down the phone and keyboard and then went to put the coffee on.

She passed Constable Schilling in the squad room on her way to the coffee room. "You're here early," Chantel said, eyeing the empty desks that surrounded the young officer.

Schilling looked up distractedly. "Huh? Oh, yeah." She tapped the keyboard of one of the computers.

Chantel walked closer, her high heels echoing on the floor. She always felt like she towered over Schilling, especially in heels. Schilling was short, and while she had a fair enough figure in civilian clothing, she always looked squat in her uniform. Chantel looked at the belt, loaded down with all that gear, which seemed to press uncomfortably into Schilling's ribs.

"They weren't thinking of women when they designed those things, were they?" she asked.

Schilling laughed and shifted in her seat. "Definitely not. They weren't thinking about women with a lot of stuff in the RCMP." She tapped something more into her keyboard, and the image on the screen shifted. "There," she said.

"What are you working on?" Chantel asked.

Schilling stood and gestured to the coffee room. "A bit of a long shot. It hit me in the middle of the night, so I came in early to try to find some answers."

"Can you tell me what it is?"

Schilling shook her head. "Let's just say, sometimes being a woman in the RCMP is an advantage," she said. "You notice things that the guys wouldn't necessarily pick up on."

They reached the coffee room. "Like what?" she asked. She didn't want to be nosy, but she could tell that Schilling was dying to tell her. Chantel could keep a secret. She poured the remains of the old coffee down the drain and started fixing a fresh pot.

Schilling just laughed and shook her I'm-trying-to-look-just-like-a-guy hair. "Let's just say I'm working the lingerie angle."

Chantel raised an eyebrow. "You mean on the dead girl? Oh, good thinking. I've never seen a bustier like that. I mean, I only saw the pictures, but—"

Schilling pointed a finger at her and winked. "Exactly what I thought. I knew if I ran it by Resnick, he'd make a big stink about it. So I'm not going to say anything at all. Unless, of course, I find something out."

Chantel laughed and pretended to zipper her lips closed. "Won't say a word," she said.

It felt like she was in a dream when she arrived at the brewery. The air reverberated with the hum of machinery. The tiny staff room was packed and Evie was jostled as she went in to get a coffee. Someone had brought in doughnuts.

"Is she gone?" Evie asked Gemma.

"She's gone," Gemma said with a smile. She ripped open a small packet of artificial sweetener and stirred it into a white ceramic mug that read "I'm the Real Boss Around Here."

Evie's mug was printed on the outside to look like a can of Campbell's soup. Most days she would have coffee in it in the mornings, and then heat up some soup in the same mug at lunchtime. Now she filled it with hot coffee from the urn and added some milk and sugar.

"Nice to see you come in at a regular time," Gemma said.

Evie felt her face reddening. Was she imagining it or did the whole room fall quiet at that moment? She felt oddly exposed. She was usually in the office hours before anyone else.

"I took the dog for an extra-long walk this morning," she said. Which was true: she had. She'd driven home just before dawn. She'd had more sleep on Bern's couch than she'd had in all the nights of the past week put together. She felt on solid ground, sure of herself, rested. But the thought that her black SUV had spent the whole night in the brewery parking lot niggled at her. Someone was sure to have noticed.

"Well, it suits you. You look great. You should do it every day."

Too much time in the office isn't good for anyone," Gemma said.

Karl appeared in the room as if from nowhere. His golf shirt was steel-blue today, worn with pressed jeans. In keeping with his recent international theme, his shirt sported the logo of one of the oldest brewing companies in Austria, which had recently joined the BevCo fold. Space seemed to appear around Karl in the crowded room. Evie reached for a doughnut and leaned against the wall, nibbling on it, watching.

Karl grabbed a doughnut and looked around. "Good, everyone's here. Let's have a quick briefing before we get back to work," he said. He took a big bite of doughnut between his teeth and kept talking as he chewed it.

"Great news is that the WSB officer is gone. She signed off on the bottle shop startup last night and said she was assured that there was no machine malfunction. It will be some time before we see her report, but I have reason to believe it will fall on the side of operator error. Evie has been told to expect a major overhaul of procedures, but for the meantime, it's business as usual," he said.

"We had technicians working through the night last night to get everything ready for startup. We dumped the caustic. And we removed and disposed of all the bottles that were in the bottle washer at the time of the incident," he said. Karl nodded to Conrad to pick up from there.

"There was no finished liquid involved, since the machine jammed up right away," Conrad continued, pushing his glasses up his nose. "We emptied all the bottles that were in the machine and the first thousand that had come out, and we crushed them. We had a maintenance crew working through the night, giving the machine a tune-up, and uh—" He paused for a moment and coughed into his hand. "Sorry . . . uh, the crew hosed the machine down and sanitized it—on the inside, that is. Then they filled it and got it ready to go." Conrad fell silent.

Everyone looked down at their feet for a few seconds without saying anything, taking in the facts behind his words. Any remains of Gavin left in the bottle washer had been hosed down the drain.

Evie put her doughnut down on a napkin. Karl took another bite of his and started talking again. "It is now Thursday morning. We haven't produced anything since we ran two hours of new glass on Tuesday. It's time to put all this behind us and make some beer."

Conrad stepped forward, his beak nose prominent under the harsh fluorescent lights of the staff room.

"As a way to turn over a new leaf, I'd like to invite you all to a potluck at my place tomorrow night. Six o'clock. Bring your spouses," he said.

Someone giggled, and Evie saw Karl looking pointedly at her.

"Shush," Gemma said. "Leave her alone."

"What?" asked Evie.

"Just wondering which spouse you'll bring," Karl said, his voice edged like a razor. "Will we get to meet your new boyfriend?"

Evie's mouth opened, but no sound came out. "New boyfriend?" she mouthed.

"So innocent," Karl muttered.

"We were just talking about the case," she said.

"The case? It's a case now? And what are you, the detective?" Karl asked.

"All right, all right, that's enough," Conrad said. Somehow it seemed worse that Conrad had to jump to her defense.

Karl coughed slightly. "Thanks for the invitation, Conrad. It's an excellent idea, and Felicia and I will definitely be there. I hope you all will as well," he said with a finality that made it sound like failure to appear would impact their annual performance reviews. "By the way, Evie, we need to find time to talk about that environmental audit. As soon as you get that accident report done and sent off to corporate, you'll need to take over the file."

Evie blew a breath out of her mouth, and a lock of hair lifted from her face and fell back down again. She brushed at it angrily with her hand. "I'd love to take over that file, Karl. I've been trying to get the file from you for weeks now. I can't do anything until I get that."

Karl's smile was quick and easy. "You need the environmental file? Why didn't you just say so? No problem at all, Evie. I'll get someone to bring it to your office by the end of today. And once you've looked through it, I'd be happy to sit down with you and go over any questions you might have," he said.

Evie stared at him in disbelief. She'd been emailing him and leaving him messages for weeks trying to get her hands on that file. Karl was looking at her curiously. Evie realized that her mouth was open and her hands were clenched.

She loosened her fingers. "That would be great, Karl. Thank you. If I'm not there, just leave it on the chair by the door." Her face felt like it would crack from the effort of smiling. She picked up her coffee cup and left the room. She was halfway down the hall before she heard their hushed voices start talking again.

SOLDIER'S ALLY

=========== August Issue ===========

CIVILIAN TRIAL DENIED IN MERCY-KILLING CASE
Editorial
by Troy Thompson

Captain Marcel Alais appeared before a judge last month in a closed-door hearing. The officer, who is imprisoned while awaiting trial, is charged with disgraceful conduct in the shooting death of a mortally wounded Taliban soldier in Afghanistan.

Soldier's Ally magazine has learned that Alais's civilian legal team submitted a motion to have him tried in civilian court. The Judge Advocate General denied the request, stating that military law requires a soldier to be tried before his peers. Alais's lawyers are afraid that their client will become the scapegoat for a faulty military mission and the ongoing tug-of-war between the current government and top brass. Military culture has historically—at least off the record—condoned mercy killing in the field, and some commanders have been known to look the other way. However, military doctrine officially denounces the practice.

But as many soldiers know, and what the government fails to understand, is that what sounds reasonable on paper, and in theory, may not apply at all to the realities soldiers face in theater.

Readers may remember that thousands of citizens descended on Parliament to protest the charges against Alais. The young captain came across a wounded Taliban soldier while on patrol in Afghanistan and deemed there was no hope for his recovery. Medical aid was too far away, and the injured insurgent was dying slowly and in excruciating pain.

Alais does not deny his actions. During a recent visit to his prison cell, I asked him why he shot the injured soldier. He said simply: "I hoped that someone would do the same if it was me."

Here at *Soldier's Ally* we will continue to follow this story closely. Will Alais become another scapegoat, taking the blame for more senior officers who are trying to keep the realities of the Afghan mission from the politicians in Ottawa and the Canadian public?

Our government sends soldiers to the end of the earth to take a stand for peace and freedom—all in the name of politics. But God forbid if, when put in an impossible situation, a soldier makes an honorable decision.

Readers, I want you to know: I am a former soldier, and I have been there. I understand. Those of you who are still serving can't speak out, can't ask questions, and can't search for the truth. But I can, and I will.

The first question, of course, is: Where is Alais's former commanding officer? We are hearing stories of backroom deals and golden handshakes. The name on everyone's lips is Lieutenant-Colonel Bern Fortin. Why the sudden retirement? Where has he gone? And will he come back to defend his subordinate's actions?

Soldiers, I am on a mission to bring you the truth. I will not stop until I have given you a full accounting of what really happened.

14

Evie was gone by the time he woke up. She'd neatly folded the blanket he'd spread over her; there was not even an indentation on the couch to show where she'd slept. There was no note. Almost as if she hadn't been there at all. Except that he knew she had been.

There was something about her that stayed with him. At first she'd reminded him of someone from his past, and he smiled now at the fleeting memory of Madame LeClerc. She was both similar and quite opposite to Evie—all fluff and softness on the outside, while on the inside she was all cold efficiency. Evie's exterior seemed to be constructed of the regulations, systems, and compliance she was in charge of managing. But under all that Bern was sure there was softness, acceptance, and space.

He thought about her as he dressed in what he considered his office clothes—corduroys and a dress shirt, instead of his usual jeans and flannel shirt. He knew he wanted to see her again. And soon.

He walked the few short steps into the kitchen and turned on the espresso maker. While he was waiting for the water to heat up, he opened the patio door and surveyed the garden. The plants looked cool and plump after the late-night watering he had given them. The tomatoes were ripening faster than he could harvest them, and more were ripe this morning, despite the harvesting Mrs. K. had done the day before.

He made his triple espresso in a travel mug and went back on the deck for a few minutes to enjoy it. It was another perfect day. There was no hint of summer abating, though fall would be waiting expectantly in the wings. He was beginning to understand the suddenness of scene changes between seasons in the mountains. Fall would arrive like a curtain dropping. The same curtain that lifted between spring and summer.

Coffee finished, he set about a shortened morning routine. The garden inspection would wait. He could get away with a day or two of not splitting wood. But he had to check on Mrs. K.

She was sitting at the table when he walked in, her hands on her knees. The counters were spotlessly clean and bare. She was in a going-to-town dress, her hair in curlers. It took her a moment to look up at him when he walked in, and she was quickly on her feet.

Bern sat in the chair next to the one she'd vacated. "You can sit with me, you know," he said. "You don't need to bustle away."

She grunted but did not reply. She poured a coffee from the metal percolator on the stove and doctored it just the way coffee should be. She placed it in front of him without saying a word, then set about making him toast from her homemade sourdough bread. He watched her as he sipped the overly sweet coffee.

"Going to town today?" he asked finally.

"Couldn't get groceries yesterday. I need pectin. To teach you to make jam," she said.

"Ah," he said with a nod. "Fall fair."

She made a guttural clucking sound in her throat. "Mrs.

Grandini's niece moved here from Cranbrook. Says she's going to enter the best chiffon cake." Mrs. K. slid a plate of toast in front of Bern.

He circled her wrist with his fingers gently and pulled her toward the chair. "Sit with me. Please," he said. He tilted his head at her. "I need company."

She looked at him with one raised eyebrow, a look made almost comical by the halo of curlers that framed her stern face. She walked to the cupboard for another coffee cup, prepared it, and came back to join him.

"So is that what's bothering you?" he asked. "Mrs. Grandini's niece and her chiffon cake?" He looked up at the rows of fall fair plaques that were carefully displayed on the wall above the kitchen table. The keeper plaques, Mrs. K. had once explained to him, were even more prized than the much more elaborate baking trophy, which she kept polished in the upstairs sitting room. Those, she got to keep forever. The trophy had to be returned at the end of the year.

Mrs. K. snorted into her coffee. "I have won chiffon cake for . . . what? Twelve years? Fifteen? And anyway, I've had her chiffon cake. Too spongy." With a wave of her strong hand, she dismissed Mrs. Grandini's niece and all other contenders for the chiffon cake keeper plaque. Then she fell silent.

Bern knew better than to ask, so he just waited. He watched as her eyes became shiny with tears, and her mouth set with a determination not to let them fall.

"I called my granddaughter, Katie," she said at last. "Just to see—to make sure—" Her voice broke.

"To make sure it wasn't her you found yesterday," Bern said quietly.

Mrs. K. nodded. "My daughter and I—we haven't spoken in years," she said.

Bern nodded. "That happens sometimes."

"But her children, Katie and Brian . . ."

"Do they live close by?" Bern asked.

Mrs. K. waved vaguely off toward the garden. "Up on the hill. In the new subdivision. House is so big, no room for a garden," she said.

Bern chewed slowly on a piece of toast, waiting for her to tell him what had happened when she called the too-big house on the hill.

"Katie left for college last week," she said at last. "She's safe, at college in Kelowna."

Bern nodded, feeling the pain in the space between her words. The weight of the words she did not say: Mrs. K. hadn't known that her granddaughter had left for college. She'd left without saying good-bye.

"I'm glad she's safe," he said.

"Me too," said Mrs. K.

"And what about Brian? Is he safe?"

She nodded slowly. "Last year of high school. As safe as he can be."

After breakfast, Bern made himself another espresso and walked the short distance to the RCMP station. He ran through the events of the day before and wondered where the best place to start would be. See what the officers came up with in their door-to-door and their search of the brewery, he thought. Maybe they know who she is by now. Although if they had figured it out, they likely would have called him.

From his vantage point along the road he could see the trampled grass where the recovery of the unknown woman's body had taken place. It was another bright day; the mountains cut a crisp profile along the expanse of blue canvas that was the sky. It was hard to believe that anything bad could happen in such a beautiful place.

But Rwanda had been beautiful too, of course, as had Bosnia. And terrible things had happened there. Bern often thought of those few months he had spent living in a small house in the hills outside Kigali, before war had broken out in earnest. A peaceful time, in retrospect. The slope of those mountains was gentler and dotted with tea plantations. The mountains piled up in the distance looked blue in a certain light, making the landscape inviting but mysterious at the same time. Roads to unknown destinations led away from every central place. Roads to desolate and remote locations where atrocities were committed that might never come to light.

Bern could see Resnick outside the station, watching his approach.

"About time you got out of bed," Resnick said. He butted his cigarette into the metal ashtray by the door. The crease between his eyebrows deepened as Bern got closer.

Bern shrugged and raised his coffee cup. "Cheers," he said. "I've got my poison, and you've got yours." He pulled the door open and held it for Resnick. "Have you figured out who she is yet?"

Resnick grunted and stalked through a door off the main lobby, while Bern turned to check in with Chantel.

The receptionist smiled with all her teeth and tapped a folder on her desk. "I've got the notes you wanted," she said.

Bern picked up the file and leaned against the back of the reception counter, a few feet from her desk. He flipped open the file.

Chantel raised a plucked eyebrow at him. He smiled at her, taking in her crisply pressed white shirt, as white as her teeth. Her lips were painted a full, bright red. He was sure the rest of her outfit was black: a cropped jacket would be hanging in the staff closet, black pants and high-heeled boots tucked demurely under her desk. She tended to favor a glamorous toreador look.

A cell phone twittered somewhere in the space between them.

"Yours?" she asked.

"No, yours," he said.

It chirped again, like a wayward bird. "I don't have a cell phone," Chantel said.

Bern moved closer to her desk and listened for the sound. When it came again, he lifted a stray sheet of paper and pointed to a small silver phone underneath. Chantel reached out and picked it up. Her fingernails were painted a neutral shade, though he knew she preferred bright jewel colors on the weekends. She flipped the phone open.

"Hello?" she said.

Bern moved back to the counter and began to read the file again. Two major crimes officers had been to every house in the neighborhood behind the brewery last night. Conrad Scofield had taken a third officer through every nook and cranny of the brewery. It seemed that no one had seen anything.

"Are you serious? Like the singer?"

Chantel's side of the conversation cut into his thoughts.

"No, ma'am," she continued. "This is the RCMP detachment in Kootenay Landing, British Columbia. This cell phone was found by someone and turned in. So if you tell me it belongs to Belinda Carlisle, I'll do my best to get it back to her."

Bern stepped up to the desk. "Who is it?" he mouthed. Then he motioned impatiently with his hand and she handed him the phone.

"Who is speaking, please?" he said.

"This is Gemma Burch at the brewery." Bern recognized the smooth tone of her voice.

"Gemma," he said. "This is Bern Fortin. Who are you trying to reach?"

"This is the number that I have for Belinda Carlisle—Gavin Grayson's next of kin? I tried calling her yesterday but didn't get through. I just got in the office and thought I would try again."

Bern was silent, thinking. "I'll call you back, okay, Gemma?"

He hung up the phone and placed it gingerly on Chantel's desk.

"How many people have touched that?" he asked.

She shrugged. "No idea. Why? Do you think—"

"I think we'd better talk to Resnick."

Resnick listened to Bern's story. Bern could practically see the moment when the light went on and he figured it out.

"You think it's her?" he asked.

"Well, let's look at what we've got. We've got a dead woman no one recognizes, which means she's likely new to town. She has no personal effects on her, and there is no indication of where she came from. And we know that there is someone called Belinda Carlisle, who is the girlfriend of the worker who was found at the brewery. She was supposed to be arriving in town, but no one has actually seen her. And now we have her cell phone. But not her."

Resnick nodded slowly. "Unless we do have her—and she's the one being autopsied right now." He paused and tapped his pen on the edge of his desk. "Easy enough to find out, I suppose. Call up her driver's license."

"Yes!" The exclamation came from the other side of the room. "Staff Sergeant Resnick, come see this," Constable Schilling called out.

Resnick looked at Bern and they walked across the room together. Every available inch of table space had been taken over by the visiting major crimes officers. They had spread papers across the desks and tacked maps to the walls; several were hunched over computer terminals and laptops as Bern and Resnick walked past. Schilling was perched at the corner of a desk on the far side of the room, a laptop open before her. She stood as they reached her and started talking all at once.

"I came in early to follow a lead, sir," she said. "I thought if it panned out, great. If not . . . well, no harm done." She looked at Bern and shrugged one shoulder lightly. "It has to do with the dead woman. Her bra—I'd never seen anything like it before. A bustier. So I thought I'd chase down the manufacturer's information right away, you know? See what I could come up with."

Bern saw Resnick's eyes narrow at this. He wasn't sure that Resnick would consider such independent action to be an admirable trait in a subordinate. "And what did you find?" Bern prompted.

"Well, it's like I thought. A new design, just out for fall. It's only been on the shelves at La Donna—that's the store brand that was on the label—for two weeks," she said.

"I won't ask how you know their inventory so well," Resnick said. "So next you'll fax them a photo of the woman and see if any staff members from the stores recognize her?"

Schilling scrunched her face in a cross between a cringe and a smile. "Well, actually, I went ahead and did that. Their head office is in Toronto, eastern time and all that; they've been up for hours. So I emailed them the photo, and they sent a copy to all their stores out west. And we got a hit!"

She hiked her police belt up so she could sit in front of the computer. "Here it is: a copy of the credit card receipt. West Edmonton Mall, last Friday, a Mr. Brad Acer bought two hundred thirty-eight dollars and fifty-one cents' worth of lingerie for his girlfriend, including one Royal Renaissance bustier. Matching underwear too." She clicked on an icon and a scanned copy of the receipt popped up. "In the email, the store manager says the photo I sent is definitely the girlfriend."

"Brad Acer," said Resnick. "And I suppose you know where to find him?"

Schilling shrugged. "Well, we can check with the credit card company to be sure. But I checked the phone book online and it looks like he's in Kelowna."

"I'm going to Kelowna tomorrow. I could go talk to him," Bern offered.

"Well, tomorrow is a long time in the world of police work, Mr. Fortin. I can have a team out to his place in minutes. Maybe tomorrow you can go visit him in his cell at the station." He nodded curtly to Schilling. "Good work," he said, and walked away.

Leaving the police station, Bern found himself reluctant to head back home to the paperwork that was waiting for him. The sun was warming up and chasing every last overnight cloud away from the valley. The mountains held on to the blue sky, and it teased back: there would not be many more days like this one.

He walked past his house and followed the road to the brewery. He had seen the houses along this road hundreds of times, but he really looked at them for the first time now. Each was similar, but different in its own way. One house boasted a bird feeder made out of tin cans and other recycled odds and ends, all nailed together and carefully painted to look like a farmer. Evidently the birds enjoyed it. Bern could see them eating out of an old tin plate, painted yellow, which made up the top of the farmer's straw hat. Someone had taken time and care to make that. Bern wondered if it was the owner or a gift from a friend. Maybe he would stop one day and ask.

A few of the houses were like his, small with large gardens. Others had started as small bungalows but had been renovated to add open-plan kitchens, extra bedrooms, and enormous family rooms that took over the space where the garden used to be.

He reached Leroy Ostikoff's house, and it was different from all the rest. Still small, but here the garden had been covered over with sod, which was carefully trimmed and perfectly green. Bern walked up the two steps to the small front stoop and rang the bell. There were no decorations to be found. And while the door trim was carefully painted and the stoop swept, there was something closed and uninviting about the house. A single lawn chair was the only item on the stoop.

Bern was about to press the bell again when the door opened a few inches. Leroy stuck his head out and glared at him. His face was rugged from a lifetime of hard work, but his full head of dull blond hair and slight frame made him look like a younger man.

Bern nodded. "I came back to ask you those questions," he said.

Leroy didn't answer. He just closed the door. Bern took a step back, leaned on the railing and waited. A few minutes later, Leroy opened the door far enough to slip his tiny body out. He closed it firmly behind him and shuffled over to the lawn chair, where he sat down with a grunt. It was the only sound Bern had heard him make so far.

"So how are you enjoying your retirement?" Bern asked him with a smile. When Leroy didn't answer, he just kept talking. "I recently retired myself, you know. Must say, it took some getting used to. In fact, the first thing I did was to go out and get myself a job." He laughed. "And what a job it is."

Leroy was looking out over the railing, his eyes scanning the brewery yard. He was wearing a long-sleeved navy-blue shirt and blue work pants, the same color as the Bugaboo-issue blue coveralls that employees were required to wear. He pulled at the cuffs, tugging them down to his knuckles. One side, then the other.

"You see all the activity around here yesterday and today?" Bern asked. "We found the body of a young woman. Over there in the grass," he said. He gestured to the tract of land that spread from the edge of the brewery, over the railway tracks to the police station, and all the way to his own house.

"Police already asked me," Leroy said. His voice was harsh, though Bern suspected it was more from lack of use than strong emotion. "Don't know anything about it. None of my business." He didn't look at Bern as he spoke, kept his gaze somewhere over the left of Bern's shoulder.

"You keep an eye on things over there?" Bern asked him.

Leroy tugged at his right cuff with his left hand, then his left cuff with his right hand. "The way they've got that spent grains tank rigged, they're going to have an awful mess to clean up," he said.

Bern turned to look over his shoulder. He could see half a dozen tanks; two of them were at least three stories high. Another was sleek and white and protected by its own chain-link fence. There was one suspended in the air, attached to the side of the building by a complex metal frame. He had no idea which one of these might be the spent grains tank, but he nodded slowly anyway. "I bet," he said. "I hear you were a poet with those machines."

Leroy grunted.

Bern tilted his head and leaned closer. "What's that?" he asked.

"Like things a certain way." The words came as though squeezed from a rusty pump.

"Who does? You or the machines?" Bern asked.

Leroy tugged at the collar of his shirt, which was buttoned to the top, then crossed his hands in his lap. "Machines. These young guys don't listen to the machines. Think the machines are all the same. They'll tell you what they need if you listen right."

"So is that what happened to Gavin? He didn't listen?"

"Wouldn't know. Never met the guy," Leroy said. "But I bet not, seeing as what happened."

Bern asked, almost in a whisper, "Do you miss it?"

He waited out the silence that followed. Leroy worked at the sleeve of his shirt, then smoothed it in place. "Not the people. Never was good with people," he said finally.

"The machines?"

"Yeah."

"I bet you were good with the machines, Leroy."

He nodded. "Only thing I was good at."

Bern let the sadness of those words hang in the air between them. He watched Leroy, who was now staring at the space between Bern's boots. One shoulder was hunched higher than the other. Bern scanned the older man's body and saw that the hitch was coming from his hips, which were twisted in the seat, no doubt to accommodate pain. One of his wiry legs was bent to hold the hip in place and the other splayed out in front of him, almost touching Bern's foot.

"So what do you think happened to Gavin?" Bern asked, still keeping his voice low.

"Idiot. Went in. By himself. Didn't lock out. Didn't tell anyone." Leroy spat the words out. "Got filled up."

"By whom?"

"Wouldn't know," Leroy said with a grunt.

"Not in touch with anyone there still? Not hearing things through the grapevine?" Bern asked.

Leroy looked at him now for the first time. Bern held his gaze, surprised by the color of his eyes, a pale, clear blue.

"Now you're asking stuff you already know the answer to," Leroy said. He looked away and stood.

"Do you remember losing one of your locks, Leroy?"

"What are you talking about?" he asked. It was only a step to the front door. Leroy held the handle, ready to go in. Bern was sure he would not be invited to follow.

"For locking out," Bern said, his voice louder now. "One of your locks is missing."

Leroy laughed. "Barking up the wrong tree there," he said. "That thing got lost ages ago. Doesn't matter—you only ever need seven locks." He opened the door then and walked inside without saying another word. As the door closed, Bern got a whiff of stale air. He turned and stood for a minute, watching the workings of the brewery from Leroy's front stoop.

• • •

Evie left the mountain of paperwork on her desk at six o'clock sharp and headed home. The accident report had big holes in it, but she'd done as much as she could that day. The audit was going to take a week of long days to prepare for, but she needed the environmental file before she could get started. She decided, with an excited thrill, to take a night off. She would not work all evening, and she would come in at the civilized hour of eight o'clock the next morning for the second day in a row.

As she drove down the main street of Kootenay Landing, she took a new interest in the shops. They were closed up for the night already. Evie marveled at the fact that in all the years she had lived there, she had never once strolled the shops on Selkirk Street. She thought it might be time to take a longer lunch one day, or a Saturday morning off, and do just that.

It was also time to make some decisions, she thought as she drove out of town on the short strip of highway that took her home. About Dirk. She turned into the curve of her driveway. Funny that Rory didn't come running out as he usually did. Evie parked her SUV and got out.

"Rory!" she called.

There was no answer. She looked over into the neighbor's yard and saw his dog asleep by the back door. Evie turned the corner to the side of the house; there, on the strip of tarmac where Dirk used to park his truck, was a white pickup. She froze for a moment—Dirk had been gone for long enough that he could have gotten a new truck, though his taste ran more to brand-new and this one was a well-preserved relic—but then she recognized it as Bern's.

"Hello?" she called out. She walked along the tarmac to the back of the house. She could hear some scuffling and scraping. Behind the house was a massive deck with a panoramic view of the fields below. Just past the deck, on the small patch of grass that topped the cliff that Dirk's nephews had climbed, was Bern. He was tossing a stick from hand to hand. He looked more dressed up than usual, in cords and dress shirt. He stood over Rory, tall and lean, arm stretched high, waiting to throw the stick. Rory gazed up at him expectantly, his tongue lolling. It looked like they'd been at this for a while.

"Rory! Here, boy!" she called.

Rory looked away from the stick and stood. She slapped her hands on her thighs and he came, though a little reluctantly. He ran toward her and leaned against her legs. She patted his head and rubbed his ears. "Good boy," she whispered. Then to Bern she said, "Some guard dog!"

He laughed and came toward her. "I called your office, but there was no answer. So I thought I would pop out to see you. Hope you don't mind."

"I was planning to take Rory for a walk. Would you like to come?" she asked.

"Sure," he said.

She fed Rory first, then grabbed his leash but didn't put it on him. They headed down the driveway and walked along the highway, which was quiet at this time of night. The road was dotted with houses, most set way back in the middle of two- and three-acre lots, like Evie's. They were often advertised as hobby farms, though Evie's topsoil consisted mostly of bedrock, and she'd never been able to grow much on her two acres, except the occasional geranium in a pot.

"I mostly just wanted to check that you were okay," Bern said. "You were gone when I woke up."

"I had to come home and feed the dog," she said. "And walk him. The neighbor looks after him when I'm not here, but I prefer to do it myself."

They walked on in silence for a moment. Bern took short steps to match her stride. Evie looked up at him quickly and back at Rory, who was weaving off the road and skirting the ditches, following a promising scent. Her stomach felt fizzy and unsettled, like it had in junior high when a boy had asked her out to a movie. She'd wanted to go but was so overcome with shyness she'd never answered him. He'd met her at the bus stop every morning, his hair carefully brushed, his clothes tidy, and they'd sat next to each other, not talking. Eventually the school year ended and put an end to her dilemma. The next year they were at different high schools, and she never saw him again.

"Did you find out who it was yet? The girl next to the train tracks?" she asked. She didn't want to say body—it sounded so harsh.

He nodded. "We think so. The RCMP are talking to a person of interest. I probably shouldn't say too much, but it is so odd, I wonder—" He broke off, and they walked on for a minute before he continued. "It looks like the young woman we found was Belinda Carlisle," he said finally.

Evie stopped walking and looked at him. "Belinda Carlisle? Gavin's girlfriend? We've been trying to call her."

"Yes, that's how we figured it out. Someone turned in a cell phone—a teenage boy had found it. And then it rang and it was Gemma, looking for Belinda. We were able to get a copy of her driver's license picture, and we're reasonably sure it's her, though we'd like someone who knew her to identify the body," he said. "None of this is confirmed yet, and we're not releasing this information to the public. I probably shouldn't even be telling you."

"So why are you?" she asked without looking at him.

He laughed. "Because I get around you and I talk more than I should," he said. "And because I want to ask you what you remember Gavin saying about Belinda."

"We should turn back. It's starting to get dark," she said. The setting sun washed the sky pink in the final moments before it dropped behind the mountains. She whistled to Rory, and they turned and started walking back toward her house. Their shadows spread in front of them—his long, hers short. "I don't remember much. I know that he had a girlfriend, and he was excited that she was coming but nervous too. I got the impression things weren't necessarily smooth between them, but he was hoping it would work out," she said.

"Do you remember anything else?" Bern asked.

"Not really. I only spoke to him a few times. What I do know is just from comments he made, chitchat while I gave him his safety orientation his first few days."

"Do you know if he was close to anyone? Any of the workers?" he asked.

Evie thought for a minute. "Maybe Steve Ostikoff? I'm not sure how close they were, but I know Steve invited him up the lake to a party his dad was having."

"The employee barbecue?" he asked.

She nodded. They were approaching her driveway now. The walk back always seems shorter, Evie thought.

"It's so . . . well, *strange* hardly seems the word. But that both of them should die—what are the odds of that?" she asked.

"Not very likely, but it seems to be what happened," he said.

"Do you know how she died?"

He shook his head. "Not yet. It will take a few days for the preliminary autopsy results to come in."

They turned up her driveway and started walking toward the house.

"You sure you're okay?" he asked. "I have to go to Kelowna tomorrow, just for the day."

"That's a long way to go for a day," she said.

"Yeah, I'll leave early and get back late. But you know my door is unlocked if you need a couch to sleep on," he said.

She looked up at him and smiled briefly. "Thanks. I had a good sleep on your couch," she said.

He held up his hand, the dog leash dangling from it. She reached for it and felt the cool stillness of his fingers brushing hers. She could feel him looking at her, but she couldn't bring her eyes up to meet his.

"Good night," she mumbled, stepping back. The sun had slid behind the mountain, taking most of the light and heat with it. "C'mon, Rory."

They were almost inside when, from the corner of her eye, she saw Bern move toward his truck. His headlights swung past the window in the front door just as she was bolting it.

BEVCO ACCIDENT/INCIDENT PRELIMINARY INVESTIGATION REPORT	
Drafted by: E. Chapelle	Date: 09/10
Edition: 1	Page: 1 of 2

Brewery: Bugaboo Brewery (Kootenay Landing, BC)
Location within brewery: Bottle washer
Department(s): Bottling, Maintenance
Date and time of incident: Monday, September 7 (time not known)
Number of employees involved: 1 injured. (It is believed that 1 other employee was on the premises at the time, not yet identified.)
Names of employee(s) impacted: Gavin Grayson
Type of injury: Fatality—exposure to caustic
Was the injury a fatality? Yes
Type of accident (use BevCo Hazard Criteria to identify): 72-B: Exposed to, or in contact with, a harmful substance (NaOH—sodium hydroxide—3% solution) 84-B: Drowned or asphyxiated
Summary of incident (attach diagram and/or any other information as needed): Employee on a weekend overtime shift entered a confined space (bottle washer) and remained trapped inside when machine was filled with 3% caustic solution. Body of employee was discovered at startup on Tuesday, September 8.
Is there evidence that BevCo management or an employee knowingly and seriously contravened the Occupational Health and Safety Act and/or regulations? Management: No evidence of contravention by management. Employee was fully trained in working-alone, confined-space entry, and lockout procedures, as per BevCo standard. Reasonably practicable steps were taken to prevent such a situation from occurring. Employee: Though a relatively new employee, he was trained in all the relevant procedures. Entering a confined space without locking out and in a working-alone situation is clearly prohibited in brewery procedures, as per BevCo standard.

Should the employee and/or manager have reasonably known that the site conditions, work processes, or actions of management or workers at the time of the incident seriously contravened safety regulations and/or accepted industry practice?

Yes. Employee should have been aware. He had received recent training in all applicable hazards and should never have entered a confined space while in a working-alone situation. He was provided with a full set of locks for use during routine maintenance on equipment, but he did not lock out the machine before entering it.

Is any further action required to encourage future compliance?

Working-alone, confined-space, and lockout procedures will be fully reviewed with all applicable employees during next 30 days.

Include any further relevant information here:

At the current time, the RCMP, WSB, and Coroners Service are all investigating this incident. Bugaboo management is fully cooperating with their efforts. The person who filled the bottle washer has not, as yet, been identified. Mechanical failure has been ruled out as a possibility. Regular production has recommenced.

15

Evie pushed open her office door, and a waterfall of paper collapsed on the floor. She could barely get the door open. When she did manage to create a space wide enough to slip through, she found the chair beside the door stacked with papers. They spilled over the arms and covered most of the floor of her pocket-sized office in a flood of paper.

She picked up a document at random. *BevCo Environmental Policy: Leading the Way in Green Brewing,* it read. She sighed.

The phone rang. She carefully took one step into the puddle of paper and fell into her chair. She grabbed the receiver.

"Hello? Evie Chapelle here," she said breathlessly.

The line crackled. "Evie, is that you?"

"Yes!" she exclaimed. She was so happy to hear Bern's voice. "I thought you were going to Kelowna today."

"What? Kelowna? What are you talking about, honey? I'm coming home to Kootenay Landing!" the voice said.

"Dirk?"

"Yes, of course. Who else would it be? Listen, I'm going to run out of cell battery here in a minute. I'm just leaving Edmonton.

I'll be there for dinner. Don't work too late, okay? I'm dying to see you," he said.

There was a knock on Evie's door, and Conrad stood in the doorway. He motioned to the papers quizzically. She held up a finger to him and mouthed, "One minute."

"Conrad's having a potluck tonight. Will you be up for that?" she said into the phone.

"Oh, great! For sure. Let's do that. Tell him I've got a hankering for some of his home brew." He chuckled. "See you when I get home."

The crackling sound stopped as the call was dropped. Evie hung up the receiver. "Dirk is coming home tonight," she said to Conrad.

Conrad leaned his tall frame into the doorway. As usual, his safety glasses hung uselessly from a chain clipped to his shirt.

"That's great, isn't it?" He paused when she didn't say anything. "Isn't it, Evie?"

She bent over and picked a few documents up from the floor. She made a tidy stack of them and placed them on the corner of her desk.

"I don't know, Conrad. I don't know what I'm supposed to think," she said.

"What do you mean, you don't know what you're supposed to think? He's coming back. It's great. He went away for a while, to think things through or whatever, but now he wants to come back to you!" Conrad raised his arms in the air and shrugged. "That sounds pretty good to me," he finished.

"But what about me, Conrad? What about what *I* want?" she asked.

Conrad looked at her incredulously. "This is about that guy, isn't it? That coroner? You've got the hots for him, don't you?"

Evie was surprised by his vehemence. It was nice to think it mattered to someone that she and Dirk stay together. But she was not sure it mattered to her anymore.

She straightened up wearily. "It's not about Bern," she said. "Don't jump to conclusions."

"Jump to conclusions? Someone said they saw you go into his house two nights in a row. And your car was in the parking lot here all night the other night. And don't tell me you were working!"

Evie shrugged. "Don't believe everything you hear, Conrad. Especially in this fishbowl." She gestured around her office. "Karl kindly brought me the environmental file. I've got a little work to do."

"Well, you asked him for it." Conrad barked a laugh. "Look, I'm sorry. I'm just happy Dirk is coming home. I've missed him."

"Yeah, I know you did," Evie said. "We'll see you tonight, okay?"

"Yeah, sure. Okay," he said as he pushed himself up from the doorframe and turned to leave her office.

"And Conrad?"

"Yes?"

"Please put your safety glasses on before you go back into the bottle shop," she said.

He stood still and stared at her, then blew his breath up so that his bangs flopped on his forehead. "You never stop, do you?"

"We've just had a fatality, so no, I see no reason to stop," she replied.

"It might be news to you, Evie, but Gavin was wearing eye protection when he died. It didn't do him one bit of good," he said.

Evie took a slow, deep breath. "You're right, Conrad. Safety eyewear did not help Gavin. But following procedure would have. And our first procedure is to wear safety glasses on the bottle line."

He slid his safety glasses over his hook nose and walked out, closing the door firmly behind him.

"See you tonight!" she called after him.

Ogden Kumar's office in the new headquarters of the Interior Division of the BC Coroners Service was cool and expansive, a refreshing change from the pressing heat outside. Bern liked his boss; in general, they got along. He didn't think it was because they were the same height, though they were both well over six feet tall. It was a nice change to be with someone as tall as he was—comforting somehow. As if they were equals in that and so it made it possible for them to find other areas where they were on equal footing. Bern followed the chief coroner to a sitting area in one corner of his office. A waft of new upholstery smell rose to greet him as he sat down on a pale-gray, cube-shaped chair.

"I thought we'd have lunch in today," Ogden said. Bern nodded, taking in Kumar's impeccable charcoal-gray suit of a light woolen weave. A pale-blue linen shirt peeked through at the ends of his sleeves. He was not wearing a tie. Casual Friday, Bern supposed.

"That's fine. I want to get back anyway," Bern said. He

stretched his jean-encased legs out in front of him and crossed his feet at the ankles. He hoped there was no dirt on his boots. "So?" he said.

Ogden held up one finger. "Just one moment, please," he said. He leaned back in his seat, stretched out his own equally long (though infinitely more elegant) legs and closed his eyes. He sat there in silence for a moment, his finger in the air, his eyes closed, waiting. Then there was a knock at the door. "Come in," he said.

Claire bustled in carrying a tray. Her flowered skirt swung as she crossed the room, and the air around them was soon filled with the smell of her perfume. She put the tray on a round side table, which she slid closer to them. She fussed with the sandwiches and moved a bowl of dip from one side of the tray to the other. Then she stood and tucked a lock of hair behind each ear and smiled at them.

"You like tuna sandwiches, I remember," she said to Bern with a smile. Then she nodded briskly. "I'll bring you coffee in a little while."

Bern watched her leave the room and knew that his coffee, when it came, would be superb. He could hardly wait.

They did not begin their discussion until they had eaten all the dainty tuna sandwiches, plump baby tomatoes, and crisp, fresh grapes on the tray. Bern enjoyed every bite, but when he saw Ogden fold his napkin, tap the sides of his wide, brown lips with it, and place it on a corner of the tray, he knew it was time to talk business.

Ogden began to speak, in a lilting, precise accent that brought to mind colonial mansions and servants behind palm fronds. "So let's begin, shall we? Tell me how things are going."

Bern shrugged. "Fine. It's all going fine. I could have told you that on the phone."

Kumar waved his hand in the air as though whisking a fly from a bowl of rice. Bern wondered when Kumar had last left the Kelowna city limits. To ask someone in from Kootenay Landing for a meeting, as if it were a four-minute, not a four-hour, drive . . . well, he seemed to have no idea how big this province was. "Soon you will say there is too much snow to drive that distance, and by the time the snow melts, it will have been over a year since you started. And so here we are. And my message for you is simple—" Kumar looked toward the door of the office. "Can you open the door? Coffee is here."

Bern crossed the room in three strides and pulled the door open. Claire was standing there with another tray, this one of coffee, and was trying to find a way to knock on the door. She beamed at him and he followed the roll of her round hips and the swish of her skirt back into the office.

The coffee was perfect. Kumar nodded curtly to Claire, who took the sandwich tray and left without saying a word.

Kumar cleared his throat and started again. "As I was saying, my message for you is simple. Coroners Service, RCMP, Workers' Safety Board—sure, we each have our own mandates. But in the end, the reality is that we all take our money from the same pot: the government. And we all answer to the same person: the taxpayer."

He leaned forward and put his coffee cup down on the table, then sat back and crossed his legs. He pulled on the crease of his trousers so as not to wrinkle them too much, then tented his long fingers and looked at Bern over the round moons of his nails. "As I'm sure you've heard, the government is in a deficit position.

We have been told, clearly, that we must balance our budgets. No overspending. None."

Kumar paused, as if waiting for a comment from Bern. He did not say anything, though he, like everyone else in the Coroners Service, knew that the chief coroner had accepted a hefty pay raise earlier in the year. There had been no increase in funds from the government to offset that expense. And the move to the new offices—while long planned—was not being funded to the expected level. Kumar would be looking for pennies under gravestones to balance his budget.

"So what are you saying?" Bern asked.

"What I'm saying is this: the WSB, the RCMP—they are our partners. Let's let them do as much as they possibly can." Kumar lifted his shoulder and cocked his head. "There is no harm in waiting for their reports to come in, in letting their officers take the lead."

"The RCMP think someone from out of town committed this crime. They've got someone in for questioning—a guy from Kelowna," Bern said.

"Yes, I'd heard that," Kumar said with a nod. Bern realized that he had probably been fully briefed on the situation in Kootenay Landing already. It irked him to think of Kumar keeping tabs on him through Resnick. It had to be him; no one else knew the cases that well.

"I don't see the problem with this," Kumar said.

"I'm not so convinced," said Bern. He sighed and took a small sip of his coffee. "We're talking about a small town. A *really* small town. I can't pick a tomato without a neighbor seeing me—"

"Yes, I've heard that you are developing a bit of a reputation as a lady's man," Kumar interrupted with a raised eyebrow.

Bern clenched his coffee cup. "See what I mean?"

Kumar shrugged and flicked a thread on the hem of his pants. "Not really," he said.

"That girl was held against her will for at least a few days. And somehow, she escaped and made her way—by crawling, it seems—through a residential neighborhood in the smallest town in the world. No one saw her. No one noticed a thing. If I can't so much as smile at a lady without the whole town talking about it, I don't see how a stranger could pop into town, carry off a trick like that, and then head home!" Bern sat back and took a deep breath.

Ogden Kumar looked at him, his eyes watchful under perfectly shaped brows. "How's the stress level?"

Bern exhaled sharply. "Fine. It's fine."

"This is more than you're used to. You normally handle natural deaths: sudden heart attacks, grieving widows—that kind of thing. You are good with that," Kumar said.

"I'm good with this too," said Bern. "I've done it before."

"But not here."

Bern shrugged. "True."

Kumar leaned forward and picked up his coffee cup again. He took a small sip before speaking. "You know, we took a chance on you—with your background. Your references were good, but they said you shouldn't be under too much strain. Two unnatural deaths in one week would strain anyone."

"I never said I was under strain. I just said I wanted to get to the bottom of this." Bern's voice was tight with restrained anger.

Kumar stood and walked to his desk. Bern stared out the window at the city traffic below. He could see where the vineyards began, just a few blocks from downtown. Kumar came back and stood before him, blocking his view. He handed Bern a sheet of paper. Bern looked it over.

"Thought you might want to see this," Kumar said.

"Preliminary result of forensic autopsy . . . You got this already?" Bern asked. He put down his coffee cup and leaned closer to read the paper. The words seem to swim before his eyes. *Preliminary cause of death . . . asphyxia . . . foreign matter . . . awaiting results of toxicology . . .*

"Asphyxia," he said.

Kumar nodded. "She choked on her own vomit, Bern."

"But what about the abrasions on her wrists?"

Kumar shrugged. "Some people do strange things and call it fun."

"Cigarette burns?"

"You know, I saw that on *Oprah* one time. Self-harm, they call it. Lots of young women are doing that these days. A coping strategy."

Bern closed his eyes and called up the picture of Belinda's body. *Tortured.* That's the word that came to mind. Not self-inflicted harm. "So are you saying not to investigate this?"

"Look, all I'm saying is don't rush in. Let our partners do their work. Give them some time, and some space. Take the lead from them when they ask for your help."

Kumar stayed standing as he spoke. Bern took this as a sign that their meeting was over. He took the last sip of his coffee and stood as well. "And in the meantime, I stick with the old ladies and widows?"

Kumar smiled and held out his hand. When Bern shook it,

the chief coroner clapped him on the back with his other arm. "Stick with what you know. You're very good with the old ladies and widows," he said.

They walked together to the door, keeping pace with each other's long strides. Kumar opened the door for him and Bern stepped outside, where he found Claire waiting for him. He realized he still had the preliminary autopsy report in his hand.

"Keep it," Claire said when he turned back to the door. "I can get him another copy."

"Thanks for the lunch," Bern said to her. "And that coffee— worth driving all that way for a coffee like that."

"You headed straight back?" she asked.

Bern smiled at her and winked. "Pretty much."

Monica Acer swung the door wide open before Bern even had a chance to ring the bell.

"Come in," she whispered. "We have to be quiet."

He stepped out of the heat of the day and into the closed-up air of the entryway. A folded baby stroller took up most of the available floor space. Overflowing laundry baskets took up every other inch. The whole room had the faint smell of sour milk. Behind half-shut folding closet doors he could hear a washing machine churning through a small portion of the laundry that awaited it. He followed Monica Acer's sweatshirt-clad back to the kitchen. It was the first in a chain of rooms, each open to the next. Every surface in sight was littered with the evidence of life with a baby. A high chair took up the only available floor space in the kitchen; the counters were piled with dishes—many of them of multicolored plastic and bearing trademarked cartoon characters that Bern failed to recognize.

Piles of half-folded laundry and an odd assortment of fragile items—several wine glasses, a crystal vase, a porcelain figurine of a Bavarian man playing the accordion—covered the dining room table. He could only assume they'd been placed out of baby's reach. He could see clear through to the living room, where baby toys and contraptions dotted the floor, couch, and coffee table.

They sat on bar stools at the kitchen counter. The sound of the baby monitor hissed in the background like a shortwave radio that had gone off its station.

"He's finally sleeping," she said.

Bern smiled gently at the woman and took in her appearance. She had been beautiful once. The bags under her eyes and the lank brown hair that was overdue for a cut could not hide the sharp cheekbones that made her otherwise long face striking. Her eyes were dark as well, though red-rimmed from lack of sleep, or perhaps tears.

"What's your baby's name?" he asked.

"Hunter," she said. "A boy. There's a mom in our tot music class who named her daughter Hunter. Hopefully they don't end up at the same school. That would be a bit rough, don't you think?" She looked anxiously at Bern.

He shrugged. "They say those sorts of things build character, but I've never been truly convinced of that."

She laughed. "Listen to me worrying about school at a time like this. Brad's been gone all day. You're with the police, right? Can you tell me when he will come home?"

Bern handed her his card. "I'm with the Coroners Service. I'm helping the police look into the death of a young lady. It seems that your husband was seen in her company not long before she died. Can you tell me what you know about that?"

The tears started flowing then, telling Bern all he needed to know about her red-rimmed eyes. "He's away so much," she started. "I thought it was possible, that . . . well, that he'd stray. But now I know." The last word came out as a wail, which she quickly suppressed with a furtive look at the baby monitor.

"Why is he away so much?" Bern asked.

"Work. He's an engineer. He works two weeks on, two weeks off for an oil rig in Fort McMurray. What with the baby and everything . . ." She looked down at her sweatshirt, the white letters of the local college spotted with stains. "I guess I've let myself go. But it's all so much more than I expected. Hunter cries all the time. He won't sleep. I try to keep him quiet when Brad's home, but it's just so hard. And the house—" She stopped talking suddenly and looked around helplessly. The tears continued to run silently down her face. "Do you know how long he was with her?" she asked him.

Bern shook his head. "I really know very little about it. Except that he bought her some lingerie in Edmonton."

"He brought the leftovers home to me! And then I felt so badly that none of it fit—this baby weight is just not coming off—but it was never meant for me in the first place. What am I going to do?" She broke down completely then. Bern rubbed her shoulder gently, then sat silently and waited for the outburst to run its course.

"What did you take in college?" he asked.

She looked down at her sweatshirt. "Oh, um, nursing. I'm a nurse."

Bern looked at her until she lifted her head and looked back at him. "So you're going to be just fine. You will go back to work in time. You will look after yourself and your baby. It may be difficult—it certainly will be difficult—but it is possible. And looking back, it will be a turning point. Perhaps not one you would have chosen, but an important one nonetheless."

He thought of his own mother, raising him alone. She'd been a teenage mother from a well-respected Catholic family—hardly an easy fate in Montreal in the 1960s. Bern nodded solemnly. "I know you can do it," he said. "Now, I always say, pick one thing to get started. So how about I help you wash the dishes, while you tell me everything you know about what Brad did last week?"

It turned out she didn't know all that much. Hunter and his needs had swallowed every shred of her attention, but two things did stick out in her mind. Brad came home a day later than usual—Monday, instead of Sunday—and in a rental car, rather than by air, as was his usual habit. And when he got back, he was mad.

"I thought it was something I did," she said as she wiped the last plastic bowl and stacked it on top of a pile of others. She picked them all up and placed them in a cupboard above the sink.

Bern gave the counter one last wipe, then folded the dishcloth and hung it on the edge of the dish drainer.

"But then I heard him tell the police that she stole his money, and that's why he was mad." She bit her bottom lip. "God, I can't believe how selfish I'm being. She's really dead, isn't she?"

Bern nodded. "One more question before I go: Did you tell the police about the rental car?"

She nodded. "Yeah, I did." Just then, a wail broke through the house. Panic took over Monica's eyes. "Oh, God. I'm just so tired."

"You'll be fine," Bern said. His voice was barely audible over the baby's cry. "It's cooled down a little outside. Why don't you put him in that stroller and go for a long walk? It will probably do you both some good."

"But what about Brad? What if he comes home?" she asked.

Bern shrugged. "Let him fend for himself," he said. "You go look after your baby. I'll see myself out."

16

It was another clear fall night, the last twinkling promise of summer in the breeze. The leaves, though still green, sounded a little drier as they brushed against the wind, a little more ready to turn and fall. Evie stood away from the others, leaning against the railing on the back balcony of Conrad and Lisa's place. They lived up on what was commonly called Manager's Hill, overlooking Kootenay Landing. Evie could see clear to the brewery parking lot, which was still full; the afternoon-shift production lines would be running for a few more hours. Once the shift was over, at eleven o'clock, there would be a complete shutdown for the weekend. No one working alone, thought Evie. She closed her eyes and rubbed them, then ran her fingers through her hair. No chance of anyone's getting hurt.

"Rough week?" Dirk came up behind her and put his arms around her waist. Evie put her hands lightly on his wrists, opened his arms, and extricated herself by moving two feet to the left along the railing.

"Yeah," she said. She smiled tightly.

"Want to talk about it?" He leaned against the banister, holding an unmarked bottle of Conrad's home brew loosely between his fingers. He looked good. Tanned and tight-muscled. His jeans were loose where he had lost weight from hard summer work. He had a few more gray hairs since the last time she had seen him, and they stood out against the black of his hair, which was longer than she remembered. He was wearing a new shirt, one she'd never seen before—lime-green and red stripes on a white background. It was more colorful than the shirts he normally wore.

"You look good," she said flatly.

"Yeah, I feel good." He brushed the hair out of her face and rested his fingers on her chin, tilting it until she was looking up at him. "You look like shit."

She laughed and turned her head away. "Yeah, I feel like shit."

He leaned his tanned arms on the railing, looking out over the view, and began to talk. Somehow it was easier to listen to him when he wasn't looking at her directly.

"It's good there, you know. Good jobs, good pay—great pay. You could get a job there like that." He snapped his fingers and held his arm up in the air for a moment before letting it drop. "They need safety professionals like you would not believe. And they pay well, way better than BevCo. We could build a house. Close to my sister and the boys. It's nice to be near family, real nice."

Evie took a sip of her beer, to keep her hands busy and so she wouldn't have to look at him. She inspected the view until she found the back gate of the brewery and began mentally counting the cars in the lot.

"You don't have to do this anymore, Evie. Come with me to Fort McMurray. We can start a new life, a better one for you, for us. You can find a new job, or hell, not work at all. You can do whatever you want. No more transfers, no more stress." Dirk laughed. "You can learn how to cook, like you've always wanted to, and garden, though I guess there's not really much gardening up there. Scratch that, you can cook—"

"And clean and have babies?" Evie fell silent again. Sixteen more cars now; sixteen more people to make it home safely. Sixteen more people she was responsible for.

"Well, why not?" He looked directly at her now, waiting for an answer that did not come.

Evie's eyes followed the well-worn track that was made in the strip of grass along the road by the back gate to the plant. It had been made by generations of workers shuffling from their little bungalows to work and back. If she followed the road straight and then slightly to the left, she could see Bern's little house, the last one on the block, with its siding made to look like brick, its small, covered back deck, and the large garden that stretched down to the creek.

"Evie, are you going to answer me?"

She just stared off in the distance at Bern's back porch, as if she hadn't heard the question. She felt that if she stared hard enough she could be there, drinking tea on that shaded porch, rather than here, in the bright evening sun, drinking beer she hated in a place she did not want to be.

Conrad's voice broke the impasse.

"Guys! Dinner's ready!" he called out to them.

"C'mon, let's go eat," Evie said.

"I want to talk about this later," Dirk said.

"Okay, so we'll talk about it later."

$$\bullet \quad \bullet \quad \bullet$$

It was getting dark by the time Bern reached Kootenay Landing's main street. The lights on the cinema flashed on and off, signaling that the night's showing was about to start. It was a popular feature, judging by the numbers of teenagers crowded around the glassed-in ticket booth. The night was warm and those restaurants with outdoor patios were doing brisk business. Bern slowed to a stop at the second of the three traffic lights in town and watched a group of teenage girls cross the street. They stopped and hugged each other in the middle of the crosswalk, laughing. Bern smiled at their youthfulness: life had barely made an impression on them yet.

He drove slowly through the next block, debating with himself. At the last moment, he swung the truck up a side street and pulled into the back lot of the Kootenay Landing Hotel. Its crowded bar was the local hot spot on a Friday night, and as tired as he was, Bern knew that if there was news to be had about recent events, this was the place, and the time, to hear it.

Once inside, he could barely see through the crush of bodies. He made his way slowly to his regular seat at the bar. Leigh was working, and Bern watched her easy movements. Her strong arms pulled pint after pint of the only beer on tap: Bugaboo Brew.

Bern loved watching women of a certain age; the age between forty and fifty particularly appealed to him. It was a time when many women seemed to shed the insecurities of youth and get on with the business of being themselves. He knew the story of how Leigh was raising a boy on her own, her husband in jail after some kind of a breakdown. He could see the plotline written in the strain around her eyes, the severe fold of skin between her eyebrows, the extra padding at her hips and waist.

She looked at him now and cocked her head in question. He nodded once and a moment later a glass of whiskey appeared before him.

"Don't you have anyone to help you?" he asked before she could walk away.

She began pulling pint glasses from an overhead shelf and lining them up on the counter.

"I can't seem to keep waitresses these days. Had another one quit just a few weeks ago. Wouldn't come in on Saturday after she made over two hundred bucks in tips on Friday night," she said. She pulled on the handle of the draft. It was in the shape of a mountain range and emblazoned with a letter B. "I just don't get it."

She placed the glasses on a tray, ducked under the bar, and lifted the tray once she was on the other side. Soon Bern could not see her at all, only the tops of the glasses on the tray as they made their way through the crowd. A moment later she returned and was back behind the bar. She stashed some dirty glasses and pitchers into a bus bin and started the process all over.

"Did you recognize the girl? From the pictures the police showed you?" Bern asked her.

She nodded. She picked up a clean pitcher and began to fill it. "She was here last Saturday night for a while. She was a real mess—high on something," she said.

"Do you know who she was?"

"No, I'd never seen her before—or since." She placed the pitcher on the tray and started on another one. "She left before closing, I know that much. It got super busy, and then when things quieted down again, she was gone."

With that Leigh was gone too, disappearing once again into the crowd. Bern took a sip of his drink and looked around. He recognized quite a few workers from the brewery—people he'd interviewed earlier in the week.

"The police asked me all this already," Leigh said as she returned once again with a tray of dirty glasses.

"What did you tell them?" he asked.

"Just what I said—she was a mess. Falling all over the place, laughing, flirting with people, but in a desperate, end-of-the-line kind of way," she said.

"You've seen that before?"

She shrugged. "You see everything in here."

"And what did you think?"

"When I see that, I think of crack. Hyper and desperate, you know?"

"Did you tell the police this?" he asked.

"I can't remember. But I did tell them about the car," she said.

"What car?"

Her hands paused midmotion. "The red Firefly with Alberta plates in the parking lot? It's been there all week. Didn't think much of it, until that girl's body showed up and Jason found her cell phone. They're out there now," she said. She pulled down another pitcher and began to fill it.

"Leigh! Bring us beer!" someone hollered to her from the crowd.

She smiled at Bern apologetically. "Got to get back to work." A moment later she was making her way through the crowd, a full tray balanced expertly on one hand.

Bern took a last swig of whiskey. He placed a ten-dollar bill under his empty glass and stood up. He made his way through the crowd toward the back door to see if he could find Resnick and a little red Firefly with Alberta plates.

•   •   •

Evie lay on the couch fuming. The ease with which Dirk had
reinserted himself into her life, after almost a two-month absence,
with no explanation or discussion, amazed her. He had plopped
his suitcase in their bedroom, used her toothbrush when he had
forgotten his own, and hopped right into their queen-sized bed
like he belonged there.

Evie hadn't slept well for years, but if she had been a sleeper,
she would not have been able to sleep with Dirk in the bed. And
this made her too angry to even try. She shifted onto her side
and pulled the thin wool blanket up to cover her shoulders. She
would have an uncomfortable night on the couch, and it would
be his fault.

Sensing her restlessness, Rory reached down from his bed
between the plants and placed a paw on her shoulder.

"Good boy," she muttered. His tail began to thump, even in
sleep. He sighed a contented dog sigh and a gust of deluxe dog
food breath blew across her cheek. "You are my baby," she said
with finality.

Evie had never wanted to have children. It seemed most
women she talked to—women like Conrad's wife, Lisa; women at
the office—did not feel complete until they had children, but Evie
had never felt that way. She had always felt complete, an entity unto
herself, an island really. If anything completed Evie, it was her job.
Her job had always been there for her. The orderly inventory of
tasks gave her days meaning and gave her enormous satisfaction.

Even marriage had been a surprise. She and Dirk had met
at the Winnipeg Laundromat where they both went on Sunday
afternoons each week. Week after week they met over the folding

table until one day Dirk brought lattes for them both. After that it was a standing date, each Sunday at two o'clock. They talked about work mostly—Evie was lab manager at the brewery in Winnipeg, Dirk a heavy-duty mechanic at a local construction company. This went on for months, these weekly coffee meetings over laundry, both of them too hesitant to make the next move. Something had to happen, and eventually it did.

Evie bought a small house in a neighborhood along the Red River. Two bedrooms on the main floor, with a small eat-in kitchen attached to the living room. There was a side entry from the driveway that had a utility room, complete with a washer and dryer.

Dirk started coming over on Sunday afternoons to do his laundry. It took longer with only one machine, and he would often stay for supper and a walk along the river while the final load dried. He started coming to Evie's work parties, and she suddenly stopped dreading them; they became an enjoyable part of her job with Dirk at her side. For the first time, she used up her annual allotment of free beer, a perk that she had always ignored but now became a joke between them—you only date me for my washer and free beer.

They were married a year later at city hall, in a simple ceremony attended by his mother and her new boyfriend. His sister sent flowers from Fort McMurray. Evie's father sent a check for one thousand dollars, which they used to buy a new dining room table. Her mother never knew that she had married. It was why Evie kept her maiden name—if her mother ever wanted to look for her, she would find her—though she did not tell anyone this was the reason.

Dirk and Evie never talked about having children. They were

just happy to have company, each other's, or so Evie had thought. A few days after their second wedding anniversary, the summons had come: promotion to assistant quality manager at the Bugaboo Brewery in Kootenay Landing. They jumped at the chance: for the price of their small Winnipeg house, they could buy several acres with an attached shop. Dirk could run his own business and be closer to his nephews, though they were still a ten-hour drive away.

It was after a few years in their new location that the topic started to come up. Dirk was restless. Business was slow, the clients cheap. It seemed Kootenay Landing folk were adept at making do with their own repairs rather than getting them done properly by a certified mechanic. Why pay someone else to do what you can do for yourself?

Dirk started to make more frequent trips to Fort McMurray. He liked to visit his nephews, who were growing fast, and drum up some work while he was there. Evie was making more than enough for both of them, but that wasn't the point. A man has his pride, Dirk would say. They still went to the parties together when he was home, though Evie often wanted to leave early, citing work the next day. Once the promotion to safety manager came, she often worked late into the evening and brought work home on the weekends. Dirk had become good friends with Conrad, and the two of them often went to the parties together, Lisa home with the babies and Evie too busy working.

Dirk seemed to think that a mini-Dirk, someone to follow him around the shop and learn the trade, was just what he needed. He did not seem to understand that they might have a child who was not a born mechanic. He assumed the baby would come fully formed and with the same temperament as his nephews, who loved to learn about motors and hung on their uncle's every word. But Evie wasn't cooperating. It was the first rift in their otherwise companionable marriage.

It wasn't that Evie didn't like children. Her only exposure to them had been their visits with the nephews and dinners at Conrad and Lisa's. Evie liked other people's children just fine, but she could not imagine having her own. She felt a wave of indifference at the thought of it, as well as a deep tiredness, as if her body was unwilling to even contemplate such an action.

"But look at what a nurturer you are!" Dirk would exclaim. "You love your plants like they were humans, and we have the best-groomed and -trained dog known to man!"

Evie knew she could not handle it. Her own nurturing had been incomplete; her basic biology was flawed in some way. Her mother had seen it, had not been able to love her.

No, thought Evie. Children should go to people who want to have them. Not to people like me. A dog I can handle, some plants too. Even one hundred childlike employees. But not a child of my own.

Evie sat up on the couch and pushed off the blanket. She reached for her jeans, which were folded on the arm of the couch, and pulled them on. She left a note in the kitchen for Dirk: Gone to work. The clock on the stove said 11:24.

"Find anything?" Bern asked.

Resnick was supervising two officers who were searching the interior of a small red car with flashlights. He nodded toward a large Dumpster next to the car. "No one noticed it tucked behind there," he said.

"Is it hers?"

"Yeah, we found her wallet. Driver's license, credit cards, and a wad of cash," Resnick said. He handed Bern a sealed plastic bag.

"Ah," said Bern. "Acer's stolen cash."

Resnick looked up sharply. Bern could not see his expression in the dark, but his annoyance came across clearly with a sharp shake of his head. "How did you know about that? Jesus."

"Kind of puts an end to the theory that he killed her for the cash," Bern said. He held the bag up to the streetlight and took a closer look at the driver's license. "Wouldn't you agree?"

"I'm not convinced, but I had to let the bugger go. Couldn't hold him for more than twenty-four hours," Resnick said. "I still like him for it, though. There's something twisted about that guy."

They stood together and watched in silence as the flashlight beams dueled with each other inside the car. The evening air was still warm. The sky held on to a pale echo of blue light, which was gradually being eclipsed by night. Behind them a truck started up and roared out of the lot. Bern watched it go, wondering how the driver would do on a spot Breathalyzer test.

"Did you go and talk to him?" Bern asked.

"Acer? No, I just listened to the interviews. You know we can email those things now. Pretty amazing, hey?" Resnick shrugged. "He claims he took Highway One, which means he didn't even drive through here. We've got a gas station attendant in Revelstoke who can back that up."

Bern thought of the two routes that stretched from Calgary to Vancouver. The Trans-Canada Highway was the faster. Kootenay Landing was along the scenic route, off the beaten track. Kelowna could be reached by either highway.

"Could he have come here first? Then driven home by the Trans-Canada?" Bern asked.

One of the officers backed out of the rear seat of the car and stood and stretched. Bern recognized Constable Schilling.

"Depends on the time lines. Alive and well Saturday in Edmonton. Alive and a little shaky on her feet Saturday night in Kootenay Landing. Dead on Wednesday morning. You know when Acer got home?" Resnick asked.

"Monday. Supposed to be Sunday," Bern said.

Resnick shook his head. "Freaks me out, really, how you know this stuff."

Bern shrugged. "It's my job. What else did he say?"

"Sounds like they partied pretty hard in Edmonton. Out of the oil patch and all that. Acer likes his lingerie. And his coke. Says they had a great time. He was surprised as anything when he woke up and found her gone. With his cash."

"Hmm. Anything else?"

"Yeah, he used a condom," Resnick said.

He thought of Monica Acer and her little baby, Hunter. How upset she'd been that the lingerie didn't fit. "What a guy," Bern said.

"Yeah, what an asshole. Didn't show up in the autopsy yet?"

Bern shook his head. "Spermicide? Not in the preliminary."

They watched the yellow stripe of Schilling's uniform pants approach them. "Doesn't look like much happened in that car," she said. "A coffee cup from 7-Eleven. Maps, wallet, winter chains. A whole lot of personal effects in the trunk—mostly clothes."

"We'll have to get the major crimes guys to go through the lot," Resnick said.

"Not looking like the primary scene?" Bern asked.

Resnick shrugged. "What do we know about the primary

scene? She may have been tied up. She may have had some sex, may have smoked some crack and a few joints."

"Preliminary autopsy report found fibers on her bra. Brown polyester-wool blend," Bern said, ignoring Resnick's tone. "Similar to couch upholstery from the late nineteen seventies."

They both looked to the young officer.

Schilling shook her head. "Vinyl seats," she said, nodding toward the car. "Unless we can find something to match it in the clothing."

Resnick nodded. "This will probably take all night," he said to Bern. "I'll call you if we find anything." He walked off with Schilling to the passenger side of the car, where the other officer was standing. Bern could not see who it was.

He won't call, thought Bern as he headed back to his truck. And that's all right. This will keep him tied up for a while.

"Are you alone?" Bern asked.

Kelly John looked up with a start. Eyes. Bern was waiting for those. Deep green and steeped with common sense.

"I didn't hear you come in," she said. She pressed a buzzer under her desk to unlock the side door, which separated the main lobby from the offices. Bern came through the door and entered her domain. He stood back from her desk a bit and leaned against the reception counter, which was empty at this time of night.

Bern smiled at the receptionist. "I just saw Resnick at the hotel—searching that car. Had a little idea and thought you might be able to help."

She sat up straighter and smoothed her hands along the lines of her flowered blouse. She smiled, showing him slightly crooked teeth between lips shiny with gloss. "I can try," she said. She looked uncertainly around the station. "There's an officer here somewhere. Maybe you'd better ask him?"

"Well, let's see if you can help me first. It's about the cell phone," he said.

"Belinda's cell phone?"

Bern nodded. "Is it still around?"

Kelly chewed off some of her lip gloss while she thought. "I can't get it for you. It's in evidence. Staff Sergeant Resnick could, though, or—"

Bern waved off her suggestion. "Have they checked it for messages?"

"Oh. Yeah, they had to get permission from the cell phone company. Constable Schilling transcribed them this afternoon."

"Ah, that's what I'm after," he said. "Could I have a look at them?"

Kelly shrugged quickly and looked at her computer screen. Bern could see the uncertainty in her eyes. She didn't want to say no, but she didn't want to get Resnick mad at her either.

Bern smiled and took a step back. "I know I should ask one of the officers. In fact, why don't I wait until tomorrow? I'll come back in the morning and ask Resnick," he said.

Kelly took a deep breath. "The thing is," she said, "I have them right here, on my screen. But you'd have to get an official copy from Resnick." Then she smiled. "I was just about to get a cup of tea. Would you like one?"

He nodded and said quietly, "Yes, thank you."

She stood and smoothed out her corduroy skirt. She reached

over her desk for a china teacup and turned the screen toward him. "Wait here until I get back, in case anyone comes in."

He sat on the edge of her desk and leaned toward the computer screen. It looked like the messages spanned a three-day time period. And there were a lot of them. As he scrolled through the transcript, his cell phone rang. He picked it up quickly.

"Fortin," he said.

"*Oui, c'est moi.*" The voice came through the line, words slurred. "*Ça va?*"

"*Oui, oui. Ça va, Colonel,*" Bern said. He scrolled through another block of messages. Most of them were from Gavin to Belinda, their tone increasingly desperate. "*Et vous?*"

"*Oui, ça va. Encore une autre journée.*" *Yes, fine. Yet another day.*

"*Oui, une autre,*" Bern replied slowly, caught up with trying to read in English as he was speaking in French.

"*T'es occupé.*" *You're busy.*

Bern sat up straighter and answered slowly. "*Il n'y a pas de quoi,*" he said casually. *It's nothing.* But Sauvé must have heard the hesitation in his voice.

"*Et bien! C'est beau. À bientôt.*" *It's good. We'll talk soon.* Sauvé hung up before Bern could reply.

Bern hooked the phone back to his belt and let out a slow breath. A clatter of dishes reached him from the staff room. He leaned toward the computer screen again and quickly began scanning the messages before Kelly came back.

TRANSCRIPT OF VOICE MAIL MESSAGES   **FILE #: 2009-7-924-3**

CELL PHONE BELONGING TO: Belinda Carlisle

TRANSCRIBED BY: Cst. Schilling   **Location: Kootenay Landing**

VOICE MAIL: New message. Sent on Saturday, September 5th, at 12:37 p.m.

MESSAGE CONTENTS: Belinda. It's Gavin. I thought you were going to call me before you left? I hope you're on the road by now anyway. Drive safe through the mountains, okay? I don't want to distract you while you're driving, so just call me back when you take a break. And take it easy. Roads can be busy on a long weekend like this. Don't drive too fast, okay? Uh, okay. That's it. Call me later. Bye.

VOICE MAIL: New message. Sent on Saturday, September 5th, at 2:01 p.m.

MESSAGE CONTENTS: Belinda, where the hell did you go? You stupid bitch. I can't believe you took all my cash. Shit. Now what the hell am I supposed to do? Aw, Christ, Belinda. Don't call me or you'll get me in serious shit. But you're in serious shit already, aren't you? I want that money back.

VOICE MAIL: New message. Sent on Saturday, September 5th, at 3:13 p.m.

MESSAGE CONTENTS: Hey, it's Gavin again. You must be on the road. Can't think of why you wouldn't have called otherwise. Listen, I forgot to tell you something. I picked up an overtime shift on Monday. It's only four hours, but triple time. I don't like to leave you by yourself, but it will give you a chance to get to know what it's like when I'm working, right? A half day, before I go back for real on Tuesday. So hurry up and get here. But drive safe. Call me when you get this.

VOICE MAIL: New message. Sent on Saturday, September 5th, at 5:47 p.m.

MESSAGE CONTENTS: Hi, it's Gavin. Hey, I thought you'd be here by now. Call me. I'm getting worried.

VOICE MAIL: New message. Sent on Saturday, September 5th, at 7:02 p.m.

MESSAGE CONTENTS: Okay, so now I'm really worried. Do you even know my address? I thought for sure you'd call by now. Just call me when you get to town. I'll come out and meet you.

17

Following some instinct she could not name and did not want to look at too closely, she parked on a strip of dried grass in front of Bern's house. The house was dark and his truck was not in the driveway. Evie turned off the engine of her SUV and waited for a few minutes, thinking. Finally, she made a decision: go get a bit of work done and come back later when Bern was home.

She walked down the dirt road to the back gate of the brewery grounds. She climbed a set of fire escape stairs and entered the building through the brew house, planning to do some spot inspections on her way to her office.

The only lights on in the brew house were those of the emergency lighting system, which automatically activated whenever the main overhead lights were shut off. Here the multiple layers of hallways were inhabited only by row upon row of fermentation and chilled aging tanks—alcoves and corridors that might not see an employee for days on end.

Evie loved the scientific orderliness of the brew house. As long as the huge tanks of liquid were provided with the right conditions, the outcome was predictable: it would become beer within five to seven days. Conditions that were measurable; that could be tracked on a daily basis through testing; that could be adjusted along the way, if need be, to give a standard result: Bugaboo Brew.

Once she entered the cellars, drafts of cold air chilled her through her fleece vest, and the roar of the refrigeration units was deafening after the silence of the rest of the fermentation hallway. She descended a set of metal steps and stood for a moment at the bottom, surveying the lower hallway. Something was off, though she could not figure out what it was. Her gaze roamed over the rows of tanks, each one a full story high. Some held fermented liquid, slowly turning it into beer; others held chilled water; and still others, concentrated beer ready to be diluted and bottled.

Then she found it. At tank number seventeen, the tube that was suspended from the top of the tank, allowing workers to siphon off samples for the lab, had come free from its anchor and was dangling in midair. Drops of finished liquid were slowly dripping from the tube onto the tiled floor below. If left to drip all weekend, they would produce a slick puddle of beer at the entrance to the cellar hallway, a treacherous greeting for the next worker headed this way.

Evie walked over and slipped the tube back onto the clip that held it in place and tightened the dripping tap. Taking one more visual survey of the room, she shivered involuntarily. Then she made her way out into the stale air of the warehouse and back to the quiet of the rest of the brewery, where the production machines lay sleeping.

Once in her office, Evie dialed the call center to register that she was working alone. A formality really, since the most significant hazard that she faced in her office was eyestrain from staring at the computer screen.

"Kootenay Landing Answering Service," a sleepy voice responded.

"Hi, sorry to wake you," Evie whispered into the phone. "I'd like to register as working alone—"

"Can you speak up, honey? I can't hear you."

"Dolleen, is that you?" Evie asked.

"Evie, honey, that you? What are you doing calling me in the middle of the night?"

"I had to come in to work. What, do you work the night shift too?" Evie asked.

"Girl, I work all the time. It's what I do," Dolleen said.

Evie knew from her previous conversations with Dolleen that she was in a wheelchair and virtually housebound. She had started the answering service as a way to earn a living.

"Yeah, me too, Dolleen," said Evie. "Me too. I'm the only one here tonight. So I'll call in every two hours, okay?" Evie felt bad knowing she would be interrupting the other woman's sleep when she was unlikely to leave the safety of her office.

"No problem, Evie. I've got you covered."

As soon as she was gone, he stepped out from behind the tank. He had a half-filled beer bottle in his hand and he took a bitter swig. That was close. There was no escaping her. It was like she was on constant patrol, looking for the slightest thing out of place, like that spout loose from the tank. He looked at his watch and shook his head again. Midnight on a Friday and there she was, wandering the brewery, tormenting him.

He pictured how close she'd been when she bent over and picked up that spout. From the shadows behind the tank, where he'd ducked when he first heard her footsteps, he could have spit on her. Or worse. He smiled at that thought.

He gripped the beer bottle like a weapon and let his arm fall to his side. The bottle slapped against his brown coveralls with a small thud. Time to get the job done and get out of there.

He emptied the beer into the drain on the concrete floor and left the bottle on the counter in the control room, neatly lined up with the other sample bottles, waiting to be washed. He headed down the dark hallway and descended the concrete stairs to the basement. It was rarely used, abandoned to the technology of the upper floors. No one ever went down there, especially in the middle of the night. Not even Evie Chapelle. He would have time to finish the job that he needed to do.

By the time Evie cleared off the surface of her desk, her eyes watered from the strain of reading under fluorescent lights. The environmental files were, for the most part, off the floor and divided into semiorganized piles on various surfaces throughout the room. Evie had categorized everything, with a pile for each environmental impact area: water usage, waste products, plastics, glass, cardboard. Her task over the next two years would be to reduce consumption according to the new BevCo standards. But her immediate job was to get up to speed on the files. In just two weeks the auditors would arrive. They would survey every document and every inch of the brewery, and never once crack a smile. They would make Susan Byron look like an officer from the clown patrol.

Might as well start with the water file, Evie thought. The brewery used so much water that even a small reduction made a big impact. She brought the water papers down from the top of the filing cabinet, plopped them on her lap, and started reading.

Half an hour later, she put down the last document in the pile and started again from the top. This time, she stopped when she got to a chart showing water usage numbers for each month of the year to date. There had to be a calculation error, she thought.

She reached over with the tip of her pencil and started tapping the numbers into the adding machine that was perched on top of a pile of binders at the back of her desk. Then she zeroed out the total and added them again.

Definitely something wrong here. She reached for her computer mouse and logged on to the online database that tracked every measurable aspect of every BevCo brewery across Canada. Here she once again found the same total for water usage. How could this have escaped notice?

Evie thought back to the basic brewing training she had taken as a new recruit to the company. Brew school, they'd called it. Unless there had been some major change in the brewing process since Evie's brew school days, there was something off with these numbers. They showed a water usage level that was well below what it should be. Specifically, they showed that the amount of water going to the drain was way too low. The Bugaboo plant generally, and Karl Ostikoff in particular, were touted by head office as the place to beat because of its low water consumption year after year. But too little water could also mean not enough sanitation—and that could be bordering on dangerous.

Evie sat back and sighed. It was no wonder Karl didn't want to hand this information over—unless there'd been a mistake. She thought of the one day when Karl had deigned to show her the ropes regarding energy consumption. He had taken her down to the basement and shown her the meters where the water numbers were collected on a weekly basis. Evie checked her watch. She still had a half hour before she needed to check in with Dolleen. It would be easy enough to get this sorted out before then.

Bern smiled when he saw Evie's car parked on the edge of his front lawn. Glad I left the door unlocked, he thought as he pulled into the driveway.

Except she wasn't there. Not in the house, not on the deck, and not in the garden either.

He crossed the garden to the tap and turned on the sprinkler. A good, deep watering is what it needs, he thought. The heart-shaped sprinkler attachment started to spin and jettison water across the garden bed. It looked as though Mrs. Kalesnikoff had harvested some more tomatoes, but still more had ripened while he had been away. He picked one now, as large as his palm, the skin smooth except for a tiny blemish on the blossom end. It would be perfect for a bacon-and-tomato sandwich. He'd make them when Evie got there.

The steps to the basement were cold and eerily quiet. The corners of the steps were dark with dampness, and the air smelled cold and moist. Evie passed the paint room, where shelves were piled with half-empty cans of paint. The room was secured with a chain-link fence and locked. Evie brought it up at every safety meeting: the paint room needed to be cleaned out. She always got the same response: no manpower, no time, not a priority. That will change after the audit, she thought. The hallway was dark and quiet, save for the buzz of an overhead emergency light. Evie reached for the light switch and it too began to buzz as it slowly warmed up. She felt the small, downy hairs on the back of her neck rise as though a cold wind had passed through the hall.

"Is anyone there?" she called. She turned to face the abandoned length of hall. The lights were still not bright enough to show anything. Enormous vats of chemicals glowed white in the dim space. Pipes rose to the ceiling in long, silvery strands that, on production days, would carry the chemicals through miles of piping in an intricate process, dilute them to the correct ratio, and flush the lines, bottles, and machines that allowed for the sanitary production of beer. The undiluted liquid caustic that had caused Gavin's death was in the largest container on the right.

The feeling of unease did not leave Evie as she turned to the old refrigerated cellar where the water meters were kept. The bulbs were barely beginning to shine as she lifted the long metal bar latch that lay across the heavy door and pushed it slowly open. The lights inside the room were incandescent and responded immediately to the flick of the switch. She left the door ajar as she entered the chilled room, its walls lined with old tanks that were no longer in use. There was evidence of rust along the base of some of the tanks, and a trickle of water dripped from a back corner. But a few of the tanks seemed to be in better shape than the others, with relatively new piping and sample tubes. The smell was of closed-up beer, beyond stale. The dull rankness permeated Evie's nostrils. She edged slowly into the room, keeping an eye on the half-opened entry door. A small chalkboard hanging on the wall let her know that the tanks eleven through fourteen had last been filled on October 28, though there was no indication of the year.

Evie reached the last tank and ducked between its side and the corner of the wall to read the water meter. She could barely see the numbers. She fumbled for her notebook.

Just then, the door began to swing shut. Evie heard its creaking groan just as her pen started to trace out the first number from the meter. She dropped the pen and notebook and ran to stop the door from closing. It shut with a thud as her fingers touched its cold surface. She heard the metal bar slide into place on the outside. And then she heard footsteps walking down the hall and away from her.

The closest Dolleen could come to pacing was rolling her wheelchair back and forth over the square of linoleum floor between the kitchen counter and the television. She had the television tuned to the weather channel. She knew there must be other people who, instead of sleeping, kept track of the weather in far-off places in the middle of the night. But she felt as if she was all on her own. A woman with a tidal wave of blond hair and a paunchy, balding man were telling her that it was going to be another very hot day in Georgia.

Dolleen twirled again, rolled to the kitchen counter, and grabbed another handful of corn chips. She washed them down with a sip of cold coffee from the mug on the counter. She had made the pot of coffee almost two hours ago, when Evie had called from the Bugaboo Brewery. Knowing her sleep was done for the night, she figured she might as well stay up and fret. Dolleen's sister had long ago told her that she'd be better off learning to knit or taking a course in classical literature—that her fretting didn't help anyone—but Dolleen still fretted.

She often worried about the weather. She watched now as the weather channel flashed to a picture of a trailer park, rows of run-down trailers that looked liked they'd been parked on a military landing strip—not a tree in sight. They were the kind of trailers that got washed away in floods and ravaged by tornadoes; trailers on the brink of existence. The people who lived in trailers like that would have flocks of kids and then would be too busy working or drinking to look after them properly. Dolleen worried about the kids. She worried that they'd go out and play in the caked and exposed fields that bordered the edge of that trailer park without sunscreen or hats. A kid could get just one bad sunburn and be at risk for skin cancer later in life.

She paused in her wheeled pacing and checked her watch. It was after two o'clock and Evie had not phoned back. Dolleen fingered the logbook for the Bugaboo Brewery and reviewed the terms of her contract, though she knew them by heart. The worker is to call and check in every two hours, and also to call when he was leaving, to log out. Once he logged out, it was not Dolleen's job to worry about him anymore.

Evie had not logged out. And she had not called in at the two-hour mark. Dolleen picked up the phone and dialed the number

Evie had given her. A distant ringing came over the phone, followed by Evie's voice on the voice mail message.

"Evie, honey, it's Dolleen. You never called in for your two o'clock. Just checking on you. Give me a call and let me know you're all right," Dolleen said. "I'll call you back in fifteen minutes."

Dolleen pulled out the list of emergency contacts for the brewery and reread the procedure. The instructions were very clear: if she was not able to get Evie on the phone within half an hour, she was to call down the emergency contact list until she reached someone and then let that person know there was a worker missing in the brewery, potentially in an emergency situation. She had never had to call before.

Dolleen had never met her in person but she'd been amazed at how much work Evie had put into developing this procedure. Dolleen handled working-alone situations for bigger companies with higher hazards than the brewery, companies that were happy with a simple record book and Dolleen's scribbling account of what went on. For them it was a case of covering their asses. In the event of an accident, they could prove due diligence to the WSB. Evie was not like that. Evie would call, no matter what—unless she was in trouble. Dolleen swung around and began her wheeled pacing again.

Evie tucked her hands into her armpits to warm them and to keep from looking at them anymore.

Her legs ached from pacing on the concrete floor. The cold had taken hold of her, squeezing her heart into pumping faster, her breath into a shallow, panicked rhythm. She could not sit down in the black slime that covered the concrete, so she paced, stomping her feet and swinging her arms to keep the circulation moving.

Had she heard footsteps? She went over the sounds again in her mind: the whine of the door as it rolled shut; the slam of the metal bar as it locked into place. The metal bar was heavy, and it didn't slide into place on its own. There had been footsteps, she was sure of it. Or was she? Was she imagining things, picturing evil and conspiracy when there was only her own stupidity? Had she locked herself in after all?

Who would want to lock her in here? And who else would be in the brewery in the middle of a weekend night? Evie mentally reviewed the discussion at the last production meeting. She was sure that Karl had said there would be no weekend work. A complete shutdown for two days, to give everyone a rest from the shock of what had happened the week before. She should have listened to him and taken a break too. She should have stayed home with Dirk.

No, she thought, turning quickly midpace and heading back to the door. She imagined herself as a stay-at-home mom in Fort McMurray, having coffee with her sister-in-law and pushing a stroller through the snow and cold. She imagined holding a baby and the fear almost paralyzed her.

"All new mothers are afraid," Dirk's sister had said once when Evie had asked her about it. "You get over it; you get used to it. And you realize that it's not about you anymore. It's about the baby, about being a mother. So it doesn't matter if you are afraid; you just do what you need to do."

That had sounded like good advice to Evie, but general

advice for life, not something she would ever apply to mother-
hood. She never wanted to be a mother. She knew now with a
calm finality that her relationship with Dirk was over. The thing
that he wanted more than anything was the one thing she would
never give him. She saw their relationship suddenly as one of
convenience. They had both needed companionship—a warm
body—but that need could not overcome the basic differences
between them.

I could sure use a warm body now, Evie thought. She started
to recite the procedure for working in extreme temperatures and
she felt a little calmer. She had drafted it over a year ago, but it
was hung up in the safety committee, waiting to be finalized. The
sticking point was hats, she remembered. She had suggested that
anyone who spent more than half of his shift in a refrigerated area
should be required to wear a toque. Evie laughed now, thinking
of this. The members of the safety committee had refused to sign
the procedure, knowing that the guys on the floor would refuse
to wear the hats: they were afraid to look like idiots. And yet, if
they were ever to get locked in a refrigerated room, a hat would
likely save their lives.

It took Evie a moment to register this thought and then
another moment to extricate her hands from under her tightly
folded arms. She was wearing a tank top under her long-sleeved
shirt. She took off her fleece vest and hugged it between her
knees to keep it from falling on the floor. In a maneuver reminis-
cent of a child at the beach changing behind a towel, she fumbled
to take off the tank top while not exposing too much of her
skin to the cold air. She stumbled as she pulled it over her neck,
almost dropping the vest on the ground. She wrapped the tank
top around her head, tying the spaghetti straps with her numb

fingers so that her head and ears were completely covered. This task completed, she sat down on the stainless steel pipes for a rest, leaning her covered head against the frozen wall and allowing her eyes to close.

She went through the past week in her mind. Clearly, someone was up to no good. It had started with Gavin, obviously, but then Belinda was found too. And now Evie was locked in the basement. Someone had locked her in.

Behind her closed eyes, she saw the image of Gavin's signed training sheet, a signature she had known was forged the second she looked at it. All she had felt at the time was relief. Coldness filled the pit of her stomach like a stone. Lying to the WSB officer had come so easily: how could Susan Byron be expected to know if one single sheet of paper, in among so many hundreds, was legitimate?

Now Evie saw clearly. Hers was just one small lie in a web that was concealing a dangerous killer. She fumbled and moved slowly, trying to stand, but with each movement the cold air swirled around her anew. She wrapped her arms around her body and leaned her head back again. Dolleen would have called for help by now. They would comb the brewery until they found her. *I'll just rest for a minute, until they get here. And then I'll tell them.*

At twenty-eight minutes past two, Dolleen started calling down the list. At the third number she called, a man grunted into the phone.

"Yeah?"

"This is Dolleen at Kootenay Landing Answering Service. There is an employee who called in to register a working-alone situation and has not checked in, in two and a half hours. I am calling down the emergency response list to summon help. You are the first one who has answered." She spoke loudly and with authority—in what her sister called her no-bullshit voice.

"What time is it?" the man asked.

"Two thirty," Dolleen responded.

"Okay," he said slowly. His words were starting to come more clearly. "But it's Friday. The plant is closed. There is no one scheduled. Who called in?"

"Evie Chapelle" was Dolleen's response.

"Ah, Evie." He whistled on an exhale. "Okay, run it by me again. What time did she call in?"

"She called at"—Dolleen paused to check her logbook—"eleven fifty-seven p.m. So I was expecting her to call again before one fifty-seven a.m., or sooner if she left the premises. She has not called and has not responded to my calls at the number she gave me."

"Did you try her house? Maybe she just went home," the man said.

Dolleen took a deep breath and let her no-bullshit voice boom through the phone. "Do you know this woman? I have only talked to her on the phone, but I feel certain that Evie Chapelle would not call in to a working-alone situation and then go home and forget to log out."

"Okay—"

Dolleen continued, interrupting him. "And I do not believe that she would fail to check in at two-hour intervals, as is outlined in the procedure. She wrote the procedure, for God's sake! She knows what it says!"

"So you think—" he started.

"I think you'd better get your sorry ass down there and check on her, Mr. . . . , Mr."—Dolleen ran her finger down the call list to find the name of the person she was talking to—"Mr. Conrad Scofield. Because if she's not calling me or answering her phone, then something has happened to her. Got it?"

"Okay, okay, I got it," he said.

"And call me back to tell me if she's all right," Dolleen said as he hung up on her.

Conrad shut off his cell phone and tapped it on his chin. He spun a slow circle in the brewery parking lot. Evie always parked right between the beer store customer parking and the brewery manager's spot, and no one else dared park there. Park in Evie's spot and you were sure to have your department audited the next day with an attention to detail normally reserved for a military drill. But Evie's spot, like every other one in the deserted parking lot, was empty. Except his, of course.

He opened the door to his truck and climbed in. His head pounded and his stomach churned. He'd had too much to drink last night, and he knew he probably should not be driving. Looking for Evie was the last thing he needed to be doing.

He started his truck and wound down the window. He waved his passkey and the chain-link gate retracted. He pulled out onto the road, tires squealing, before it was open all the way. It was a god-awful time of night. Anyone with any sense at all was at home sleeping, which was where he planned to be shortly. There were precious few hours before the kids would be hanging off him and the whisper of the hangover he felt now would be in full bloom. And of course, Lisa would be harping at him about something, like she always was. Wanting him to make up for something, some failing, as though working at the fucking brewery twelve hours a day just wasn't enough. Maybe he could find some way to escape, if only for a few hours.

He circled the block. He would check the back parking lot on the way home, but he didn't expect to find anything. The thing was, Conrad liked Evie. And he liked Dirk. They'd had a lot of good times together, and judging from the tension between the two of them at dinner earlier that night, those times were all but over.

The back parking lot was empty too. He drove right up to the gate and shone his high beams into the empty lot. He backed up without looking again and took the back road toward home, through the lazy dispersion of streets that flanked the brewery. Half a block later he stopped short.

"Son of a—" Conrad exclaimed. Evie's car was parked at the side of the road. He braked and backed up until he was side by side with the black SUV. "I don't believe it."

He sat thinking for a moment, looking straight ahead. Evie's SUV was parked in front of a small house covered in siding that was made to look like brick. Cheap-looking stuff, he thought vaguely. He knew whose house it was. There were no lights on.

"I don't believe it," he said again. Conrad popped the clutch, eased his truck forward, and headed for home. "He must be something if she's forgetting her own procedure." He chuckled to himself.

Conrad sped up as he crossed the train tracks, wondering vaguely if Dirk knew, and whether he would care. He wondered how long Evie and the coroner had been going at it. Maybe I'll just give Dirk a call. And with that thought he picked up his cell phone again.

TRANSCRIPT OF VOICE MAIL MESSAGES   FILE #: 2009-7-924-3

CELL PHONE BELONGING TO: Belinda Carlisle

TRANSCRIBED BY: Cst. Schilling   Location: Kootenay Landing

VOICE MAIL: New message. Sent on Sunday, September 6th, at 3:14 a.m.

MESSAGE CONTENTS: I can't believe you're still not here. Are you even
coming? I don't know what's happening here, Belinda. I thought this was
a new start for us. How the hell can we have a new start if you won't even
call me back?

VOICE MAIL: New message. Sent on Sunday, September 6th, at 11:47 a.m.

MESSAGE CONTENTS: Hey, Belinda. It's me. Just woke up. I'm thinking I
must have got the days wrong, or something got fucked up. You're leaving
today. I must have heard you wrong. Right? I'm getting all set up to watch
the game. First time in four years we won't watch it together. But that's
okay. You're on your way, and that's what counts. So can you just call me
to tell me what time you left? I'm still kind of worried. Okay. Bye.

VOICE MAIL: New message. Sent on Sunday, September 6th, at 2:12 p.m.

MESSAGE CONTENTS: [hang up]

VOICE MAIL: New message. Sent on Sunday, September 6th, at 4:38 p.m.

MESSAGE CONTENTS: [hang up]

VOICE MAIL: New message. Sent on Sunday, September 6th, at 6:16 p.m.

MESSAGE CONTENTS: [hang up]

VOICE MAIL: New message. Sent on Monday, September 7th, at 1:46 a.m.

MESSAGE CONTENTS: [hang up]

VOICE MAIL: New message. Sent on Monday, September 7th, at 11:16 a.m.

MESSAGE CONTENTS: [hang up]

18

Lève-toi maintenant.

The voice in his dream was loud and angry. The voice of a nun—his seventh-grade teacher. Sister Marie-Ange. Such a beautiful name, but such a brittle and angry woman.

Lève-toi! Maintenant, Bernard. He drifted back into the dream. *Get up! Now.*

Is it a sin to lie at confession?

Of course it is a sin.

Sister Marie-Ange was always exasperated with him.

Then I can't go to confession today. I have not sinned. It would be lying to confess to sins I have not committed.

In that moment between wakefulness and sleep, he could see it again. It was like he was watching himself on television but was inside his body at the same time. She'd pointed to a spot on the floor, next to her desk, in front of the blackboard.

Kneel here until you think of something. You are a sinner. Just like everyone else. Learn from Bernard, boys. There is never an absence of sin. It is always lurking. Now, return to your reading.

They hadn't, of course. The other boys stared at Bern and his tangle of limbs. They stared as the points of his knees pressed into the floor. They stared as a jolt of pain lodged itself in the wide wedge of his hips. He rolled back on his toes to give himself a moment of relief, but the pain soon entered his ankles and bore into their hinges until he fell back on his knees. After an hour of this aching dance, it was time to leave for confession.

Bernard, are you ready to confess your sins?

Yes, Sister. I sinned while I knelt here. He looked straight into her dried-up eyes. *I sinned thinking I am not a sinner. I thought it over and over again until I believed it was true.*

So now you get up. And confess. Lève-toi maintenant.

But Bern could not get up. His knees creaked under the long unfolding of his preadolescent limbs. He had to lie on the floor, stretching out the cramps, while the class was led by a furious Sister Marie-Ange to the chapel.

Bern stood up from the couch. His knees creaked and his ankles ached, and he thought that his forty-five-year-old body was not unlike his twelve-year-old body after all. He could tell, without looking at the clock, that it was that time just before dawn when night gave way reluctantly to morning. He thought if he sat in the garden, he might sense that exquisite moment when the dew shifted and began to rise.

He slid open the patio door and listened to the calling of the chickadees that inhabited the willow tree at the edge of his property. Under that was a hissing sound. The sprinkler.

Bern moved quickly, his bare feet soaking up the cool water that had pooled in the rows between garden beds. He turned the tap and the hissing sound stopped, though he could hear trickling as the excess water found its way to the creek at the edge of his property.

The birds stopped their cries too, chastened momentarily by

the sudden change in the sounds of their environment. In the seconds before they started clamoring again, Bern remembered Evie.

He squished along the side of the garden, wet topsoil clumping to his bare toes, and began to jog when the ground dried out. He went out the side gate to the front yard. Her car was still there. Could she have come in while he slept on the couch? But where would she have gone?

He went in through the side door, tracking his muddy feet through the house to his bedroom. He opened the door. There was his bed, made with military precision. No Evie.

He pulled a pair of socks out of a drawer and put them on his wet feet. He grabbed a sweater and pulled that on over his button-down shirt—the same one he'd worn for his meeting with Kumar yesterday. At the back door he slipped on sandals— no time to lace up his boots—pulled a flashlight from his box of camping gear and headed out the door.

Both his road and the one that led to the brewery were unpaved. They'd been leveled and prepared for paving in the spring, then covered with a layer of sand, which neighborhood residents complained about. The dust from the sand drifted through tiny, unseen cracks and made its way through tightly sealed windows, leaving a veil of dust in their immaculate houses. The town council had promised the roads would be paved before the first frost.

But Bern was glad it hadn't been done. He started at the driver's-side door of Evie's black SUV and shone his flashlight on the firm-packed dirt of the road. By the light of its beam he was quickly able to pick up the trace of her footprints, heading away from his house.

He could see how it had happened. She'd come by and he

wasn't home. Maybe she'd waited for a while, but when he hadn't shown up, she'd decided to go do some work. But now it was almost dawn. Surely even Evie would want to kick off work for a while?

He tracked the light impressions of her footprints to the back gate of the brewery. What would he say when he found her? *Are you okay? I've been thinking about you. I noticed that quad in your garage and wondered if it's yours? I was just about to make a bacon-and-tomato sandwich and wondered if you wanted one too?*

He stood at the back gate and looked at the punch combination lock. The whole neighborhood knew the code, Evie had said. But Bern didn't. Maybe this wasn't such a good idea. *If the lady wants to work all night, why not let her?* But he felt an urgency that he could not define. Two dead bodies so far this week. Despite Kumar's budget worries and Resnick's theory of good times gone bad, Bern could not shake the feeling that someone was up to something. And the brewery seemed to be at the center of it all.

The fence was easy to scale. He jumped down the other side without snagging his jeans and landed in a strip of weeds next to a pile of broken pallets. A few exterior lights showed the outline of the grounds.

Bern made his way to the door by the boiler room—the one that had set off the alarm on the day Gavin's body was found. He thought back to the set of Evie's delicate jaw, how frustrated she'd been, and how angry. Perhaps there was something she wasn't telling him.

The door swung open easily. He waited a moment in the entry, expecting to hear the alarm sound. Nothing. He closed the door behind him and listened again. No alarm. Even the boilers were shut down. But there had to be someone there. You couldn't just walk off the street through a back door and into a brewery.

He shone his flashlight on the floor and around the doorway. There was no trace of dirt that he could see. Even if she'd wiped her feet at the door, he would expect to find a few grains on the floor. She must have gone in another way. But then who had left this door unlocked?

Three doors led away from where he was standing. To the right, he knew, was the entrance to the boiler room. He could only assume the door on the left reached the bottle shop. He couldn't imagine Evie having business there before dawn on a Saturday morning. The door in front of him was the one, then. He opened it and entered a giant room, two stories high and filled with an intricate system of stainless steel pipes, interspersed with the occasional tank. He recognized two small units as centrifuges. Had he walked through this room before with Evie? They must have come through here on the night the alarm went off. Somehow it led to the office area.

He shone his flashlight around and picked a path through the tanks and pipes. Halfway across the room he saw an exit sign on one wall. He headed that way and out through a swinging door. He found himself in a small warehouse. Bern played his flashlight across the space. Two forklifts were parked next to each other, with pallets full of boxes stacked up next to them. Just ahead he saw a flash of white. He headed toward it and at last knew where he was. He stood at the same crossroads as he had on that first day. In front of him, a yellow-painted pedestrian pathway led through the bottle shop. Beside him were the white-painted cinder blocks, lined with awards, that led to the offices. He took this route.

"Evie?" he called out when he opened the door to the front

office area. It was silent. He ran his light along the floor, slowly. He got down on his knees, keeping the flashlight close to the floor. He crawled around Gemma's desk and a few feet down the hallway, looking for the slightest speck of sand or dirt that might show Evie had passed by.

A few grains of dirt. And then a few more. He'd found her. Bern stood and followed the minute trail down a warren of hallways. At last he found a lighted room.

The sign outside the door had two slots: one for the occupant's name, the other for her title. Both signs were designed to slide out easily. In case of staff changes, Bern supposed. It said loud and clear that in this place, people were interchangeable. And could easily be replaced. Evie Chapelle, Safety Manager, the sign read.

Her office was tiny, as small as Bern's kitchen pantry. The door was open and the light was on. A generic three-dimensional cube moved about and changed color on the computer screen.

"Evie?" he said again, though it was clear she was not there.

He looked about some more. There were piles of paper covering every inch of her desk. It looked a mess, but from what little he knew of her, Bern was certain there would be some sort of logic to the assorted piles. He put one foot in the room and leaned over the top pile. Numbers, row upon row of them, trapped in tiny boxes on the page. *Water Use, Bugaboo Brewery* was written in a large font across the top.

Bern leaned against the doorway. It did not look like she had packed it in for the night. He shone his flashlight into the hallway again. He tried the doorknobs of the two adjacent offices. Both were locked, and no light came through the crack at the bottom of either door.

A third door gave way as he pushed it and he found himself in the bottle shop. A conveyor belt formed a corridor at eye height. Lighting the floor he got down on his hands and knees again and followed where it led. He hardly expected to see it, but almost ten steps later he found some crumbs of dirt. The floor must have been hosed off at the end of the shift; it was relatively clean. But still, could those few specks of dirt really lead him to Evie? Evie somewhere in the brewery, tallying water numbers for her report and wondering what he was doing, crawling around on the floor like an infantry soldier hunting down the enemy.

Paranoia. Reactions out of proportion to the situation at hand. He could recite the list of post-traumatic stress symptoms from memory. He stood up, careful not to bash his head on the conveyor, and headed farther down the corridor. He looked down at yesterday's clothes, wool socks in sandals, a flashlight in his hand. He looked ridiculous.

Before long he was back in the warehouse, the two forklifts at the ready for Monday morning startup. But there. There. On the floor was more dirt. He could barely make it out, must have missed it on his first time through. And next to the forklift, he hadn't seen that before either—a doorway.

Opening it, he found himself on a small landing with stairs heading down. At the bottom of the stairs, a light was on.

"Evie?" he called.

He sniffed. It smelled like wet cement. As he went down, the air seemed to get colder and more damp. At the bottom of the stairs was a hallway. To his right was a chain-link fence, and behind it rows of paint cans. The hallway was brightly lit from above by fluorescent lights.

"Evie, are you there?" he bellowed it this time.

Silence.

"Evie?" he called again.

Farther down the hall, on the right-hand side, was a door; it looked like the door to a walk-in freezer at a butcher shop. Except this door was old and made of wood. A heavy metal bar held it closed. Beads of light made their way through a space where the door met the frame.

"Evie?" he called out again. And there it was: slow, faltering taps from the other side of the door. He pulled the bar up and pushed the door open. In two steps he was next to her.

"Can you stand? Are you all right? Here take my sweater." He spoke all at once, and when she had trouble moving, he picked her up. Her tiny body was frozen, past shivering. He breathed into her blue lips to warm her from the inside. He wrapped her in his sweater and wrapped his shirt around her head. He rubbed her limbs. When she could talk just enough to say she was all right, he carried her outside. He held her to his bare chest like an injured bird all the way to his house. Ignoring her mild protestations, he slid her into the passenger seat of his truck.

19

"Shandra, I'm counting on you," Leigh's voice pleaded over the phone. "I know you quit. I know all that. But I really need an extra set of hands tonight."

Shandie twirled a lock of wet hair around her finger and sat on the white chenille coverlet of her bed, which her mother had come in and made while she was showering. That used to annoy her, but now it seemed like just another fact of life, something she would do for her own kids someday.

"Shandra, are you there?" Leigh asked.

"Yeah, I'm here," Shandie replied. "Just thinking."

"Are you going out with Steve tonight? Is that it?" Leigh asked.

"No, we went out last night."

"So you have no plans? Can you give me a good reason why you wouldn't come out and make a little extra cash?"

Shandie cinched the belt of her bathrobe tighter and wrapped her free arm around her belly. Some extra cash would come in handy.

"I have to go to church on Sunday," she told Leigh. "I can't be out too late."

"Okay, no problem. I'll close up; you can go home after the big rush has died down. Around midnight? That okay?"

"Sure," Shandie agreed reluctantly. "And Leigh? Can I work behind the bar?"

After she got off the phone, Shandie towel-dried her hair. When Steve called, which he did every day, she would ask him to pick her up after her shift. And she wouldn't drink anything while she was there, not one drop. She wasn't taking any chances.

Her dark hair lay in long, wet shanks across the white terry-cloth shoulders of her robe. She listened for sounds in the main part of the house but didn't hear anything. Her mother must have gone downstairs to bring her father some more coffee. Shandie's dad spent most of his day in a reclining chair in the basement, keeping track of the sports scores and collecting disability for chronic back pain. The pain made him grumpy; the pills for it made him sleepy and gave him ulcers. Shandie tried to stay away from him as much as she could.

She slowly opened her bathrobe. The scars seemed to be healing. She inspected them carefully. The red of the outside rim had slowly faded to a dull pink. The centers still glowed white, though they stood out less. The circles dotted her abdomen, hips, and inner thighs. There were twenty-eight of them in total.

Shandie opened the drawer to her bedside table and pulled out a small tube—an all-natural burn remedy from New Zealand. She had paid a fortune for it over the Internet. She squeezed out a thick blob of the cream and began to dab it on the small wounds, one by one.

"Honey?"

Shandie tugged her robe closed and wrapped her fist around the tube of cream.

"Yeah, Mom?"

Ingrid Greene's perfectly coiffed brown head popped in the door, followed by her trim, forty-five-year-old body. Ingrid could, and often did, wear Shandie's clothes. Today she was dressed for the golf course in a pair of tidy pastel-yellow shorts and a matching golf shirt. "Can you get Daddy his lunch today?"

"Sure, Mom, no problem." Shandie tied the belt of her robe tightly as she spoke. She slipped the tube onto the bedspread and crossed her legs, angling them so her mother couldn't see the cream from the doorway.

"You okay, hon? How was your date last night?" Ingrid leaned against the door and smiled at Shandie.

"Good, it was nice. We went to the movie, then had a drink with Steve's parents after," Shandie answered.

"Well," Ingrid said with a laugh, "normally that would be a big deal, right? To meet his family, that is. But of course you've known them your whole life, so you're practically part of the family already!"

Shandie just smiled and shrugged. "I told Leigh I would work tonight," she said.

Ingrid's eyes narrowed. "Hmm, well, you know what I think of that."

"I know, Mom, but she needed help. And it does pay well."

"But what do you need money for? You've got all that money saved, and any day now Steve's going to pop the question."

"I thought I'd save up for a nice honeymoon," Shandie said.

"Just don't let anyone get the wrong idea while you're there. You're not going back to your old ways."

Shandie picked up the towel again and started to rub her hair. "I'll get Steve to pick me up, and Leigh said I could finish early. It'll be all right."

"You'll be up in time for church tomorrow?"

"Yes, I will. And I'll bring Daddy his lunch." Shandie smiled at her mom. "Go on. Have a good game."

Shandie waited until she heard her mother's car start in the driveway before she began, once again, to carefully anoint each cigarette burn with the special cream from New Zealand.

Sometimes, when he wanted a good sleep, he stacked boxes on the inside of the door to his little hideout. They were stacked all around him anyway: he'd had to move them out of the way when he set up the room. It helped him to relax. If someone opened the door, they would only see stacks of boxes—a document storage room. And since that's what they would expect to see, they would go no further. They would not walk around the boxes to find his couch, his work desk, and his television with full cable hookup.

It had been hard work, and his arms were sore. But it was worth it. Worth every risk, and every minute. It was the right thing, he thought. He lay down on the brown couch that had been in his parents' rec room for years. It didn't take long for him to fall asleep, and for the images to come. Brandy. The old farm dog, a golden Lab.

Didn't see her there, Sparky had said. *Ran her over with the tractor.* But Sparky was lying, as usual. Brandy's old body, crippled by arthritis, lay still. Her soft tummy was covered in red welts, dozens of them. Cigarette burns. Her neck lay at an odd angle. Sparky liked to burn things. He needed to. He couldn't help himself.

Help me? Sparky asked him, but then he walked away, through the frozen field. Help me, to Sparky, meant deal with it.

And he had, as usual. The ground was too frozen to bury her, so he'd wrapped her heavy body in a burlap sack, weighted her with sandbags, and dropped her in the river. The sound of the splash woke him from his dream.

"Just an old document storage room," said a voice outside the door. A voice he knew well.

"So open it." Another voice, one he didn't know.

He lay still and quiet but not overly worried. A weak ray of light filtered through the boxes as the door opened.

"Boxes," the voice he knew said.

The other one grunted. Then the door closed and they were gone.

It took two hours to search the brewery from top to bottom. Bern had wanted to charge into the building and search without staff help, but Resnick had held back and waited. Sure, to protect evidence, they could search without permission, but the practicality of it was that in such a massive building, they were likely to get lost without staff members to guide them. They split into two groups: Bern, Constable Schilling, and Karl Ostikoff in one; Resnick and Gemma in the other.

They met back at the rear entrance door that Bern had entered the night before. The brewery yard looked different in the light of day. Objects that had seemed foreboding at night were just objects now. The sun pushed through heavy clouds with a brightness that made Bern's tired eyes squint. There was a rank smell to the air.

"What's that smell?" he asked Karl.

"Spent grains. Once the brew is mixed, the grains get sent to that tank up there." Karl pointed to a stainless steel tank suspended off the side of the building, the bottom of it a good twelve feet from the ground. "It must be full—that's when it really smells. A dump truck will come on Monday, park right under there, and take it away."

"Where does the truck take it?" Constable Schilling asked.

"To some farms in the valley. Cows love the stuff," Karl said with a laugh. Then he clapped his hands. "So we just about done here? I'll make sure that the lock gets changed on that back door, and that it stays locked—don't you worry about that for a minute. And I can change this combination on the gate here right now."

The brewery manager, with his salesman good looks and relentless get-it-done attitude, was getting on Bern's nerves. He stepped away from the group and allowed his eyes to roam to the back gate. On the other side he spied his truck, a police cruiser, and two other vehicles, which he assumed belonged to Karl and Gemma. Beyond that were the tidy streets of his own neighborhood, where a killer roamed.

As he watched, another police cruiser pulled up and an officer got out. It was the officer Resnick had assigned to stay at the hospital and keep an eye on Evie. He walked though the open gate, his steps energetic, unaffected by having worked all night and into the next day.

"Aren't you supposed to stay with Evie?" Bern asked him as he approached.

The young man looked uncertainly at Resnick and then shrugged at Bern. "I did stay with her. She slept for three hours and then woke up. So I took her statement. The doctor said she was fine and should go home and get some more sleep."

"And then?" Bern asked.

He narrowed his eyes at Bern, his shoulders rising up again. "Then I drove her home."

"You drove her home? And left her there all by herself?" Resnick was looking at him. They all were. He didn't care.

"The doctor told her she'd be fine. Besides, she said her husband's home and will look after her if she needs anything," the constable said.

Bern opened his mouth and a sound escaped, like he was being choked. He felt as if the ground were shifting beneath his feet. "What about her car?" he asked.

"She said her husband would drive her back in to get it," the officer said. He walked away from Bern and began talking quietly with Resnick. The staff sergeant motioned Schilling over as well, and the three of them conferred for a moment.

Bern felt frozen in time. The chirp of his cell phone seemed to come from a million miles away.

"Fortin," he barked into the receiver.

"Ah, Lieutenant-Colonel Fortin. I found you." The voice on the line was smooth and lazy. Unfamiliar. Bern watched as the officers started to head toward the gate. Karl followed.

"Who is this, please?" he asked sharply.

"Troy Thompson, *Soldier's Ally* magazine," the voice said slowly. "I'd like to interview you. About Captain Alais and the charges against him. Do you have plans to come back and defend your subordinate's actions?"

Karl followed the others out the gate. Only Bern was left now, alone in the brewery yard. He could feel the others looking at him. He could hear the jumble of words from the stranger on the phone. He knew he needed to move, but it was as though he were free-falling through a shifting of roles, expectations, and realities. Lieutenant-Colonel Fortin. Coroner Fortin. Bern Fortin. Could he be all three in this moment?

And all the while, the words the officer had said echoed in some empty chamber of his brain. *Her husband will look after her if she needs anything. Her husband will look after her.*

Bern started walking toward the gate as though in a dream. "This isn't a good time," he said.

"When would be a good time, then? How about I'll call you back in an hour for an interview?"

"Interview me in an hour?" Bern asked. What was the man talking about? He walked past Karl, who was bent over the combination lock on the gate, resetting it.

"Why wait to set the record straight? I mean, one of your men is in jail, right? No doubt you want to speak up for him."

Bern didn't answer. He opened the door to his truck and got in.

"Lieutenant-Colonel Fortin? Are you there? A bit of a shock maybe?" The man chuckled. "I'll call you in an hour."

Bern clipped the phone back to his belt and drove the two blocks to his house. Evie's black SUV was still parked out front, but he pulled into his driveway without looking at it. Once inside his house, he turned off his cell phone, stripped down to his boxer shorts, and fell into bed.

20

At first, Evie thought they'd been robbed.

"Rory?" she called.

Her voice echoed in the entryway, her footsteps on the bare floor. There was usually a small carpet in the entry. Dirk had bought it in Turkey, when he'd traveled there before they were married. Her purse was back in her office, so she'd let herself in using the spare house key from the garage. She went to lay it on the small shelf by the door and it clattered to the floor.

"Dirk?"

Nothing.

"Rory!" she called again. Her voice sounded harsh in the silence. Had they gone for a walk?

It was early afternoon. Evie had been at the hospital for hours. She felt exhausted and wound up at the same time; her limbs drained of energy, her mind unable to rest.

"Rory?" she called more quietly this time. She kept her shoes on and walked down the hallway toward the living area.

The computer was gone, as were the stereo and the couch. Coffee table, desk, portrait above the mantel, large stand-up vase full of silk flowers—all gone. All that was left in the living room was a rocking chair—the one Evie's mother had left behind when she'd run away when Evie was a child—and the pots of plants on the window seat, carefully circling the place where Rory's bed had once been.

Evie walked around the room slowly, taking inventory. The CDs were almost all gone: Dirk was the music lover, not her. The dining room table was there, the one they'd bought with the money Evie's dad had given them when they got married. But they'd kept the chairs from Dirk's old set, which were comfortable and in good shape. The chairs were gone now.

She walked into the kitchen. She remembered how, when they had first moved in together, Dirk bought all new pots, pans, dishes, and cutlery. "A fresh start," he'd called it. Now the cupboards were empty. Dishes, pots, mixing bowls, even the food processor were gone. Only Evie's collection of assorted BevCo beer glasses remained. She didn't go upstairs to check the bedrooms, knowing what she would find: Dirk had bought new sheets, blankets, and towels for their fresh start as well.

Evie pulled the rocking chair up to the window. She sat on its hard seat and put her feet on the window seat, between the plants. A tapestry of fields spread out in the valley before her. Golden squares of harvested hayfields stacked up against those green rectangles yet to be harvested.

She could not believe he had taken Rory. He knew that Evie loved that dog more than any of the people in her life. Rory was the one who could always pull her out of her work, could get her out of a meeting to take him to the vet, could lure her away from the laptop on a Sunday morning to go for a walk. Rory understood her like no human being had ever done. And now he was gone.

• • •

The ground outside her window was dry as bone. His soft-soled slip-ons left no trace. He had to get up close to see through the small space between the curtains. He chewed on the end of his cigarette as he watched her talk on the phone. Her fingers twirled her long, dark hair, her features relaxed into a smile. She hadn't been smiling much lately, he'd noticed. Her normally pretty face seemed drawn and pale.

She was dressed to go out, in jeans and a V-necked Bugaboo T-shirt. The time they'd gone out together she'd worn a red tank top under her jean jacket, a pair of white pants, and a chain around her neck with a good luck charm that secreted itself under the seam of her shirt. He'd stared at it all night, wondering what it was. Later, when she'd laid the talisman, warmed from her skin, so casually on his bedside table, he'd found out it was a small silver dolphin.

He noticed she wasn't wearing any jewelry tonight. She hung up the phone and started brushing her hair roughly. She spun her head upside down and brushed from underneath in long strokes, then stood up and shook her head.

He'd seen her do this so many times, he knew what would come next. She'd dab a small amount of cream of some sort and smooth it through her hair so it lay perfect and shiny and so soft that anyone who went near her would want to touch it. A tap of shiny lip gloss to her lips and that was it. She did not need makeup.

Headlights spun around the corner and he dipped behind the shrub beneath her window. A black truck—could be anyone, but he knew exactly who it was. Steve Ostikoff, the lucky bastard. He bit his bottom lip to keep from crying out in frustration, and watched as her mother opened the door and drew him into the warm glow of the house. Moments later, light and swift, Shandie hopped down the stairs and into his truck. He didn't even open the door for her. How could she settle for so little?

The phone on the other end of the line rang three times and then switched over to voice mail. A man's voice. *You've reached the home of Dirk and Evie. We're not here to take your call. Please leave a message.*

Bern snapped his cell phone shut and placed it on the bar. He signaled to the young girl for another whiskey. Leigh had managed to convince someone to come in, he noticed, but the girl stayed behind the counter while Leigh ran orders out to the packed house. He watched her as she came closer: jeans that fit like a glove and a Bugaboo T-shirt that she kept tugging at, to cover the inch of abdominal flesh it wanted to expose. She flashed a quick smile as she put the drink in front of him: perfect teeth, dark hair that glimmered, and eyes that looked sad. No—scared, Bern thought. Eyes that looked scared.

He took a sip of golden liquid and let his eyes roam the room. Saturday night at the Kootenay Landing Hotel was a whole lot like Friday night at the Kootenay Landing Hotel. The whiskey soothed its way down his throat and loosened some part of him that had been clenched as tight as a fist since he'd found Evie that morning.

The image of her there, cold and helpless, hugging a pipe

to stay upright, would not leave him. Because the floor was so dirty, she'd said at the hospital. And another image: Evie wrapped in the warming blanket, with Dr. Sinclair at her side, her eyes closed. She opened them, looked straight at Bern, and told him to phone someone named Dolleen to tell her she was all right.

Another half hour in that cellar and the outcome might have been different, Dr. Sinclair had said. Was she all right now? He had no way of knowing. Was this Dirk, her husband, taking proper care of her? The whiskey was going down too smooth, and he knew he needed to be careful. He knew that sensation of warmth and lifting that he felt now would turn later, and the images would come to him. Africa, in all her dark and haunting splendor, would visit him in his sleep.

His cell phone rang. He stared at the words on the screen. *Incoming call,* it read simply. Sauvé? Or Troy Thompson? He had no way of knowing. He let it ring.

He watched the girl behind the bar remove a draft glass from a dishwasher tray and slide it onto a shelf above the bar. She did it over and over again. With each motion came another—a tug on the T-shirt that kept riding up. Reach. Flash. Tug.

Bern found himself staring at the inch of exposed, then covered flesh, waiting to see it again. There it was. And again. Could it be? There was only one thing Bern knew of that could leave a scar like that. He waited to see the flash of skin again, but it did not come. He looked up at her face. She was staring at him, eyes wary, both hands pulling on the shirt hem, smoothing it along her hips.

There was one way to make her come closer. He nodded to his empty glass.

• • •

Why do we have to walk so far in the rain?

It won't be long now. We're almost home. Then you can have a nap.

I don't want to have a nap. I'm big. I don't have naps anymore.

Evie sat up with a start. It was dark. She had a painful kink in her neck from falling asleep on the rocking chair. She whistled for Rory. The sound echoed in the empty living room.

The dream had been so real; it was like waking up into that childhood moment all over again. She had fallen asleep that long-ago day. When she woke up, her hair was sticking up from sleeping on it while it was still wet from the rain. She was thirsty. She went to the kitchen to find her mother. There was no one there, so she drank from the tap in the bathroom. Then she sat down to watch TV.

Her father came home at the usual time but did not say anything. He just sat on the couch with her until the children's shows ended and the news came on. Evie waited for the news to explain why her mom wasn't home. But all it talked about was the flooding caused by the heavy rains. Nothing was said about where Evie's mother was.

Finally Evie said she was hungry, and her father heated up a can of soup—Scotch broth. It was never her favorite after that, although they continued to have it every Wednesday night for the next thirteen years, until Evie left home.

It wasn't until she went to high school and had to walk by the bus station every day that Evie realized where she and her mother had walked that day. Her mother had bought her ticket in advance—had put Evie down for that nap knowing she would not be there when her five-year-old daughter woke up.

Evie sat in the rocking chair in the dark, listening to the night sounds: an occasional car on the highway, the wind blowing raindrops against the window. The quilt of the fields below was indiscernible in the darkness.

She was hungry now too. She could call Bern, tell him what happened. He would probably even bring her some soup and listen to her for a while, if she asked him to. She stood slowly from the rocking chair. She was wearing the same clothes as last night, with Bern's scratchy wool sweater, smelling like wood smoke and fresh-turned soil. Her bones ached. She moved like an old woman to the nook next to the kitchen. She reached out for the phone and found a smooth expanse of countertop.

A small cry escaped her lips and she let her arm fall. She held her hand relaxed, slightly cupped, expecting Rory's nose to come nuzzle in her palm like a thousand other times. The phone. It would never have occurred to her that the phone was Dirk's, but thinking back now, she remembered. Their old phones in Winnipeg had been rented from the phone company. When they'd moved to Kootenay Landing, Dirk had gone to the local electronics store and spent a small fortune on a cordless phone set with three receivers—one for the kitchen, one for the upstairs bedroom, and one for his shop in the garage.

She moved quickly through the dark hall, the ghost of Rory's footsteps padding along behind her. She stood helplessly by the front door, next to the hook where she normally hung her purse. It wasn't there. She'd left it on the floor of her office last night. In it would be her cell phone—which by now would be intermittently chirping a low-battery sound—and her car keys.

The reality of the situation flooded her all at once. She

remembered the sound of the heavy door handle falling into place and the definite echo of footsteps walking away from the closed door. Someone had shut her in there. Yesterday, someone had tried to kill her.

And now here she was, alone at home. No Rory to alert her to danger. No phone to call for help. And no vehicle to get away.

She checked the lock and moved away from the door. She was cold and her joints felt stiff. She needed to stay warm. She thought of the emergency kit in the supply closet. A flashlight with spare batteries, a three-month supply of water and two massive down sleeping bags, rated to minus twenty degrees Celsius.

She moved quickly now, turning lights on as she went. The waterproof case was there, at the very bottom of the closet. She hauled it out and pulled out one of the sleeping bags. For the first time since coming home, she went upstairs. She turned on every light and unraveled the sleeping bag as she went. The bed was still there, with no sheets or blankets but one pillow. She lay down and wrapped herself in the down bag, waiting for her body to heat it up and keep her warm. She lay there, with every light in the house on, to wait for morning.

He'd have to finish up another time. It was dawn, but there was still work to be done. Another crack had appeared—out of nowhere, it seemed. And a soft spot in the floor, in the basement under the bottle shop. The thought of waiting until the next shutdown weekend to look after everything formed an angry fist of frustration in his stomach. It could be weeks away.

He dared not risk working through a Sunday. Someone might come in to do some overtime. Or some overzealous manager might come in to catch up on paperwork. The steam engineer would be in at some point to start the boilers. He couldn't risk getting caught. *By someone like that meddling Evie Chapelle. Should have killed her when I had the chance.* But no. He was trying to protect them. He wasn't a killer—not really. Despite what had happened. And what they might think now.

He turned on the hose and watched a stream of water make its way to the drain. Then he hosed out the hopper of the portable cement pump. It had been an investment, but it was worth it. When the last clump of wet cement had floated away, he folded the hose and placed it on the grilled screen on top of the hopper. Then he lifted the handle and rolled the cement pump down the basement corridor on its two back wheels, careful to avoid the area he had just patched. It rolled as smoothly and easily as a wheelbarrow.

It was a long walk from one end of the cavernous basement to the other. Hardly anyone ever came down this far. Closer to the main steps there were a few storage tanks, the paint storage room, and, of course, that old aging cellar where Evie had spent some time last night. The thought of this made him chuckle. But the area under the bottle shop was deserted, for the most part. Left to him to look after.

Evie woke up to the pale light of dawn, sweating inside her arctic sleeping bag. She took a much-needed shower. When she got out and Rory was not there, waiting for her, a wave of grief slammed into her again.

She dressed in some clean clothes and went downstairs. She could use the neighbor's phone to call for someone to help her. Or ask him to give her a lift to town. But it was too early for that: the sun was barely up.

She heated some water in a BevCo glass in the microwave and made herself a cup of tepid tea. Then she sat on the rocking chair and watched the sunrise spread across the western sky while she waited for the full light of day.

From: bernfortin@bccoronerservice.bc.ca
To: capitaineallouette@hotmail.com
Re: re: re: re: re: re: re: Bonjour
Sent: Sunday, September 13 7:32 a.m.

Capitaine,
I am glad you are taking a course. Philosophy will be use-
ful somehow, I have no doubt. Now that I am a civilian
for what feels like the first time in my life (the Catholic
Church of my upbringing had more rules than the army
in some ways), I find myself faced with a stunning array
of decisions each day. Maybe a philosophy course is what
I need too.

It is still a struggle for me to understand the clash of
duty and honor with rules and law. Does a person's own
morality ever supersede the law? I know that will be a
question at your trial, but I do not think it will ever be
answered. Troy Thompson has been calling me as well,
asking this type of question. I have no answers for him.

If you find an answer, please tell me. I am afraid,
though, that when you do, you may also find that I have
failed in my duty as your commander.

But enough pondering. Time for some action. We are,
after all, soldiers at heart. The garden plants are waiting
to be put through their paces.

Bonne chance,
Bern

21

The gunshot rang out just as Bern stepped out of the car. Instinct made him crouch down low. The echo of the blast resonated in the morning sky. Several crows protested loudly from the branches of an enormous fir tree at the edge of the driveway. They flapped and cawed, flew in a circle, and then settled back down in the thick-needled branches. The shot had come from the log house next to the driveway. The house was angled to take in the mountain views, and Bern could only see the back door and the side of a wraparound deck.

A man's voice bellowed. "Fucking crows! Shut up!"

"Resnick?" Bern called out. He stood up again.

"What?" Resnick's voice shouted back.

"Don't shoot!"

Resnick appeared on the deck and walked toward Bern. He stood there in his boxer shorts, rifle in hand, and laughed. He motioned to Bern to come around to the front of the house, and Bern followed a well-worn track through the unkempt grass. He turned the corner and drew in a breath at the view. The house backed against the mountains; miles of farmland spread out below. The western mountains shimmered in the distance.

Bern whistled. "Nice view."

Resnick grunted. "Told the real estate agent I wanted to be able to shoot and piss off the front deck." He shrugged and laughed. "This is what I got! One hundred and sixty acres of farmland and a shack. You want a coffee?"

"Sure," Bern replied, stepping onto the porch and folding himself into an Adirondack chair. "You own this place?" he called through the screen door to Resnick.

"Yeah, I love it. Lease out the land, of course. Pays for some of the mortgage. I may even hold on to it when I leave, rent out the house." He pushed the screen open with his shoulder and emerged holding two steaming mugs of coffee. He'd pulled on a T-shirt and a pair of sweatpants over his boxers, and the rifle was gone. "Hope you like it black. That's all I've got."

"Sure thing." Bern smiled, taking the mug. He brought the steaming cup close to his face and inhaled deeply before taking a sip. "You leaving, then?"

Resnick sat in a chair next to Bern. He put his feet up on the deck railing and lit a cigarette.

"We all go eventually. I put in for a transfer. Probably in the next six months or so," he said. They fell silent. A plane made its way along the western edge of the valley, leaving a white cloud trail in its wake. "But you didn't come here on a Sunday morning to talk about my career path. What's up?"

Bern swallowed a bitter mouthful of coffee and asked lightly, "Anything happening on the girl's case?"

Resnick looked out at the faraway mountains as he spoke. "Nothing since Friday. The car wasn't the primary scene—if you are of the opinion that there *was* a primary scene, that is. I'm not convinced."

The silence fell between them again, and Bern relaxed comfortably into his seat. He put the coffee cup on the wooden arm of the chair. He could happily wait out a silence longer than most people.

"Why, you got something?" Resnick finally asked.

Bern allowed a sliver of a smile to cross his face. "Just a thought," he said.

"Okay, let's hear it." Resnick sighed.

"I think there is a serial rapist at work in Kootenay Landing." Bern tented his fingers and tapped them on his chin.

"What?" Resnick sat up and looked at him. "You're kidding, right? Where the hell did you get this?"

"I just got thinking, from a few things I saw at the bar," Bern replied.

Resnick laughed as he exhaled a lungful of smoke. "Well," he said, "don't believe everything you hear at the bar! Especially in this town."

Bern kept his voice calm and authoritative. "I didn't say things I *heard* at the bar. I said things I *saw* at the bar."

He let the silence fall between them again. After a moment, he continued.

"Did you notice that Leigh was the only server there on Friday night?" When Resnick grunted in acknowledgment, he continued. "She can't get anyone to come in. Girls can make two hundred dollars a night working there—cash—and they won't come in. Ever wonder why?"

Resnick shrugged. "Not really."

"She talked a girl into coming in last night. Pretty thing. Shandie is her name. Skittish as a cat at bath time. Wouldn't look at anyone. Refused to wait tables and would only serve behind the bar. Does that make any sense to you?" Bern asked.

Resnick took a sip of his coffee and smiled into his cup. "It makes perfect sense. You've got to know this town a little better, that's all. She's landed a big fish, see? Girls like that, in this town—pretty girls? They want a hockey player from the B team or a brewery worker. They land one of those, they've hit pay dirt. So they play around a little, sure—work in the bar, go out with this guy or that. Hell, some of 'em even go out with police officers." He snorted. "But they land the big fish, it's all over. Those pretty ladies know which side their bread is buttered on, believe me."

"So you're saying that Shandie has a boyfriend, and that's why she's scared?" Bern repeated.

"That's exactly what I'm saying. Steve Ostikoff. Brewery worker, son of the brewery manager. That's like Kootenay Landing royalty. To a girl like that, barely got through high school and only has her looks going for her? That's like a guarantee for life: nice new house, two-point-one kids, new minivan every three years, and ladies' golfing every Tuesday night till the day she dies." Resnick stubbed his cigarette into a black plastic ashtray tucked beneath his chair.

"I still don't get it," Bern insisted. "Why would she be afraid of working in the bar?"

"Oh, that's easy. Doesn't want any rumors to start. Doesn't want to mess it up for herself. And with you especially. You've got quite a reputation as a ladies' man. She probably didn't want you to think you could hit on her."

"I don't hit on women," Bern said quietly.

Resnick laughed again. "So what do you call it, then?"

"Appreciation." Bern smiled. "I appreciate them."

"Okay, then, let's say she didn't want your appreciation. Doesn't make her a rape victim, though."

The silence fell over them again. They both watched the unfolding of yet another perfect day in the valley. The rain from the day before gave the air a thick, fresh smell, like towels hung out on a clothesline. In the distance a tractor circled a field.

"How do you know all this?" Bern asked.

Resnick shrugged and sipped at his coffee. "Learned it the hard way. She's too young for me, of course. But by God she's something to look at. Breaks a man's heart looking at a girl like that, don't you think?"

Bern tilted his head. "I prefer women with more experience in life. I find it makes them more, let's say, interesting."

Resnick laughed. "Well, good for you. But me? I like 'em just as gorgeous as in the magazines." Resnick raised a strong, tanned arm and rubbed at his crew cut with his hand. "Made a complete ass of myself, of course. I'm over forty and she's barely twenty. Idiot."

"That doesn't explain the marks, though." Bern watched Resnick carefully as he said this.

"Okay, I'll bite. What marks?" he asked.

"Little circle-shaped scars on her stomach, the size of cigarette burns. She kept pulling her shirt down, but you know how the young ones dress these days. Lift an arm up and you can see everything. I saw the marks when she was putting away glasses. I counted ten of them."

Resnick thought for a long moment. "No. I'm not convinced. Could be anything, right? Hives, chicken pox, allergic reaction. Who knows? Shandie's a good kid. She's snagged her fish and she's not going to let anything mess it up. Whole other story from Belinda. We got toxicology back on her, I tell you that?"

Bern tilted his head and raised his eyebrows.

"Everything in her system. Unbelievable. Alcohol, cocaine, Valium. Fact of the matter is, she choked on her own vomit. And no wonder."

"So you think she did this to herself?" Bern asked.

"Nah, nah, of course not. There was someone else involved all right. We just don't know that there was foul play. Here's my theory: She was in over her head in Fort McMurray. Gavin's gone, Brad Acer turns out to be a mean bugger, and her crack habit is getting out of hand. She decides to give up the party life, runs back to her boyfriend—Gavin Grayson, her own big fish. She gets to town here, and she stops for one last drink at the bar, maybe a hit of something. Meanwhile, Brad's mad as hell because she dumped him and stole his cash. He chases her down. They have one last party somewhere here in Kootenay Landing, it all gets carried away, and she dies. End of story. People from out of town bringing their problems here and expecting us to figure out their messes for them. That's what this is about. Nothing home-grown going on here—especially no serial rapists."

Bern did not reply, just sat, sipping his coffee. Finally he said, "If you say so, Resnick."

"I say so."

"You got the Grayson thing all worked out too?" he asked.

"Matter of fact, I do," the officer replied, standing up. "Operator error. It's what I told the WSB lady when she called me on Friday. Stupid idiot didn't lock out and it's his own damn fault. She agreed. It won't be long before they file their report."

"You don't think there is an awful lot happening around that brewery? Gavin dead in the bottle washer. His girlfriend found in the neighboring field. An alarm going off mysteriously. Evie—" Bern stopped himself. He didn't want to talk about Evie.

"We've searched that brewery top to bottom twice now. We've found nothing. No crack pipes, no brown couches, no serial rapist. And no evidence of what happened to your Evie." Resnick looked right at Bern with his dark, shiny eyes. "You got some evidence that shows otherwise, you come back and see me, okay? Meantime, my investigation shows two things: one, an idiot who didn't lock out when he should have, and two, a party that got out of control."

Bern stood and nodded. "So back to the garden and the old ladies for me, right?"

"Damn straight, Bern. Stick to heart attacks and strokes. And ladies with life experience, as you call them, and we'll be just fine."

Bern thanked Resnick for the coffee and hopped down the two steps to the grass, loping along the worn trail back to his truck. *If only it were that simple. If only.*

Constable Schilling was the only one at the station when he arrived. She nodded to him from behind the receptionist's desk.

"Help you?" she asked.

Bern smiled. "I was just out at Resnick's, talking to him about the cases," he said.

"Yeah," she said. "Slow day around here today too. Major crimes guys got called back to Cranbrook. Might be a few days before we see them again. If ever." She shrugged and hitched her belt up.

Bern was amazed she could breathe with that thing strapped to her. She looked like a little girl playing police dress-up. "You happy with the conclusions being reached in this case? Young woman with a crack addiction and a party gone wrong?"

Schilling narrowed her eyes at Bern. "In police school, they teach us to listen to orders and follow where the evidence leads."

"And ignore your womanly intuition?" he asked with a smile.

She smiled back. "Sometimes it's good to listen to that. But sometimes it gets you in trouble."

"But the whole lingerie thing—that worked out, right?" He leaned on the front counter and played with the edge of a pile of victim assistance brochures that were stacked there.

She tapped something into the keyboard in front of her. It looked to Bern as though she was done with this conversation. But he wasn't.

"Have you tracked down their families yet?" Bern asked.

She stopped tapping and looked up at him. "You were just talking to Resnick?" she asked.

He nodded but did not elaborate further. He *had* been talking to Resnick, after all. She didn't need to know that her superior officer had been less than forthcoming.

"Sad, really. Gavin doesn't have much family to speak of. An elderly aunt in a care facility outside of Saskatoon. Belinda took off from her family in New Brunswick the day after she finished high school. This is the first they've heard of her in over seven years," Schilling said. She rolled her chair back and looked up at Bern. "Tragic, really."

"How'd you find all this out?" he asked.

"Belinda's old roommate. She was a fountain of information," she said.

"Oh, really?"

She nodded. "I'm not going to risk following my intuition

on this one," she said. "But since you're the coroner, I can't deny your official request for a copy of my investigation notes." She tilted her head at him. "Are you requesting?"

"I'm requesting," he said.

She nodded and stood up, holding her notebook. She left through the door that led to the squad room and came back a few minutes later with a sheaf of photocopied pages.

"Roommate's phone number is in there," she said as she held the stack out to him.

It was close to noon by the time her neighbor dropped her off at the back gate of the brewery. She stood outside and took in the deserted lot. Not one car. It would be hours before the first workers showed up and started up the boilers for the week's production.

Inside that building were her car keys, her wallet, her cell phone, the passkey that would get her into the building itself, and her laptop, which would give her something to do at home, other than stare out the window. She had felt many things about the brewery over the years she'd worked there. Usually it was pride—pride in the company, pride in the team she was part of, and pride in the product they brought to market. Other times she'd felt wonder at the intricate system of which she was such a small part. Many times she'd felt annoyed by or downright angry at some safety violation that she'd come across while walking into work: the driver of the spent grains truck not wearing a high-viz vest or a transport truck parked in front of the fire hydrant.

She had never before felt fear. But she felt it now.

She punched the code into the gate and pulled the handle. It did not open. She tried it again, with the same result. She punched the numbers in hard a third time and pulled the handle. When the door did not open, she fell back on it in frustration. Of all the days to change the security code.

She closed her eyes and leaned her forehead against the gate. She could call her neighbor back from a pay phone—there was one not far away—and get a lift home. But then what? Spend the afternoon and evening staring at the bare walls, broiling bread in the oven to make toast, and boiling water in the microwave for tea? She needed to get on with life, and with work. And in order to do that, she needed her purse, her keys, her laptop, and her vehicle.

She lifted up her head and squared her shoulders. She would not cry. She would not. There were plenty of people who would be willing to help her; she could go to almost any house in the block behind her and ask one of the employees to lend her his passkey. But then she'd have to explain. And she really did not want to do that.

She scrunched her eyes shut, but the tears started to fall anyway. There was really only one place she could go. One place where she would not have to explain. She turned from the gate and started walking along the path at the side of the road. She'd taken only a few steps when the rear bumper of her SUV came into sight. A few steps more and she could see the fake brick siding of Bern's house and the back of his white truck, which was parked in the driveway. He was home.

· · ·

"You don't sound like a Kitty," Bern said to Belinda Carlisle's former roommate when he got her on the phone.

She chuckled and said, in a strong voice infused with intelligence, "What do I sound like?"

"Let me see. You sound more like . . . an Anne or a Joan." Bern wished he could meet her in person, to see for himself. But Fort McMurray was a long way away.

"A Catherine, maybe?" she asked.

"Yes, I suppose a Catherine. Is that your real name?"

"Well, it was my name when I was born. But I've been called Kitty for so long, I consider it my real name now. So what can I do for you, Mr. Fortin?"

"I'm just looking into a couple of questions around Belinda's death," he said.

"You know that the police were here and asked me all about it? And I spoke with another officer on the phone?" she asked.

He put his feet up on the coffee table and leaned back on his couch. "I have the notes from their talk with you. There are just a few things I want to ask. Okay?"

He heard her whisper to someone else in the room, but he couldn't make out the words. A few seconds later she came back on the line. "Sorry about that, my niece is here. She's glad you called, because I'm going to let her watch TV while we talk. So we're all set. I've got exactly eighteen minutes to talk to you," she said.

Bern laughed. "Thanks. Can you start by telling me about Belinda? You said to the police that she had changed in the past few months. What was she like when you first knew her?"

There was silence on the line for a moment. When her voice

came, it was strong and clear. "When I first met Belinda, I would have described her as a tomboy. Which is funny, because she looked so girly—I mean, she was all blond hair and blue eyes and curvy figure. Looking at magazines and movies, you would get the idea that guys go for skinny girls. But I can tell you that guys around here went crazy for Belinda."

"How did she take the attention?" Bern asked.

"To tell you the truth, she thought it was funny. Belinda was really into football. She loved watching football and talking about it. She could talk about it for hours, like one of the guys."

"That must have made her pretty popular," Bern said.

Kitty laughed. "Yeah, it did. But I don't think that's why she did it. I just think she really loved football. That's why she and Gavin got along so well. He loved it too."

"Tell me about them," Bern said.

"Oh, it's so sad to think they're both dead. I still can't believe it. Gavin was like a big teddy bear, and just as innocent. If I had to think of a word for him, it would be *well-intentioned*. He just wanted people to do well and be happy, and if he could help, then he did. He was simple too. I mean, he was happy with simple things. He didn't want all that much out of life that he couldn't have," she said.

"What did he want?" Bern asked.

"He wanted to have a job that he did well at, a good income, a nice house, a few kids. And he wanted Belinda."

"Did Belinda want the same things?" he asked.

She sighed. "Well, that's the sad part. I think she did want the same things—eventually. But Gavin wanted them right away. I think Belinda just wasn't there yet. And the more he pressured her, the more she rebelled. It went on for months. There was a lot of drama—fights and breakups. And that's when Belinda discovered cocaine."

Bern waited to see if she needed prompting or would just keep talking. After a moment, she started up again.

"You know, this is the oil patch. There's lots of coke around. People working overnights and long shifts—they do what they can to stay awake. And it spills out in the town—the bars, the social scene. It's easy to find if you want it."

"Did Belinda want it?" Bern asked.

"Yeah, she did. It's funny, because it was Gavin who first introduced her to coke. He was on his way to a twenty-four-hour shift and shared some lines with her before he left. When he got back, she was still awake. And her addiction—like that." Bern heard her snap her fingers into the receiver. "Instant addiction. She went downhill fast."

"Did she stick with coke?" Bern asked. He thought of the concoction of substances listed in the toxicology report.

"No, she did whatever she could. Alcohol, coke, but later crack, amphetamines, Valium. Within two months, she went from a fun tomboy to a sniveling crackhead." Kitty's voice faded away for a minute.

"And Gavin? How did he take it?"

"Gavin got the job in Kootenay Landing, and he thought that would save them both. Clean living, away from the pressure of the oil patch. But he left over a month ago. Belinda still had to work for a month—not that she was doing much of anything. Gavin didn't see what the last month was like for her," Kitty said. "Or for me, for that matter," she added. "If she hadn't told me she was leaving, I would have kicked her out. My brother is a single dad, and I help him out when he's on night shift. My niece is here a lot. Belinda and I used to be close, but by the end, I didn't want her anywhere near me or my family."

Bern allowed the silence to fill the line, waiting to see if she would say anything more.

"Look, my eighteen minutes are almost up," she said finally. "And most of what I've told you, I've already told the police."

"Yes, I know," Bern said. "But it really helps to hear it from you directly. Can I ask you about one last thing?"

"Uh-huh," she said.

"Did Belinda go for rough sex?" he asked.

"The police asked me that too, and I'll tell you what I told them. The Belinda I knew, my friend Belinda, was looking for a companion. Someone to take care of her, someone to laugh with, and someone to beat in the football pool. Her sex life—it was just part of the package, and from what I know of it, pretty ordinary. But the other Belinda—the one on a downward spiral that no one could stop—she would have done anything for more drugs. Anything," she said, her voice fading away.

When she spoke again, her voice was choked with tears. "I was hoping that she would turn it around when she got to Kootenay Landing. That she would clean up her act, and they would work it out. They were good together, Gavin and Belinda."

"I'm really sorry you lost your friends," Bern said. He stood as he said it and wandered over to the window. Evie's SUV was still parked in front of his house, and he wondered yet again if she was doing all right. But just as he thought it, he saw her walking toward his house. Her shoulders were hunched and he saw her brush at her eyes.

"Look, my time's up. Was there anything else?" Kitty asked.

He had forgotten he was still on the phone with her. "No, that's it. Thanks for your time. You've been a big help," he said as he hung up.

He took long strides to the door and was out on the steps in his bare feet. He watched Evie approach, tears streaming down her face.

"I'm sorry," she said, when she reached him. "I had nowhere else to go."

He took her arm and led her inside. "Then I'm glad you came here," he said.

From: Troy Thompson [tthompson@soldiersally.ca]
To: Bern Fortin [bernfortin@bccoronerservice.bc.ca]
Re: The real story
Sent: Sunday, September 13, 5:42 p.m.

Dear Lieutenant-Colonel (Ret.) Fortin,
You can answer my questions by email, if you prefer.

Is what they are saying true? I've attached a piece
we ran on some unconfirmed reports about the circum-
stances surrounding your retirement.

I can't believe you would walk away from Captain Alais
like this. I've spoken to some of your men. They speak
highly of the principled officer you used to be. What happened to the man they knew?

I plan to find out.

Troy
Troy Thompson
Editor in Chief
Soldier's Ally Magazine

22

She slept well into evening. Bern sat in the armchair adjacent to the couch and kept watch, staring out the front window. He could see the intricate roofline of the brewery from where he sat. Gradually the sky behind it turned to a deeper blue and melded with the mountains in the background and the geometric roof in the foreground.

He turned his head and watched Evie's sleeping figure. She was a quiet sleeper, peaceful. He suspected it was the most sleep she'd had since the Wednesday before, when she'd spent the night curled in that same position, on that same couch, under that same throw.

He dared not turn on a light, or even move around too much, for fear of waking her. He laid his head back, closed his eyes, and allowed the images to come. They were upon him instantly and it was almost a relief to let them be.

They made a familiar parade. Rwanda came first, showing herself in thick lush forests, rows of tea crops lining the hillsides, groups of smiling children in the countryside, innocent and unaware of what was to come. Like flipping a calendar page, the scene shifted. April 6, 1994. The bodies were before him again.

Bloodied and piled in ditches by the side of the road. Some still blinking, injured beyond hope, terrified, waiting silently for death to take them. The weight of the limbs as he took them in hand, the slick of blood, the stench—no passing of calendar days would erase these from his mind. He touched them not to help them— they were beyond help—but to pull them out of the middle of the road so that their UN jeep could pass. He laid them as gently as he could at the side of the road with a whispered "God our Father." He could not remember the whole prayer, and in any case it was too long for so many dead. He did not have the time.

The images came frame by frame and he did not resist, though he tensed as the haunted slideshow progressed. He knew what was coming. The child.

The ringing of the phone tore him from his gruesome reminiscence. He was on his feet in seconds, crossing the room in two bounds before it could ring again and wake Evie.

"*Oui, allô?*"

"*C'est moi.*" The voice on the other end of the line was subdued. "*Ça va?*"

Colonel Sauvé. "*Ce n'est pas une bonne journée aujourd'hui,*" Bern said, equally subdued. *Not a good day today.*

"*Moi non plus.*" *Me neither.* "*Mais je suis toujours là.*" *But I'm still here.*

A thread, thought Bern. Frayed and delicate, but strong enough, perhaps, to hold them both. "*Moi aussi,*" he whispered. *Me too.*

"*Bonne nuit, Lieutenant-Colonel.*"

"*Toi aussi, Colonel.*"

Bern hung up the phone and stood quietly over his desk, breathing deeply. The emotions passed through him like a bullet, the pain burning and coursing its way through his torso. He forced his breath to steady and slow and hung on in his mind to one small thought: it will pass. His eyes settled on Evie. The peaceful rise and fall of her breathing, her tiny features, almost unformed like a child's, more relaxed than he'd ever seen them.

It did pass, but the shame left in the wake of the violent emotional ambush was stronger than ever. Like a tourniquet compressing his ribs. *How could you?*

"Who is that who calls you every night?" Evie's voice seemed to float from another world.

He turned, his heart pumping fast, his throat as dry. He took a moment to focus on her face in the shadows. Her hands moved to pat her hair and she laughed. "Good thing there are no lights on," she said. She stood and made her way slowly to the bathroom.

While she was gone, Bern paced the house. He turned on a few lamps, closed the blinds, and ended up in the kitchen, where he pulled out a cutting board and a skillet. Gradually, he could breathe more freely, but the weight was still there. Manageable, but there. The weight of guilt and shame. The weight of the dead.

"You must be hungry," he said as she came back into the room. "Come sit at the table and keep me company. I'll make us a little snack."

He felt her watching him as he worked. The tomato he'd picked on Friday night, in anticipation of a midnight snack with her, was still sitting on the counter.

"Are you a vegetarian?" he asked.

She shook her head.

"Good," he said, "because what I am about to make you has been known to make at least three vegetarians change their minds."

He liked the sound of her laugh. He opened the fridge and

pulled out a paper-wrapped bundle from the local butcher shop. He heated the skillet and laid thick slices of bacon across it when it was spitting hot.

"Are you going to tell me who calls you every night?" she asked. "An admirer?"

Now it was his turn to laugh. He lifted the corner of a slice of bacon with a fork and then laid it back down. "It's my former commanding officer. From when I served in Rwanda," he said. "We check on each other."

"Every day?" she asked.

He looked at her and nodded, felt the tears building up behind his eyes. He turned each piece of bacon with a fork and moved them around in the pan. Center to the sides, sides to the center.

"When was that?" she asked.

"Rwanda?" he asked. When she nodded, he said, "In nineteen ninety-four."

She didn't say anything more, just watched as he laid tomato slices thick as flak vests on a plate. Next he sliced four even thicker pieces of bread from a loaf Mrs. Kalesnikoff had left him earlier in the day. He put these on the plate next to the tomatoes and brought it to the table. Returning to the kitchen, he turned off the bacon and set the pieces on some paper towel to drain. He put pepper and salt grinders on the table, along with mayonnaise, butter, two knives, two plates, two wine glasses. He uncorked a bottle of cabernet franc and left it on the counter.

"One important ingredient left," he said.

"Must be lettuce," she said with a smile. He picked up a small metal bowl and a tiny pair of clipping scissors.

"Come with me," he said.

The night garden drew them in. The soil soft under their bare feet, they made their way through the jungle of tomatoes to the rows of greens.

"How do you know where you're going?" Evie whispered behind him.

He chuckled. "Practice," he said. He put a hand back as he stopped at the row of mesclun greens. Her shoulder pressed into his palm and she stepped back in surprise. "Hold the bowl?" he asked. He handed it to her and she crouched down next to him as he filled it with lettuce. Then he reached a little further into the row and snipped a few fragrant leaves from a neighboring plant.

"What's that smell?" she asked.

"Secret ingredient," he said. "When combined with the bacon, it gets the vegetarians every time."

"When we get back inside, you'll have to tell me what it is," she said, standing. He stood too, towering over her by more than a foot. They were quiet for a minute, and Bern felt a breeze blow over them. The branches of the willow tree by the creek rustled and swayed. He sniffed.

"Can you smell that?" he whispered.

"What?" she asked just as quietly.

He took another deep breath and let it travel through him. He felt the weight on his chest loosening a little more. "Fall," he said. "It smells like fall. Come on, let's go inside."

Once there, they assembled their sandwiches. "They say you should eat whole grain bread," Bern said. "But with a true BLT like this, I find it's best with the whitest bread you can find."

"And basil," she said, digging through the pile of rinsed greens and rolling a leaf between her fingers. The scent filled the air between them.

She took the first bite and smiled. He nodded then and took

a bite of his own sandwich, watching her all the while. She ate slowly and seriously, the sandwich bigger than both her hands. The dark circles under her eyes seemed darker than when he'd first met her, but apart from that, she seemed to show no ill effects from her ordeal. At least none that he could see.

When she pushed away her plate, a few crusts still remaining, he looked at her seriously. "Now we need to talk," he said. "Tell me about your husband."

She looked up at him with those impossibly lavender eyes. "I was going to tell you sooner," she started. "At first it didn't matter, and then, when I thought it might matter, it seemed too late to say anything."

"And now?" he asked.

"And now he's gone. Again. He left nearly two months ago to visit family in Fort McMurray. Then he decided to stay. He wants me to move up there with him."

He pushed his own plate away. He'd barely touched his sandwich. "Do you want to go?"

She shook her head slowly, her face sad. "No. No, I'm not going. But he left while I was locked in the brewery. He took everything that he considered his: the couch, the sheets, the kettle." Her eyes filled with tears as she whispered his final transgression: "He took Rory."

They sat with this terrible truth between them. Finally, Bern said simply, "He took too much."

She nodded and smiled through the tears that had spilled over. "That pretty much sums it up."

He stood and gestured for her to do the same. He filled their wine glasses and they moved to the living room. She took a seat on the couch and he sat across from her in the armchair.

"Do you want to tell me more about him?" Bern asked once they were settled.

She shook her head firmly. "I don't want to talk about it anymore right now."

He looked at her over the top of his wine glass, the circles under her eyes even darker in the lamplight. He wished he could spare her, but there was more they needed to discuss. "Can we talk about something else, then? About who would want to kill you?"

She looked away, then up at him. "I've thought about it nonstop. I just don't know what happened," she said.

"But you heard footsteps?" he asked. "You heard the bar fall into place?"

She nodded slowly. "I thought I heard those things," she said. "No, I'm sure I did. And when I was in there, I thought about all the strange things that have happened—with Gavin, and then the alarm that went off that night, and—" She paused, looking up at him with wide eyes.

"And?" he asked.

"And Belinda," she said thoughtfully. "That happened so close by."

"Anything else?" he pressed. He thought he saw her flinch.

"Nothing else," she said firmly.

"Has anything happened in the past that seems to fit in with these events? I mean, something that maybe seemed odd at the time but stands out now?"

She gave this some thought, fingering the stem of her wine glass. "I can't say that I can think of anything. We've had trouble with that back door before, with it getting left unlocked. It's just carelessness, though. Lots of people go in and out that way.

People who live around here and walk to work. And employees who smoke—they go out that door to take a smoke break."

"How many people have a key to that door?" he asked.

She shrugged. "Conrad will have a record of that. Lots, though. Most of the employees, staff. Just about everyone. It's a key card, though, not an actual key. Programmed for the different doors, depending on who uses what door." She sighed and took a sip of wine. "It all seems so unreal. I mean, it's a brewery. We make beer. What is there to kill someone over?"

Bern shrugged. "I've seen people killed for less," he said.

"I'll keep an eye out and see if anything strikes me as odd. But unless someone is mad because I made him wear safety glasses or audited his department . . . I mean, that's the kind of thing I do that pisses people off." She broke off and yawned. "I can't believe I'm still tired," she said.

He stood quickly. "You'll sleep here," he said firmly. "All night this time, so you get some decent rest."

She didn't argue with him. She just nestled back into her spot on the couch. "I was hoping you'd say that," she said. She yawned again and lay down, pulling the blanket up around her. "For some reason I have no trouble sleeping here."

Bern turned out all but one of the lights and sat in the armchair again. "Shall I tell you about Colonel Sauvé?" he asked.

"Please do," she replied.

And so he began, the words rolling off his tongue effortlessly in French. He did not know if she understood a word, but it didn't matter. She was already asleep.

From: Karl Ostikoff [plantmgr@bugbrew.ca]
To: All employees; all staff
Re: Brewery security
Sent: Monday, September 14, 7:03 a.m.

Hello everyone,
Due to several events of a concerning nature over the
past few weeks, we are stepping up security precautions
at the brewery.

Please see Conrad in the lounge during your break
today to have your key card updated. You can also get
the new combination to the back gate lock at that time. If
you must be at the brewery off shift or over the weekend,
please remember to reset the alarm and lock all the doors
when you leave.

We are counting on every one of you to take steps to
keep this brewery secure at all times. Thank you for your
cooperation.

Cheers,
Karl
Karl Ostikoff
Manager
Bugaboo Brewery—A BevCo Company

23

God, but the smell was disgusting. Monty Osgoode raked the spent grains from the bottom of the enormous trough. The mounds of sticky, fermented barley fell through the tines of the rake and into the wheelbarrow. The smell wafted around Monty in a thick cloud. He held his breath and raked faster.

Behind him, the cows crowded around the closed gate, pressing up against each other and watching Monty with their slow, careful eyes. They knew when the grains truck was coming, though Monty could not figure out how. Maybe they felt its rumblings along the flat dirt road that stretched from the farm to the base of the hillside that led to town. Or maybe the wind carried the smell down to them when, up at the brewery, the grain truck driver opened the valve of the spent grains tank and started filling the dump truck that would bring their favorite treat to them.

Fucking cows. Monty couldn't wait to be free of them. Just one more year. Of course, his dad didn't think so. But Monty knew he was never meant to be a farmer. He liked books and science. Farming is science, his father told him. The science of food and soil. There's no more important science than that.

Monty scraped the flat edge of the back of the rake along the bottom of the trough. Several black clumps clung stubbornly to the edge. Monty pressed at them impatiently.

The cows stared absently back at him. Stupid animals. It was their fault he was stuck on this farm in the middle of nowhere when all his friends, and Sheila Watkins, the girl he'd been dating for two weeks, having had a crush on her for three straight years, lived way up on the hill in town. Town kids, his father called them dismissively. You are a farm boy.

He'd known, when he stayed in town after school every day last week to study in the library with Sheila, that his dad would give him extra chores to do. "Get it real clean. Don't want the cows getting sick," his father had said. Monty, who knew the trough hadn't been cleaned in several months, bit his tongue. If the cows were going to get sick, they would have done so by now, he thought.

The cows began to murmur impatiently behind him. The fog of the morning pressed up against him, wetting his clothes, even though it was not raining. Normally he could see the fence of mountains behind town, could pick out Sheila's large house on the ledge of the hill. Today he could not even see to the main road. The cows hemmed in closer to the gate, their rumps bumping into each other. The truck must be getting closer. He quickly grabbed the hose and started to hose down the last bits of grain.

One lump of grain refused to budge. He held the hose directly over it, poking at it with his gloved hand. A hard object moved beneath his fingers. He held the hose closer and watched as the blackened grain fell away. Monty looked, trying to make out what it was. He reached down to pick up the object just as the dump truck backed into view.

A moment later, Pen jumped down from the truck. He wore the same blue coveralls that all the brewery workers wore. He had a skinny, greasy ponytail of gray hair that hung out the back of his Bugaboo baseball cap.

"Mornin', Monty," Pen called out cheerfully. "Help me with the gate?"

Monty walked up and unhitched the gate. He swung it open from the inside.

"How come you're not at school?" Pen called back to him.

"Had to muck out the trough," Monty called as he slid the leather strap over the gatepost to hold the gate open. The cows watched their movements deliberately, knowing from experience not to get in the way.

"Old man givin' you trouble?" Pen asked, coming around the truck and handing Monty a delivery slip. Monty folded it carefully and slipped it into his pocket.

"Nah, he's all right," he replied. "Say, Pen?"

"Yeah?"

"I found this in the trough. Any idea what it is?" He held out the lock for Pen to see.

"Well, I'll be! Good thing one of the cows didn't eat it." Pen rubbed it against his coveralls until most of the spent grain was gone from the lock. "There, good as new. L. Ostikoff, it says. Hell, Leroy hasn't worked there in months. Well, it's a brewery lock for sure. Wonder how it ended up out here."

Monty shrugged. He had to get a move on if he was going to get to school before the end of first period. He was definitely going to have to go in and shower. Sheila would not sit anywhere near him at lunchtime, or ever again, if he went to school stinking of spent grain.

"Can you get it back to them, you think?"

"Sure thing, son. No problem. Now you get going. I'll finish up here and close up the gate when I'm done."

Monty hesitated, but only for a moment. He nodded. "Thanks, I'll do that."

He walked around the cows and out of the gate. He'd parked his beater truck off to the side, and he jumped in it now and headed back to the farmhouse. His dad liked someone from the family to stay for the delivery, but if he hurried, Monty might still make it to school on time.

Evie's next trip to the basement was quick and uneventful. Armed with a notebook, a pen, and Conrad, she ducked down the stairs just before the end of the day on Monday.

"Stand right there and hold this door open," she said to Conrad. She pulled on a toque, switched on the lights. She shivered as she walked to the end of the cellar.

"So how do you think you got locked in here?" Conrad called to her.

She didn't answer right away. Nothing had changed since Friday night. The same stale beer smell, the same rusty old tanks. She quickly noted the numbers on each of the water meters. On her way back out a flash of metal caught her eye and she once again noticed the shiny piping on the old tank.

"Thanks," she said as she pulled off her toque. "Are these tanks still used for production? They seem awfully old."

Conrad shrugged. "Sometimes in the summer, when we're

running at full capacity. We'll drop a smaller brew, like an ale or something, to age in here."

Evie jumped as the door groaned closed behind her.

"That was quite a scare you had. You sure you're okay?" Conrad asked as he secured the door.

Evie nodded slowly.

"Thing is, this lock really sticks. Someone would need to shove it down to get it to close," he said. "I just don't see how that could have been an accident."

"Me neither," she said. "And I don't want to talk about it anymore."

"Okay, fine. So is that it?"

"No. One more thing. Follow me." She led the way up the basement stairs and through the circuitous route of hallways that would take them to the maintenance supply room. Conrad talked the whole time.

The supply area was deserted. Evie felt silly dragging Conrad around with her, but she wasn't going to take any chances.

She went to the metal cabinet where all the workers kept their locks. The door was half open. She pulled it open all the way. The locks were on the top two shelves. Each worker had a set of eight, individually labeled with his name. Evie looked over all the locks and scanned the names. They were all there, including the set assigned to Leroy Ostikoff, which were the ones Gavin had been told to use.

She leaned forward into the cabinet and stared at the locks as if they might tell her something. Gavin had liked things just so, and she wondered whether he would have used the locks if someone had taken the time to change the labels and put his name on them. She took a deep breath and let it out with a sigh. Then she sniffed inside the cabinet. She sniffed again.

"Can you smell spent grains in here?" she asked Conrad.

He came closer and sniffed. "Ooh whee, can I ever. What are you looking for anyway?" he asked.

"I'm not totally sure," she replied.

She pulled out the small tray with Leroy Ostikoff's locks on it. She placed the tray on the counter and carefully inspected the locks. They had been sitting in the cabinet for years, used only on occasion.

"That's funny," Conrad said.

"What?"

"Leroy's locks. When I checked these the other day with the coroner"—he winked at her and waggled his eyebrows up and down—"one of them was missing. That one," he said, pointing to a lock at the front that was shinier than the others.

She picked up the shiny lock and turned it over. She sniffed again, then brought the lock right to her nose and smelled it. She held the lock up to the light and tried to look into the keyhole. "Smells like spent grains." She put the lock down again and reached for the key. Each lock had its own key tucked in next to it on the tray. Except for the shiny one. "Eight locks and seven keys," she said.

She picked up the key to the lock next to the shiny one and tried it on the shiny lock. It snapped open. She tried the same key on another lock at the back of the tray, and it opened too. She brought the key back to the cabinet, pulled up another tray of locks and picked up the first lock she could reach. She tried the key on that one, and it worked as well.

"Did you know about that?" she asked.

"What?"

"All the keys work on all the locks," she said quietly. "Anyone who has a key can open any lock."

"That is weird, Evie. Look, we'd better go. Karl wants everyone up in the lounge for that announcement. Five o'clock sharp," he said, looking at his watch. "Which is right now. C'mon, let's go. You don't want to be late."

Evie picked up the tray of locks and slid it back into the cabinet. She closed the doors and turned the handle to secure them.

"Thanks for your help," she said.

He nodded and led the way to the lounge. Evie walked behind him, thinking about one key that fit many locks and the implications of what she had just found.

A big-screen TV was set up in the lounge. All the management and staff were milling around it, beer in hand. On the screen was the smiling face of Dave Porteous, western vice president of BevCo. "I've called you all here for an announcement," he started, just as Evie and Conrad came in. "As you know, Karl Ostikoff has been the force behind Bugaboo's exemplary energy numbers for years. He's innovated a reduction in water consumption that is leading the pack in BevCo breweries worldwide. Really something to be proud of." Dave paused. "And now, I am pleased to let you know that Karl has been named the new vice president of energy for BevCo."

A murmur spread throughout the room. Several people near Karl started to clap him on the shoulders.

"Karl will be traveling to breweries all around the world,

advising them on how to follow Bugaboo's example of reduced water and energy consumption," explained Dave. "Congratulations on this well-deserved promotion. Here's to Karl!"

The room came alive with the buzzing of voices. Evie found an armchair slightly away from the crowd and sat down. She rested her glass of beer on the wide wooden arm.

"We'll be announcing your new brewery manager soon, so stay tuned for that news. And I have more news to share," he announced. "I made a call to the head of investigations at the WSB this morning—a guy I used to play squash with when I worked out west." He laughed. "Good to have friends in high places at a time like this. Anyway, he assured me that the report the WSB is working on will likely find the cause of the recent unfortunate accident to be operator error. Gavin Grayson did not lock out. The police are going to continue to investigate, to see if they can find out who started up the machine, and we will help them in any way we can, of course. But as far as my contact in the WSB is concerned, our safety management system was found to be thorough, complete, and beyond fault. And that is largely thanks to your own Evie Chapelle."

Everyone around her—Conrad, Gemma, and even Karl—raised their bottles and turned to face Evie. A chorus filled the room: "Here's to Evie!" Evie kept her smile firmly in place and took a sip of her beer. She held the liquid in her tightly sealed lips and swallowed it reluctantly.

From the screen, Dave continued: "Now, I know she probably drives you all crazy sometimes, with her procedures and her forms and her training. But this is why she does it, folks: for our own protection. We all know some people will go ahead and do their own thing, with tragic results, as we've seen here. It's Evie's job to protect us from all of that. And it's a job she does very, very well, I might add. We at corporate have noticed, Evie. And with that, I'll sign off now. Enjoy your celebration," he said. And the screen went blank.

Evie anchored the smile on her face and watched the party gear up around her. Conrad sat on one arm of her chair and held out a bowl of chips.

"They're baked, not fried," he said, smiling at her.

She took a handful and popped a few in her mouth. She hadn't eaten all day but was nowhere near hungry.

"Good work, Evie. Good work. I know we give you a hard time sometimes, but it's all in good fun, hey?" Conrad said.

"Just doing my job," she said hollowly.

"Ah, c'mon, Evie. Aren't you glad? It's all going to be okay. What's wrong now?"

"Nothing. Nothing's wrong, okay? It's just been a long week— and weekend. I'm tired." Evie crossed her legs and squeezed over to the far side of her chair.

Conrad looked at her seriously. "I've been wanting to say this to you all day, but I wasn't sure how." He ran his fingers through his hair and gave her that smile that got her every time. "Look, I'm sorry. When I got that call from the working-alone lady, I should have broken down every door until I found you myself." Evie watched a frown tug at his normally carefree features. "And when I saw your car outside his house, all the lights off, three in the morning, I drew my own conclusions. I called Dirk and then and went home to bed," he said. "I'm really sorry about every-thing."

Evie closed her eyes. "You know that he left, right? He took everything." Her voice broke. "He took Rory."

"Oh, Evie. I'm sorry. I didn't know he'd do that," Conrad said. "I was just mad. I was really hoping you two would make it, you know?"

"I know you were," Evie said. She ate a few chips and glanced around the room. Karl sat in another armchair across the room, deep in conversation with Gemma. He gestured grandly and almost knocked over a small wooden table holding a group of old trophies from Bugaboo-sponsored events. The largest of these, topped with a brass bathtub, was a remnant of the Bugaboo Bathtub Blazer—an event where teams soldered skis to ancient bathtubs of various shapes and sizes and raced them down the local ski hill.

Evie shook her head. Corporate would never let them get away with that kind of competition anymore, no matter how many waivers the participants signed. It just wasn't safe. She looked up to find Conrad studying her closely.

"You know, Evie, it doesn't have to be a bad thing. This WSB report—it'll be your ticket out of town. Corporate will sit up and take notice. Where do you want to transfer to? Head office? Travel the world doing safety audits? You can start all over again."

She stood up from her seat and turned to him. "Gavin died, Conrad. He can't start all over again. As far as I'm concerned, getting off the hook for his death is nothing to be proud of."

Evie walked away. She had to get out of there. But she only made it three steps before she bumped into Karl. His hair was perfectly brushed and his skin deeply tanned. He beamed at Evie with his too-white teeth. He pumped her hand up and down, dislodging a swag of bangs that fell in front of his eyes. There is something unnatural about a fifty-year-old man with a full head of blond hair, Evie thought. She clamped her smile back in place.

"Congratulations, Evie. Congrats. Good work." He continued to hold her hand and wrapped his other hand around her wrist, pulling her closer to him. Close up she could see lines around his eyes and the wrinkles across the width of his forehead. These were paler in the creases, where the rest of his face had tanned. There was puffiness under his eyes that she had never noticed before.

"You getting enough sleep, Karl?" she asked innocently.

"Ha!" Karl exclaimed. "Well, I was worried, I admit that." He tapped her gently on the forearm with his free hand and released her arm. Evie rubbed her wrist where he'd held it. "So I guess we should get this handover done, about the energy stuff. You got the files, right? I'm leaving in a week or so. Should we meet?" he said.

Evie bit back what she wanted to say. "That would be good, Karl," she said. "Sometime tomorrow? The audit is next week."

"Sure, sure, Evie. No resting on your laurels, hey? They'll like that in Toronto, or wherever you end up. Good for you. Sure, we can meet tomorrow," Karl replied. "How about after taste panel? I'll catch you there."

You never go to taste panel, she wanted to say. But she didn't. She followed him with her eyes as he walked away. She watched the line where his dress shirt tucked into his designer jeans until it was swallowed up by the crowd.

From: [capitaineallouette@hotmail.com]
To: [bernfortin@bccoronerservice.bc.ca]
Re: re: re: re: re: re: re: re: Bonjour
Sent: Tuesday, September 15, 6:35 a.m.

Lieutenant-Colonel,
I have only a minute. The class starts today and I have
only thirty minutes online every day to get things done.
I hope that those plants marched to your orders, and
that those tomatoes aren't giving you any more trouble.
Maybe when I get out I can come with Jeanette and the
girls to see you. I can give you a philosophy lesson, and
you can teach me how to be a good civilian, just as you
taught me to be a good soldier.

But first, I need to get out. I have to ask you, Lieutenant-Colonel—will you come and speak for me? Maybe you
will have no choice, if the lawyers have their way? But
what will you say? Everything depends on you.

Until next time,
Marcel Alais

24

After his breakfast with Mrs. K. and a full briefing on his duties and obligations over the coming days with respect to the fall fair, Bern set out on foot. Paperwork would still be there when he got back. He cut through the field between his house and the police station, pausing only briefly at the place in the trampled grass where Belinda's body had been found almost a week before. For most people who passed by here, life had returned to normal. He followed the path and allowed it to lead him past the park where the weekly farmer's market was held, to the back of the local community college and behind the grocery store.

He skirted the edge of the store and found himself in the parking lot. One block farther and he was on Selkirk Street, that odd and charming mix of storefronts that served the everyday and year-round needs of the population of Kootenay Landing, as well as those more whimsical needs of tourists just passing through. A person could pick up a roll of duct tape, some lumber, a hunting license and rifle, a pair of flowered rubber boots, a lawn ornament featuring a family of quails, jasmine-scented hand cream for gardeners, artfully packaged snacks of dried apple and pear chips, and a harvesting combine, all within one short block.

He was tempted to stop at Mountain Station, the gathering place for breakfast and lunch that was home to the only espresso maker in Kootenay Landing that Bern knew of, other than his own. He decided against it, though. He didn't know how much time he had.

He kept walking, picking up his pace. He moved off Selkirk Street onto a side street that slowly angled uphill. He passed the hospital and was soon on the wide, leafy residential streets that flanked the town. The suburbs, he chuckled to himself.

He found the house easily enough. It was, as Mrs. K. had said, quite large. Modern, tidy, and, as far as Bern could tell, rather ordinary. The clapboard siding was freshly painted sage green, the trim painted a deep green-brown color. The combination was appealing, and Bern paused to look at it, wondering if something similar might work on his own house. He'd been meaning to replace the fake brick siding ever since he'd moved in, but he was hampered by his limited knowledge of the options available. The desire for a home of his own had come to him rather late in life, and even then it was the garden, not the house itself, that had tipped the scales. But looking at this property, he could see the promise of something—something tidy and orderly—that he wanted for himself.

There was no garden to speak of with this house, just as Mrs. K. had said. But there was something welcoming about the artful arrangement of shrubs in the front yard, the carefully swept colored concrete pathway, and the folk art welcome sign hanging by the front door. This was the home of a family that was doing just fine.

Just then he caught a movement out of the corner of his eye. A lanky boy of about sixteen or seventeen was walking along the side of the house pushing a bicycle. He was wearing a helmet, the straps hanging loose around his pointed chin. The boy stopped when he saw Bern.

Bern smiled at him and held out his hands. "Brian?" he asked.

The boy looked over his shoulder and back, as though Bern might be talking to someone else. Bern walked toward him and stopped at the edge of the driveway. The boy's straight brown hair was raggedly cut and hung down past the edge of his helmet. His deep brown eyes were sunken into the hollows of his long cheekbones. He was almost as tall as Bern, and painfully thin. Bern was reminded of the ravenous hunger of his own teen years just looking at the boy: no matter how much he ate, he'd be thin and hungry, at least until he grew into himself.

"I came here to see you. Do you mind walking your bike for a bit so we can talk?" Bern asked.

Brian looked around again. "Okay?" he said.

Bern waited for the boy to reach him, and they walked together down the wide street toward the high school.

"My name is Bern Fortin. I'm your grandmother's neighbor," he said.

Brian looked up at him, eyes wide. "My mom and my grandma don't get along," he said.

Bern nodded slowly and waited for the boy to say more. When he didn't, Bern said, "I gathered something like that. How about you? Do you get along with your grandmother?"

He shrugged. "She's okay, I guess. She's kind of bossy. But she's sure a great cook," he said. "My mom gets so mad around her, though. It's just easier, you know?"

Bern nodded. "I know. I know what mothers can be like."

It wasn't a long walk back into town. A boy whizzed by on a

bike, headed fast down the hill. "Hey, Bri!" he called out. Brian looked around again, for a way out this time.

"I know you need to get to school. Listen, let me just ask you something: What if your grandmother needed help? Would you help her?" Bern asked.

Brian shrugged again, holding his bony shoulders up to his ears while his hands pushed down on the handlebars. He dipped his head down. "I guess," he said. He looked up impatiently, then stopped walking.

Bern nodded. "Good," he said. "Because she does need help. She needs help chopping wood."

"Chopping wood? What are you talking about? She can chop wood just fine," he said.

Bern shrugged slowly and raised his hands helplessly. "I know she says she can. And maybe she can. But me? I have trouble with the idea of a seventy-year-old woman chopping her own logs," he said. "I help her when I can, but the fact is, she misses you. You and your sister." He tilted his head to catch the boy's gaze. He looked at him carefully. On the surface, he did not look like his grandmother. But that glint of stubbornness in his eye was familiar.

Brian swung his leg over his bike and mumbled something as he adjusted the straps on his complicated backpack.

"Sorry, I missed that?" Bern said.

"I don't know how," Brian said, his voice low. "I don't know how to chop wood. She gets mad and tells me I'm doing it wrong." He snapped the helmet into place as he spoke.

Bern smiled. "Of course she does. But tell you what—how about I'll teach you? Just leave for school a little earlier a few days a week. Chop a few logs for your grandmother. Believe me, the cinnamon buns alone are worth it."

"Cinnamon buns?" he asked. His brown eyes brightened within the saucers of his cheekbones.

"As big as your helmet. Sourdough bread, pastries." He shrugged. "Chiffon cake sometimes, but only if you're really lucky." He jutted his chin toward Brian's backpack. "What have you got for lunch in that bag of yours?"

Brian grunted. "Didn't have time to make it today."

Bern nodded. "No doubt your grandmother would pack a lunch fit for a logger if she saw you out there chopping wood for her."

Brian hopped on his seat, placed his feet on the pedals, and squeezed the brakes, balancing himself in place. He smiled for the first time. "Okay. I will. One day soon, okay? Maybe next week."

Brian loosened his grip on the brakes and momentum took him swiftly downhill. With a few pumps of his legs he was at the corner of Selkirk Street, where he turned and was quickly out of sight.

Bern continued at his same slow pace. The view from this vantage point was one he rarely saw—the whole village and surrounding fertile valley in its lush green, late-summer splendor, safeguarded by mountains as far as the eye could see.

He pulled out his cell phone and punched in a speed-dial code.

"Claire?" he asked when the chief coroner's secretary answered her phone. "Can you do something for me?"

"Bern, is that you? Of course I'll help if I can," she replied.

"Is it possible to have call display set up on my cell phone?" he asked.

She laughed. "As long as you still answer when I call, then yes, of course. I can have it on there by this afternoon."

He thanked her and hung up. He allowed the slope of the hill to draw him into the idyllic scene that spread before him. He had time now for that cup of coffee.

The pounding became part of his dream. He dreamed of Gavin—the blistered stump of Gavin's arm, trying to pull itself out of the tank. Gavin was still alive, thrashing about in the caustic bath. If Steve could only get to him in time, he might keep him from being eaten alive by the chemical bath. But there was the sound of pounding, and as he approached the side of the bottle washer, he saw the angry eyes of his union brothers, pounding the side of the machine, yelling, "Killer!" Killer!" They blocked him from reaching the ladder and saving Gavin.

He woke up, drenched in sweat. The sound of shouting voices died away, but the pounding continued. The sun pushed up against the blinds and peeked in through the cracks, throwing an eerie light around the room. He looked at the clock: 8:57. He'd gotten off night shift at 7:00 a.m. and had been asleep for barely an hour.

"Steve! Open up!" a voice yelled from the front door.

Still shaken from the dream, he fumbled into a pair of jeans and crossed the living room. He eyed the empty beer bottles and dirty dishes on the coffee table, the pale comforter trailing off the drab couch and onto the floor, and the pair of dirty work socks lying on the unvacuumed carpet. All of it was evidence of how Steve spent his hours between shifts when he worked nights.

The brightness of the day, which flooded the dim room as he

opened the door, almost pushed him back. Karl Ostikoff stood on the stoop and flashed his brilliant-toothed grin at his son.

"You look like hell," he said, pushing past him and coming into the house.

"I'm on night shift," Steve said. "I just got to sleep."

Karl stepped over the socks, pushed the comforter away, and sat on the sagging couch. "So? Night shift is no reason to let yourself go all to shit, you know." He gestured around the room. "Your place is a mess!"

Steve didn't answer. He rubbed at his eyes and sat in the armchair across from his father, hanging his legs over the side.

"I don't understand why you had to buy this place anyway. It's not like we didn't have a comfortable place for you at home— your own apartment in the basement, for God's sake. Home-cooked meals provided for you, and someone to clean your place every week. I hate to see you living like this." Karl waved a hand over the mess as though he could make it disappear. He tugged at the creases in his jeans and sat forward, pointing a slender, tanned finger at Steve. "Your mother is heartbroken, you know. It just kills her to know that you live in squalor when she worked so hard to make your life nice. What kind of gratitude is that?"

Steve's mind clicked slowly through the possible answers. He finally settled on one and was forming the words in his sleep-starved mind when Karl continued as though he had never asked the question.

"You know, I did night shift for years. I loved night shift. I used to ask for it. The guys all knew that if they didn't want their night shift, I would trade with them. You, on the other hand, don't seem to be able to handle it. Two days into a week of nights and you're falling apart. I don't know if you have what it takes to work at the brewery in the long run. And God knows you're never going to make it in management, so you'll be doing shift work your entire career. Are you going to fall apart every three weeks for the rest of your life? I'm beginning to wonder if I should have recommended you for the job when you asked me to!"

At this, Steve sat straight up in his seat. Karl's eyes flashed and he sat back, brushing imaginary lint from his BevCo corporate tie. Seeing the gleam in his father's eyes, Steve took a deep breath and slouched back down in the chair.

"Why are you here?" he asked sullenly. "What do you want?"

"Ha! What do I want? I take time out of my busy day to come see you, and all you can do is ask what I want? Maybe I just wanted to come see my son, huh? Can't I just come see my son sometimes, since he never seems to come home anymore?" Karl said.

"What are you talking about? We just saw you guys the other night. And no, you can't come see me anytime. You can't come first thing in the morning when you know perfectly well that I'm on night shift!" Steve shouted. God, but he wanted to sleep for three years.

His father's version of events seemed to shift and change with the wind. Steve could never keep track, had stopped trying to figure it out. All he wanted was peace and quiet and a normal life. Sure, the house wasn't much, but it was his, and it was peaceful, except for when Karl decided to drop by unannounced. "So you pretty serious about that sweet little thing?" Karl asked.

Steve rolled his eyes and slouched some more. He did not want to talk to his father about Shandie. He shrugged. "She's nice."

Karl leaned forward on the coffee table and began to idly

sift through the piles of papers and magazines scattered on the scratched wooden surface. "I'm sure others would say the same." He chuckled under his breath, his voice so low that Steve could barely make out the words.

"What? What did you say? She's a nice girl, all right? A nice girl. That's all I want to say about it. And maybe you'd just better get used to the idea of her being around!" Steve sat up, his fists clenched. Karl simply chuckled again, sifting through the papers.

"Half the town knows where her tattoos are, that's all I'm saying. But look, you want to spend the rest of your life with a girl like that, go right ahead. That's not what I came to talk to you about," he said. He set aside the previous week's edition of the local paper, which had a four-page feature on the accident at the brewery. It had gone to press before Belinda's body was found. The local reporters, who normally covered curling bonspiels and kept the townspeople up to date on bridge and whist scores, were having a field day.

"So you did come for a particular reason?" Steve said finally.

Karl shrugged. His fingers closed around a sheet of white paper covered in drawings in black ink. Steve sucked in his breath and waited. He knew what was coming next.

Karl laughed out loud. "You still making your little comic books? You should give this up, you know. It's kid's stuff. You want people to take you seriously? You want people to know you are a grown man now, with prospects, a job, a house?" Karl looked around him with disdain. "Well, an investment anyway. And a girlfriend." Here he stopped and chuckled. "Anyway, you got to stop with this stuff. If the guys at the brewery knew you drew little pictures on your days off, they'd think you were the biggest pansy going. Get a hunting license. Go buy a quad for that truck of yours. Face the facts, Steve. This is your life now. Don't embarrass me and your mother. Christ, don't embarrass yourself." He curled his lip and tossed the page back onto the tumbled pile on the table.

Steve imagined the words floating off him, bouncing and scattering around him. He would not let them in. Not this time. He sat back up and pulled his hands out of his hair. He was sure he looked a mess; his hair was sticking up and he had a thick scrub of stubble across his cheeks. Looking a mess was the ultimate transgression to his perfectly groomed father.

"What did you come to talk to me about?" Steve asked.

"The lock," Karl replied.

Steve's eyes widened. "What lock?" he asked.

"It's okay. That's what I wanted to tell you. I looked after it. Little Monty Osgoode found it in the spent grains trough on his farm and sent it back up to the brewery. I just wanted you to know that I intercepted it before there was a fuss. I looked after it. It's all taken care of." Karl threw his hands up lightly, as though the problem were a fleck of dust, now scattered to the wind.

Steve exhaled and felt his bowels loosen. His stomach gurgled under his sweatshirt. "That's great, Dad," he said. "Of course, I have no idea what you're talking about, but I'm glad it's all looked after."

Steve stood and started walking to the door. Karl stood as well. "I know it was you, son. Who pulled the trigger, so to speak." Karl chuckled. "Pushed the start button that killed Gavin. Everyone knows it was you. But we're covering for you. You're part of the brewery family now, so don't worry about a thing. We'll look after you." He followed Steve to the front door. His polished shoes gleamed on the gray carpet.

Steve blocked the door. "Great speech about family and all,

Dad. But it wasn't me." Steve looked his father right in the eye as he said the words.

Karl flicked his hand impatiently, gesturing for Steve to move out of the way.

Steve glared at him steadily. "It wasn't me!" he cried out.

Karl laughed. "You didn't want me here, and now you're not going to let me go? What is this, Steve? You're not making much sense."

His stomach churned. He jerked the door open and let Karl pass. "It wasn't me," he said again lamely. He slammed the door behind his father and ran to the bathroom.

When the doorbell rang, Evie was hunched over a laptop at the makeshift workstation she had set up in the kitchen. A reflection of Bern's curls, magnified in shadow, bobbed on the strip of glass next to the front door.

When she opened the door, he cocked his head and smiled. He held a large cardboard box in his hands. "I hope you don't mind. I tried phoning. I wanted to make sure you were all right."

"Come in," she said, opening the door wider.

He followed her into the kitchen and placed the box on the counter. "My neighbor—I don't think you've met her? Mrs. Kalesnikoff is her name. She heard about what happened to you. She was worried, so of course she prepared food for an army and asked me to bring it to you." He unpacked the contents of the box as he spoke. "Borscht, of course. Believe me, this will cure what ails you. Sourdough bread, pickles, cookies . . . oh, and peaches. And the icing on the cake, so to speak." He reached into the box and pulled out two large jars. "Tomato soup. That's from me."

She stood watching him—so at home anywhere, it seemed, especially around food. Even in her kitchen, where he had never been before, he was perfectly at ease, putting food away and chatting as if he were in his own home.

He stopped talking and looked at her. "I'm sorry," he said.

"What? No, it's okay," she said.

"I just barge into your house and start talking away, opening your cupboards—which are very empty, I might add—like I live here." He put the loaf of bread he was holding down on the counter. "How are you, anyway?"

She laughed. "I'm fine, really. I am. Your neighbor is very sweet to do all this. But it's really not necessary. I'm okay."

He watched her carefully as she spoke, as though reading the undercurrent of her words. She must have passed some unspoken test, because he nodded and moved closer to her. "Can I make you a cup of tea?" he asked.

"How about I make you a cup of tea for once?" She stepped around him into the kitchen. The words came out automatically, then she regretted them. She was not sure she had anything to make tea in. She dug around in the back of the pot cupboard and pulled out a small double boiler. She'd bought it one time, planning to learn how to make chocolates.

Bern sat on the bar stool next to Evie's. As she stood, double boiler in hand, she saw him look around her bare house.

"He really didn't leave much, did he?" he said.

She filled the bottom part of the double boiler with cold water and placed it on the stove. "I finally talked to him. He's gone for good," she said. She came around the counter and sat on the stool next to his. She stacked up a pile of papers and placed them on the keyboard, then pushed the laptop out of the way.

"And Rory?" he asked.

"He says he's keeping Rory," she said. The tears started again, great silent ones. It was like a faucet was turned on every time she thought about Rory or heard his name.

He swiveled her stool seat toward him so their knees were touching. She looked down to see her sock feet dangling in the air, his firmly on the ground. He put his palm ever so gently on the side of her head, then slid it down slowly to cup her chin. They sat like that for a moment, without moving or talking. Evie closed her eyes.

The water boiled over and started to hiss. She jumped up to turned off the stove, then she clattered through the cupboards and pulled out two BevCo beer steins and a few tea bags.

"Blueberry tea," she read. "That's all I've got. It seems a shame to make it in these." She gestured to the beer mugs, then took a deep breath. "But they're all I've got as well."

"He took all the kitchen stuff too?"

She shrugged. "He mostly looked after the house. He bought everything for the kitchen—for the whole house, really. I just worked. And brought home beer glasses. And beer. I have lots of beer if you would prefer that?" she asked.

He laughed. "No, no. Tea is fine. But I'm betting you haven't eaten, and I haven't either. So how about I put together a little snack for us?"

She smiled. "That would be nice. And you can tell me how you've been. How are the cases going?" she asked. She handed him a beer stein of tea, then sat down and wrapped her hands around her own glass to warm them. She still felt cold all the time. She watched him as he made himself at home again in the kitchen. First he made a quick inventory of the minimal pots, plates, and utensils available. And then he got creative. He filled the lower part of the double boiler with borscht and set it on the stove to heat.

"I've mostly been concentrating on Belinda. Not sure if I'm getting anywhere. It's always kind of like that with an investigation—seems like you're going nowhere for a long time, and then all of a sudden you get somewhere." He sliced peaches as he spoke, using a cheese knife, and arranged them in the inverted lid of a butter dish. "Or you don't."

"Do they still have that guy from Kelowna in custody?" Evie asked.

He shook his head, his hand on his belt. At first she thought he was reaching for his cell phone, but he pulled out a pocketknife. "They had nothing on him. In fact, they can place him in Revelstoke a few hours before she died. The forensic pathologist puts her time of death sometime after nine at night. And he filled up with gas in Revelstoke at eight thirty. It doesn't look like he was ever here."

"No other leads?" she asked.

"Well, I spoke to Belinda's old roommate in Fort McMurray. She said that Belinda was on a short, fast downhill track with crack. And that Gavin got fed up with it. He came here to start again, and it sounded like she was going to join him and straighten herself out," Bern said. He sliced pickles with the pocketknife and arranged them in the lower part of the butter dish.

"And now they're both dead," Evie said thoughtfully. "It just doesn't make sense."

"You're right, it doesn't," Bern said. He reached over for a sip of his tea. He found two eggcups in the cupboard and took them out. Then he looked over at her. "Say, do you know someone named Shandie?" he asked.

"Sure, she gives tours of the brewery."

"And she works at the Kootenay Landing Hotel," he said. He sliced some cubes of cheese and filled one eggcup with them. He reached back into the box and came out with a handful of snap peas. These he rinsed and arranged in the other eggcup. "I was there the other night when she was working, and I noticed some scars on her stomach and lower back. They looked an awful lot like the cigarette burns on Belinda."

Evie pressed her hand to her mouth and looked at him in surprise. "You think—"

"It's hard to say. I told Resnick about it, but it doesn't sound like he's going to follow up. He likes the idea that Belinda was partying and it got out of hand. I might just talk to Shandie myself. But she lives with her parents. Maybe I can catch her at work?"

Evie moved her glass out of the way and pulled the laptop forward. She tapped quickly into the keyboard and opened a file. "She's working tomorrow, all day. You can probably catch her between tours," she said.

Bern smiled. "You give me an idea. Maybe I'll just go for a tour myself." He found the one plate that Dirk had left her and filled it with chunks of bread. Sipping the last of his tea, he gestured toward her cup. "Drink up," he said. "I need your glass."

Evie finished her tea as he arranged the various dishes on the counter. "It looks wonderful," she said. "You can put together a beautiful meal, even in an empty kitchen."

He served the borscht in the beer steins. "*Bon appétit!* You seem to have only one teaspoon. But luckily, I carry my own utensils wherever I go," he said, folding out a mini-spoon on his pocketknife.

They ate in silence for a few minutes. The borscht was thick and rich, with the tiniest hint of spice. "I can definitely see how this could heal the sick and wounded," Evie said.

Bern laughed. "I'll tell Mrs. K. that it brought you back to life. She won't be surprised, of course. But secretly she'll be pleased." He pointed to the laptop and the pile of papers that she'd pushed aside when he arrived. "What about you? I see you are working on something quite different. Water usage? Have you set aside the safety investigation?"

"BevCo procedure is that I need to submit a preliminary accident report within forty-eight hours. I sent that in last week. I can't do much more with it until we find out who started up the machine." She gestured with an open palm around the empty living room, dining room, and kitchen. "Meantime, I need to keep myself busy. I'm the lead on the environmental audit, which is coming up next week. So I'm getting ready."

"Do you want to talk about it?" he asked.

"Well, it's funny, you know. I was looking into the water numbers on Friday night. When I got locked in the cellar."

"Yes, I remember you told me that's why you were down there." His eyes did not move from her face as he spoke.

"I went back and checked the numbers yesterday. And there is really something off," she said.

"What kind of something?" He pushed his soup mug aside.

It would be good to talk it through, she thought, say her ideas out loud. "It used to take nine or sometimes ten liters of water to make a liter of beer. That's always been pretty standard in every

BevCo brewery I've worked in," she started. "It's called hectoliter per hectoliter—how many hundreds of liters of water it takes to make one hundred liters of beer."

Bern shrugged. *Fill your boots,* it seemed to say.

Evie continued: "It's a standard measurement in any brewery—not just BevCo. Everyone from the managers to the janitors knows it's an important number. Make the target—whatever it happens to be that year—and get a bonus."

"How do they measure it?" Bern asked.

"Well, that's the interesting part. At Bugaboo, it's by adding up all the water that goes out of the brewery—that is, the finished product and what went to drain at every stage of the process. We've always measured it going out—not coming in—and in one big lump volume. But the new measures that BevCo is implementing are going to change all that. They are separating it out into two numbers: how much water goes into making beer, and then how much wastewater is produced. So they need a new way to measure what comes in and what goes out."

Bern nodded. "Okay, I get it," he said.

"And not only that, but they want us to reduce both numbers—by a lot. The target was between nine and ten liters for ages. But they want to get it down to less than seven liters. Most breweries are struggling to get close to eight, but Bugaboo is already below seven. And we are the toast of BevCo. That's what this audit is about. They want to find out how we are doing it." Evie sighed. "And I'm going to be the one who has to tell them."

"You think the numbers are fudged somehow?" Bern asked.

"I think there is water missing somewhere, and people are asking the wrong questions. They think it's so great we've reduced our water usage, but they're not looking at how," Evie said.

"But how can they not be asking how? I mean, wouldn't they look for that right away? Look for problems and rule them out?"

"You see, that's one of the things I was thinking of when I was locked in that room. In this company right now, everyone is so busy trying to spin their numbers to corporate office, no one's really taking the time to look at what the numbers really mean. Every brewery, in the whole BevCo worldwide family, has been put on notice. Produce or we shut you down. We are pedaling as fast as we can just to keep up, for our own survival. They would never shut Bugaboo down if we've found a way to make a liter of beer using less than seven liters of water. Can you imagine if they were able to replicate that worldwide? What a savings it would be. And what a marketing coup—the world's greenest brewer! Imagine the market share, the profit."

"But you don't think it's right?" Bern asked.

"I don't see how it can be. The new measures come with masses of protocols—incremental changes in the brewing and bottling process. Tiny decreases in water use that add up over time. So that's what I'm doing now. Going back over time, through department meeting notes and process indexes for the past five years, trying to see how this reduction happened. And why." Evie scooped the last of the soup onto the teaspoon and savored it.

"Can you get that guy Karl to explain it to you?" Bern asked.

She laughed. "You know, he came to me yesterday about a meeting. Wanted to meet this morning after taste panel to go through it all. And of course, he never showed up. I looked everywhere in the brewery for him—I walked through each department—and it seems I just missed him wherever I went. It's been like that for weeks."

"So what do you think it is?" Bern asked.

"I think that somewhere in the system, water is going missing. There is more water coming in than is going out. That would explain the apparent low water consumption." Evie paused for a minute, thinking. "And once the upgrade happens, which is scheduled for a few months from now, and we start measuring both the water coming in and the water going out, we're not going to be able to hide it anymore. Corporate is going to come to me looking for answers."

As she'd been speaking, he'd quietly started cleaning up the kitchen. He arranged a plate, covered it with plastic wrap, and put it in the fridge. "A snack for later," he said. Then he continued: "See, that's what I don't get. I guess I just don't see the big deal over some water."

"Ah, but that's the thing. We're not talking about water. We're talking about money—a lot of money. If this blows open and it turns out that Bugaboo is underperforming, it would spell disaster for the employees—for the whole town of Kootenay Landing. BevCo could just shut the place down."

"So do you think someone is trying to keep this from coming out?" Bern asked as he wiped down the counter.

"I don't know. I've been thinking about this since I was locked in that cellar. I wondered why someone would want to lock me in there. But this would be a reason. If someone is trying to hide this," she said.

"Any idea who that might be?" he asked. The dishes done, he came and sat next to her again.

She looked up at him, wide-eyed, and shook her head. "None," she said.

"When it's about money, I always say look for the interest. Whose interest would be threatened if this came out?"

"If the Bugaboo Brewery were closed down, the managers would all be transferred elsewhere—other breweries, corporate office. But the employees would all be laid off. Over a hundred people. The ripple effect of that, in a town this size, would be disastrous," she said.

"So what are you going to do?"

Evie looked over his shoulder, out the dark windows. She'd thought of little else since she'd started piecing this together. "Do you remember when you asked about doing what my job said was right versus what my heart said was right? I thought about that a lot."

He shrugged. "I say a lot of things. Best to take them with a grain of salt. I'm certainly not one to be giving advice," he said.

She dipped her head and spoke quietly. "It wasn't advice. It was a question, or maybe an observation. A good one. And I've been thinking about it. I want to do what's right. The right thing. Not the right thing for the team or the company, but the thing I think is right."

He nodded. "Are you really prepared for that? The right thing is not the easy thing. And it looks like somebody is actively trying to stop this from coming out."

"I know," she said. "I'll be careful, but I'm not going to keep quiet for the good of the team anymore."

"Careful but brave. That's a fine line to tread," he said, shaking his head slowly. Sadness seemed to tug at his features, elongating his face. He looked at her straight in the eye. "I tried to walk that line one time, and I'm afraid I failed terribly. I erred on the side of careful."

"Is it too late to do something about that?" she asked.

"I'm not sure. It might be for me. But maybe I can redeem myself by helping you. Is there anything I can do?"

"There may be one thing," she said.

He raised his eyebrows and shrugged, as if anything she asked would be a simple matter he could take care of easily.

"I could get in so much trouble for this. But I know it's the right thing," she said. "Okay, here goes: I think that Gavin's training document was faked."

"Which one?" he asked.

"Working alone."

He nodded slowly. "And if I wanted to know more about this document, I would talk to . . ."

"Gemma Burch," Evie said.

Bern smiled. "Well, looks like I'll have a few people to visit at the brewery tomorrow. And I'll be able to go in by the front door for once."

They fell silent. After a moment, Evie said, "It's getting late."

Bern looked around. "Are you all right by yourself? I would offer to sleep on the couch, but . . ." His voice faded off as he looked to the empty living room. "Or you could always sleep on my couch," he said quietly.

She looked up to find his dark eyes roaming the edges of her features with a tenderness she was not expecting. She leaned forward and so did he, their foreheads brushing softly together. They stayed like that, forehead to forehead, for a long moment. He smelled like crushed leaves and soap. She thought of the quiet security of his couch, the soothing comfort of his voice lulling her to sleep. But there was work to be done. She took a slow, deep breath and felt him do the same.

Evie straightened up. It was as if an invisible cord between them tightened and then slowly released.

"I'm going to stay up for a bit and try to figure this out," she said, standing slowly.

He stood too and they walked together to the door.

"Thanks for the tea," he said ever so quietly.

"And thank you for the food," Evie added. "Please say thank you to your neighbor. It was very kind of her."

He opened the door, then turned to look back at her. "I would like to know that you are all right. May I phone you once a day, to check on you?" he asked.

"I'm fine," she said. "Besides, I'm not your responsibility."

"No," he said. "You're not. But I want to check anyway."

He closed the door quietly behind him. Evie leaned against the wall for a moment, thinking about how his hair had felt when it touched the skin of her cheek—softer than she'd expected. She put her hand down and imagined Rory's nose nuzzling her palm. Then she turned the dead bolt and headed back to the kitchen, and back to work.

From: Karl Ostikoff [plantmgr@bugbrew.ca]
To: Shandie Greene [tourguide@bugbrew.ca]
Re: Notice of Termination
Sent: Wednesday, September 16, 8:59 a.m.
1 Attachment: SGreeneLetter.doc

Dear Shandie,
As a follow-up to our conversation, I have attached a formal notice of termination.

As you know, the tour guide position is a student position. As such, it is reserved for students who are attending, or are planning to attend, college in the fall.

I would like to thank you for all your hard work, and for everything that you did to make this tourist season a success. If you do decide to attend college after all, please let us know. We would be happy to have you back on the Bugaboo team in the future.

Cheers,

Karl
Karl Ostikoff
Manager
Bugaboo Brewery—A BevCo Company

25

It was past three in the morning before she finished up for the night. She'd combed the notes of three years of energy meetings, departmental meetings, and strategic plans, and as far as she could tell, no concerted efforts toward water reduction had been implemented. Nonetheless, over the past five years, Bugaboo's hectoliter per hectoliter number, always low, had been consistently decreasing.

If what she suspected was true—if water was going missing somewhere within the brewery—then the amount had been growing over time. The issue would become immediately clear once the new water meters were installed.

A thought struck her. She returned to her makeshift desk and called up the employee phone list. This was the BevCo way: the home number of every manager in the company was available to every other manager. You could fill out a form to request that yours not be listed, but that would show that you weren't really a team player.

She reached for her cell phone and punched in the home number of her counterpart in Halifax. She knew the Halifax brewery had installed the new metering system just a few months ago—the first BevCo brewery in Canada to do so. She glanced quickly at the clock by the stove and calculated the four-hour time difference. It would be seven in the morning there. There was a chance that Howard Allister had not left for the office yet.

"Hello?" A woman's voice came on the line.

"Hello, may I speak with Howard, please?"

"Yes, one moment." The woman's voice had quickly become clipped and resigned. Evie could hear the sounds of young children in the background. Another family breakfast interrupted by a work emergency.

"Hello, Howard speaking," the voice said.

"Howard! It's Evie Chapelle calling, from the Bugaboo Brewery. I'm so sorry to be calling you at home," she said.

"Evie, it's been a long time. I hear you're in my old job now. How's Bugaboo treating you?" Howard asked.

"Pretty good, pretty good," she said. "I'm assuming the energy portfolio as of now. I'm preparing for an environmental audit next week," she said.

"Evie, isn't it the middle of the night there?" Howard asked. "And didn't you have a fatality last week? Surely you have other stuff on your plate than an audit?"

"Yeah, I know. Listen, Howard, please. I wouldn't be calling if it wasn't important. There's something off with our water numbers. And I know that Halifax just got the new intake meters installed. I was just on the system and noticed that your most recent numbers aren't up yet—for the last two months," she said.

"No, we only have to put them up quarterly," he replied. Evie could barely hear him over the sounds of kids screaming in the background. Then suddenly the sounds faded away. "Sorry about that," he said.

"Hey, that's okay. I'm the one calling you at home. Listen, any chance I could have a look at your most recent numbers? I want to see how things break down after the intake meters are installed. It might help me figure out something that's been bugging me."

"Uh, sure. I mean, it's no problem. I can email them to you when I get to the office. But I've got to say that Kootenay Landing's numbers are the best in the country—and always have been, even when I was there. Halifax's are the worst. I can't imagine you'd have anything to learn from the way we do things."

Evie paused; she was not sure how much to tell him. "Can you remember anything about the water file from when you were here?"

"Anything like what? What's up, Evie?"

"I can't really say. I'm just trying to sort it out. It could be nothing. Can you just tell me what you remember?" she said.

"Well, it was Karl's baby, even back then. I can't imagine he's having an easy time handing it over. But I expect the promotion to VP will help with that," Howard said.

The BevCo world was a small one. It always amazed Evie how fast news traveled.

Howard sighed. "This is really important, right? Does it have something to do with the guy who died?"

"It might. I'm not sure, really. Let's just say, I think someone is actively trying to stop me from figuring it out," she said.

Howard laughed. "I pity that poor person, Evie. Okay, I'll send you the numbers as soon as I get in. And I'll let you know if I think of anything else."

"Thanks, Howard," Evie said, but he had already hung up.

• • •

Shandie folded the letter into a small square and slid it into the back pocket of her jeans. She fought back tears as she approached the half-dozen senior citizens who would make up her last tour of the Bugaboo Brewery. She bit her lip and smiled at them. Three couples, dressed for the golf course.

"Good afternoon," she said with a broad smile. "My name is Shandie, and I'll be your tour guide today." She knew from the past few months that it was hard to smile at first, but it got easier. "Are you all ready to head out?" she asked.

After a chorus of yeses, she checked that they were all wearing closed-toed shoes and started handing out safety glasses.

"So you'll look as stylish as everyone who works here," she quipped. She handed glasses to a pear-shaped woman wearing a bright red golf shirt.

"Last minute addition to the tour," a voice next to the woman said.

Shandie looked up and saw the man from the bar on Saturday night. He was tall, with curly dark hair and kind eyes. He smiled down at her and held out his hand for a pair of safety glasses. She handed him the last pair. Automatically, she looked down at his shoes. He was wearing hiking boots.

Shandie looked over at Gemma Burch, who would take over the rest of her shift and cover the tours and the shop until they found a college student to replace her. It was all so embarrassing. She knew Steve's dad had to fire her; he had no choice. But the only reason he knew she'd decided not to go to college was that she'd mentioned it when they'd all gone out for drinks.

"Follow me in single file, please," Shandie called out to the group, and led the way out into a light rain. She walked quickly through the parking lot, wishing she'd thought to bring an umbrella. She turned to look back at her group. Several of them had pulled on sweatshirts, and the lady in the red golf shirt was unfolding a pocket-sized rain poncho. "Won't be long and we'll be inside," Shandie told them.

She led them along the edge of the building, where the overhang would keep them dry. The mountains were invisible through the thick clouds in the sky. Looks like any other place when you can't see the mountains, she thought. College had been in her plans when she took the job last spring, but things had changed after that day in May. She led her increasingly damp charges to the side door of the brew house and turned to them. "Please put your safety glasses on now, if you haven't already," she said. She pulled her own on and waited for them to do the same. The tall man smiled at her from the back of the group. "Have you had your workout today?" she asked cheerfully. "Because we are about to go straight up three flights of stairs. Please take your time. We'll wait for everyone to get to the top before we start."

Shandie was almost at the second-floor landing when the entry door slammed shut. She jumped at the sound, then paused for a minute and held her hand to her heart, which was beating wildly.

"You okay?" the lady in the red golf shirt asked. She had kept pace with Shandie but was breathing heavily.

Shandie nodded and smiled. "That door always slams, and it always takes me by surprise," she said. "You'd think I'd have figured it out after so many tours."

She kept climbing but slowed her pace. She knew she had to calm down. "Jumpy as a cat," she'd overheard her mom say to her dad last week. The fear was with her all the time now. The pain in her body had gradually faded away—the scars on her skin would be gone soon—but the fear threatened to gnaw her very foundation.

She'd never decided *not* to go to college. After that day, she hadn't made any decisions about her future at all. The acceptance letter had arrived, as had the information about courses and student loans. She'd been planning to get out of Kootenay Landing for as long as she could remember. But suddenly, the simple act of walking to the post office to mail off her tuition fees was too terrifying. What if whoever had done this to her saw her?

She reached the third-floor landing and pushed open the door to the brew house. The woman in the red shirt was a few steps behind her. Gradually the rest of the group straggled in, with the tall man pulling up the rear. He was watching her closely.

"Welcome to the brew house," she began. "This is the place where we turn water into beer." She paused while they chuckled and then continued with the spiel she had memorized so completely she could say it in her sleep. "The brewers are behind that glass, keeping an eye on what is mostly a computerized process. They make about two hundred eighty-five hectoliters of concentrate beer every two hours, and the brew house runs twenty-four hours a day, five days a week. How are your math skills?" she asked, smiling as they laughed again. Then she looked up at the tall man. He was staring at her again. "Any idea how many liters that is in a week?" she asked him.

He smiled slowly at her. "About one-point-seven million liters in five days. A little more."

She nodded. "That's right. And for those of you who are American, a liter is about the same amount as a quart. So it's a lot of beer," she recited cheerfully as she fingered the letter in her pocket.

It's my own damn fault. She'd been too afraid to go to the post office to mail the package that would have gotten her out of town. It took too much effort to do anything through the confusion and fear. She went with whatever came her way. Steve asking her out, her mom pressuring her to go to church—it just seemed easier that way.

My own fault. My own damn fault. That one thought was with her always. That thought and the shame that permeated it could be distilled down to a single fact, which tormented her to no end: to cause the burns, someone had to have taken off her jeans. And her underwear. When she'd woken up, at home, in her own bed and with no memory of what had happened, she was wearing her jeans. But no underwear. *Someone has a pair of my underwear. And I don't even know who. It could be anyone.*

The group was looking up at her expectantly.

"Sorry, where was I?" Shandie asked them.

"Something about a lottery ton?" the woman in the red shirt prompted her.

"Right, sorry," said Shandie. "The lauter tun. Does anyone know what a lauter tun is?" she asked. She led them across the floor of the brew house to a large stainless steel vessel. She pointed to a window in the machine and they approached one by one to look inside.

"Lauter tuns have been used for centuries in brewing. Their role is to extract all of the sugar from the grain," she said.

"Excuse me, how do you spell that?" a man in a backward

baseball cap asked. He had dark gray hair and a heavy crease on his forehead that made him look like he was frowning.

Shandie smiled as she spelled *lauter tun* for him. Then she continued: "When the lautering process is done, the grains are separated from the liquid, which is now called wort. The spent grains are sent to a special tank, then collected and used for cattle feed. The wort is then boiled and piped downstairs for fermenting."

She had to get through this, stay focused. The tall man was watching her closely. She looked up at him again. He didn't mean her harm, did he?

"Your own damn fault," her mother would say. And she would be right. She'd had too many one-night stands, too many thoughtless affairs, too many men she'd laughed at, not taking their advances seriously.

She'd thought about going to the police, but what would she say? "Something bad happened to me, but I don't know what." She would sound ridiculous, paranoid. Besides, she'd slept with more than one of the officers. They'd laugh at her, behind her back if not to her face. *Your own damn fault.*

"Let's go back downstairs now and have a closer look at the fermentation process," she said. She kept her voice light and cheerful. They smiled up at her and followed her without question back to the stairs.

Bern followed Shandie and her flock back to the Bugaboo Pub and Store. She led them through the door and straight to the bar, where she started pouring complimentary glasses of draft.

"Better get in there and get your free beer before someone else drinks it," a voice next to him said.

Bern turned to see Gemma standing behind the cash register by the door. The counter and shelves around the register were stacked with Bugaboo souvenirs and T-shirts. He smiled at her.

"Are you waiting to free them of some of their hard-earned cash before they go?" he asked.

Gemma laughed. Her perfectly painted lips parted slightly to show very white teeth. "Everyone likes to bring gifts back to their loved ones—especially after they've had a glass of our fine product," she said.

Bern's smile faded and he leaned toward her, keeping his voice low. "I wanted to come see you today, as a matter of fact," he said.

She pointed a manicured index finger to her chest and raised her eyebrows. "Me?"

"Yes. About Gavin Grayson. I hope you don't mind me asking this. It's just that I like to tie up all the details, you know? Staff Sergeant Resnick and Officer Byron, and even my boss, the chief coroner, have all referred to a document, a training document. Its existence suggests that Gavin knew better than to do what he did," Bern said. The skin around her eyes was thin as paper. He could see a light dusting of powder.

"Um-hum," she said. "What about it?"

He shrugged. "It's just that I must not have been there when this document was shown to Officer Byron. And everyone seems to have seen it and to understand its implications—except me. I wondered if you might explain it to me? And perhaps show it to me as well?"

Gemma seemed to think for a minute. Then she shrugged.

"Sure, no harm in that. Follow me," she said. "Be right back!" she called out to Shandie.

She led him down a long hallway that ended at the main office area. Gemma tapped a code into a keypad lock and pulled open the door to a storage room adjacent to her desk. "We call this the vault," she said as she opened the heavy door. Inside were rows of filing cabinets. She pulled open a drawer on the one right next to the door. "We keep all the training documents in here."

She flipped through the files and pulled out the one labeled Working Alone. "See here? Gavin reviewed the training document. He answered all of the questions correctly and signed that he understood what was required of him, on the eighth of August," she said. She handed him the single sheet of paper. "He should have known better."

Bern held the paper up to the light. On the top right-hand corner, the name Gavin Grayson had been written in script by someone who was left-handed. The true-or-false questions had been answered, with black ink circling the letters T and F down the page. Someone had put little red checkmarks next to all the answers. A signature, which Bern could only assume read G. Grayson, was scrawled on the bottom line.

"Who wrote this?" he asked, pointing to Gavin's name at the top of the page.

"That's Evie's handwriting," Gemma said.

Bern leaned his elbow on the side of the open drawer. He held the paper up again, then looked at Gemma. "Tell me how the process works. How does this paper get here, and what steps does it take along the way?" he asked.

Gemma crossed her arms. "If you're suggesting—"

"I'm not suggesting anything. I just want to understand how the process works," he said.

Gemma sighed. "Well, Evie keeps a pretty close eye on things. When a new employee comes, she makes sure the managers know what to train him on. And she keeps at them until it's done—phone calls, reminders, emails, meetings. She can really drive people crazy."

Bern smiled faintly. "So why would she have written Gavin's name on here?"

"Oh, well, she probably did a whole pile at once. She prints out all the training documents that need to be reviewed for each department and then writes the name of the employee who needs to review them across the top of each one. Then she gives them to me, and I distribute them to the department managers," Gemma said.

"And then?" Bern asked.

Gemma laughed. "Well, in theory, they come back signed a few days later, and I enter in the system that they've been completed and then file the document."

"But in practice?" he asked.

Gemma shrugged. "In practice, they don't always come back right away. So that's when Evie starts to do her thing."

Bern nodded. "Thank you," he said. "That's all I needed to know. Except perhaps I might have a copy of this?" He held up the sheet. "It sums everything up so nicely. I'd like to include a copy in my report."

"Well, of course," she said. She left him there and went to the copy room next door. He fingered the open file drawer before him and found a label that read Maintenance Orientation. He grabbed the last paper in the file and pulled it out. He looked at it quickly, then folded it in quarters and put it in the back pocket of his cords.

"There you go," Gemma said, handing him a copy of the training sheet. "We'd better get back to Shandie. And your free beer," she said.

"No whiskey here," Shandie said as she placed the beer in front of him.

"Not smiling anymore?" he asked.

The corners of her lips raised slightly. "My last tour is all done. I never have to smile again if I don't want to," she said.

He raised his glass and said, "Well, here's to wanting to."

He took a sip and watched as she polished glasses and put them away. The bar was made from one solid piece of wood, varnished to a brilliant sheen. The bar stool on which he sat looked like it had been handcrafted from wrought iron. Bern swiveled the stool to see the last of the tourists make their purchases from Gemma and head out to the parking lot.

"Gemma!" called a voice from the hallway to the main office. A head of blond hair appeared, and Bern recognized the brewery manager, Karl. "I need you in here for a minute," he called.

Gemma hurried the last customer out the main door and walked over to Karl. She looked up at Shandie and flashed five fingers. "Five minutes, sorry," she said, and was gone.

"Are you in a rush to get somewhere?" Bern asked.

Shandie shook her head. "They're in a rush to get rid of me. I wasn't kidding—that was my last tour. They just fired me."

Bern looked at her quizzically. "They fired you? Can they do that?"

Shandie raised her shoulders up and let them drop. "It's a student job. They gave it to me because they thought I was going to college. But then I never went, so they have to fire me now. Something about the funding they get for the job. Students only." Then she tipped the glass she had been polishing and filled it with draft. "What the hell," she said. She pulled up a stool and sat down across the bar from him. "Might as well let them buy me a farewell beer."

Bern took another sip of his drink. "Why did you decide not to go to college?" he asked.

"I didn't exactly decide; I just didn't go," she said. They watched each other over the rim of their beer glasses for a moment.

"Did that have anything to do with the scars?" He spoke quietly into his glass. The words seemed to echo in his ears.

She answered so quietly that he had to lean forward to hear. "I'm scared," she whispered.

"I can tell," he replied.

"I thought it would get better, but it hasn't." She brushed at her eyes with her hand and then stared at the floor.

"What happened to make you afraid, Shandie?" he whispered back. The store was silent except for the hush of their voices.

"I don't remember what happened!" she whispered fiercely. "I can't remember," she said, emphasizing each word.

"Tell me what you do remember."

"I remember being at work, at the hotel. It was a really busy night—a Friday—Apple Blossom weekend," she started hesitantly. "You know Apple Blossom weekend, right? It's the busiest weekend of the year. We got slammed at around nine o'clock. So many people came in all at once that time just seemed to speed up, you know? There were two other girls working, and Leigh was behind the bar," she said. She took another sip of her beer and leaned closer him. "The weird thing is, I don't remember finishing my shift."

She closed her eyes for a moment, as though trying to remember. Her long hair glistened under the spotlights above the bar, and the bright-blue Bugaboo T-shirt hugged her curves appreciatively. Bern could see why Resnick had called her perfect. He watched as she slowly shook her head.

"The next thing I knew, it was morning. I was in my bed, but I had no idea how I got there. I could hear my mom in the kitchen, telling my dad to be quiet because I had worked late and needed to sleep in. My body was sore, and everything just hurt. And my head—I felt hungover, but I don't remember drinking anything," she said.

Bern listened quietly, wishing he could do more. He waited to see if she would continue, and when she didn't, he asked, "Could you have been drugged?"

"Sometimes we have a drink, you know, at the end of the shift, the last hour or so. It does no harm and helps us relax. Everyone else is so drunk by then anyway, no one notices. Someone might have put something in my drink. I just don't know."

A tear rolled down her cheek, and then another. She reached for a paper towel and rubbed at her eyes. Her voice was hoarse when she spoke again. "When I woke up, it was like a nightmare. Something had happened. But I didn't know what, or where, or with who. Everything hurt and I didn't know why. And then, when I finally managed to get up, I saw the marks."

"Cigarette burns?" Bern asked.

She nodded. The tears started again. She put her beer glass down and hugged her stomach. "They hurt so much. That was the scariest thing," she said. He could barely hear her voice.

She cried quietly for a moment. He wanted to go around the bar and wrap his arms around Shandie, but he knew that would probably make things worse. So he just watched her and waited, ready to listen if she had more to say.

"No," she said, her voice ragged with tears. "That's not the scariest thing." She wiped her eyes with the now balled-up paper towel. "The scariest thing is not knowing who did it. And exactly what they did."

The door opened then and Shandie stood up quickly. She poured what was left of her beer down the sink and started washing the glass. Bern picked up his glass and took a few more sips.

"No idea who it was?" he asked while Gemma was still out of earshot.

Shandie shook her head. "None."

Gemma looked at Shandie. "Oh, sweetheart, I'm sorry. I tried to talk to them, but they wouldn't listen to me. You know we'd have you back in a snap; it has nothing to do with you or your work. You know that, right?" She'd made her way behind the bar and wrapped her arms around the girl. Shandie's shoulders tensed at the older woman's touch.

"I'm fine. I'm sorry. It's okay—it really is," she said, pulling herself away. She looked up at the clock above the bar. "I told Steve I'd meet him at three."

As if on cue, the door to the store opened and Steve walked in. He smiled at Shandie. "You ready?" he asked.

"Just going to freshen up," she said cheerfully. She ducked

around Gemma and opened a small door behind the bar. Staff Only, Bern read as she shut the door behind her.

Steve came up to the bar and sat next to Bern. "Don't suppose you'll let me have one of those, will you, Gemma?" he asked, nodding at Bern's draft.

Gemma laughed. "No way! Never hear the end of it if I did."

Bern swirled the last of the beer in the glass like it was a tumbler of whiskey. It was warm now and tasted sour. The slight buzz it had given him had faded, and now he felt let down. He held his breath and quickly drank the last of it.

He turned to Steve. The young man had bags under his eyes and looked disheveled.

"Everything okay?" he asked.

Steve looked at him, bleary-eyed. "Yeah. Just night shift. Gets to me," he said.

"Did you think of what it was you wanted to tell me?" Bern asked cheerfully.

"Huh?"

Bern shrugged. "That day you found Gavin. I thought there was something more you wanted to tell me. That's all," he said.

Steve leaned his elbows on the bar and dropped his head into his arms. "Nothing," he said. "I have nothing to tell you."

Shandie came out then, her eyes clear, her hair brushed, and her lips shiny with gloss. "Are you ready to go, Steve?" she asked.

He was up in a shot. He looked her over and smiled. "I'm ready. Let's go."

Bern and Gemma watched them leave. "I don't know how I'm going to manage without her. But I guess we'll find a way," she said.

Bern suddenly wanted to be away from there. But there was

one more thing he needed. He watched Gemma as she cleared his glass off the bar and washed it. She was lovely, really, in a put-together way, her grooming a shell that covered her completely. What he was about to ask was not so unlikely, though he hated to do it.

He smiled at her. "You know, I often go down to the Kootenay Landing Hotel on the weekends and enjoy a drink there," he said. "Do you think you might like to join me sometime?"

The fine creases at the corners of her eyes deepened slightly as she looked up at him. "But . . . well," she said, "I hate to pry, but what about Evie? Aren't you and Evie . . . ?" She didn't finish her sentence.

Bern tilted his head and smiled. "I have many friends. Evie will not mind if I have a drink with a friend. May I call you?" he asked.

Gemma wiped her hands on a towel. "Sure. Would you like my home number?" she asked.

He nodded once. She took a small business card from below the bar, wrote something on it and handed it to him. Bern took it and turned it over in his hands as though inspecting it before slipping it into his pocket.

"This will do just fine," he said. "Thank you."

And with a wave, he headed out the door. It was still raining outside and he felt a slight relief that the rain would water the garden for him. He could go home, sit on his covered deck, and think through everything he had learned that afternoon. There would be a lot to think about.

From: Troy Thompson [tthompson@soldiersally.ca]
To: Bern Fortin [bernfortin@bccoronerservice.bc.ca]
Re: re: The real story
Sent: Wednesday, September 16, 2:35 p.m.

Dear Lieutenant-Colonel (Ret.) Fortin,
It seems that you no longer answer your phone.

I've done some more research into your sudden retirement. I received some documents through access-to-information requests that show you were weeks away from a promotion to colonel at the time you left the service. This brings up so many questions.

Why would a well-loved leader like you step aside just before a major promotion like that? You'd already climbed the greasy pole and were about to grab the brass ring. What happened? I've heard some people say you could have made it right to the top—Chief of the Defence Staff.

Lieutenant-Colonel, at some point this story is going to break wide open. You won't be able to stay hidden in your garden out west. I've spoken to some of your men. They say you were never one to hide in the trenches when you could be leading an offensive. This is no way to go down.

Troy

From: Howard Allister [safety@BevCoHalifax.ca]
To: Evie Chapelle [safety@bugbrew.ca]
Re: Water Numbers
Sent: Wednesday, September 16, 3:14 p.m.
1 Attachment: HalifaxWater07–08.xls

Hi Evie,
As requested, I have attached our water numbers for the
last two months. Our new intake meters were installed
mid-June, so July is the first full month using the new
metering system.

Hope this helps,

Howard
Howard Allister
Safety Manager
BevCo Brewery—Halifax

26

Paperwork could wait just one more day. Bern went into the garden just after dawn and had every intention of exhausting himself, body and mind.

First he tilled each row until the tines of his rake moved through the soil as easily as a fork through a rich chocolate cake. It had been a few days since he'd tilled—enough time for some ambitious weeds to take root. He was merciless with these, collecting them in tidy piles and then dumping them in the compost.

Once the tilling was done, the sun was fully up. He stopped only to take a sip of water from the hose, and then got on with harvesting. That would take most of the morning. Tomatoes, peppers, cucumbers, squash, potatoes, peas. Carrots he could leave a while longer. He set some of each aside, to prepare for his fall fair entry and so he could harvest seeds from them later. With the exception of the tomatoes, of course. Mrs. K. had already delivered her verdict on those.

The abundance of it all was hard to fathom. Not just because of the work involved, though this was considerable. What really amazed him was that everything he had harvested had come from a few tiny handfuls of seeds that Mrs. K. had carefully saved from her own harvest the previous year and handed to him over the fence. She had handed him the world folded in tiny squares of recycled paper.

On days like this, with his full focus on each task before him, he could see his way clear. He could even find comfort in his formerly held religious beliefs. The waning of the garden, of the plants, of the seasons was part of an inevitable cycle—out of human hands. Death was part of this same cycle. Who was he to rail against such a powerful force? But death by human hands? Death by his own hands? Who would account for this?

You must confess your sins. Sister Marie-Ange spoke to him from the roots and tubers, from the crumbs of turned soil, from the decaying heap of the compost.

But to whom? Who could hear his confession and not be infected by the horror of it? Who would hear his failings and not turn away? He thought of the people close to him and could not imagine burdening them with this horror. Mrs. K., he suspected, stoically carried her own unshared burdens through each day. Evie?

He paused, remembering her voice, so controlled and focused on the phone. Working long hours to prepare for the audit, as thorough as Mrs. K. had been the time he'd watched her strip a chicken carcass of meat before making stock. He closed his eyes and remembered how Evie smelled, like paper and blueberries. He'd wanted so badly to raise his fingers to touch her cheek, the point of her chin. To feel the soft pulse at her temple.

But who was he to stake a claim on such tenderness? The seeds Mrs. Kalesnikoff had gifted him were precious and rare: with care and attention, they were capable of unlimited growth.

But the seed of what he had done in Rwanda more than fifteen years before was still inside him, and would be forever. It corrupted some part of him. No good could come from sharing what was inside him with others. Even God did not want to know this sin.

On this, he must keep his own counsel, tend his own garden. Sister Marie-Ange was wrong.

By the time the sun was high in the sky, he had finished harvesting. Another sip from the hose, a red pepper eaten whole, and he was ready to move on to the next tasks: chopping wood and preserving food for the long winter ahead. And saving seeds, in hope of another spring.

"Evie, it's Howard in Halifax. I hope I'm not calling too late. I figured you'd be up."

"Howard? What are you doing? It's—" Evie checked her watch and quickly added four hours to the local time. "It's almost three in the morning there!"

"I know. I just woke up and remembered something. It's been a really long time since I worked at Bugaboo, five years or so. Maybe this is nothing, but maybe it will make sense to you."

"Okay, shoot," said Evie.

"Well, it was kind of a myth at the time. I was safety manager, just as you are now, and Karl was maintenance manager back then. We didn't have environmental standards like we do now. Nothing was tracked. This was before the new municipal treatment plant was put in, so things were even more lax."

"That's just around the time I came here," she said.

"So do you remember the smell?" he asked.

"What smell?"

"Well, it started in the aging cellars. Remember that old cellar in the basement that's been there since the brewery opened? It's got about five small tanks in an ancient refrigerated room?"

Evie shuddered at the thought of it. "Yes, I know the room," she said.

"Well, the smell down there was really bad—rotten, stinking beer. But it was coming from under the floor. It wasn't a leaking tank or anything like that. And then it spread. The main filtration area started to smell too. That's on the main floor, but it doesn't have a basement under it. And then the fermentation hallway and the control room."

"So what happened?"

Howard laughed. "Well, it came up at a few management meetings. The brew master was all upset about it; something needed to be done about the smell. He was concerned about the integrity of the product, as if the smell would get in the tanks and turn the beer. He didn't much care that the employees were almost sick from the stink. Anyway, the plant manager was Eddie Von Sickle. Remember him?"

"'Deal with It' Eddie," Evie said slowly.

"Yes, that's right. 'Deal with It' Eddie!' He didn't care what went on as long as he didn't look bad." Howard laughed again. "A lot of the breweries that Eddie managed are still feeling the effects of that approach. Meanwhile, he spends half the year golfing in Ontario and the other half golfing in Arizona—drinking BevCo product all year long. Anyway, Eddie told Karl to deal with it. There was talk of a broken water main or a leaking storm sewer, and the employees started making noise about a sinkhole. And then the smell went away. Gone. Karl dealt with it."

"How?"

"I don't know the details. Remember, I was safety, and it wasn't environment and safety at the time—just plain old safety. But I remember some complaints, a few workers who had to leave their shifts early because of inhaling fumes. There were a few days when the smell of bleach was really strong throughout the brewing department. You can look them up; the complaints will still be in the system."

"And after that?"

"After that, it all went away. And soon after, I was transferred. You still in that closet of an office I was in?"

"Yes." Evie laughed.

"Did anybody ever clean it out? Because there was a report floating around at the time. Some engineers came and did an assessment of the integrity of the water system and made some recommendations. I seem to remember something, anyway. It was right around the time of the BevCo takeover."

The line fell silent as Evie thought over what Howard had said. "What would that mean, Howard? In a climate of takeover, to have a report like that?"

"Well, it wouldn't be good. Bugaboo's always been a bit of an outsider, even before BevCo came on the scene. It's the only brewery that's not in a big center. It's got a geographically dependent product line—brewed with mountain water and all that—and that makes for an expensive product. Everyone wants to make products that can be brewed as close to market as possible, to reduce shipping costs. And then the volume matters too.

Bugaboo is a small brewery, and the production volume could easily be made up by running an overtime shift once at week at one of the bigger breweries, like Toronto or Montreal or Halifax. So if there was a need for a big repair to the fabric of the brewery . . . well, BevCo might just look at shutting it down."

"But it's the biggest employer in Kootenay Landing!" Evie exclaimed.

"Yes, that's true. But in terms of BevCo, it's tiny potatoes. Frankly, I'm surprised Bugaboo has survived as long as it has."

"So do you think I could get my hands on that report?"

Howard was quiet for a moment. "I know I had a copy buried in my filing cabinet, in what is now your office. When I transferred, I left everything in there . . ."

"Ah," Evie said. "I moved all that stuff to long-term storage when I took over this job. It's down in the document storage room in the basement."

"Yeah, well, you didn't hear it from me, got that? My wife hasn't left me yet, and it looks like the company might keep me on long enough to get my pension. I don't want to do anything to mess myself up at this point in my career. Life is good, so, Evie, you didn't talk to me, all right?"

"Sure, Howard, no problem," she said. "And Howard? Thanks."

From: evidence@bccoronerservice.bc.ca
To: bernfortin@bccoronerservice.bc.ca
Re: Handwriting analysis
Sent: Thursday, September 17, 3:52 p.m.

Hi Bern,

I had a quick look at the handwriting samples you sent in. Here is an unofficial summary.

Sample 1: Signature on document entitled "Maintenance Orientation."

This signature is distinct from the other two that were provided. The overall form of the handwriting indicates that a person held the writing implement in a fist-type grip. Notice the heavy press into the paper at the start of each word. Though the letters are cursive, I believe this was written by someone under the age of forty, as they do not have the firm grasp on cursive writing someone of an older age might. (Cursive writing has fallen out of favor in schools in the last thirty years.) However, this might point to socioeconomic levels, literacy, and/or education, rather than age.

Sample 2: Signature on document entitled "Working-Alone Procedure."

I have no doubt that this signature was forged to imitate the one above. While at first glance it may be similar, upon closer inspection, it is clear that the person who signed this was trying to hide the characteristics of his or her own writing style. However, this person has an innate ability with cursive writing, as evidenced by the smooth upward strokes at the beginning of each word. This natural flow is masked by frequent hesitations and pen lifts, as he or she stopped to compare his or her attempt to copy the signature from the above sample.

Sample 3: Name Gemma written on a business card.

While much more fluid and natural than sample 2, this is identical to it in the upward stroke of the cursive *G*. Given that similarity, and the similar shape to the letter *A*, I would conclude that sample 2 and sample 3 were written by the same hand.

I hope this is helpful. If it's a criminal case, we will need to submit these samples to the RCMP for independent handwriting analysis. This informal report is for information purposes only.

Regards,

Ted

27

"Well, I think she's sweet anyway," Felicia said as she pressed Steve's jean jacket into his hands. "I wish she could have had dinner with us."

Steve smiled at his mom. As always, she had something nice to say. And as always, she looked like a perfect doll. The white dress accentuated her tanned skin, and the high-heeled sandals lengthened her tiny frame. He never could figure out why she stayed with his dad.

"She's back working at the bar, getting pawed over like yesterday's baked goods—that's why she couldn't make it," Karl muttered.

Felicia patted Karl on the chest and then turned her back and leaned against him. She took his arms and wrapped them around her own waist. "Oh, stop, you old grump," she said with a laugh. "Shandie's a sweet girl—and she's smart too. And determined as anything."

"Yeah, determined to land our son."

Steve pulled his shoes on so quickly he almost fell over. He tugged on his jacket. "Bye, Mom," he said as he closed the door behind him. He did not look at his father.

He sat in his truck for a few minutes before turning it on.

He knew how things would go in his family home over the next hour. It would start in the kitchen. His mom would do the dishes while his dad sat in the adjacent family room, flipping through the sports channels and shouting out angry comments.

He watched as the lights went out in the hallway. Moments later, his mom's face appeared over the kitchen sink. She does too much, he thought, and then wondered for the hundredth time why she didn't slow down and simplify now that the kids had left home. If anything, she'd gotten busier. It used to be that she would cook to feed the hungry masses—Karl, Steve, and his sister, Angie—and any brewery people or friends they happened to bring home. It was all good, simple food in volume. Tonight she'd made a port-cranberry sauce to go with the pork roast. "Oh, it's nothing, dear," she'd said when he commented on it.

After a while of making upbeat replies to Karl's ranting, Felicia's voice would become strained, and it would be more difficult for her to keep smiling. Steve remembered one time after a party at the trailer. The crowd at the campfire had dwindled to just a few stragglers. Karl had an audience and was carrying on about his favorite topic: girls who went to college and got too smart for their own good. They managed just fine when they didn't know anything at all—just look at Felicia, he'd said with pride. Angie had sat through the whole thing, staring straight ahead. It was the summer before she went into grade twelve, and Steve knew she secretly pored over college catalogs in her room and hid them under her bed.

Steve had gone into the trailer to use the bathroom, and he spent a few minutes in there, trying to talk himself out of being drunk. When he came out, Felicia was standing at the counter, holding a paper plate in each hand. She stood perfectly still. Her head was tilted and she was staring at a spot on the ground. All the muscles that normally held her smile in place were slack. The skin seemed to sag, leaving a terrifying mask of deep sadness.

When she saw Steve, the elastics snapped back in place again. "Don't pay any attention to him, dear. No attention at all," she'd said. He tried to hug her, and she just patted him and sent him back to the campfire. "Send Angie in here to help me clean up," she'd said.

It was that night, Steve learned later, when she'd told Angie about the money. Felicia explained that she had set up an appointment with a college savings plan salesperson when Angie was born, but Karl had refused to let him in the door. Ever since then, she had been stashing away a percentage of the grocery money every week—for college—and Karl knew nothing about it. Of course there was college money for Steve too. But when the time came, he couldn't stand up to his dad. And he didn't want to leave his mom. Because that's what Angie had done: she'd gone off to college at the coast and never come home again.

Felicia now moved away from the kitchen window and out of view. Steve stared at the golden rectangle of light and the gleaming farmhouse kitchen it contained. He waited for his mother to reappear, but she didn't. He knew that one of two things would come next: either she would cajole Karl out of his chair and they would head up to bed together, or if his mood was too black, she would leave him there and head up to bed by herself. After she was asleep, Karl would often leave the house and get in his truck. Steve knew this pattern like his own breath. It had been ingrained in his sleep as a child, a twisted sort of lullaby: the duet of voices through the wall, raised and angry, then abruptly quiet; the soft swoosh of the back door closing; the rumble of his father's truck.

Steve started his own truck finally and followed the pitted farm driveway to where it met the trunk road. On the road he backed into a tangle of cottonwood trees that edged the river, turned off his headlights, and waited.

Shandie placed Bern's whiskey on the counter and walked away without looking at him or saying a word. He opened his mouth to call out to her but then shut it again. Let her come in her own time.

The usual crowd had gathered for another Friday night at the Kootenay Landing Hotel. Leigh was working the floor again, happy, he was sure, that Shandie had agreed to come in at all, even if she would only work behind the bar.

He took a sip of his whiskey. Only this one, he promised himself. After two full days in the garden and the kitchen, he was as sure on his feet as he could ever expect to be.

He'd put them out of his mind, but now his thoughts returned to the brewery cases as they would to a complex battle plan. Not much longer now and the final details would fall into place. Though Bern had his suspicions, he could not be sure quite yet. Like a sniper in the desert, he knew the insurgents would give themselves away if he was patient enough.

He allowed his mind to wander over all the facts of the cases as he swirled tiny sips of whiskey on his tongue and watched Shandie go about her work. He thought about the individuals in each case, sifted through them in his mind as though he were shuffling a deck of playing cards. He paused as one player flashed by, and then he dealt that card again and looked at it more closely.

He nursed his drink in this way for over an hour. At one point his cell phone, which he'd placed on the bar, began to buzz. He recognized the reporter's number and let it ring. Shandie studiously ignored him the whole time. When Resnick hadn't shown up by eleven o'clock, Bern signaled to her that he wanted to pay. He looked directly at her as she walked toward him, and smiled.

"Look," she said, "I'm sorry I told you, all right? I was having a bad day, the worst day," she said. Then she paused. "Okay, well, not the worst day, but a rotten day. I just . . . I just need to know you won't tell anyone else."

"I'm not sure I can do that," he said. He reached forward and touched her wrist. She jerked her hand away as though he had burned her.

"I'm sorry. Sorry," he said. "I wasn't thinking. It's just . . . have you thought about the fact that this person is still out there? Belinda Carlisle died, and other women could be at risk—*you* could still be at risk. Have you thought about that?"

She nodded. "I think about it all the time," she said.

"I think it's time to go to the police." He said it quietly, and she leaned closer as he spoke.

"No! No, you can't!" she gasped.

"But don't you want to put a stop to this?" he asked.

She leaned right over the bar, so close to him he could smell her shampoo. "What if it's one of them?" she asked. Then she pulled away.

He sat back and mulled that over for a moment, then shook his head. "Resnick?" he mouthed.

She looked around quickly. Then she leaned close again and spoke quietly. "I only went out with him once, but he called me for weeks after. And then, right after it happened"—she snapped her fingers—"he stopped calling."

"Do you want me to find out for sure?" he asked.

She reached out to take the ten-dollar bill in his hand, her eyes wide. She nodded, and as he watched her walk away, his cell phone buzzed again. This time it was Colonel Sauvé, and this time he answered.

It was just after eleven when Evie pulled her SUV into Bern's empty driveway. She took a small backpack out of her car and went to his door. She knocked quietly, and when no one answered, she tried the handle. It was unlocked.

She sat down to wait for him. Dropping her head back on the couch, she thought through everything she had done that day. The auditors would arrive on Thursday, and even if she worked every minute between now and then, there was no way she would be ready.

If she could just get her hands on the document—the one Howard had told her about—she might find the answer to the water question. Water leaking out of the system was the only thing that would explain those numbers. But what if the company—or someone within it—had been hiding that leak for years?

She needed to know the truth—whatever it was. If she was going to face this on her own, she'd rather do it on her own terms: find out the truth now, and tell the auditors as soon as they arrived. Risky, but her only option. Her career was on the line. And with Dirk and Rory already gone, her career was all she had left.

She paced the small space that made up Bern's house. He'd

been busy in the kitchen again. A row of jars lined the counter. "Salsa," the neatly printed labels read. Evie touched her hand to one jar. It was still slightly warm. The rest of the kitchen— the rest of the house, even—was spotless. She ran her hand along the edge of the kitchen table and walked into the open area off the living room that made up his office. She read the spines of the books that lined the built-in shelves on either side of the window: gardening, beekeeping, composting, food preserving. A man with many interests. She thought of her own bookshelf, or rather, her own books, which were now piled on the floor next to where the shelf used to be. Loss prevention, industrial hygiene, compliance manuals, hazard assessments.

She pulled a book off the shelf—about cooking straight from the garden—and plopped down on his brown velvet sofa. She'd always wanted to learn how to cook. Maybe it was finally time.

After twenty minutes of flipping through the book, she shut it with a sigh. It looked complicated. She had no doubt she could safely oversee the production of any kind of mass-produced food. But she didn't know that she could ever make a chiffonade of fresh basil for a marinade.

She thought about the document again. She'd tried checking for it during her workday, but every time she headed down to the basement, there was someone around. She didn't want anyone to know what she was looking for—at least, not until she knew what she was dealing with. On her third attempt, she gave up. She'd gone home at the end of the day as usual and decided to wait until the afternoon shift ended, which was exactly half an hour ago. The brewery was sure to be empty by now.

The more she thought about it, the more convinced she became. She needed to see that document. It was the only way to get to the bottom of the water question. The only way to get through the audit with her reputation, and possibly her career, intact. I want to do what's right, she'd told Bern the other night. His voice echoed in her head: *Careful but brave. That's a fine line to tread. I tried to walk that line one time, and I'm afraid I failed terribly. I erred on the side of careful.*

Evie reached into her backpack and pulled out her cell phone. She knew what she was about to do was certainly not careful and it was likely more foolish than brave. But without the answers, which she felt sure were in that document, she knew she'd be hung out to dry by the auditors—and Karl. She dialed Bern's number and waited. After only one ring, it bounced to voice mail.

"Hi, Bern. It's Evie. I'm at your house. I'm going to pop over to the brewery for a few minutes. There's something there I need. I'll be back here in ten minutes." She slipped the phone back in her pack. Then she went out the door and walked the block to the brewery.

Once there, she went directly to the basement. The document storage room was a little closet of a space inside the paint room. She avoided looking in the direction of the cellar where she'd spent last Friday night and kept her focus instead on getting the padlock open on the gate. Once she'd managed that, she swung the gate closed behind her. She'd always thought of it as "the dreaded paint room" and half expected some eerie music to start playing in the background as she opened the door.

Her backpack was a reassuring weight on her back. In it were her cell phone, a flashlight, and a toque. Just in case. She pulled out the flashlight now and shined it at the rows of shelves, which held gallon cans of paint for various industrial uses.

Something caught her eye. Evie turned the light off for a

moment and leaned back against a metal shelf. The smell of paint was very strong. But there was another smell that she couldn't place. She listened for a full minute. When she was sure everything was quiet, she turned the flashlight on again and scanned the back wall.

"What the hell?" she whispered. She approached the odd form she'd seen. As she got closer, the shadows separated themselves from the light. She made out a stack of sealed paper bags, piled up to shoulder height.

"Cement," she said quietly. She tapped the top bag with her flashlight. Each row was about a dozen bags long and ten bags high. Now that she was closer, Evie could see that the rows were two deep. She quickly did the math. What in the world would someone be doing with 240 bags of cement?

At the end of the row of bags was the door to the document storage room. Evie held the long-handled flashlight under her armpit as she searched through the keys on the ring. Three of the keys were marked "Storage Room."

Her hair fell in front of her eyes as she tried the first key. No good. She swung her neck to try to get the hair out of her face and tried the next key. Nothing. Stopping for a moment to put the flashlight down, she pulled the toque out of her bag and tugged it onto her head. With her hair out of her eyes, she picked up the flashlight and tried again. The final key slid into place and the knob twisted smoothly under her hand. Evie shone the flashlight around until she found the light switch. No way was she going to do this in the dark. The room had been shut up for so long, who knew what might be waiting. Evie pictured walking through cobwebs or tripping over mouse droppings—or worse, disturbing a nest of bats. She turned the light on, and froze.

The room that came into view under the dim bulb was

spotlessly clean. There was not a cobweb in sight. The document storage boxes Evie had expected to see were pushed aside and stacked neatly along the walls, stretching almost to the ceiling. In the center of the space was a sofa, dark-brown-and-mustard plaid, like the sofas that had populated every 1970s rec room. At the foot of it a flat-screened TV was bolted to the wall.

Evie took a step forward as she slowly took in the rest of the space. There was a desk and filing cabinet in one corner and a wood-paneled stand that held a microwave and a coffee maker by the door. Everything was surrounded by the boxes of old documents, stacked in rows along the wall. It looked like the clubhouse of a very tidy bachelor.

What was going on here? Whose room was this? Thoughts flipped quickly through her mind, one after the other. It wasn't a safety violation but a human resources one. Not her department. Then she thought of the weekend before and felt once again the chill in her bones from the sticky concrete floor of the refrigerated cellar. The heavy latch sliding into place. The footsteps walking away. The search of the brewery that had turned up nothing. Had they looked in here?

Get the document and get out.

She turned to the first stack of boxes. She scanned the front row, looking for her own handwriting in thick black marker. She found three boxes marked "Safety Documents" next to the couch, amid some labeled "Production Schedules."

She slid the first box of safety documents onto the couch and sat down next to it. She ripped off the packing tape that held it shut and riffled through the yellowed papers crammed in there. She found training manuals for machines that had long since been replaced and instructions for manually adding caustic soda to the bottle washer even though the automated system had been in place for at least a dozen years. *Get the document and get out. Get in and get out.* The words circled in her mind, making her heart race and her fingers fumble.

She put the first box back and pulled down another. This one held training records. The top one certified that Norm Vincent was fully trained to handle both a forklift and a pallet jack. Norm had retired more than four years earlier.

She was just about to close the second box when her fingers caught on an elastic band. She pulled out a fat dark-brown folder, across the front of which was scrawled, in her own handwriting, "Howard's Docs." She ripped open the folder and flipped through its pages. The report was halfway through the thick file. Sent to Karl Ostikoff from an engineering firm. She scanned it, and as the significance of the words sunk in, she felt the breath leave her body.

She collapsed back, forgetting where she was for a moment. She let the report drop to her lap and her hands fall to her sides. She started circling the edges of a rough spot in the fabric of the couch with her index finger as she thought. It was all starting to make sense now.

TAYLOR, ECCLES AND STRONG
PROFESSIONAL ENGINEERS
Calgary * Kelowna * Vancouver *

April 12, 2004
Karl Ostikoff
Maintenance Manager
Bugaboo Brewery
Kootenay Landing, BC

Dear Karl,

Thank you for giving us the opportunity to assess the structural work of the proposed canning line adjacent to the existing Bugaboo Brewery building. Our report will be complete and sent to you before the end of the month.

While on site, you asked us to have a quick look at some cracks and softening in the concrete basement of the original brewery. Our technician was particularly concerned about one hole, the size of a rabbit hole, which one of your managers stated had grown over the past several weeks.

As you know, our technician took several soil samples, and the results of the tests conducted are attached. Briefly, we believe these results show significant sinkhole activity beneath the brewery building. We would need to conduct more extensive testing to determine the exact cause and nature of the activity. However, these initial tests lead us to the conclusion that this is a serious situation that merits further investigation.

The geological aspects of the land make it unlikely that this activity is related to natural rock and soil formation. It is more likely due to broken or leaking pipes beneath the building itself. As the building is almost sixty years old, it seems a likely explanation that there is a large quantity of liquid runoff from the brewery, in the form of wastewater and beer, continually leaking out of the pipes and saturating the soil beneath the building, causing the foundation to shift.

A short-term remedy would be to pump concrete and gravel into the holes and fill them. However, until the old pipes are dug up and replaced, this would be only a stopgap measure. A permanent solution is to dig underneath the brewery and replace the broken and aging pipes. We would be happy to provide a quote for this work. More testing would be needed to determine the full extent of the damage, but in our opinion, because of the suspected instability of the soil beneath the building, the facility would need to be shut down while the work took place. The magnitude of the project would depend on the depth of the sinkhole and the state of the soil. Our initial estimate is that the work would take anywhere from two to six months.

Please do not hesitate to contact me if you have any questions about the attached soil test results, or if our firm can be of service in addressing these concerns further.

Yours sincerely,
Chuck Strong, P.Eng.

28

In the dark, it was hard to tell where the driveways were. It was hard to tell much of anything. All Bern could see were the two beams of the truck's headlights and the dim edging of farmers' fields. Mown alfalfa was interspersed with the occasional fence where one farm ended and another began. He slowed a few times before he found Resnick's driveway.

As soon as he turned off the main road, his cell phone started beeping—the sound it made when it was out of range. He followed the rutted road to the log cabin and parked behind Resnick's patrol car.

When he turned off his cell phone, the beeping stopped. He unfolded himself from the truck and stepped outside. It was completely quiet. He rounded the path to the veranda and knocked on the front door of the house. When there was no answer, Bern moved to the side and looked through a crack in the curtains. He could see Resnick on the couch, staring absently off into space. He was in uniform. His shirt unbuttoned, his holster across his lap.

"Resnick! Open up!" Bern pounded on the door again.

"Go away!" Resnick shouted back. Bern watched him

through the crack in the curtains. Resnick reached for a bottle of beer on the coffee table and took a deep pull. He kept his eyes closed the whole time. He sat back on the scratchy plaid sofa and began to caress the smooth, hard leather of his holster.

"Resnick, I want to talk to you!" Bern said again, knocking on the door.

The sergeant opened one eye and looked toward the curtained window. "Fuck off," he yelled from inside.

Bern laughed. "I will as soon as you answer my question. Are you going to shoot me if I come in?"

Resnick mimed a shocked look. He slid his holster onto the coffee table and held his hands up in the air. "Come on in, Mr. Coroner," he said.

Bern eased into the room, which was lit only by a small lamp on a wooden side table next to the sofa. The air had a sharp odor, as if the kitchen garbage hadn't been taken out in a few days. The dark-paneled walls and heavy woolen curtains made it feel like an oppressive cave. Bern sat in a plaid armchair, the cousin to the couch that Resnick was holding down. The sergeant did not look up at him.

A silence grew between the two men. Resnick sipped his beer and watched Bern's feet under hooded lids. Eventually, curiosity seemed to get the better of him and his eyes slowly slid up the coroner's long legs in their pale trousers to a dark gray wool sweater with three white buttons at the neck, the kind worn by loggers and snowmobilers. Bern smiled brilliantly when Resnick finally met his eyes.

"I've been talking to Shandie," Bern said. He kept his voice light as he spoke. "Is there anything you want to tell me?"

Resnick cast his dark eyes toward the holster. His head and

face were freshly shaven. He looked almost like a new recruit, except for the sagging shadows under his eyes and the drawn, weary lines of his face.

"I didn't want to hurt her."

"Tell me what happened."

Once inside the brewery, Steve listened carefully for sounds. With the boilers off, it felt like the whole building was asleep. Then a sound started up, like someone vacuuming. It seemed to be coming from under the brew house, so Steve cut through the boiler room and started down the stairs. He stuck close to the wall, wanting to stay out of sight, but he wasn't too worried. It might be funny if he scared his dad a little.

He was getting closer to the source of the sound. To his left were the circular metal steps that led up four stories to the top of the malt elevators. Steve sniffed. Over the smell of chemicals and malt, he could smell wet cement. The high ceilings caused the sound to echo and reverberate against the concrete floor and walls.

He reached the intersection of two hallways and tucked his head around the corner. It took him a moment to make sense of the picture before him. The first thing he saw was the machine. It was a small concrete pump, bright yellow and, by the looks of it, very powerful. Attached to it was a long hose that stretched about twenty feet to the end of the hallway. Holding the hose was Uncle Leroy. There was no mistaking his stooped-over frame and slight limp as he aimed the hose and moved from one place to another, spraying concrete. He was wearing brown coveralls, the kind everyone had worn up until ten years ago, when they had switched to the blue ones they wore now. Next to him, using the flat side of a rake to smooth the concrete and wearing a pair of coveralls identical to Leroy's, was his dad. They both had their backs to Steve.

"Leroy!" Karl shouted. "Shut that thing off a minute." When Leroy didn't hear him, Karl came closer. He tapped Leroy on the back of his coveralls. Steve could see the thick gold stitching on the shoulders and, when Leroy turned, the corner of the crest on the chest pocket, which had the old Bugaboo logo on it. Old, like from the 1980s at least.

Leroy pulled off his earmuffs and tilted his head. "What?"

"You done?"

Leroy rubbed at his ears. "It looks like we're going to have to do this whole area, under the tanks and everything. It's gotten bigger."

"Yeah, well, like I been telling you . . ." Karl muttered. "So what now?"

"Well"—Leroy pulled at his earlobes again and rubbed them—"I'm going to fill this crack up. Then we can smooth it down. We can block it off with a rope or something. It'll take a few days to dry. Looks like it's moving that way, toward fermentation."

"How long?"

"I don't know. I don't know if it's going to hold anymore."

Steve couldn't figure out what they were talking about, or what they were doing. But then he saw his dad lean on one hip. Even without seeing it, Steve knew what this pose looked like from the front. Arms crossed, his dad was no doubt staring intently, a vague, almost friendly look on his face. He was about to say something devastating.

"Time to wrap it up, Leroy."

Leroy turned to face Karl, but he wouldn't look him in the eye. Uncle Leroy, the loyal dog. He'd turned the machine off and now he laid the hose at Karl's feet, then stood, tugging at the sleeves of his coveralls. Steve knew why he did that. He'd stopped by Leroy's place one time with an invitation to dinner from his mom. Leroy was not expecting him. In the privacy of his backyard, and in the heat of the sun, his uncle had unbuttoned the top two buttons of the dark-blue work shirt he always wore and rolled up his sleeves. He'd closed his eyes and fallen asleep in the sun, and Steve had seen the awful truth: his uncle's forearms and what he could see of his chest were covered in thickly whorled scars. Some were old, healed to white, but others were more recently healed and dark purple. And a few were brand-new—raw red circles that stood out on the ruin of his skin.

No wonder he'd never married, Steve had thought at the time. He'd backed away quietly, climbed into his truck, gone home. When his mom asked about dinner, he said he'd forgotten to go by Leroy's, and that was that. Though he'd never looked at his uncle the same way again.

"We've got to cover it over, Karl," Leroy said, still not looking him in the eye, "or it's gonna open up."

Karl barked a fake laugh. Steve ducked back around the corner at the sound before realizing that his father was not laughing at him. He peeked his head around again, just enough to see and hear what was being said.

"So I guess you haven't heard the big news," Karl said with that fake laugh again. "Word finally came through. I'm getting a promotion. Moving to the big time. C-fucking-O. Corporate office, man!" He clapped one hand on Leroy's shoulder.

"Moving?" Leroy asked. To Steve he looked like a lost child, all small and bent over and confused.

Karl laughed again. "Well, not actually moving. Can you imagine Felicia living anywhere else but here? Nah, but I'll be traveling everywhere, breweries all over the world. China, South America, Asia. And get this! I'll be advising them on how to save water!" Karl threw his head back and laughed hard. "Don't you think that's kind of ironic?"

Leroy shrugged. "I guess it's funny in a twisted sort of way." He gestured into the dark basement. "So what about it?" he asked finally.

"What about what?"

"You know. Our little problem. The sinkhole."

"What sinkhole?" Karl asked. "No sinkhole, just a few cracks in the foundation is all. Old building like this, happens all the time." He narrowed his eyes. "Right, Leroy?"

Leroy didn't answer, and in the silence between the two men Steve tried to figure out what the hell had just happened.

"It's time to let it go, Leroy. Time to move on, retire. Take up golfing. Buy a boat, sit in the sun." Then Karl tipped his head back again and laughed. The sound was full of cruelty. He nodded to the work they'd done. "This is good enough. We'll leave it like this."

"But Sparky," Leroy said. Steve winced at the whine in his uncle's voice. Didn't he know, after all this time? Hadn't he learned? Begging just made it worse. "You said we'd look after it. That new crack will open it up for sure. You said—"

"I changed my mind. We're done. Clean it up."

Steve watched them work. It was odd looking at his dad from this angle. He looked younger as he tied off the area with a yellow hazard ribbon, Steve thought, jauntier than he'd been at dinner. But Leroy looked like all the life had seeped out of him. He washed off the end of the concrete hose with another hose normally used to wash the floor. He was bent almost double, and as he followed a rivulet of gray water to the sloped drain, his limp was more pronounced than ever. Steve followed the stream with his eyes as well, watched as it headed straight toward his own feet. Too late, he looked up to see Leroy staring at him.

Get in and get out.

How long had she been there? It seemed like hours but no doubt had been only a few minutes. She'd become so absorbed in reading the document, she'd forgotten her surroundings. As usual, Dirk would say.

She had what she needed. Time to get back to Bern's place. He should be home by now, and they could talk it through. He would know what to do. She picked up the letter and folded it carefully in four. She slid it into the back pocket of her jeans and put her hand flat on the couch to stand up.

That's when she felt it again. The rough patch under her hand. She ran her fingers over it. Then she found another, and another. She leaned forward to look more closely at the marks. Tiny circles of fabric, puckered and hardened. There were dozens of them. Cigarette burns.

She stood quickly, taking in her surroundings again. What the hell was this place? Right next door was the cellar she'd been locked in. Just up the stairs was the back door that was always left unlocked. And not far from there was the field where Belinda was found. *With cigarette burns on her belly and hips.*

She moved to the desk. On it was a fake-leather three-sided calendar, the kind that insurance agencies gave out at Christmas-time. The pages for each month up to the current one had been carefully ripped off. And each day in September had been crossed off with an *X.* Including today.

The top drawer of the filing cabinet slid open smoothly when she pulled it. Inside was a set of tabbed folders, each one marked simply with one letter of the alphabet. *A* was empty, but when Evie slid her hand into *B,* she came across a plastic sleeve from a three-ring binder. She pulled it out slowly, then dropped it with a yelp.

The sheet protector slid to the ground and a pair of purple embroidered underpants snaked out and slid to the concrete floor.

In two steps, she was back at the couch and had her cell phone out of her backpack. She called Bern's number first and left him a terse message when he didn't answer. Then she dialed 911. "I need the police at the Bugaboo Brewery. Right now," she whispered into the phone as soon as the operator picked up. "Back gate. I'm going to go open it right now. I'll wait by the back gate."

"Ma'am, what is your name? Are you in danger?"

"I'm Evie Chapelle. Tell them I've found something. About Belinda Carlisle," she said, keeping her voice low. "I'll be at the back gate."

She hung up the phone with a shaking hand. Was she in danger? She looked at the calendar again, then at the underpants crumpled on the floor. Today's date had already been crossed off.

She was in the paint room and moving toward the hallway

when she heard a scraping sound. She moved slowly behind a row of paint shelves. Had she left the light on in the hall? She couldn't remember. There was the scraping again. The sound of the cellar door opening—or closing. A sound she would never forget.

There were footsteps then, and she heard the sound of something rolling along the floor, clinking. Bottles. Evie would recognize that noise anywhere. The sound of dozens of empty beer bottles making their way along a conveyor belt to the filler. But how could that be? She was in the basement. There were no conveyor belts here. The clinking got closer, along with the footsteps and, inexplicably, whistling.

The clinking stopped once the footsteps reached the cellar, but the whistling continued.

"Steve?" Leroy said. He took a few steps down the hall. "That you?"

"Stupid bugger," Karl muttered behind him. Then, in a more cheerful voice, he said, "Son? What are you doing here?"

Steve stepped out of the shadows and Leroy saw a younger version of Karl, and of himself. Young and healthy and not ruined—yet. The boy shrugged at them. "Stopped by to see what you were up to."

Karl moved toward his son, still holding the rake in his hand. He smiled broadly. "Just in time for a beer, my boy. As always, huh? Show up when the work's all done." He laughed, but Leroy could hear the edge in his voice.

Steve looked at his watch and shook his head. "No time. I'm

just on my way to pick up Shandie. Dad, why are you carrying a rake?"

It was the last thing he asked. With a movement as sure as slapping a new bag of concrete to burst it open, Karl knocked his son square on the top of the head with the flat edge of the rake. Steve crumpled to the floor.

Leroy did not move. Karl stood watching his boy for a moment. Then he pulled a set of keys out of his own pocket. He threw them at Leroy, who caught them easily.

"Go pick up the little sweetheart from work. Bring her back here. Tell her Steve is working late."

Leroy ducked his head down. Best not to look Sparky in the eye when he was in this kind of mood.

"She likes mango juice," he said as Leroy walked by. Karl handed him a tiny square of folded paper.

He didn't need to say more. Leroy knew just what to do.

29

"She wouldn't see me anymore," Resnick began at last. "I couldn't get her out of my mind. She was so beautiful. It was only one night, I know. But I wanted more." He paused and drained his beer bottle. "Pass me another one?" he asked, tilting the empty bottle toward Bern.

Bern shook his head. "Depending on what you tell me, I may need you to be sober," he said. He got up and went into the tiny kitchen. The counter was piled high with several days' worth of dishes. "I'll make coffee while you talk."

Bern rinsed and filled the coffeepot and emptied the grains from the filter into the overflowing garbage can. Once the coffeemaker was plugged in and had begun to gurgle, he emptied the sink of dirty dishes and began to run hot water and soap into it. "Carry on," he said as he found a cloth and began to wash the crusty plates and forks.

"It all started because she left her necklace here. We spent one night together." He reached into his pocket and pulled out a delicate silver chain with a tiny silver dolphin pendant dangling from it. "I had to get it back to her, but she wouldn't return my calls. So I went to her house. I walked over after my shift. It was just getting dark, that time of day when the lights are on but people haven't closed their blinds yet. Her room is at the front of the house, and there are bushes under her window. She was in there. I could see her as I walked up." He paused and lifted the empty beer bottle again and placed it down absently, as though seeing for the first time that it was empty.

"I couldn't help myself. I went up to her window and watched her. She was getting ready to go out," he spoke quietly, almost in a trance. He raised one hand to his head and brushed it down toward his shoulder. "She was brushing her hair over and over until it gleamed. I could remember what it felt like, how soft it was, how good it felt." He looked up at Bern, his eyes haunted hollows. "I couldn't stop myself. I went almost every night. Sometimes the blinds were closed, and as winter ended and it got to be light later, it was riskier. But I didn't care about that. I didn't care who saw me. I felt invisible. I knew I was risking everything, but I didn't care."

Bern searched under the sink for the dish drainer and laid it on the counter. He pulled the plug, and as he waited for the soapy water to drain, he wiped his hands on a towel. He rinsed a soapy mug and filled it with coffee and brought it to Resnick. "So what happened?" he asked.

"Something happened to her. I'm not sure what. It was sometime in May. She stopped going out. Her blinds were closed all the time; she stopped working at the hotel. I stopped calling her altogether, even though I was worried about her. But I still kept an eye on her. Then she started dating this Steve character. Serious, right from the start." The silver dolphin in Resnick's hand clinked against the mug as he took a sip of coffee.

"So you don't know anything about what happened in May?" Bern asked.

"No," Resnick replied. "Do you?"

Bern nodded.

"Can you tell me?"

Bern shook his head once. "I can't tell you. But it scared her pretty bad. Real bad," he said.

"Why didn't she report it to the police?" Resnick asked.

Bern didn't answer right away, choosing instead to let the words echo in the room. Resnick took another sip of coffee, and Bern watched as the thoughts ordered themselves in his mind.

"Shit," he muttered. "Oh, shit. She doesn't know who did it, and she thinks it was me?"

Bern nodded.

"Date rape drug?" Resnick asked.

Bern shrugged. "Seems to be. No way to know for sure."

He filled the sink with water and began to rinse the dishes. Resnick sat quietly. He fingered the chain and sipped his coffee. When all the dishes were stacked neatly in the draining board, Bern wiped the counters and brought the coffeepot to Resnick to refill his cup.

"I've really fucked up, haven't I?" Resnick asked.

Bern tilted his head to one side. "It's never a good thing to confuse desire with need," he said quietly. He remembered Evie's forehead against his own. The fleeting echo of the memory left an ache of longing behind. "Especially when other people are involved."

Bern returned to the kitchen and searched through the drawers until he found a clean dish towel. He began to dry the plates, using slow, circular motions.

"Are you going to report me?" Resnick asked.

Bern thought about this for a moment. "If it was one of your officers, how would you handle it?"

Resnick rubbed his scalp and sighed. "Two weeks' suspension without pay, counseling, and tell him to stay the hell away from the girl."

"You do that for yourself and I won't report you. Donate the two weeks' pay to the rape crisis center," Bern said.

"Belinda." Resnick groaned. He put his coffee cup down and covered his head in his hands. "A serial rapist." He looked up at Bern, his hands on either side of his head distorting his features. "Do you know who it is?"

Bern shrugged and put a stack of plates in the cupboard. "I have my suspicions."

"And? Aren't you going to tell me?"

"Why don't you go have a shower and put on a clean uniform. Do you think you'll be straightened out after that?" he asked.

Resnick nodded and stood up.

"We'll go to town and get it all sorted out," Bern said. He opened another cupboard door and started to slide mugs into the empty space, one after another.

The wind blew through the alley behind the Kootenay Landing Hotel. It picked up bits of castaway paper and plastic bags from the darkest corners and whipped them up in the air. The parking lot was deserted.

"You want a lift home?" Leigh asked.

"It's okay. Steve's picking me up." Shandie shivered and hugged the front of her cardigan closed. Her eyes roamed the barren parking lot and the adjacent street, looking for the headlights of Steve's truck. She checked her watch. It was past one a.m., their agreed-on meeting time.

"I'll wait with you," Leigh said. She locked the door of the bar and pulled it to test the bolt. She leaned next to Shandie on the wall and sighed. "Busy night," she said.

"Yeah," Shandie replied. Her eyes stung from the smoky air; her ears were filled with the sound of voices calling out for more beer. It felt like every man in town had had his eyes on her that night. Eyes that followed her around the room, lingering and caressing the letters decorating her chest. Shandie just wanted to get home and have a shower.

"Maybe I'll go with you after all," Shandie said. The two women crossed through the gritty wind of the parking lot to Leigh's car. Leigh slid into the driver's seat just as a truck's headlights swung into the lot. A black Ford truck. Steve's.

Shandie backed away from the open passenger door. "There he is!" she called to Leigh, who had already started the engine. "Catch you later." She closed the door, the sound swallowed by the low rumbling of Steve's truck, which pulled up alongside her.

Leigh waved in response and pulled out of the lot. The brake lights of her compact car flashed briefly as she pulled into the deserted streets of Kootenay Landing. Shandie felt clean and safe for the first time all night, now that Steve was here.

She approached the truck from the back and noticed the decal right away. A little cartoon character taking a little cartoon pee on the Chevy logo. Shandie paused. Steve did not have a decal like that on his truck. The other differences flooded her senses all at once: the paint was really dark blue, rather than black; a gold stripe ran along the side; the side mirrors were extra wide, designed for a truck that pulled a trailer. It was not Steve's truck.

"Shandie?" a man's voice called out. It was not Steve's voice.

Shandie started to back away. She looked around her. Leigh was long gone. She did not have a key to get back into the bar. There was no way she could outrun a big truck like that.

The driver's-side door opened. "Shandie?" the voice called again. The twin spotlights of the truck's headlights illuminated two triangles of the parking lot. She could see in their glare road dividers blocking vehicles from accessing a dank corner of the lot. She began to move in this direction, keeping out of the path lit by the headlights. The voice laughed, a low echo of a sound. "Shandie, where are you?"

She froze. She'd heard that voice before.

"Shandie? It's Leroy. Are you there?"

It took a moment for her to relax her tightened limbs and allow the words to register in her mind. Leroy. Uncle Leroy. Steve's uncle. Steve had told her about him. Hopeless but harmless, he'd said.

She let out the breath she had been holding. "Leroy?" she said. It came out in a croak.

"There you are. Steve got tied up at the brewery. He asked me to come drive you home." Leroy had stepped out of the truck and moved in front of it now. Shandie could see his wiry, bent-over body in the dust-swirled light. He wasn't all that old, but he'd spent so much time in awkward positions, repairing machines at the brewery, that his body was creased and folded in stiff lines of pain and he looked like a much older man.

Shandie stepped into the light. "That was nice of you to come get me," she said. She pulled open the passenger door and climbed up into the idling vehicle. It was a relief to escape the gritty wind. Leroy got in the driver's seat and put the truck in gear.

"Steve said to give you this." He held out a jar of her favorite juice—organic mango and pear. Shandie took it with a smile. It was cold, and she was thirsty after a long shift without drinking anything. It was nice to know that Steve had thought of her, even if he had gotten called in to work. She took a deep sip, and then another.

"How come Steve had to go to work? I mean, it's the middle of the night." She leaned her head back on the soft leather of the seat and took another sip of her drink.

"Something came up," Leroy said.

It was only a two-minute drive to Shandie's house, but it seemed to be taking a really long time to get there. Leroy was driving very slowly, checking each deserted intersection for cars, his truck hugging the curb. It occurred to Shandie that he might be drunk. She thought she should be worried about that, but she was too tired to care. She drank the last of the juice and rested her head on the cool window.

Bern turned his cell phone on as soon as he pulled out of Resnick's driveway. He saw the headlights of Resnick's cruiser pull out after him. Less than a minute later, his phone started chirping that he had a message. He looked at the dashboard clock. He had been with Resnick for over an hour, longer than he had planned.

He punched the speakerphone and tapped the button to listen to his message just as Resnick's siren started up and the cruiser sped past him. The sound of Evie's hoarse voice filled the car as he followed the speeding cruiser through the deserted streets to the brewery.

The whistling continued.

Evie moved around the paint shelf and stood by the chain-link fence. There was no one in the rectangle of space that she could see. She ducked her head around the fence. The hallway was empty. The door to the refrigerated cellar was open, and the light was on. The whistling was coming from there.

The police would be waiting outside for her by now. She had to get to the back gate. Had to get away from this person, whoever he was and whatever he was up to.

If I can't see him, he can't see me, she thought. Move.

She took two steps into the hall and was moving away from the sound when the whistling stopped. She froze midstep and turned. The clinking started again, and there, at the entrance to the cellar, stood Conrad. He was pushing a rolling cart filled with beer bottles. He tilted his head to make his bangs flop to one side, a movement she'd seen him make a thousand times.

"Evie?"

She ran. She heard him push the cart out of the way and start to run after her.

"Evie! Wait!"

But she was gone. Up the basement steps. All she had to do was go out the back door and run to the gate. But he was catching up. Almost behind her. At the top of the landing there were four doors: outside, bottle shop, cellars, and boiler room.

She pushed open the door to outside and let it slam. Then she opened the door to the boiler room, went through it, and closed it ever so quietly behind her. She pressed her back up against the door and tried to quiet her breath.

Conrad reached the top of the stairs. "Evie?" he called out. "Where did you go? Shit." He chose the door to outside and headed into the brewery yard, calling her name.

Evie closed her eyes and slumped against the door. Conrad. It had been Conrad all along. She thought back to the week before, when she'd been locked in the cellar. He hadn't needed to go looking for her. He'd known where she was all along. And the secret clubhouse, the cigarette burns, the underwear. She shuddered.

She had to get to the gate, to explain to the police. She knew Conrad. He could talk himself out of anything. She had to get to them first.

She pictured the quickest route in her mind: through the boiler room, up the malt elevator stairs, and through the brew house. It was just a short sprint from there to the back gate. The police would be there by now.

She headed through the boiler room, moving quietly in case Conrad came back inside looking for her. She turned into the brew house basement and ran smack into Karl.

"Karl! Thank God you're here! It's Conrad! He's the one who's been doing all this. Where are the police? Did they send you in here looking for me?"

Karl's face barely registered her jumble of words. Something passed over his features that she took for a smile. He let out a low chuckle and kept his body close to hers, angling her toward the malt elevator steps.

Evie looked around, trying to make sense of the shapes she could see behind him. Where were the police?

"You brought the police, right? Where are they?" She looked over his shoulder and caught a flash of yellow ribbon and a long hose, much wider than the ones used to hose down the floors in this department. And a small yellow machine she'd never seen before. Evie went to move around him but he edged closer.

"I was just heading out to meet them. They're back the way you came," he said. He was standing too close. Evie looked up quickly, trying to see over his shoulder again, then she glanced back the way she'd come. Conrad was back there.

Karl chuckled again. "It's okay," he said. "I'll keep you safe."

He put his hands on her shoulders then, and Evie jolted at his touch. He took a step back so he could spin her around, and in the space that opened up between them Evie could see more of her surroundings. In the gap under his right arm she caught a glimpse of the machine again. A concrete pump. He turned her again, and in the space between his left elbow and hip she caught a glimpse of a shoe, a calf in jeans, a white T-shirt not tucked in.

The images didn't make sense. They didn't have to. Karl was behind her now, his hands pressing heavily on her shoulders, pushing her forward. She raised one leg and, with a solid kick, pushed her steel-toed shoe behind her and into his kneecap.

"Motherfucker!" he cried out. And she ran.

She dodged around him again, past the prone body that she could now see clearly was Karl's son.

"Steve?" she called out. But she didn't stop. She reached the circular staircase that led to the top of the malt elevators and started climbing, the metal steps ringing with each footfall.

• • •

Leroy parked the truck. Steve's girl was already asleep. This new stuff that Karl had given him worked fast. The wind whipped around in the parking lot, blowing raindrops up against the window.

He watched her for a moment. So trusting. Pretty thing too. He reached out and touched her hair. It felt so soft under his fingers. A waft of flowery smell made its way to him and he sniffed. The smell filled him with a sense of dread. He knew what was coming for this little girl and her pretty-smelling hair.

The dread grew as he sat back and watched the outside of the building. It was lit by floodlights every ten feet or so, and from where he was sitting he could make out different areas: the brew house, the steam room, the side of the bottle shop. Like the profile of a familiar and well-loved face. Except there was no person, no face that Leroy had loved like he loved that brewery. The orderly process of making beer was all he'd ever known. It was his legacy—the only good thing he'd ever done.

He ran through the building in his mind: the warm vibrations of the brewing process; the quiet expectancy of fermentation, long hallways filled with potential beer; the cold readiness of the cellars; the complicated, sensitive machinery of the filter room. He closed his eyes as he thought of the bottle shop and the exquisite timing between machines that he knew better than any person, except for maybe his brother. He sighed when he thought of the boiler room, the hub that fed the whole process and kept all the machines powered, year after year. He'd spent his whole life caring for those machines, keeping them running. And his father before him. It had always been that way.

The machines themselves had changed over the years, but ever since he was a young boy, Leroy had understood each one, its role, its purpose in the grand scheme of making beer. And it wasn't the making of the beer that was important to him. It was the way, if you timed it right, if you tinkered with the parts and the cogs and the conveyor belts just so, you could get all those machines working together in a beautiful, perfect system.

It was as if those machines spoke to him. By their grinding and groaning and squeaking, he could tell what they needed. It was something that the new guys and the managers, with their targets and measurements and automation, would never under-stand. His machines were not safe under their care.

That's why he'd had to stop Gavin. It was easy. Take off the lock. Press start. The guy had tried to take his place. He'd taken Leroy's tool cabinet, his set of locks, his locker. He'd taken his spot on the payroll, on the Christmas gift-exchange list, and in the hockey pool. And just like that, with the press of a button and a gurgle of hot water mixed with liquid caustic solution, Gavin was gone. Erased.

He'd learned the hard way: no one could replace Leroy.

Leroy had started looking after the machines as a child. He and Karl. They'd gone to work with their dad as often as they could. Or at least Leroy had. Karl was a natural with the ma-chines, but he'd had other interests, other drives, from when he was very young.

Leroy could do a complete boiler overhaul on his own before his twelfth birthday. He'd been looking after those machines for forty years. What would he do without them? Without Karl? Be-cause as much as Karl tormented him, tortured him, he'd always been there. A constant. The only person in Leroy's life. Without

Karl and the machines, the days, months, years stretched uselessly before him. Empty.

He had tried. Lord knows he'd tried his whole life. By the time he was five, he'd known there was no stopping Karl, so he'd done his best to minimize the damage his younger brother could do. Look after your brother, his parents had said. And he had; his life was testament to that fact.

What life? He knew some would ask that. But those same people—his niece and nephew, his sister-in-law, his coworkers—were free in their lives because of Leroy's sacrifice. He had given his life, his career, any hope of relationships. He had given his very body to protect them from Karl.

He looked over at the girl now, so pretty. So tired from the drug Karl had given him to give to her. There was no stopping his brother when it came to the girls. So Leroy stood by, tried to keep them safe. He'd loosened Belinda's restraints, hadn't he? Left the door unlocked so she could get away. Wasn't his fault she hadn't gotten far. He'd done what he could.

Leroy got out of the truck now and locked the doors behind him. He'd made his decision. Let the poor girl have her sleep. Safe from Karl and his need to inflict pain, to watch others suffer. To scar.

Karl was moving on. And with Karl gone, there would be no one to stop the Evie Chapelles of the world. All those changes they talked about: increased security, a guard at the gate letting people in and out, certified contractors for all maintenance work, and safety rules so sticky that a guy could spend his whole shift filling out paperwork just to keep track of what he was doing. He'd be locked out of the brewery forever. He wouldn't be able to look after the sinkhole. And once they found out about that, they would just shut the place down for good.

He limped over the tarmac to the railcar and looked up to the roofline. The tops of the fermentation tanks, the rounded steel edges of the bottle-ready beer tanks, and the highest point of the brewery—the malt elevators. Above them, on a system of steel bars and cables that he had helped rig, was the fluorescent letter *B*, for Bugaboo.

That was the place. Karl might be moving on, but there was no moving on for Leroy. He would stay right here, with his machines, where he belonged.

There were four trucks in the parking lot, but the gate was locked tight.

"Don't worry, I've done this before," Bern said as he scaled the fence. He jumped down to the other side and opened the gate for Resnick. The officer had left his cruiser lights flashing as he got out of the car.

"Backup will be here in a minute. Should we wait?" Resnick asked.

"No," Bern said, thinking of Evie's pinched voice on the cell phone message. "Let's just go find her. But where the hell do we start?"

They were crossing the brewery yard when a stooped figure emerged from the shadows by the railcar. At the same moment, the back entrance slammed open and a man appeared on the steps, scanning the yard. Bern recognized him immediately.

Resnick turned to Bern, a question in his eyes. Bern jutted his chin at Conrad. "You go talk to him, get him to help us find Evie. I'll go after that guy, see what he knows."

Bern walked close to the edge of the building, but he could no longer see the limping figure. He pictured the man's walk again. Leroy Ostikoff, he decided. But where had he gone?

He heard footfalls above him. Scanning the side of the building, he saw the start of a staircase that seesawed back and forth up a part of the building that was taller than the rest. Bern climbed one flight and then another. Above him he could still hear Leroy climbing. "Leroy?" he called out, and heard the man's steps speed up. By the time Bern reached the roof, he was out of breath. The wind howled around him; dirt and raindrops blew into his eyes and hair. Above the roof, suspended from enormous steel cables, was a giant fluorescent *B* casting an eerie glow in the night sky. Thick clouds obscured the moon and the stars, and what little light was on the roof was tinged a cold blue from the Bugaboo sign.

Bern took a few steps onto the deserted roof. Bits of cardboard and cast-off beer labels scattered in the wind. He rubbed at his eyes, which were itchy with grit. The corners of the roof were in shadow. He could not see Leroy.

Below him, and stretched all around him, the lights of Kootenay Landing twinkled. Most people lay sleeping in their beds. The wind would be pressing up against the sides of their warm homes, weaving its way through their gardens. The dancing swirls of dust on the road in front of his house would no doubt prompt another rash of complaints to town hall; maybe the road would get paved at long last.

Just then he caught a movement in the shadows. His eyes darted from place to place until he spotted Leroy approaching the steel cables that rose up another story at the end of the roof. The man began a halting climb up the ladder attached to the side of the metal frame that held up the fluorescent sign.

"Leroy! Wait!" Bern called out. With his long strides, he quickly reached the bottom of the ladder and started to climb after him. "Wait!" Bern called again. "Stop! It can't be that bad." Panic gave his legs a surge of strength and he raced up the ladder.

"No more!" Leroy called out. He was almost at the top.

It happened then, like the click of a shutter. The child, in Rwanda. Always that same child. His accusing eyes fused Bern to the ladder. *But nothing is as it seems in Rwanda, Fortin,* Colonel Sauvé always said.

The child stepped away from the tree that had camouflaged him. If he was ten, it was barely. He stared at the two soldiers. Bern had never seen such a look, never mind from a child. Anger, disappointment, disgust. *Why didn't you stop this?* He seemed to be shouting it, without saying anything. But he was alive. Alive and alone and they could help him. He was the only one to have survived the slaughter that surrounded them.

"He's alive," Sauvé whispered.

The boy's eyes, round and brown, seemed to stare right through Bern, who had stepped out of the jeep to move a body that was blocking the road. *Nothing is as it seems.* The boy looked past Bern to his commanding officer in the passenger seat of the jeep. The gun came from nowhere, a rifle, as long as the boy was tall. He aimed over Bern's shoulder, and with an instinct born of years of training, Bern had his own weapon in his hand, the bullet out and moving. It crossed paths with the boy's bullet at some midpoint predetermined by chaos.

The boy's bullet shattered what was left of the windshield and entered in through Colonel Sauvé's upper arm and out through his shoulder blade.

Nothing is as it seems.

"Sauve-le. Sauve le garçon!" Sauvé had cried out. *Save the boy.*

Time seemed to slow down as Bern made his way to the side of the road, sliding over corpses like so many speed bumps. He became aware of the stench and the slick of bodies. Of the buzz of flies over an otherwise heavy silence. Of the inexplicably lush green of the leaves on the trees that grew right to the edge of the road. He reached out his hand to part the branches. He had to find the boy, but as always happened at this moment, the shutter switched again, dropping Bern back into the present, breathless and lost.

Leroy had reached the top of the ladder. For a moment, the clouds broke apart and the moon illuminated the sky and the dark shadow puppet that was Leroy. He bellowed down to Bern.

"It was—" His voice faded away, swallowed by a strong burst of wind.

"What?" Bern yelled up at him. He gripped the ladder, willing himself to move but not trusting his limbs to hold him.

"It was *me!*" The next gust of wind carried Leroy's voice to Bern. He climbed as quickly as he could. He saw Leroy step over the outside edge of the metal safety railing, all that separated him from a five-story drop to the tarmac below.

In one moment he was a waving silhouette, perched on the railing. The next instant he was a dark speck, as light as a fluttering piece of litter in the sky. The clouds blew over and obscured the glare of the moon, and he was swallowed by darkness.

30

The smell of dry, roasted barley filled her nostrils. The steps and banisters were covered in a fine cream-colored powder, the residue from the malt mill above. Evie left footprints in the soft white malt dust with every step. Mentally she scanned each level of the brewery above her. She passed the doorway to the second level without stopping. She imagined the storage rooms of ingredients on that level—hops, calcium, syrup—all of them harmless. She needed something to protect herself with.

She heard thundering echoes to her steps coming from below. Karl was following her up the staircase, but slowly. She stopped to listen for a moment. His heavy steps clanged beneath her, and over the top of their resounding echo he was calling to her: "Evie!"

She slowed her steps to make less noise. When she reached the third level, she pulled the door open and slipped into a dimly lit area. It was a relief to get away from the bright lights of the stairway. She faced the cavernous space and considered her options. To her left was a tiny storage room filled with more boxes of obsolete documents. Evie knew that the lock gave if it was pulled hard enough. But she'd spent far too much time hiding in small rooms already.

She crept through a wide-open area lit only by emergency lights. On her right, a ladder led up half a story to the malt mill above. Evie was about to move past this when she saw the sulfuric acid.

She grabbed a face shield and neoprene gloves that hung on a pipe by the drums of battery acid and pulled them on. The wording from the safety procedure rang through her mind: *extremely corrosive, causes serious burns, harmful by inhalation and skin contact, ingestion may be fatal.* She approached the fifty-gallon drums with caution. The area always smelled sharp and funky at the same time.

A small plug at the top of the current drum had been removed and a pump on a long wand filled the opening. With each brew that passed through the pipes, a tiny amount of sulfuric acid was pumped in, to keep scale from forming on the insides of the pipes. Once diluted through hundreds of hectoliters of concentrate beer and diluted again to bottled liquid, the acid left in an actual bottle of beer was too minuscule to be measured.

A door slammed behind her.

"Evie!" Karl's voice sounded calm now, like he was cajoling an angry child who had run away from home. "C'mon, Evie. Why are you hiding?"

Evie loosened the pump with a gloved hand. It made a small popping sound as it came free. She pulled the wand out of the drum and held it away from her body, pointed forward like a gun. The smell of acid was overpowering. She took a few steps to the side to avoid directly inhaling it. Drops of acid fell from the end of the wand and onto the floor.

"Evie, I just want to talk to you! Evie?" He rounded the bend. Even in the semidarkness, she could see how disheveled he was. He was breathing hard and the flap of blond bangs at the front of his head was sticking up.

"There you are . . . What? What are you doing?" He walked up to her, arms extended in question. She held the wand up.

"Don't move," she said.

"Holy shit. You wouldn't." He stepped back.

"I said don't move." He stopped moving. "Take two steps forward," she commanded. He did. The pump was still attached to the main piping system by a thin, flexible line. She couldn't go far. She wanted him close enough to be able to reach him with the wand if she needed to protect herself.

"What are you doing, Dragon Lady?" he asked.

Evie laughed. "So it was you who started that, was it?"

"Yeah, and why not? It's true. No one can do anything around here without filling out seventeen forms and sitting through five meetings with you. We're just trying to make beer, not launch a nuclear rocket!" He sounded like he was trying to make a joke, but his voice was edged with anger. "Dragon Lady," he spat.

"So what about Gavin?"

"What about him?"

"Who started the machine?"

The edge had returned to Karl's laugh. "Gavin was an idiot. It's his own damn fault he died."

Evie thrust the wand forward. "Was it you? Playing at maintenance? Coming in on the weekends to . . . what? Relive the good old days?"

Karl jumped back. "You are completely crazy." He shook his head and twirled his index finger at his temple. "Totally nutso."

She tilted her head and shoved the wand forward again. "Did you start up that machine knowing Gavin was in there?" she asked.

"Ha! That's a good one. My fault. That's right, blame it all on me. You always have. You've been trying to hang everything on me from the start. Can I help it if people act like idiots? Can I help it if my crazy brother likes to entertain himself by sneaking in when the brewery is closed to repair machines? To fill cracks with cement? To work for free? He's sick in the head, obsessed. It's all he's ever done his whole life. And he lost it all—thanks to you again, and your regulations."

Evie shook her head. "This isn't about me. I have no explaining to do."

Karl laughed. Evie jabbed the wand closer to him and he stopped. Then he took a step back. "What a joke! You wouldn't hurt a fly." He took another step, and then another. Evie felt herself losing her advantage over him. She moved around the drum and pulled the wand along with her. She took a deep, acid-filled breath and stabbed the wand forward. It stopped abruptly a full foot from Karl's chest. She pulled again, but the pipe that led to the main line had reached as far as it would go. Drops of sulfuric acid splashed on the floor.

"Crazy, Dragon Lady." Karl shook his head. "Crazy."

She stood there helplessly, holding the wand, aware of the ridiculous position she had put herself in. Somehow, once again, she was backed into a corner and on the defensive. Was he right? Was she being crazy? Karl was her boss. Sure, she'd never liked him, but was he really going to hurt her?

"Tell me about the sinkhole," she demanded.

Bern watched the red flashing lights join the blue and red, and the growing number of black spots moving about on the tarmac below. They moved together and spread out, milled in a circle, seemed to reach some conclusion and broke into small groups. One cluster stayed with the black, unmoving stain that was Leroy.

He knew he needed to get down there. His legs still shook as he edged slowly down the ladder. The wind chilled him now that the heat from the flashback had left him. Fully in the cold reality of the present moment, he was still six feet above the rooftop when the wave of shame tore through him and pinned him in place. He gripped the steel frame of the ladder and laid his head on a cold rung.

Nothing is as it seems, he heard Colonel Sauvé's voice again.

"That may be so. But Leroy is not coming back," Bern replied out loud. "And neither is the boy."

"Are you going stand up there all night talking to yourself? Or are you going to come down and do your job?"

Bern turned to see Resnick below him on the roof, an unlit cigarette in his mouth. He found his legs in a hurry and clambered down the ladder, but he could not look at the other man. The wind whipped at his hair and face, making his eyes tear up. He rubbed at them, hard, lest Resnick think he'd been standing up there, weeping.

"Did you find her?"

Resnick shook his head. "We're splitting up to search for her. She told dispatch she'd meet us at the back gate. Never showed. Schilling's got the basement. Conrad's got the bottle shop. I've got this brewing part." He pulled a white plastic card out of his pocket and they started across the roof, back to the staircase. "I've searched this place so many times, they're giving me my own key now."

"Let me help," said Bern, walking behind Resnick. The wind

blew at them hard, but it felt good to be moving. Taking steps on something solid.

Resnick shook his head again and yelled over the wind. "Not sure that's advisable, Mr. Coroner. You're a bit of a mess, if I can say so. Personally involved. Plus, you've got a new customer waiting for you down below."

They'd reached the top of the stairs. Bern grabbed Resnick's arm and forced himself to look the other man in the eye. He kept his gaze steady. "The dead can wait. I can't handle another customer tonight. Let me help."

Resnick looked back at him and finally raised his hands in a helpless gesture. "Fine, whatever. You take this thing," he said, gesturing to a nearby entrance. "Malt elevator, four stories. I'll go in through the door one floor down and search the rest of the brew house."

Resnick swiped the white plastic card along a black metal box by the door, and Bern pulled it open.

"Don't do anything stupid. Got it? Meet you by the back door when you're done," Resnick said. Then he tapped Bern on the shoulder. "You okay?"

Bern nodded, though he didn't know the answer to that question. Would he ever be okay? He just had to keep moving. Had to take action. That much he knew. And he had to find Evie. He gave Resnick a little wave as the police officer headed down the stairs toward the brew house. Bern stepped out of the wind and allowed the hushed dark of the brewery to draw him in.

The smell hit him first. A clean, dusty smell. The space was dimly lit and he used the pathway illuminated by the emergency exit lights to orient himself. He was standing in a hallway. To his left was a bright white cylindrical tank, which he assumed was the malt elevator Resnick had mentioned. A white metal staircase led down from it. The way out.

In front of him was some sort of platform on which stood a machine as old as time. A mill, he realized as he approached it. Everything around him—the platform, the railings, the mill itself—glowed from a thin coating of pure white dust. It was slippery too. Bern's foot slid out from under him and he grabbed the railing as he stepped forward.

He almost cried out, but he swallowed the sound as he heard voices below. He crouched down low and moved slowly around the mill. The malt dust tickled at his nose and he pinched his lips together to hold back a sneeze.

"Dragon Lady," he heard a voice say with a low chuckle.

The mill was on a platform that formed a loft. A metal railing kept wayward workers from falling to the level below, where the voices were coming from. There was an opening in the railing where a ladder led down to the lower level. *Another ladder.* Bern moved behind a garbage can that stood next to the opening. Crouched, he held his breath to keep from sneezing and listened. Waiting for his moment to act.

It took a minute for his eyes to adjust to the light so he could pick out the players in the scene below him. Finally he placed Evie, alive and well but backed into a corner. She stood next to an enormous barrel, holding a metal stick out in front of her and wearing a welder's face mask. She looked like a kid playing dress-up as a knight.

Karl paced back and forth in front of her, tracing a semicircle around the drum. Bern barely recognized the slick senior manager who'd so annoyed him only a few days before. He seemed to have unraveled.

"Sinkhole?" Karl muttered. "There is no sinkhole. A few soft spots, that's all. Dealt with," he said. He ran his hands through his hair and across the stubble on his cheeks as he spoke. He passed by Evie again and she jabbed the stick out uselessly: it did not reach him. That's when Bern realized it was attached to the drum by a thin line. She truly was backed into a corner.

"No sinkhole?" she asked. "So what about that report?"

Karl stopped pacing. "What report?"

"The one from the engineers," she said. "'Significant sinkhole activity,' 'a serious situation that merits further investigation,' 'two to six months' to repair," she quoted. "That report."

Bern wanted to yell at her to shut up. To run. But he wasn't sure he could get down there in time, and maybe she was right. Maybe the best plan was to keep Karl talking. He shuffled forward to check the ladder, then ducked his head back again. As soon as he put one foot on that thing, Karl would see him. He'd be putting both of them at risk. He looked around for a weapon.

"My, my, you've been busy, Dragon Lady," Karl spat out.

"What were you going to do when the auditors came?" she asked.

"I knew you'd handle them, Evie. Take one for the team. You're always so good at that." He threw his head back and laughed, a sound that chilled Bern to the core. He saw Evie shake her arm and rub at the front of the mask. She was getting tired. How long had they been at this standoff? Think, Fortin. No weapon, but what is your tactical advantage?

Below him the conversation continued. "What about when the intake meters get installed? How were you going to hide it then?" Evie asked. Her voice was getting that pinched tone she took on when she talked about work.

"Couldn't care less." Karl moved closer, but he was still out of reach of the wand, taunting her. "Not going to be here, remember? VP Energy, my ticket to corporate. Flying out next week, thank you very much. If there's a sinkhole in this shithole . . . well, so what?"

He saw Evie's hand sag from the effort of holding up the wand. Karl did not seem to be armed. But if Bern headed down the ladder, Karl might attack him—or worse, Evie.

"Gavin," Evie said simply.

Karl leaned back and rolled his eyes. "If you must know, it was Leroy. He just lost the plot, okay?" he said. "He got forced into long-term disability, which we all know is early retirement. Young buck comes along and takes his job, his locker, his life. You've got to understand my brother. He's not all there. This job was his whole life. You know?" Then he let out that low laugh again. "But of course, you of all people know what that's like. When was the last time you just relaxed, hey, Evie? When was the last time you let off a little steam?"

Bern stood up then. "Up here!" he yelled.

Both of their heads swung in his direction, but they could not see him. Karl started walking toward the ladder, but Bern saw Evie lay the wand carefully on the drum and back away.

"Who's up there? Steve? Is that you? Don't you go telling stories out of school. We'll keep family in the family. Like we always do."

Karl was at the base of the ladder now, and Bern could see his advantage clearly. It was so simple. He waited silently as Karl climbed one rung. And then another.

"Leroy? Steve? You up there?"

When he reached the third rung, Bern picked up the garbage

can that had shielded him and dropped it down on top of Karl. He crumpled to the floor in a shower of white dust, sneezing and sputtering. The rubber garbage can bounced on top of him and rolled away, coming to a stop by the drums where Evie had stood. Bern scrambled down the ladder to look for her, but she was gone.

Outside, the wind howled. Lights from emergency vehicles flashed on the tarmac below as she ran down the steps as quickly as she dared. "Up here!" she called, but there was no hearing her over the noise of the wind.

"Up here!" she cried again.

And suddenly there was Conrad at the foot of the stairs, reaching up toward her, smiling, hair in front of his eyes, trying to convince her of something.

She backed away. "Get away from me! Get away!" People heard her this time. Constable Schilling came running up behind Conrad.

"Back up, back up, man," Schilling said, pushing Conrad away from the base of the stairs. "You're scaring her."

"It's okay, Evie. Just come down. It's okay," the young officer said, taking a few steps up toward her. Evie started to move down again, more slowly this time. "We've been looking everywhere for you."

Schilling reached her and she gave up. Didn't care how she sounded, whether anyone would listen to her. "Ask him! Ask him what he was doing down there in the basement."

Schilling's hands were on her arms, guiding her down the

stairs, waiting to catch her if she fell. But she wasn't going to fall. She saw the flashing lights reflected all around, red and blue, red and red. Schilling was moving her toward an ambulance. She fought back.

"I'm fine! Just ask him." She tried to push Schilling away. "Cigarette burns and underwear in files. Ask him what he was doing down there!"

"It's okay, Evie," Schilling was saying. "We did ask him. We did."

"But did you see? The underwear? The burns?"

The officer stopped walking and stood in front of Evie. The two women were about the same height, and she felt the younger woman's eyes holding hers steady. "He was making beer, Evie. He was sneaking around, yes. But he was making beer. Home brew. In the brewery. He'll probably be in trouble with his boss, but that's about it. He told us right away, and then he helped us look for you."

Evie took in the words slowly. "Making beer?"

Schilling nodded. "We need you tonight, Evie. I know you've been through a lot, but we need you to hold it together. Just a little longer. We need you to show us what you found, and to tell us everything you saw and heard. Can you do that?"

Evie took a deep breath and stood taller. "I can do that," she said.

From: Dave Porteous [vpwestern@bevco.ca]
To: Bugaboo Senior Management Team
Re: Brewery Closure—Effective Immediately
Importance: Urgent
Sent: Sunday, September 20, 11:52 a.m.

To all:

Please be advised that all operations at the Bugaboo Brewery are suspended and the building is closed until further notice. I will be in touch with each of you individually to advise you of your next steps. Please be prepared to relocate on short notice.

A team of structural engineers will be on site this week to determine the extent of sinkhole activity under the brewery building. It is unclear at this time when, or if, operations will resume. All gates have been locked and a private security firm has been hired to keep everyone out of the brewery grounds.

All human resources personnel are asked to report to the Kootenay Landing Community Centre at 7 a.m. on the morning of Monday, September 21. All union employees will be present, and the details of their compensation packages and terms of their layoff will be explained. Counselors will be available for them to speak to if needed. All other management are welcome, but not required, to attend.

This is a sudden shock to us all, but I have been assured by the national office that all our management personnel will be looked after and reassigned to other breweries.

I will send out more information as soon as it is available.

Dave
Dave Porteous
Vice President, Western Region
BevCo Canada

31

"Now do you remember what you wanted to tell me?" Bern asked.

Steve Ostikoff sat across from him at the plain pressboard table in the interview room. It was the twin to the room next door, where Bern and Resnick had spent the early morning hours questioning Karl. Their prime suspect had clammed up and would not say a word. So they were turning to Steve, a younger and slightly less disheveled version of his father in the next room. Bern suspected it wasn't the first time he'd been left to explain a mess his father had made.

Steve sighed. "It wasn't me."

"Yes," Resnick snapped. "We got that part."

"Easy," growled Bern. "We know it wasn't you, Steve. But there seems to be a series of complex events—each one perhaps innocent on its own—and the compounding of those events caused two deaths."

"A series of preventable incidents," Steve said.

"Pardon?" asked Bern.

"Evie is always going on about it in those safety meetings. An accident is a series of preventable incidents. If you prevent the incidents, you can keep the accident from happening."

A smile played over Bern's lips. Evie was asleep on his couch, with Mrs. K. crocheting in the armchair, keeping a watchful eye over her. "She would say that," he said softly. But there was more to it than that, he thought. Human action could cause a lot of damage, but to culminate in a tragedy like this one, there had to be more at play. A compounding of misfortune. And a dose of ill intent.

"Do you really think these were accidents? We think your uncle started the machine up on purpose."

Steve looked up at him, his eyes bloodshot and sagging. "It's been going on for years," he said. His voice was hoarse with fatigue. And anger, Bern suspected. "Way longer than I've worked there. Leroy would do all the weekend overtime shifts. He'd do cleanup or fill the bottle washer. He'd even start up the boilers or the brew house. Whatever needed to be done. He wouldn't get paid for it. If you were scheduled, you put in for overtime, but Leroy would actually do the work. Even after he retired, he'd still come in on weekends. He lived for those shifts.

"At first I couldn't believe it. Didn't want to go along with it. But then I got my truck and my house, and that extra four hours of double time every few weeks really came in handy. Especially if I could just sleep it off on a Sunday and not actually go in." Steve ran a hand through his hair and looked up at Bern with desperate eyes. "I knew it was wrong. But everyone else was doing it. After a while, I just gave in."

"And on that Monday?" Bern asked quietly.

"I was scheduled to come in and do some cleanup, then fill the bottle washer," he said.

"Even if it didn't need to be filled until the next morning?" Bern asked.

Steve shrugged. "Sometimes we'd fill it up on the weekend, if someone was coming in anyway. Then just heat it up the morning of. One less step."

"So Leroy came in for you that Monday. And what happened?"

"Look, I don't know for sure, okay? I mean, I wasn't there. But I can tell you what I think," Steve said.

Bern opened his hands in invitation. "Please do."

Resnick sat back in his chair, pen and notebook in hand. He looked up every few minutes to glare at Steve, but for the most part he seemed content to let Bern conduct the interview.

"I think he just snapped, you know? He got put on disability and just forgotten about. Goes in on his little overtime shift, and there's the guy who's taken over his life, breaking every rule in the book by doing a confined-space entry all on his own. I think he just thought that if Gavin was gone, he'd get his job back, just like that." Steve snapped his fingers with those words.

Bern thought of Gavin's arm hanging on to the trapdoor while the rest of his body heated up in the tank of caustic solution on that Tuesday morning almost two weeks before. *Just like that.* He closed his eyes and pushed the image out of his mind, though he knew it would be back. Another image added to the inventory in his slide show of horror.

"After I found Gavin, I went to the locker room to get myself cleaned up," Steve continued. "And there was a lock on my locker. One of Leroy's for locking out."

"What did you think when you saw it?" Bern asked.

"I thought Leroy or maybe my dad—one of them—was sending me a message: keep quiet or you'll get the blame. So I took the lock off."

"You have a key?"

Steve waved off the question. "The same key fits in all the locks. It's been like that forever. Everyone knows about it. A mistake, I guess, but pretty handy if you're trying to get some work done and some asshole has forgotten to take off his lock.

"So I took the lock off my locker, deleted the overtime from my time sheet, and went out the back door. The spent grains dump truck was there, picking up a load, and I threw the lock in the back. I never thought I would see it again, but some farm kid mucked out a trough and found it. It came back to haunt me."

Bern nodded. Evie and Conrad had both mentioned the lock to him. Steve rubbed his red-rimmed eyes, looking from Bern to Resnick. Exhaustion seemed to seep from his pores.

"Just a few more questions, Steve," Bern said. "What do you know about the room in the basement?"

Steve frowned. "Sorry, you got me."

"The room in the basement," Bern repeated slowly. He closed his eyes, feeling his own fatigue fraying the edges of his consciousness. "Next to the room Evie got locked in."

Steve tilted his head up to look at Bern from under a swath of blond hair, his eyes dull, uncomprehending slits. This would not do. Bern slammed his palm on the table.

"Damn it, I have been patient with you, but I tell you if you were one of my men, you'd be facing a court-martial." He had Steve's attention now. Resnick's too, for that matter. "Tell me about the little room." Bern enunciated each word.

"What little room? I don't know anything about a little room!"

"You don't know about a room with a dirty plaid couch covered in cigarette burns?"

Steve's green eyes, a mirror of his belligerent father's, stared back at him. "No," he said. But he was sitting up straight now.

"You don't know about young girls waking up with their bodies covered in burns and no panties to be found?"

Steve's eyes were wide, wild, but when he spoke it was in a whisper. "What the hell are you talking about?"

"You don't know about the filing system? We found seventeen files. We think by the letter of the first name. In each file, one pair of underpants." Bern modulated his voice now. He had the boy's attention. What he said next would likely change his life forever. "There were three separate files under the letter S."

It was Steve's turn to pound his fist on the table, to throw his chair back, to yell, to put his head down and weep. He did none of those things. He just stared at Bern, his fingers tapping out a rhythm on the edge of the cheap table. Perhaps he would have made a good soldier after all.

"My father did that?" Steve asked. "To Shandie? Those spots? She said it was an allergic reaction."

Bern shook his head slowly. "We think it was your dad. He won't tell us right now. Won't say anything at all. Do you know anything that could make your father talk?"

Steve continued tapping the table and didn't look up when he said, "Leroy. Leroy could always get my dad to say something. When he was alive."

"We can't ask Leroy anymore."

"He would have known it all. He was a container for a whole lot of my dad's bad shit. Which is maybe why he did what he did last night. It got too much for him." Steve stood up then. "I've got to go. I've got to go see my mom. Talk to Shandie. Where is she? Oh God."

Bern stood with him. "Easy now. Easy," he said. "You've been up all night. Officer Schilling brought Shandie home. She's safe. First thing you've got to do is get some sleep, all right?"

Bern cleared his throat and looked at Resnick. The police officer shrugged and muttered, "Fine, whatever."

"You can go, Steve. There is a lot to sort out, but as far as I can tell, all you are guilty of is claiming overtime you didn't work," said Bern.

"Just don't leave town without telling us how we can reach you," added Resnick. He walked Steve to the door, then turned to Bern. "One hell of a crime we've got here, Fortin," he said. "What the hell am I going to recommend to the prosecutors?"

His beady eyes bored into Bern's, but for the first time since he'd known Resnick, Bern didn't feel like being sarcastic in return.

"Tell them to focus on Karl. Plenty of others had a part to play. But Karl's crimes caused the most damage," Bern said.

"Well, except for taking off the lock, which Leroy did, and starting up the machine when he knew Gavin was in there. He's clearly at fault for that," Resnick argued.

"Is he, though? He'd been a puppet for his brother's sick mind for his whole life. You might say that in his own way, he was trying to protect people—the employees who worked there, Karl's family, even the girls Karl tortured. He was trying to soften the impact his brother was having, because he didn't believe he could stop him," Bern said. "And then it all went too far."

Resnick grunted.

"Sure, Leroy pressed the start button, but I think everyone had a part to play. You go down the road of what happened to Gavin, and fingers will point in every direction within that brewery. Leroy, Karl, Steve, Conrad, Gemma—they all did some-thing," Bern said. Even Evie, he thought, though he didn't say it out loud. "And Belinda too. If Leroy had let her out sooner, if Evie and I had looked harder to find the reason the alarm went off, she might have survived." Bern looked meaningfully at Resnick. "And dare I say it, if Shandie had felt safe enough to report what happened to her, it might have all been avoided in the first place."

Resnick shook his head. "So you've been bugging me for days to look into all this, and now that you have it figured out, you want me to drop the whole thing?"

Bern laughed out loud. "No, that's not it. I'm just suggesting you focus your energy. Focus on Karl," Bern said. "Leave every-thing else be."

Resnick nodded his assent. "All right, Fortin. We'll see if we can get him talking. Too bad your girlfriend didn't grill him about the room and the girls and the files. She got him talking about just about everything else."

"I think it just didn't occur to her that it was Karl. She'd just run away from Conrad down in the basement, and she assumed that part was his doing," Bern said.

"And he says he was just making beer, is that right?"

"That's what he says, and it appears to be the case—at least from what Evie can figure out. He was using some old tanks and brewing during off hours. He might be in trouble with the company for using malt and syrup and equipment without per-mission. But then, he works for a beer company. What are they going to do to him?"

Resnick laughed. "Maybe they'll market his recipe. Give him a promotion."

"I wouldn't put it past them," Bern said. "And he was in the brewery the night Evie got locked in but says he wasn't down in the basement. Sounds like it was Leroy who locked her in. We got that much out of Karl."

"Of course we'll have to look into all that again. I don't know why I'm even listening to you, since I'm supposed to be in charge. I think you can go home now."

"All right, Staff Sergeant. I'll take that as an order."

"Damn straight," Resnick said. "And get some sleep. You look like hell."

The sound of an ax splitting wood woke Bern from his sleep. Instantly he was on his feet, ready to command.

But there was only his barrack-like bedroom, the open window revealing a squadron of tomato plants standing at attention. His watch read close to eight o'clock. He'd slept in two days in a row, and Mrs. K. must have gotten tired of waiting for him to stack her woodpile. He dressed quickly and made himself a triple espresso before heading outside.

There he found Brian, still wearing his bike helmet, with the ax in front of him, his legs spread wide. Bern took a seat on a wide stump and sipped his coffee. The boy looked over at him, suddenly uncertain.

"You're doing just fine," Bern said. "Maybe just bend your knees a little more. Let the swing carry the ax through the log."

Bern kept sipping his coffee, allowing the call of the birds, the warmth of the sun, and the lushness of the garden to calm his hyperalert senses. When enough firewood had piled up around the boy's feet, Bern got up and started stacking it. They worked in silence—the boy chopping, Bern stacking—until Bern finally tapped him on the shoulder.

"I think that's enough for today," he said with a smile. "I don't know why your grandmother gave you a hard time. You can chop wood just fine. Should we go see her?" Bern led the way without waiting for an answer. "Don't take your shoes off," he said as he opened the back door without knocking.

"Who are you talking to?" Mrs. K. demanded. She stood at the counter in her work dress; it was a gardening day. The counter was covered in garden harvest—piles of tomatoes, garlic, potatoes, cucumbers, beans, and squash. Bern knew each would be carefully inspected: the best would be saved for seeds; the next best for display at the fall fair; the remainder for cooking, freezing, or preserving. She looked at him sternly, her hair pulled back in a scarf, her tanned forearms leaning on the counter.

Bern stood aside and let Brian pass. He watched her face carefully and saw the leap of joy in her eyes before she began to inspect her grandson as critically as one of the fruits of her harvest. She dried her hands on a cloth and came closer to him. She patted Brian's shoulders and pushed him toward the dining room table, into the chair where Bern normally sat.

"You chopped that wood?" she asked the boy.

He nodded seriously. Bern watched them from the door, the two sets of eyes so similar, taking each other in. They were at eye level now that Brian was seated. Mrs. K.'s eyes roamed hungrily over his drawn features, his lanky limbs, his too-big feet.

"You're too skinny," she said. "Are you hungry?"

"Always." He smiled at her with a flash of straight white teeth.

"You got your braces off."

He nodded. "Almost two years ago."

She turned then, dropped the cloth on the counter, and opened a cupboard door. She was pulling out a large rectangular Tupperware container when Bern slipped back outside and closed the door silently behind him.

He retrieved his coffee cup and walked slowly back to his own garden. There was work to be done. Mrs. K. had given him another briefing the day before on how to prepare for the fall fair. By the end of the day, he would have careful piles of harvest covering his own kitchen counters, but for now he could enjoy a few moments of the perfection of the garden.

He took a small folding lawn chair and brought it close to the broken-down fence between the two properties. He sat with his back to the fence and allowed the sweet peas to speak to him in all their bejeweled glory. The heavy sunflowers, their heads drooping over the fence, were the only indication of the inevitable waning of the season. Chickadees flitted into the enormous flower heads, pecking out a harvest of their own. There, on parade before him, stood his first season of growth: flawed, riotous, and complete.

From: Dave Porteous [vpwestern@bevco.ca]
To: Evie Chapelle [safety@bugbrew.ca]
Re: Reassignment
Importance: High
Sent: Friday, September 25, 11:52 a.m.

Dear Evie,

As you can appreciate, the sudden change in the situation at Bugaboo Brewery has taken us all by surprise. It is going to take some time for the environment and safety department to reassess and determine the best place for you. We will work closely with human resources to make sure we find a good fit.

Meantime, I see that you have over a year's vacation coming to you. It would be most helpful if you could plan to take this vacation time as of now. I understand you have been assisting the human resources team all week with some of the immediate needs of the employees, and your help has been most appreciated. However, it is my understanding that they now have this situation in hand.

I will be in touch early in the new year to talk about where we go from here.

I would like to take this opportunity to thank you for your hard work and dedication to BevCo standards and values.

Cheers,

Dave
Dave Porteous
Vice President, Western Region
BevCo Canada

32

He turned into her driveway at the appointed time. Hair trimmed, recently shaved, and wearing pressed chinos and a button-down shirt, he felt like a teenager who'd borrowed his dad's car to go on his first date.

He parked and sat for a moment, admiring how her house seemed to grow out of the rocky landscape that surrounded it. From this vantage point it looked like a small house, but he knew that was deceptive. The outcropping of rock it was built around dipped sharply and dropped a full story. The back of the house was exposed to a view that was hard to match, even by Kootenay Landing standards.

He let his mind wander to the events of the past week. The town was reeling from the loss of a major employer, a change that would impact every person in the community. And yet, there was another shift too. Perhaps he was imagining it, or perhaps it was wishful thinking, but he thought he saw hopefulness on the faces of some of the people he spoke to. Hope that not all of the changes coming would be bad. Hope that the seeds stored for winter would, if properly tended, flower and bear new fruit.

Bern knew that there was no hope for him. Not really. He

would always be accountable to the dead. Acting as coroner, he could care for the dead in a way he never had been able to as a soldier. Maybe within that accounting he could find a little space. A tiny bed of tilled soil among weeds with deep, stubborn roots. Big enough, perhaps, to plant a seed and tend it.

He did not see Evie come out until she opened the passenger door. He sat up with a start.

"I'm sorry! No, no. Go back inside. I wanted to come to the door and get you. I just got lost in thought. Go back, please. I'll be right there."

She tilted her head and looked at him, confused. "My parents are okay with this, you know. You don't have to come inside and meet them."

He chuckled. "No, please. Go back inside. I have a surprise for you."

He watched her walk back to her front door. She was wearing flowing trousers in a pale lavender, almost the color of her eyes, and a simple white T-shirt. As far as he could tell, there was not one Bugaboo logo to be seen. Her steel-toed shoes had been replaced by a pair of sandals.

Once she was back inside, he reached under the passenger seat and pulled out a white bakery box. He followed the path she had taken and rang the bell a moment later.

She opened the door with a smile. "Why, Bern, what a nice surprise," she said.

He bowed slightly. "You look lovely," he said. "And I brought you something."

She took the box from him with a smile. "Let's go sit on the deck while I open it. Since there is actually furniture there."

He followed her around the side of the house and sat on one

of the wooden deck chairs she pointed to. The valley lay below them in the golden end-of-day sunshine. The air was cooler, the press of summer heat fading. Soon it would be gone altogether.

She laid the box on the table in front of her and looked at it for a moment.

"Aren't you going to open it?" he asked.

She grinned. "I like to stretch this part out." She pulled it slowly toward her. "So have you been yet?"

"No, I was waiting to go with you," he replied.

"You don't know how many ribbons you won?"

He shook his head. "Not yet. Come on, open it."

She slid a finger under the single piece of tape that held the box closed. The lid popped open and she gasped. "Oh, Bern! It's beautiful! Is it—"

"It's a corsage," he said. "May I?" He opened the lid fully and pulled out the delicate cluster of flowers, which were attached to a soft lavender-colored ribbon by thin wire. A miniature sunflower, brilliant yellow, surrounded by a cluster of bachelor's buttons, each one the same deep blue as her eyes. He took her wrist and laid the corsage against it. "Hold this," he said, concentrating. Then he turned her hand gently. He could feel her pulse against his finger as he tied the ribbon in a small bow. He turned her hand again and held it while they both admired the result.

"Did you make this?" she asked.

He nodded. "Well, with a little help from Mrs. K. So are you ready now?"

"Not quite. I have to ask you something first," she said, taking her hand out of his.

She took a deep breath and pushed the hair out of her face. The petals of the sunflower ran along her cheek with the movement. "I'm going to leave town for a while. Next week sometime. I'm taking Shandie with me as far as Calgary. She's going to get a part-time job and get ready to start college next semester. Then I'm going to drive up north and get Rory back. After that, I'm not sure what I'll do. Maybe just travel around with Rory for a while, give things some thought."

He took this in slowly. It was not what he was hoping she would say. He watched her childlike fingers playing with the edges of the box and felt a familiar pebble of dread in his sternum. "But you wanted to ask me something?"

"Will you look after my plants while I'm gone? I know I can trust you to take good care of them," she said.

"Of course, of course. It's nothing," he said. "I'd be happy to."

"I'll bring them to your house before I go," she said.

"Yes, yes. No problem. And now, it's my turn to ask something of you." He reached out and took her hand. "Tonight, we are having fun. No cases. No Karl, Leroy, Gavin, Belinda. No brewery closure. No safety procedures or water meters. Tonight is about who grew the biggest pumpkin, who raised the best-looking quail, and who made the crunchiest pickles. Tonight, we are going to have fun."

She laughed. "I think we can manage that. For one night."

"Good," he said. "For one night." He kept his hand in hers to help her up and did not let go as they walked to the truck. He opened the door for her. "Now, let's go see how many ribbons I won."

From: Troy Thompson [tthompson@soldiersally.ca]
To: Bern Fortin [bernfortin@bccoronerservice.bc.ca]
Re: re: re: The real story
Sent: Friday, September 25, 5:42 p.m.

Lieutenant-Colonel Fortin,
You are a hard man to track down, but I've managed it.
Your garden is in a small town called Kootenay Landing.
Not easy to get to, but not impossible either. I saw pic-
tures on the Internet. Nice town. I bet those mountains
make you feel safe—like you can forget the past.

And maybe you can, but others do not have that lux-
ury. I went to Captain Alais's house. I met his wife and his
little daughters. Sad to think of them growing up with
their dad in jail. And there you are, in your little garden,
in your little town in the mountains, not saying anything
at all.

It's time to set the record straight, Lieutenant-Colonel
Fortin. You may not answer your phone or your email,
but I bet you still answer the doorbell. Time to speak up.

Troy

ACKNOWLEDGMENTS

My first thanks are to Lois Currie, who looked after my children one morning each week so that I could write. Long before there was any hope of publication, she made me promise that when my book came out, I would thank her first. Thank you, Gramma Lois.

For long walks, listening ears, and laughter, I am grateful to Alison Bjorkman, Colleen Deatherage, Brandy Dyer, Gillian Cooper, Carrie Armstrong, Amber MacGregor-Ward, Alison Masters, and Nancy Pridham. Special thanks are due to Autumn Richardson, who encouraged me to keep going, and Luanne Armstrong, who accepted me into her tribe before ever reading a word and then insisted that I finish what I'd started.

A special thank-you to Helga Stephenson, for working magic with her four-word emails, and for extending the tradition of Stephenson kindness to Colliers to another generation.

I am grateful to my agent, Sally Harding, for many things, but especially for her enthusiasm. I know I am in good hands with her, and the whole amazing team at the Cooke Agency.

Thanks to Alison Clarke and the team at Simon & Schuster Canada for all that they have done, and to my editor, Janice

Weaver, for helping make so many things better, especially the ending.

Thanks to Bart Bjorkman, Diane Dubois, Suzanne Shaw, and Michael Moore for talking to me about their work. Rita Scott read with a legal eye, and Drs. Carrie and Rob Armstrong checked the medicine. For all things military, I relied on books by Lt.-Gen. Roméo Dallaire, Fred Doucette, and Capt. Ray Wiss, MD, as well as current media and my own stint as a document reader at the Somalia Inquiry. As a civilian who has never been to war, I will never fully understand, but I did try to get the details right. Any errors are of course my own.

Thanks to my writing group: Tanna Patterson-Z, Ilana Cameron, Kelly Ryckman, and Kuya Minogue for reading and commenting on various chapters, and for the great company and food. Thanks to Joe and Katherine Fraser and the collection of misfits and creative types who hold down the couch at Kingfisher Used Books.

Ian and Elizabeth Hutton and Anne DeGrace and Phillip Jackson opened their homes to me so I could edit without interruption. Thank you especially to Anne for her friendship and her insightful reading, and for always being at the other end of an email, ready to celebrate good news with a satisfying number of exclamation points.

The Crime Writers of Canada organization supports new crime writing through the "Unhanged Arthur" Award, and I am grateful to them for shortlisting *Confined Space* in 2010. Thanks as well to my editor friends Jennifer Groundwater and Akou Connell, who helped with my submission.

My stepfather, Guy Gagnon, read the manuscript three full times before anyone else got to see it. His influence over this book, much like his influence over my life, has been balanced, logical, and kind. It is only right that my first book should be dedicated to him, since without him I never would have had the courage to write it.

My mother, Carol Collier, has believed in my writing abilities ever since I brought home that poem in the second grade. Since she is the smartest person I know, her conviction gave me a measure of confidence as I began calling myself a writer.

My husband, Ron Sherman, let me quit my full-time job so that I could write. He said, "Keep going," through the whole, long process, even though I never let him read a word. I am not sure there is a way to say thank you for the kind of steadiness, trust, patience, and support he has shown. I am lucky indeed.

To our sweet sons, Graeme and Eric, who can write (and illustrate) a brilliant book in an afternoon, and who asked me many times what was taking me so long: here it is. But you are not old enough to read it yet.

ABOUT THE AUTHOR

DERYN COLLIER grew up in Ottawa and Montreal and is a graduate of McGill University. After a short career as a federal bureaucrat she ran away to the mountains of British Columbia, where she has been ever since. She has worked in a log yard, a brewery, as a doctor recruiter, and a communications consultant. She lives in Nelson, BC, with her family and blogs about crime fiction and life in the mountains at www.deryncollier.com. *Confined Space* is her first novel. It was shortlisted for an Arthur Ellis Award for best unpublished first crime novel by the Crime Writers of Canada.